STIRLING COUNCIL LIBRARIES

D0265900

THIS BOOK IS TO BE RETURNED ON OR BEFORE THE LAST DATE STAMPED BELOW

# Over Streams

# and Squirrel Woods...

# TO TENBY

# ALYS WILLIAMS

authorHOUSE®

*AuthorHouse™*
*1663 Liberty Drive*
*Bloomington, IN 47403*
*www.authorhouse.com*
*Phone: 1-800-839-8640*

*© 2011 by Alys Williams. All rights reserved.*

*No part of this book may be reproduced, stored in a retrieval system, or transmitted by any means without the written permission of the author.*

*First published by AuthorHouse    10/25/2011*

*ISBN: 978-1-4567-8776-9 (sc)*
*ISBN: 978-1-4567-8777-6 (ebk)*

*Printed in the United States of America*

*This book is printed on acid-free paper.*

*Because of the dynamic nature of the Internet, any web addresses or links contained in this book may have changed since publication and may no longer be valid. The views expressed in this work are solely those of the author and do not necessarily reflect the views of the publisher, and the publisher hereby disclaims any responsibility for them.*

*I am deeply grateful to Jo Evans for designing the cover.*

'My life is nothing but a dream
From which I will wake into death,
which is nothing but a dream of life.'
Chitra Divakaruni ('Queen of Dreams,' p 301) 2004


'Is all that we see or seem
But a dream within a dream?'
Edgar Allan Poe. 'A dream within a dream.' (1809 – 1849)


For those who will and those who have experienced:
' incomprehensible sounds, unpredictable moods and inexpressible needs.
And all the while watching, watching the loved one simply fade away.'
Richard Eyre 'Absent Mother', Evening Standard
Magazine. 14th November 2008

*All profits from sales of this book to be donated to the
Alzheimer's Society*

# Introduction

*I*n 1998, I had no idea that there was anything wrong with my eternally healthy Mum. Then John, her boyfriend and support suddenly died and I noticed how weak she was becoming. When she was seventy she had moved to live in a maisonette overlooking my brother's house and in nine years had made few friends and had to drive to the nearest shop. We decided that she should live in Cardiff, her childhood home, to be nearer her sister Gwen and old friends. I applied to Cardiff County Council, with a recommendation from Irene (Mum's Community Care Worker in the Bridgend Elderly Team), for Mum to be 'rehoused' in a sheltered housing flatlet, with a warden on site. Letters flew back and forth, but apparently there was a 'scarcity of sheltered accommodation in the Cardiff area,' and a huge waiting list.

Then she was offered one and I took her to see it. It was completely unsuitable. A run down tiny bed-sitter, which had been empty for two years.

Mum followed me dutifully, but was silent and unresponsive. I felt embarrassed at being the one chatting to her possible neighbours and tried in vain to bring Mum into the conversation. As we were leaving and passing through the large lounge a smartly dressed resident asked: "Does she play Bridge?"

"Yes, you *do*, don't you Mum?" I pleaded of the blank faced, shadowy figure shuffling behind me, as if someone was pulling her forwards faster than she wanted to go. She did not answer in time, or smile. We got back in the car. I felt distant from her, a little annoyed at her 'otherness,' for seemingly being unaware of her switched off behaviour. I wanted her to be the charming, friendly mother I had always known. What had happened to her? I didn't understand that she had a disease that made her face expressionless and prevented her being able to think of what to say. If only I had been more patient and loving.

"You know what's best for me Alys," was all she said. Did I? Her name went back to the bottom of the list and a few months later she went to her GP about her back pain and found that her lack of facial expression, muscle weakness and faltering feet meant that she probably had Parkinson's. She was sent to see a consultant in Swansea, who prescribed Sinemet.

At some point a year or so later the diagnosis was changed to Dementia with Lewy bodies the symptoms of which, are stiffness and shakiness, visuospatial dysfunction, complex hallucinations and cognitive impairment all of which are fluctuating. Those affected have a varying ability to remember and communicate, from day to day, or even minute to minute.

The sheer horror of developing a memory disorder for both the sufferer and their carers is ill understood by those untouched by it. Just imagine the beginning stages of being unable to remember names or numbers, finding it difficult to learn new things, forgetting words, perhaps having hallucinations, depression or behaving strangely. What if your brain was insidiously overproducing the proteins, which form the plaques and tangles, which slowly and progressively starve it? It's a frightening possibility for us all and there is no cure.

The care costs to the country are huge, but inadequate. There is a focus on keeping people alive rather than happy. Dementia has been regarded as stigmatising and shameful and those who develop it have been hidden away and contained. As a society we have yet to work out how to communicate with or how best to care for sufferers. Perhaps it is thought that they don't understand what is happening to them, that they are blissfully ignorant, and maybe that is true in some cases.

However I saw that Mum understood far more than she could express. She often appeared to be aware of her thoughts, but couldn't retrieve the words, so became very frustrated and frightened at what was happening to her. The six long years from Mum's diagnosis to her death made me hope that there can be a better reality in a person's head than in the misery and degradation of their actual lives. I want to believe that there can be imagination, enjoyment and romance when health, youth and competence have gone.

Caring for people one loves would seem to be one of the most selfless and devoted tasks that one can take on. However looking after a person with dementia is daunting and there are many heart-rending books written by both sufferers and carers, which are listed at the end. The caring is a full time job and there are few rewards. I have tried to be honest about my feelings and reactions during that long drawn out time, but friends have said that I seem monstrously sarcastic, selfish and impatient in my diary entries. They were usually written after a long day of battling with Homes or hospitals on behalf of a mother who latterly didn't seem to recognise me.

This book is both about the struggle that so many of us with elderly parents have with trying to do the best for them and also what might happen to a self when the brain no longer operates normally.

What follows are my diary notes written over the six years and what I imagined my Mum to be experiencing, based on what she said to me.

# Chapter 1—Catrin. Wednesday August 2nd 2000

*J*t happened such a long time ago that I'd almost forgotten that there were two of me. Myself and the one that soared out of my body and looked down on it from high above. It's such a strange feeling, watching the scene I've just left, or haven't yet arrived at. How can I be up here and down there at the same time? Is it my soul that's leaving my body? Is this what happens when you die?

I remember that first time. I was about seven.

"Tom, you'll miss your bus! Hurry, Catrin, run after Lizzie and Gwen." Mother called from the back door, as she pulled on her boots, chicken and pig feed pails on the stone flagged floor beside her.

I shivered in the morning cool. Tom smiled. Did he smile? Probably, he was always fun, "Race you," he said, and down the road and round the corner we flew.

Then there was the peculiar sensation, a sort of falling upwards and the other me was floating like a kite on a string, *really* flying, up into the sky. I paddled my legs and pulled with my arms and saw the school playground below.

Gwen was there, and Lizzie in her new orange dress, glowing gold in the morning sun. She didn't have to wear two older sister's cast offs. A roll and a glide and the main road was beneath me, the red and white bus sitting at the stop. I lingered above trying to see if Tom had caught it. If I were a bird, I'd have been able to swoop down and look inside, and he'd have been there all right, he's a very fast runner, but I was a balloon drifting over everything and the bus moved off and accelerated round the corner.

It wasn't frightening, but unsettling, whooshing up or down with no warning. When I came back, little sparks of shock would go off in my head. Was I daydreaming events before they happened or could it have been real?

Well it felt real. Especially that time when we were coming here to Tenby for our holidays and I got measles and had to stay home with Annie the maid. They all went off in the car leaving me in bed dreaming about a magical huge stone citadel with pink and purple towers and a massive gold door, surrounded by calm blue sea where silver fishes swam. The sun shone all day on happy, laughing people, seabirds flew above and there was a clean, salty seaside smell.

A few days later Daddy came back to tend to the farm and shop, but when he set off to bring them home, I found the other me leaving too, following high above Daddy's Morris Oxford for the whole hundred miles.

Over the sun-warmed countryside, the grazing animals, fields of green and golden grain, rivers running dry, villages, trees waving in the breeze I flew, swooping and gliding in the warm air currents, leaving myself, a huddled shape in the bed I usually shared with Gwen.

I could smell the coconut gorse, the manure from the farms, the chimney smoke so lazily rising. Then as the light began to fade and the countryside below was scoured with shadows he drove down a hill towards a little walled town. No stone citadel with pink and purple doors, but glinting sea and changing colours on the rocks as clouds chased across the early evening sky. I watched my brother and sisters playing ball on the golden beach, running into the sea for a last swim and climbing up St Catherine's Rock to the fort to peep through the windows. The walls were panelled with wood and there was a sunken parade ground with a beautiful tiled floor and handsome soldiers marching up and down. Why do I have to be ill and miss all the fun, I thought, as they ate ice cream in little silver dishes in the café near the harbour and went to a variety show, 'The Tenby Follies'. I watched for a while then went back to the rented flat to see Daddy and Mother getting dressed up to go out dancing at the De Valence. Mother was flushed and humming the descant as Daddy sang. She *loved* going out; if someone had offered her a trip to the moon she wouldn't have hesitated for a moment.

And then the scene faded. I pressed my hands to my eyes and when I took them away, I was back inside my sweating and delirious body. Annie was bathing my face, her lips white, her jaw clenched.

I opened my eyes: "Praise be," she exclaimed, "I thought you were gone."

They came back the next evening:

"Move over, Catrin." Gwen pushed my legs over onto my side of the bed.

"Poor baby Catrin, we've had such a lovely time." Lizzie jumped onto the bed to give me a hug.

"Why haven't you put your clothes away? They're all over the floor again," said fussy, tidy Gwen. Even at nine she always had to do the right thing.

"Don't you care that they'll be crumpled? How many times have I told you to put them away when you take them off?" She hung them carefully in our wardrobe.

"Did you like Tenby?" I asked.

"There's five beaches, a harbour, two tiny islands and a big proper one and we went to the Follies four times! They always started by singing: 'I'm sorry I'm late, I missed the bus, I . . . '"

" . . . slipped on a banana skin." I finished, before I could stop myself, laughing and clapping my hands.

"How did *you* know that?" they said

But I didn't tell them then, or ever. Even though we played 'The Follies' for months after with Lizzie as the Director and star performer. Perhaps I thought that everybody could come out of their bodies . . . well, what else is 'deja vu?' They probably wouldn't have believed me anyway. It's been my secret.

I thought it was never going to happen again after that last time when I was in hospital having Alys. But that was . . . well; it was over fifty years ago . . . I've often wondered since if I'd *dreamt* there being two of me. I couldn't explain it, so didn't think about it any more. I wanted my life to be safe, secure, familiar, predictable, exactly as it seemed . . . no surprises. But now it's happening again.

It was only those few minutes, at the specialists, so *did* I imagine it? How do I know what's real? Perhaps at this moment I'm not really thinking through bits of my life in some timeless expanse of the night . . . perhaps I'm dreaming now? No, I can't be, I can hear the Tenby waves and see the stars through the window.

Daddy used to show me the constellations and planets on nights like this. He knew them all. I'd tip my head back and stare up at the teeming pinpricks of light in the dark blue sky.

"Look Catrin, there's the North Star. Do you see the Plough? And there, Orion the Hunter. These are other worlds," he'd say, and I'd see the stories racing behind his shining eyes, of strange people on planets far away. The words would spill out of him, soft and dreamy, lifting me up and dropping me back like waves on the sea.

I'd be dizzy with imagining those other lives in that endless space. Then Mother would call and we'd go in for hot milk and bed. He was so knowledgeable and kind, always strict, but fair. How many years ago did he die? I know he was 92. Only nine more years and I'll have caught him up, so to speak.

What was that bang? A bomb? No, there it is again and seagulls squawking . . . it's the lifeboat flares. I hope they haven't woken up Alys and Cerys. How can anyone be in trouble? It's such a warm, clear night; the sea's like a millpond.

"Mum, Mum, are you awake?"

"Yes, but why are *you* up Alys? You must be exhausted driving all that way from London so early this morning!"

"Mmm, can't sleep. Driving distances makes me feel like . . . well . . . racing."

"I told you to come last night and sleep at my house!"

"Yeh, well, I wanted to play tennis. Do you want a cup of tea?"

"No thanks, I don't want to have to get up in the night . . . I'd disturb you and Cerys."

Is that running feet already? "Those brave men must go to bed in their clothes!"

"Yeh, amazing. Wonder if Tenby has any lifeboat women? Night then, Mum."

"Good night love. Thank you for bringing me on holiday."

Oh good, she's put the hall light off; I must try to get to sleep. Breathe in, breathe out, breathe in, relax . . . Mustn't worry about anything, must *not* worry, Alys says. Makes you ill. Mustn't worry, Alys says. Mustn't, mustn't worry, mustn . . . 't. Well, wouldn't *she* worry if she had this Parkinson's and was stiff and shaky? It's frightening, can't help crying sometimes . . . only when I'm on my own though, don't want anyone else to know. Why hasn't Alys

4

worried about being an unmarried mother? Poor little Cerys . . . people must have been talking about them. I wonder sometimes what happened to my shy little daughter. I was *so* embarrassed at the specialists with her tapping her feet and sighing and saying "About time too!' when we went in.

"Please, Alys," I said, my face burning hot, my heart beating so hard I was afraid all those other patients would hear it. I was shaking and trembling, telling myself to calm down, walk forwards, follow Alys. She's not like me, our generation is more respectful, but we don't always grasp what these doctors say. Then suddenly I was suspended up on the waiting room ceiling . . .

"Lighten up, Dad," a thin young girl said. He was still moaning on and on: "This government should all be shot, and all the staff here. I can't see any of *them* hanging around for hours."

Then that nurse came in. *She* wasn't the sort anyone would argue with.

"I think that's enough, Mr Harris. There are no slackers in this hospital; everyone's doing their best. We're a doctor short and if you hadn't missed your last appointment, you wouldn't have had to come today."

He scowled as she sailed away. I had a look in the next surgery; that was crowded too. Everyone I saw seemed to be sicker than me. I wondered what they'd thought seeing me waiting in my Jaegar suit, looking perfectly healthy. I've never been ill before. Perhaps the specialist's going to tell me he made a mistake and there's nothing wrong with me. Then everything got fainter and blurry and I knew I was off back again.

"So there are absolutely *no* other options?" Alys was asking.

"Not at this stage." He looked at me. 'Any questions?"

I could feel my hands clenching the cold metal of the chair, why do I get so nervous? I stared at him, wanting him to tell me that it wouldn't get any worse, but he looked away and shuffled his notes.

"Ok, thanks then, let's go Mum."

All the words I wanted to say arranged themselves into sentences as she pushed me out of the room. Alys asks questions; she's quick thinking, confident and tries to get me the best treatment. I'm very grateful for that. I squeezed her arm; "Thank you for coming, you understand all this so much better than me."

5

"Shame I'm not a man, Mum. You and Lizzie and Gwen treat men like gods!"

"No, we don't," but I could feel my face burning.

I must go to sleep . . . Don't suppose I'll ever play tennis again. Tennis in Tenby. I loved that Sutton Street court with all the flowers and apple trees round it. Gareth and I having our annual game . . . Thirty-five years of marriage and we only ever played on holiday. It always seemed to be windy. He hit all those funny shots up into the wind, they whirled around and rushed towards me, or dropped short . . . he always won . . . sleepy now . . .

❄    ❄    ❄

What's happening? What's woken me up? It's so still and dark, are *they* here? Open eyes very wide . . . can't see. Skittering heart . . . skin cold and prickling. No, there's the chest of drawers, the chair, the door to the corridor. I'm in Tenby, on holiday with Alys and Cerys . . . my favourite place in the world . . . nothing frightening here.

"It's your insecurities," Alys said when I was at her house and shouted in the night. "They come out as nightmares, Mum. Put the light on, get up and make yourself some herbal tea. Read something happy or watch one of your tennis videos to take your mind off it."

I can't, though. After I've woken up, I'm much too terrified to move.

The air's blacker and heavier . . . there *wasn't* anything there, I checked every corner, but is there *something* now? Why *does* this happen to me, what's *there*?

The air's so thick, can't breathe . . . suffocating. It's swirling, flapping.

Pobba, pobba, pobba . . . be quiet heart . . . have to hear where they are. I *know* they're here, there's scratching and clawing. Open eyes wider, listen, help, help, why's this happening to *me*? What's that? Flapping up onto the end of the bed? Staring vicious squirrel face . . . Can I shrink inside my body? It's going to *attack* me . . . sharp teeth bite into my neck . . . can't move . . . Did I shout? No, my throat's paralysed . . . aagh . . . here it is . . . a guttural roar gushing out, deep from my chest, my pounding heart. I'll scream . . . scream.

A light . . . white thing gliding at me. The noise . . . roars, screeches, it's touching me, crushing me. "Get away! Get away! Don't touch me!" Grab it, pinch, twist; It's crying. Twist harder, dig my nails in.

It's so bright. Cerys . . . the light. "Cerys, don't be frightened, I won't let them hurt you, they'll have to kill *me* first."

"Nana, stop hurting Mummy, what's wrong with you?"

What's she saying? What? Whaaat?

The blurry shape I'm fighting slowly, so slowly . . . I'm digging my nails into Alys's arms.

I can feel all my strength draining away. Where are those squirrels? Why did *she* pretend to be one?

"Mum, you had a nightmare, you were screaming and screaming."

I smell my acrid sweat, cold on my clammy skin. Why did they follow me to Tenby? What's happening to me? I can't stop shaking.

"Please stay with me, get in bed with me." I can feel her hostility.

"It's that Sinemet. Every time he increases the dose your nightmares have been *worse*!"

She's going on and on about the Consultant not having a clue what he's doing.

"That's it, you're not taking that extra night-time one again."

I feel a bit better drinking this tea and reluctantly she's got in with me. She's turned over, she won't touch me. Cuddling against her cold, unloving back, I'm so ashamed and alone.

# Chapter 2—Alys's diary

## FRIDAY AUGUST 4TH 2000

*H*ere goes. I have decided to keep a notebook, to record Mum's symptoms, the diagnoses, the drugs she is prescribed for her Parkinson's, and as Dad died fourteen years ago and her boyfriend John, last summer, our journey together through her illness.

Was it in her genetic material, programmed from the start? Or environmental? Could the trigger have been mercury fillings, aluminium saucepans, pesticide poisoning in food? Or was it caused by the stress of my brother's divorce and her husband and friends dying around her? Could it have been the head trauma when she fell playing tennis two years ago? She certainly became too unsteady and weak to ever play again. Which of the phantoms flickering behind her could have set it off? If she had done this or hadn't done that, would it have made a difference?

When did I first notice her symptoms? I admit, I had resisted believing that she was ill because when we talked she seemed the same, always interested and concentrating on me with her steady, focussed love and unconditional support when I phoned every few days to unburden the details of my life. It has been easier to ignore the signs and put them down to aging. When she became slower, shuffled her feet and avoided things requiring effort, "It's because she's lazy, she sits down too much," I said. The more she has avoided things, the more I thought she should do them and her not doing them was the reason she was unable to.

And of course, she did have her boyfriend, John taking her out and doing so much for her.

"Would you like a cup of tea and a cream cake? I got them from Sainsburys this morning." He'd say, as he did Mum's ironing again. Outside, the hedges and lawn were freshly cut. "Have you heard about the horse who stole your Mother's lunch?" He'd make his face serious, though the crinkly lines around his smiley eyes jiggled with mirth. They always seemed to be giggling together. He knew everyone and where to get anything, that is, if he had not stashed it away at the back of his garage.

"Picked it up in a car boot sale, along with twelve left footed Wellingtons. Thought they'd come in handy."

It was such a shock when he suddenly died in a jeweller's car park. He had gone to buy Mum a present of a watch for retiring from her part time job in Aunt Gwen's dress shop.

Without his support it has become obvious that dressing, housework and going out are arduous tasks.

Mum phoned a few weeks ago and asked if I would go with her to her next appointment with her Consultant.

The resignation and slight irritation in my agreement dismayed me. I love Mum. It is just that times away from work no longer have the lustre and anticipatory frisson of freedom and adventure. They are taken up with the expected duties of my 'daughter' role.

I pictured her crestfallen, replacing the phone and sitting for a while. She sits a lot. Then slowly getting up to put on the TV and pottering into the kitchen, to make herself a cup of tea or a meal. It was a Thursday evening, so her hair would have been freshly set, her makeup carefully applied and she would have been wearing one of her smart summer suits. She would look out of her window to see if she could catch a glimpse of Robert coming or going from his house below. If he is there she would have waved, though she knows that he will not look up. Her helpless need for her son (because he is 'a man'), to consult and enlist in doing little jobs for her has ensured that he keeps away.

So ten days ago I drove from London and picked up Mum to take her to Swansea for her appointment. My heart sank as we walked into the waiting room. It was packed. My lovely, mild mannered, eager to please Mum sat down quietly in her smart clothes and full make up. After forty minutes I started to get irritated. The seats were uncomfortable, the magazines old and even more people had arrived. How could she sit there so calmly and be so resigned and patient? I found a nurse. "How much longer do we have to wait?"

She scanned the schedule. "I'm sorry but Dr Scanlon is on his own today and has to see both clinics. You're sixth on the list."

"Don't be so impatient, you've got your book and there are plenty of magazines," Mum ventured as I returned.

"It's really disrespectful not to tell people what's going on and to expect them to hang around for hours," I said loudly to my 'mustn't grumble, must be grateful mother.'

I sat down and brooded about why she is always so cautious and keen to do the right thing and why she worries about what 'the family and neighbours will think.' Her lifetime role of covering up, never making a fuss and presenting the best face to the world has prepared her well for this illness. She has been compensating for her diminishing skills, aided and abetted by John. I exhaled with frustration. Our relationship is one of exasperated affection and mutual incomprehension.

We went into the consultant's room two hours after our appointment time. I introduced myself and sat at her side. He was obviously harassed, apologised for the wait and asked her how she has been feeling. She was unforthcoming, so I mentioned her hallucinations, slowness and inability to learn new things. Explaining the results of her CAT scan, it appears that she has all the classic symptoms of Parkinson's. She scored high in the Mini-mental test, though her maths had worsened and her writing had become even smaller. He prescribed a night time Sinemet, told her to keep exercising and off we went.

Yesterday Cerys and I picked up Mum and came to our tiny flat in Tenby for a weeks holiday. We unpacked, had supper, watched our ancient TV for a while and then went to bed, Mum in the bedroom, Cerys in the tiny bunkroom and me on the bed settee in the lounge/ kitchen. Mum seemed to be having trouble getting to sleep, and I felt too buzzy after driving all day, but eventually I dropped off, and dreamed of the sun and sea.

At 4.50 as the first grey strands of light peeped around our curtains, a terrible wailing, then deep guttural aggressive shouting, followed by screaming, woke us and presumably everyone in the block. I jumped out of bed, flicked on the corridor light and rushed to her, throwing on my dressing gown as I went into the room. As I moved towards her she bellowed out, "I'll call for help if you come any nearer, don't touch me. Help, Help, Get OFF me!" I talked gently, soothingly and tried to put my arms around her to calm her, but she thrashed around violently, hitting me hard, and then dug her nails into my arms, gripping like a limpet.

"Mum, Mum, you're hurting me, let go; it's me, Alys." I begged, struggling to prise her fingers off my arm. But she was supernaturally strong and had a glinting malice in her eyes.

"Help, leave me alone! You frighten me," she sobbed.

"I'm your daughter, I love you," I kept repeating.

"No, no, you're not, you're trying to hurt me."

Her sobs grew louder as she pushed me away, her sour breath and clammy skin repulsing me as much as her physical violence.

Unable to communicate with her or calm her in any way, I called for Cerys, who appeared at the door, a strained, frightened face peering out from a tightly wrapped duvet.

"Who are *you*?" Mum demanded.

"Nana, Nana, I'm Cerys, your grand-daughter, you know me. Stop hurting Mummy, what's wrong with you?"

"Why are you dressed like that?"

But her aggression seemed to be subsiding. I helped her out of bed, as she wanted to go to the toilet. By the time she returned I had made her a cup of tea.

She looked at it suspiciously. "Why are you trying to confuse me? You're plotting against me!" Her face was twisted, eyes slit-like, skin flaccid and grey.

I explained over and over, why she is experiencing nightmares, that I was trying to help her, that she should not take the extra night-time Sinemet she had been prescribed. It seemed to have made her hallucinations worse, but she need do nothing against her will.

It was after six and other people's days were just beginning. There were the sounds of lift doors banging above us and of engines, as the traffic started its usual assault on the road outside. The bedroom was flooding with morning light, but she still did not accept that I am her daughter.

"Why is Cerys hiding there?" she demanded, pointing to a corner.

"She's in bed, Mum." I called to Cerys in the other room, who confirmed where she was in reassuring tones.

"Are you going to go back to bed now?"

"I want to get in with you," she said petulantly, starting to get up.

"The couch bed is tiny. You get into your bed, Mum."

"You come in with me then," she insisted, a 'cross child' expression on her sagging face.

I got in, reluctantly, by now, exhausted and drained, some lines from an Emily Dickinson poem going around in my head:

*'One need not be a chamber to be haunted*
*One need not be a house;*
*The brain has corridors surpassing.'*

We lay down. To my shame, I turned my back. I just could not put out my arms to comfort her. A cold, clammy claw with its bird-wing tremble gripped my arm tightly. Neither of us slept.

# Chapter 3—Walking

"Go swimming, walk for half an hour twice a day, do your exercises and then rest on the bed when you finish," that specialist said.

I'm not going swimming, all that undressing and dressing and getting your hair wet and messed up. And those exercises. By the time I've done them and then got dressed and had something to eat, the day's over.

What's the time? Is that five to three? I suppose there's still time for a walk; Alys might ring and ask if I've done it. Sunday when Mr Jones drove me back from church she said, "Why don't you walk while you can Mum, it's only 200 yards?" I'll just go down the lane as far as the post-box.

Where's my key? Coat on, careful down the steps. Well I'm walking now aren't I? If only it was tennis or golf.

I must say though everything looks pretty in the sun. Those tall, fizzy grasses, swaying in the breeze and the yellow leaves, like paper aeroplanes, twirling down.

I remember dancing through the fallen leaves, dreaming about life's possibilities. Then the war came and everything changed. All those choices I thought I had, melted away. I suppose we were happy to be still alive. I was married and the dreams I had had for my life became dreams about how the children would grow up.

Robert's always been a worry; there's just been one thing after another. He was such a sweet baby. I was so proud when his photograph won the Western Mail baby competition. If he'd tried harder in school, it might have kept him out of trouble. I don't know how I ever got through the shock of Pam saying those things about him. How could he abuse his son? She made it up and its not over now. She's so vindictive, she'll never let him go until she's had every last penny out of him, like she did with her other husbands. She's ruined those children with all those take-aways and violent videos. It's been so humiliating going into town, I'm sure people were talking. And Social Services treating us like criminals. They've got no right to still stop us seeing the children after her lies were thrown out of court. They're probably like wild animals by now.

"Come and live near me. We can buy you the maisonette at the bottom of our garden. The shop's getting too much for you," he kept saying. Perhaps it was a mistake, but I *was* feeling low after Milly, then Amy and Bob died. Too much death, it gets inside you, pushing out life. I *was* glad to go on holidays with them and I didn't mind cooking Sunday lunch or babysitting. Until she ran off with that other man . . . then everything went wrong. Robert hardly ever drops in now. It's not fair, saying I always ask him to do things. I watch him from the window, coming and going, and he never even looks up. It's so hurtful, why doesn't he come to see me? Alys's right, I am by myself a lot, but I'm pottering along, and who else can I be with anyway?

Oh, I miss John; we had such fun together.

It's been quite warm today; I can smell smoke . . . something's burning? Hate smoke smells. Reminds me of . . . I can smell it now and feel the noise, the fear rising inside me, sliding around in my head. Those warning sirens, the bangs in the distance, the whooshing and thudding, then crashing masonry much nearer. That was the last time, until the other day in Swansea hospital, when the inside me came out. There I was, hovering above, looking down at myself in the Nursing Home, shivering in my sleep of exhaustion. The wind was bullying the trees, bare and grizzled with snow, so that they rattled their skeletons against the ward window.

Those sirens got louder and more urgent:

"Hurry, Mrs Williams," the Matron said, as she half carried a woman patient to the door.

I could see myself struggling to the edge of the bed and collapsing on to the cold floor as the throb of droning planes got nearer and the voices receded away from me. I lay there, weak and forgotten.

Then that terrifying whistle and a deafening crash like a massive punch reverberated through my body. I watched the walls bulge out, the ceiling collapse and I saw myself, crawling towards a gaping void. "Where's my baby? Where's my baby?" I was crying.

My arms and legs were bleeding from the falling debris. Behind me, the paediatric wing slithered into a crater.

"Where's my baby? Where's Alys?" I was begging, as showers of orange sparks and dust drizzled around us.

The sky looked on fire as columns of flames licked upwards and there was that heat, that terrible heat. Then suddenly, the wind dropped and it was so still as if Cardiff was holding its breath. "My baby?" I was still whispering.

Long white beams of sweeping searchlights, sparkling arcs of water jets. Someone put a blanket around me and a gentle voice said: "All the babies are safe, they're all safe."

Dry flakes of snow fell in the darkness and the moon was veiled by the scurrying clouds as the invisible cord jerked me back to my body, and Alys.

Over fifty years ago and I can still remember it so clearly, hear, see, feel, smell it, oh . . . that smoky smell, it's the bonfires from the allotments. And that, what's that faint . . . aaa? I know, it's over-ripe blackberries. Mmm. My mouth's watering for one of those nice blackberry and apple tarts I used to make, with cream. I've got some biscuits, if I turn round now I can watch 'Neighbours,' by the fire with a cup of tea.

Alys's always on at me: "You need to get out and meet people Mum, you don't *know* anyone round here. Why don't you go to classes? Look here's the brochure, pick some and I'll get you enrolled."

I have tried some of the things though I don't like going to new places and it's worse now I'm old and can't get up and down so easily. I do wonder what people are thinking of me, being so slow and awkward, but she keeps saying: "You're not trying Mum, don't be so lazy."

Well, we're not all the same. I look at her sometimes and wonder how my timid little golden haired child turned into this fiercely independent woman, forcing her ideas on people. She seems to think if you cease to do you cease to be. I'm quite content not doing a lot; I just want a quiet life with no arguments and no trouble.

Why did I have to get this Parkinson's? It was such a shock . . . I mean I knew I was getting weaker, but I was speechless when that specialist said, "You have Parkinson's." I felt as if he'd cursed me. My stomach churned with humiliation, my brain a black bewildered void. I should have asked him what it meant. Will it get worse? What will I be like? Will I be able to manage? Does it kill you? What am I expected to do now? But I just sat there and all Gwen and I knew was what he said I had.

And those tests and questions, over and over again with this doctor and that.

"Do you know the name of the Prime Minister? Where do you live? What's the date? Write a complete sentence!"

I've always had a good memory, it's not quite so good now, but I can still remember events and people in the news, and when the doctors give me three words so they can ask me them again later, I always know them. I felt so ashamed though last time when I struggled with the subtraction questions. Me, who worked in the Bank and did the shop accounts. Does Parkinson's make you go stupid? I should find out.

This lane's so uneven, nearly fell then. It's treacherous today after the rain. Is it the Parkinson's making me feel as if I'm losing my balance, as if someone is moving the ground beneath me? When I was young I thought getting old would be like I felt after a busy, sporty day, but its not. Its persistent aches, poor sleep and always being cold.

Here's my road, the houses close together like teeth . . . regular, the dark doors like fillings, but . . . which way is home? There's the shop, the road bending as it goes down the hill . . . am I up or down? I'm sweating, legs gone rubbery, shut my eyes, breathe deeply, open them . . . Down, yes it's down, of course, why am I being so silly? Keep going down to my house. Walk quicker Catrin, pick up your feet . . . Lift up those feet, up, up . . . it's getting quite nippy. That mist in the valley is just like a big duvet, putting the town to bed. All those birds, winging home to roost while I stand here on my own, hands shaking, fumbling with my keys. After all these years I shouldn't be fumbling. I never thought I'd end up living on my own, having bad dreams. Why did you have to die, John? At last, got it in, open now door, oh, a big pile of brightly coloured envelopes. The post was late . . . Bending is so hard and it's not as if I'll want any of this stuff. It'll be letters offering me credit cards, time-shares, smart casual clothes, free gifts I've won if I ring this number. I'm not even going to open them, there's bound to be some begging letters with photos of poor children and animals, they're just too upsetting. Oooh, getting up hurts, lean on the wall, that's better. An electricity bill . . . I've a rush of warmth for this, the only envelope really for me. The post isn't worth having unless it's Christmas or my birthday.

Put the kettle on, coat off, where have I put the biscuit tin? Here somewhere on the worktop, with everything else I use a lot.

"This is a real mess, Mum," Alys says. "What's the point in having all this cupboard space?"

Well, why do they make them so high or so low and deep then?

The milk, Ow! How did I drop that? It's gone everywhere. And my foot, it's really painful. I may not be able to go for my walk tomorrow . . .

# Chapter 4—Support. Sept—Dec 2000

## WEDNESDAY SEPTEMBER 6TH

" *I* suspect that Catrin isn't taking off her makeup or clothes at night. A year ago she was fastidious and beautifully dressed. She's no longer looking so good, she isn't coping." Irene, Mum's Community Care worker rang me to say last week.

We have found her a cleaner, and Irene swiftly organised adaptations to her home. When I visited today I found a cantilevered table, handrails and a door lock with an intercom and her chairs, couch and toilet seat had been raised to help her get up from them more easily. Around her neck she has to wear a push button alarm: in case of an emergency.

Because she has accepted help gracefully and without complaint, I have no idea what she is really thinking. Is she frightened by her deterioration, or demeaned or ashamed because she needs help? She has for so long been navigating around her symptoms and hiding her feelings that she would never be able to tell me. Oh Mum, I'm in agony watching your increasing helplessness, but you never moan, you have always been so careful to fit in and not cause trouble. You make it too easy for me.

I worry about her living alone and not going out much. There had always been people around her, family, friends or customers to chat to. She started working in our grocers shop when I was ten, because there was not enough profit to pay a sales person and Dad had had to take a teaching job to keep us afloat. Then supermarkets came to the Gwent valleys, selling goods at the same price that we paid for them at the wholesalers. Despite Dad's business degree, he was hopeless with money. If only he had left her enough to retire on. After he died, Mum struggled on for a while, but by then her customers all had cars and drove to the supermarkets. So she closed and drove the twenty-five miles each way to work in Aunt Gwen's fashion shop for £10 a day, a very low wage even in the 1980's. My canny, elegant aunt was not impressed with Mum's knowledge of couture, but was pleased to have a good book keeper. Having survived a hard and exacting apprenticeship and slaved for years to get the capital to buy her own shop, she was a controlling taskmaster:

"Never sit down. Refold the jumpers. Check the stock. Look busy."

Apparently my naughty mother would then take so long to fold a garment that Aunt Gwen would say, "Oh, for goodness sake, let *me* do that!" in exasperation.

Mum stuck it out until she was nearly eighty, but that was eighteen months ago. It had been getting harder and harder for her, but it had provided her with people to talk to. Is she lonely now?

After a few years of Mum driving to Cardiff four days a week from her flat above her closed grocer's shop, Robert bought a maisonette overlooking his home in Bridgend for her to live in. She paid the deposit, he paid the mortgage. Yes she was nearer her job but she left behind the neighbours she knew and her few friends who were still alive. I was never sure that she should have uprooted herself. I imagine her sitting watching TV, with the sounds of the traffic roaring up the hill outside, while the days and weeks slip by.

What can I do? My job takes up most of my life. So much thought and research is needed to come up with a vibrant, exciting programme offer every year. There are 130 tutors and all their classes to visit. Not to mention my home life with Mike and Cerys. I can't live Mum's life for her. Selfish? Anyway, I have a history of failed attempts to get her to exercise her mind and body.

When she moved to Bridgend, I took her to the local tennis club Women's Afternoon, a Bridge class, Indoor Bowls, Keep Fit classes and to some pensioner's swimming sessions. She always had an excuse not to go a second time.

Now she is no longer able to play tennis she is becoming weaker, stiffer and more housebound. So when she came to stay in London I took her along to activities I thought she would enjoy.

It was so embarrassing when the Acol Bridge Club rang up as soon as I got back from arranging the class for her:

"Your Mother now says she has hardly played before, we can't accept a complete beginner. Can you come and fetch her please?"

Similarly from the Community Centre:

"Your Mother doesn't want to join in the singing class or the Keep Fit."

So I want her to go out, though not in her car. There's no public transport in her village, but I don't think that she should be driving. She has always been cautious and slow, but when she drove me to B and Q to buy some autumn plants this afternoon, I realised how weak she is. She started the car with slow, concentrated deliberation. When it gently shuddered into motion only steady forward motion seemed possible because her hands rested so lightly on the steering wheel. Surprisingly, we crawled there and back without incident.

I've written easy instructions for her to change TV channels. "Look Mum, we've coloured the Eurosport button with Tippex, just press it when you want tennis." Yet she seems unable to master the remote.

She has admitted in a thoughtful, dignified way that she often has hallucinations. "I don't mind because it's always Gwen or Cerys sitting there on the chair chatting to me. It's company really."

Why *have* I been trying to force her to do things? We are not all the same; she seems perfectly content to lead what would be for me, a quiet and uneventful life. Mum is a homely, god fearing, cake making woman, not a confident, socialising type. I remember when she and Gwen went to Paris for the weekend, a few years ago. Gwen was full of it:

"The Follie Bergere *and* a nightclub," she said. "But you know your Mother, she's got her school cert in French, but she hung around behind me and wouldn't have a drink of course. Hopeless!"

I have just rung Lizzie to see what she thinks. She is in two choirs, plays tennis, badminton and bridge and has a packed social life, so had to have three 80th birthday parties to be able to invite all her friends. She understood instantly:

"We always had to push Catrin. She was the cleverest and best at everything. Did you know that she sang on the radio and when the Cardiff chapels took scripture exams every year, she was always top? She'd get 100%! We had such a good social life at Chapel and at home. She never had to lift a finger to organise anything."

"A lot of her friends have died, or were people she played sport with and she's lost touch with them. I'm worried that now she's not going out much, she seems to be getting weaker and forgetting how to do things, like change channels on her TV. I don't know how to help her from so far away."

She tutted sympathetically:

"Catrin should invite her neighbours round for tea. She should make more effort," she said. "I'll give her a ring and talk to her about it."

I feel more cheerful, but it is true, she has never had to make much effort socially. She had a busy social life through her sport and being tall; comfortably curvaceous with a shy Princess Di smile she has been a magnet for men. But how is she going to meet new ones if she rarely goes out?

## SUNDAY SEPTEMBER 10TH

I have just rung Robert and he thinks I'm exaggerating and that she is perfectly cheerful, just getting older.

"But she's always in when I ring, just sitting, watching TV." I said

"Well where's she going to go? We're not all mad socialites like you. Most of her friends are dead and she's too old to be playing tennis or golf now."

"She's got to keep active, keep her brain and body fit."

"Don't be stupid, she's 81! And she shouldn't be driving any more, she drove into a hedge at Gwen's a few weeks ago."

We were starting to wind one another up, raising our voices, getting into an old style argument. I could hear talking and laughing in the background as he switched on his TV.

"Just because you never exercise," I paused to consider my options. I shouldn't say, she'll be as fat and unhealthy as you; I need him on side for Mum's sake. "If she'd play bowls or something at least it would get her out of the house."

"She used to be exhausted when she came back from playing tennis. I blame you for pushing.." He stopped and I heard the screech of verbal brakes. "Leave her alone. It's because you teach PE all day, you think everyone should be exercising all the time."

21

"I don't teach PE all day."

"Don't you? What do you do then?" He sounded irritable and uninterested.

"I'm in charge of an Adult Education Health Department. There are people in their 90's learning . . ." But the clapping and talking had got louder and I knew he wasn't listening. I glanced across at Mike, sitting watching the 10 o'clock news, sipping a glass of red wine. My reserved and watchful partner. While I batter everyone with words, he takes everything in, and then tactfully finds a way to peacefully achieve the same end. He is becoming very grey, but he is still so handsome, kind, such a dear, loving companion.

"I'll be down next weekend, "I said and put down the phone.

## MONDAY SEPTEMBER 11TH

I talked to Irene today and she has booked Mum into a Day Centre once a week.

Looking back on my notebook entries, I seem to be using this as more of a diary. Oh well, its probably cathartic.

## MONDAY OCTOBER 3RD

Mum's Consultant said that her PET scan shows no evidence of a stroke. He told her to carry on walking every day, doing her exercises on her bed and swimming regularly. Encouraged that she would now take this seriously, I have bought her a stationary bike for wet weather days and am taking it down at the weekend. She can take me on one of her walks.

On Friday she had a visit from an 'independent living co-ordinator' to support her in 'cooking simple meals safely.'

"I had to boil an egg and cook a 'ready meal' in the microwave. She couldn't have been more than twenty." Mum said wryly.

## SATURDAY OCTOBER 14TH

Mum has been stoically trying a more active regime, but says it takes up most of the day, and I can see that the tasks of daily living are sapping her energy. When I arrived today, I let myself in and she guiltily jumped up from her sofa crying: "Only just sat down."

The struggle to dress and undress, do her exercises, go for a walk, go out into the rushing, don't care town to buy food and then to prepare it, is filling and governing every aspect of her shrunken life.

She is still just about managing to cook meals for herself and even for me. We had poached eggs on toast for lunch. In Mum's world of domestic tasks, a woman's talent and reputation in preparing and presenting home cooked food defines her as a good housewife and hostess. Cooking for people has demonstrated her affection for them and given her dignity, self worth, her place in society. "I am renowned for my sponge," she has often told Cerys, pride swelling her voice, blooming her face, capturing her youth.

As I devoured my egg, I remembered her face as she made a sponge; it was soft, dream like and far away, as she beat up the margarine and sugar and added the egg, little by little. She sifted the flour and folded it in, "Then always add a tablespoonful of warm water to your mixture," she would instruct me. "It makes a moister, lighter sponge."

After thirty minutes, she would bend to take the two sponge tins out of the oven and turn to show me, dizzy with pride at their perfectly risen, golden evenness and light perfection.

Tennis, cooking and eating seemed to have been Mum's favourite pastimes. Robert and I sometimes talk about the concentrated way in which she spread what seemed like a quarter of a pound of butter onto half an energen roll, to eat with an apple for lunch. She was always on a diet. The spreading became almost an art form; the layer was so even and exact. Then she would bite, searing through the half-inch of yellow grease and the nasty dry ball of air, leaving the imprint of her teeth, in the piece still to be savoured.

## SATURDAY OCTOBER 21ST

Her production of meals has been slowly stalling and today we cooked chops and peas from the freezer. There were no tarts, with handmade short crust pastry, crisp on top and sweet and soggy under the apples or rhubarb, or delicious steak and kidney. No Welsh cakes or perfect sponges to eat with our cups of tea.

"There's too much left for me to finish, it wastes." she said in explanation.

Mum loves fruit, but has to buy enough for the week when she goes to town on Thursdays. Her fruit bowl always seems to be full of over ripe nectarines, bananas and grapes.

"I don't mind them like that," she said, peeling a rotting black banana for her pudding.

She always shrugs off her incapacities, her small steps, shuffling gait and unsteadiness. I am conscious that she is hanging on by a thread to her respect for her own self-image.

She says that Robert has told her that she cannot drive any more, so she will have to take a taxi into town on Thursdays. Poor, poor Mum.

## SATURDAY NOVEMBER 4TH

I arrived without warning today and looked in the fridge for something to cook for lunch. She bravely, defiantly defended her mouldering ham, smelly chops, ancient eggs and dried up cheese. "They're only a few days old," she beseeched. "I bought them on Thursday."

I thought better of demeaning her with, "which Thursday?" So drove her to one of the six nearby superstores, to replenish her stocks. Even at 81, she was determined to pay.

## SATURDAY NOVEMBER 25TH

Not wanting her to be worrying for days about what to cook for me I turned up unexpectedly again and really caught her out. I opened the fridge to be assailed by a rank smell of old, putrefying food. A black mould covered the contents, speckling the shelves and walls. I stared helplessly at the chops I had bought. The plastic packaging with its promise of 'Two for the price of one' bulged like a blown up balloon, the silvery green meat, sunk away from the bones, damp and decaying, Would she ever have tried to eat them?

The vegetable drawer was a sea of fetid liquid, black mottled beans, smelly mushrooms and a cucumber covered with a delicate white woolly mould lay marooned and helpless.

"What *have* you been eating, Mum?" I asked.

"Oh, I couldn't manage it all, we bought too much and I haven't been that hungry. Shall I make us cheese on toast for lunch?"

I glanced at the open bread bin, to see the rotting remnants of the same loaf we had bought three weeks before. Her cheerful assertion on the phone, that "I'm fine, don't worry," was a cover up, shocking me out of my 'must get back to my important, busy life immunity.' I understand with a sickening guilt that everything is *not* all right. Like her hapless vegetables she is marooned and she is not coping.

## TUESDAY NOVEMBER 20TH

I have fixed up meals on wheels. They will bring a main meal and a pudding at 11 am on Mondays to Thursdays for £1.20 a day. "You couldn't buy the ingredients that cheaply, could you Mum? When you go to the hairdressers on Thursdays, you can buy enough for the three day weekend and breakfast and supper." I explained.

She did not protest, though I feel humiliated for her in having to eat mass produced meals made for the elderly. Her identity has evolved around her pride in presenting an image of successfully managing her life. How does she feel about having to accept so much help and to be disintegrating so publicly?

## FRIDAY DECEMBER 8TH

"I think the meat is that stuff you eat," she complained indignantly when I rang this evening.

"What, Quorn? I shouldn't think so Mum. Quorn is more expensive than real meat. It's probably just a bit overcooked." I said hopefully.

I'm so worried about her; life is slipping out of her control. I am sure that she is lonely and struggling with inner fears and day-to-day tasks, but I feel that I should be tough with her, get her to try harder, keep exercising, and push herself. Apart from her Thursday taxi to town, and Monday trip to the Day Centre her only outings consist of five hundred yard walks, along a lane or Sunday mornings two hundred yards down hill to the church. Another churchgoer always gives her a lift back up; they can see that she is not managing, which I don't want to accept.

Her visual pathways seem to be failing, she can read initially, but then the words blur and go on top of one another. She blames her glasses; we've been to one optician after another in the past two years. A new prescription, new glasses, but none give her back what she craves, the ability to read.

Irene has arranged for carers to come for an hour morning and evening to help her dress, undress and shower. They come from agencies, so she is never sure who is going to arrive. Most of her better china, jewellery and silver has disappeared. I don't know if this has happened recently or in last years burglary. The police had said that the window catch had been broken from inside, so the burglar had a key. The shocking and upsetting thought that it must be connected with Robert's runaway wife, seemed to paralyse us. I never did get Mum to do a proper inventory and list what was missing.

I have been reading about 'visual agnosia' and dementia with Lewy bodies, which her consultant has now suggested might be what she has. It has similar symptoms to Parkinson's.

## FRIDAY DECEMBER 22ND

I am extremely busy at college and couldn't take a day off to fetch Mum. "It's ridiculous, me driving 180 miles there and then back, you know how much I hate driving, I can meet you off the coach at Victoria," I instructed her.

Snow and traffic made the bus two hours late. She had fallen in the bus station and had to sit for six hours with bloodied knees and elbows. She made light of it, but I was and am so anguished and ashamed that I have persisted in being fooled by the front she puts up for me. I didn't want to accept what is happening to her and have believed that she can manage if she tries. She seemed to agree with my diagnosis "try harder and you'll be OK," but she was probably just trying to be supportive. Was this an isolated incident? If she really is becoming helpless, what does this mean for her future?

# WEDNESDAY DECEMBER 27TH

Is she hiding how difficult she is finding dressing, showering, putting on her make up and walking? She has not been coming downstairs until nearly lunchtime. For the first time ever she has not offered to help us cook and wash up. She has dusted a little, but has sat for most of Christmas, reading the newspaper slowly and repetitively.

Her bedroom is next to mine and I can't sleep because of her loud, snoring breaths and cries. When she screams, I get up and try to gentle her panic and replace the bedclothes she has threshed as if struggling with a demon. I have tried shutting my door with a towel against the crack at the bottom, but still the snores saw through my head. I am sick with fatigue, but also shame at my night time rages and I am so angry at this illness for its cruel symptoms.

Today I sent her out to walk the 150yds to the hairdressers. Ten minutes later she was back between two burly builders, an ashamed, sheepish smile on her face.

"She fell love, and couldn't get up again."

# SUNDAY JANUARY 7

Mike and I took Mum to a hotel for her birthday weekend. She did not seem to enjoy it much, spending most of the time in her room. Was she struggling to dress? Should I have helped her more? I have been so sure that she could do things if she tried, and if she did not try, she would get even weaker, more dependant on others, though all the evidence is mounting that I am wrong.

I can't seem to stop talking obsessively about dementia. Am I boring my friends? They seem to be interested, but are they humouring me?

I have always imagined that dementia was a uniform ebbing of the tide of memory and knowledge, but I am learning that if she has does have DLB, the confusion varies from day to day, and even from hour to hour. It has the symptoms of Parkinson's, a tremor, rigidity, unsteadiness on the feet, loss of spontaneous movement, lack of expression in the face, difficulties with concentration and attention, frequent drowsiness and visual hallucinations, but it has been compared to the effect on a piece of fabric if it had been sprinkled with acid. Big holes appear randomly with strong areas of fabric too. Sometimes it is possible to see only intact parts as Mum folds and refolds it to hide her inabilities. Such a good analogy. How long has she been managing to distract us from all the things she cannot do? Has my tough stance with her been cruel and unkind? She must be terrified of what is happening to her. What can I do?

# Chapter 5—The Day Centre

"There you are love. *You're* looking a bit of a dish today!" The green-uniformed bus driver helps me down the steps . . . my heart soaring at the compliment. I'm not sure which door to go into. I'm apprehensive, but feel glamorous and upbeat, in my Tricoville red jacket with the navy trim and navy matching straight skirt. Plas Llwys looks like a country pub; except for 'Dyfed Morgannwg NHS Trust' across the front. The smell of May is all around. Shame the shrubs are absolutely *smothered* with that pernicious travellers joy *and* convolvulus too. Looks pretty though, like white and green clothes left to dry. Too many squirrels, hate their rat faces and their sleek bodies . . . like waves when they run. "Don't come near me!"

"Off you come my love, *you're* looking a bit of all right today."

She's so drably dressed in her brown anorak, blue pleated skirt and *pink fluffy slippers* . . . She's going through the door. I'll follow, out of the sharp sunlight. I feel rather foolish . . . deflated.

Down the blank corridor, into the yellow . . . tennis ball coloured lounge. It smells of disinfectant and . . . lunch. We're first. Blue support chairs all round the walls and backs to the view. I'll sit there in the corner. My pants feel really uncomfortable; they must be on wrong again. It's so frustrating. I held them up to make sure I'd got them round the right way, then when I lay down to pull them up I *thought* I'd got my feet in right. I get so tired and sweaty and there were still my tights and skirt and shoes to go. Alys said I spent the whole morning getting up when I stayed with her. She had to help me into the shower. I wish she would have helped me out, but I didn't dare ask. I'm going to leave my bra and pants on in bed from now on, and just change when I have a bath.

The room's filling up. What a stomach! No wonder his shirt won't do up and he has to use sticks. And that grey hair sprouting out . . . He's like a big hairy old dog.

"That's my seat," he's growling, "I always sit there."

The bustley, busty, blue overalled nurse is coming; she must be wearing a very bouncy brassiere . . .

"Now, now Jack, that's not the way to treat a new lady is it, sit here look, have a change."

All those bows and combs to hold up her big floppy bun . . . she's certainly a no nonsense person . . . Jack sat down pretty quickly. Some people are chatting but I'm not going to try and talk to him.

"How do you like your tea, love?"

"One sugar and a rich tea biscuit, please."

I'm no good at holding my cup and saucer like this, my hands don't seem to grip properly, perhaps that's why my writing's so small and shaky.

Don't drop it.

Don't..

Has it spilled on my lap?

I won't drink it, don't want to have to spend a penny.

It's funny how lonely one can be in a crowd.


"You finished love?"

"Oh, thank you. Yes, that's all I want, thank you."

This head person looks like Miss Jenkins, my first Sunday school teacher, mouse brown hair and glasses, casting a calming, ordered spell over the room.

"I'd like you all to welcome Catrin Williams and Megan Rees. Make sure you show them how friendly we are at Plas Llwys. The programme for the day is: socialising, I'm afraid the physio couldn't come this morning to give us all some exercises. Lunch, then bingo or felt-work."

Don't want to do any of it. I want to be at home. Alys said, "You have to meet people Mum. They have activities and a physio and a nice lunch."

How does *she* know it's nice?

Most of the conversations are exhausted. Why have I got to sit here in this crowded loneliness watching eyes closing and mouths dropping open . . . She really does look like Miss Jenk . . . ins . . . at . . . Sunday . . . sch . . .

*It's Sunday morning and I've escaped the pandemonium of everyone getting ready for chapel, to sit in one of my favourite places . . . on the top of the steps next to the granary door. I can dangle my legs down the wall and look at the road beneath. Not much happens there, our farm is at the end of the road, but I can hear the church bells and see the horses in the paddock, especially Diamond who won the high stepping competition yesterday, or the ducks around the farmyard fence if I crane my head round the corner.*

*Daddy's revving up his big Wolseley, to make mother hurry up. Here she comes, shouting instructions to Lizzie:*

*"Make sure you hold Catrin's hand when you cross the roads. See that Tom has washed his hands and face. Gwen, I've told you. No, you are not wearing that tight skirt!"*

*She looks beautiful in the dropped waistline, calf length beige dress she's been making all the week. The Singer machine whirring over her neat little tacking stitches, her slim fingers deftly controlling the material as she pumps the treadle. I see that Daddy's head is turned towards her. I can't see his face, but I can imagine his eyes softening tenderly, before he speeds off, down the road and round the corner, towards the lanes to pick up some of the older chapel members. We used to go to Capel Gwylm too. It's so tiny that when we were in the back room drawing pictures or having a story, all we could hear was Daddy playing the harmonium and singing at the top of his voice. "Never had a lesson," he always tells us. "When my father set up this chapel for the farm workers he said, you're always wanting to play the piano, well you can play the hymns on Sundays. So I had to teach myself and quickly."*

*I'm not much good at playing, Mother can play anything by ear. Lizzie's the best of us, but then she's thirteen and she can't sing at the same time like Mother. We sit on the landing listening to Mother when they have musical evenings. If they play whist afterwards, Daddy says she always wins. I think she wins at tennis and croquet too when her friends come for games and tea.*

*Lizzie's the same, she's good at things and she's lots of fun. Everyone wants to be friends with her and they like Gwen, though*

31

*she's shyer, she's always so fashionable and beautiful, like Mother really.*

*I liked going to Capel Gwylm, but I suppose there weren't enough other children and I didn't understand the Welsh. There's loads of us at the Baptist chapel and it's in English. Lizzie and Gwen have lots of boyfriends. Perhaps I'll have one next year when I'm ten.*

*"Catrin have you got your coat?" I scuttle down the steps and into the house to find it and we're off down the road. We've hardly started when Lizzie spots Gwen's shoes: "You can't wear those, you're not a flapper, mother will be furious. Go and take them off quickly."*

*"Mother said I could have them."*

*"Yes but for dressing up and parties, not for chapel." Lizzie's scandalised. "She'll kill you!"*

*"No she won't," Gwen wriggles uncomfortably, but isn't arguing with much conviction. She looks down regretfully at the red high peep-toes, then turns and totters in, reappearing in her sensible school shoes, but with her green cloche pulled down over her bob and her matching gauntlet gloves.*

*Tom and I are kicking stones at our high garden wall.*

*"Come on, you'll scuff your shoes, let's run, we're going to be late."*

*So off we go full pelt. I want to stretch my long legs, run fast and beat Lizzie, I'm already as tall as her. But then I look back at Gwen trailing behind holding her hat and hair in place, walking along as if she were modelling her clothes, and I slow down. Perhaps that was the beginning of not knowing which one of them I wanted to be like . . .*


"Lunch is ready everybody. Into the dining room please. Sit at your usual tables. Catrin and Megan, you can sit here with Dorothy and Mary."

This meat is chewy and gristly and the gravy watery, not like the dinners I cook. "You're the best cook in the family, Auntie Catrin," Jake always tells me. He loves my cakes and steak and kidney pie. The rich, succulent aroma when it's cooked for a day and left to stand for another makes my mouth water, just thinking about it. Pink fluffy slippers has gravy on her chin . . . and whiskers . . .

"Did you enjoy the pork?" She doesn't answer, then she splutters,

"Yes, very nice f . . ."

Her teeth have dropped . . . She reminds me of Uncle Arthur, he always had trouble with his dentures. *Food flew everywhere and often his teeth followed. You could see where he'd been sitting by the sputters of gravy and custard on the cloth. After chapel on a Sunday, we'd have two sittings in the dining room. Children eating first with our gang and then parents, their friends and relatives. Always our own meat: crisp, juicy skin and plenty of flavour and four or more vegetables from the garden. Then apple tart and custard and afternoon walks, tennis in the orchard or croquet on the lawn. Except if it was cold or wet, then we'd play cards in the granary. Daddy would be scandalised at cards on a Sunday. "Have you been to Chapel this morning?" He would ask the boys. A quote from the Bible would follow. Very religious was Daddy.*

"So, what do you think?" The puffy faced woman has finished dissecting her cake into tiny crumbs and is looking at me. I'm desperately searching around my brain for the subject matter . . . parry with a smile and a "mmm?"

She spits cake crumbs as she spoons them in: "About the transport situation."

What's she's talking about? Here's the large blonde nurse with the hair with a life of it's own.

"You've finished, Catrin haven't you? Come into my office please."

Can feel my heart sinking. Blank faced, guarded, I have to follow, for a phantom Alys stands behind me. I know the name of the Prime Minister and I can keep taking 7 from 100, but what's the date? Oh no, what's the date? Why is she looking at that form? I'm getting panicky and sweaty . . . like I've got snakes slithering inside me. What *is* the date?

The clock on the wall behind her is gulping softly, slowly swallowing the minutes. Her hair's moved itself over to her left ear; it's ready for take off.

"I have all your personal details and medical diagnosis from your doctor, how long have you been like this?"

Like what? What am I like? Shall I say always? I'm like myself, only older?

"You're having difficulty with your mobility. Are you in pain?"

"No." I've been taught never to complain. "It's not polite to moan or whine, always smile, no-one wants to hear moans," Mother used to say. I always had to fight back my tears and turn the other cheek. Especially when Miss Howells didn't give me the Maths prize. "You have won it three times Catrin, you are the best in the school, but we should encourage others. Don't you think?"

I've never complained about my lot. Alys and Robert complain to me all the time. I let them, so they can get things off their chests. "You're so sympathetic and supportive, Mum." Alys always says.

"The physio can't come in today, but she'll be here next Tuesday, so I'm putting you down for a session with her as soon as you arrive. Make sure you're wearing flat, comfortable shoes."

As if I could wear anything else with my sore back and hips . . . All my elegant heels gathering dust in the bottom of my wardrobe . . . Well I suppose I'll have to come if I get some help with my movement.

I wish they'd let me stay at home; I can sit on my chair under Auntie Dolly's mirror, with the blue and white clematis twining around the frame. I'm not like Alys; I love to be at home, watching 'Neighbours' or 'Home and Away.'

"Why do you watch that rubbish, Mum?" Alys asks. I'm always glad when Cerys is around: "Go away, Mum. We're watching and that's that."

I didn't like the idea of Social Services putting handles down the stairs and all over the bathroom, and making my couch and chairs so much higher, but it does make it easier. I can look through the window now at the hill opposite and see the cars like Robert's dinky toys slowly winding along the A 48.

No, I'm not like Alys. I like peace and quiet. I'm quite happy with my lot. I'm glad we didn't find a flat in Cardiff . . . all that upheaval! I look around at my mother-in law's old mahogany sideboard, still with the rich sweet smell of the dried dates she kept for snacks, and Mother's pink flower plates on the wall . . . everything in it's own immutable place looking back at me, and think about my happy childhood. The farm was always full of family and friends.

I sometimes have visitors even though I know they're not real. After supper wisps of something gather in the still air and Cerys or Gwen are sitting on the couch. I look forward to our evenings together. There's not too much on TV these days after the soaps are over. "Did you see the wedding, Nana?" Cerys will ask, or whatever has happened in Coronation Street or East Enders and then we have a good discussion about it.

If I ask how long they can stay, they smile, withholding, secretive smiles.

"Not long, not long, just popped in."

I don't move until they go. It's rude to have guests and leave them, so sometimes we just sit watching the TV in silence, until I look at the couch and they've left. I wait for a while in case Cerys is coming back from the kitchen . . . She always offers to make her own tea to save me getting up. Then when I'm sure, I can walk past the empty couch, with the dent in the cushion where one of them has been sitting.

"Have you got any problems managing at home?"

I shake my head, well its only driving I can't do, I suppose Robert was right stopping me . . . I'm so much weaker now. It was such a shock when we went the first time to see that specialist in Swansea.

"You have Parkinson's, Mrs Williams. I'm going to prescribe a dopamine drug for you to take twice daily."

Gwen tried to write down what he said but she's dyslexic so didn't get much and I was too frightened to take it in, so he had to say it again. He was quite cold and impatient, as if it was my fault! I never dreamt there was anything really wrong with me. There's no Parkinson's in the family.

"If you need any more explanation, I suggest that you make an appointment with your doctor."

He wasn't a compassionate person . . . didn't seem to consider my feelings and ignored Gwen. Doctors are a special breed, foreign to me; I've always been so healthy. I'm not going to run around saying I've got Parkinson's. People won't understand, they might think that they can catch it. I don't get bored at home. I'll just keep on going and hope it doesn't get worse.

"Does someone help you with your shopping?" She's asking.

"No, I manage," and I do. On Thursdays after Hazel has finished my hair, I can shop before the taxi comes. I must put a note in my pocket to use next week . . . it's embarrassing when I can't get money out of my purse quickly enough. I like being in town. No one notices me of course. But that's all right, being part of the bustle while being private and unseen.

They've finished playing bingo. "No, I won't have any tea thank-you." . . . In case . . .

I'm not going to give the bus driver one of 'my looks.' Gwen and Alys say I'm a flirt, but not today. That man at the back won't stop complaining . . . over and over . . .

"It's a waste of time, there's never any physiotherapy and the food's not up to much."

The driver's loud revs are smothering the rest of his words. Perhaps they're frothing out of the windows, trickling down the sides of the bus . . . Hope we stop at the lights next to the tennis courts . . . there's four women playing. That's Anne! I haven't seen her for over a year, not since I fell and banged my head. That was a good rally . . . We're like that bed of dahlias, some of us standing boldly, fleshily erect, bright, vibrant colours, others bent and drooping with petals on the ground. Bye Anne.

He's very polite helping me off, just in time for 'Neighbours.' Perhaps he'll forget to pick me up next week, or I'll have a cold and won't have to go . . . .

# Chapter 6—Hospital. Feb—June 2001

## TUESDAY FEBRUARY 6TH

*M*um was doing her exercises on her bed this afternoon, when she fell onto the floor and was trapped in the narrow gap between the wall and her bed. Her arms are now so weak that she was unable to get up. She eventually managed to pull the phone by the cord down from her bedside cabinet and remembered my work number. Luckily I had just come back from a meeting and was doing some paperwork at my desk. "Oh Mum, Mum, are you hurt?"

"No I don't think so, I slipped and I'm stuck."

I don't know her neighbours phone numbers, so I rang Irene who wasn't in the office, then Robert who alerted Community Care, and staff were sent to help her.

"Are you *sure* someone went straight away?" I asked him later.

'Yes, yes. Bill from over the road saw them and went and helped her up and made her a cup of tea, she's fine."

Mum answered the phone sounding calm and untroubled. If only she was nearer.

## FRIDAY FEBRUARY 16TH

Irene arranged for Mum to go to a Respite Home for a week, where people go for short-term care. I came down to see her on Wednesday and again today. She was still on the same page of her book and was chatting up a very elderly man, whose wife was having a week's holiday from looking after him. He has had a stroke and can barely speak, but was obviously thrilled by her attention. Mum was switched off from me and showed no interest in my visits. Is she traumatized at the indignity of being institutionalized? Is she embarrassed at being here so has shut off from me and it? She seems

37

so much more fully functional than those around her, but not quite the Mum I have known all my life. I'm so worried that I can't sleep, just keep thinking about her, wondering what I can do.

## MONDAY FEBRUARY 19TH

A doctor suggested that Mum should go from this place to residential care. She refused of course, so we took her home to manage with what Irene called 'an increased care package.'

This means three visits from carers each weekday to help her get meals and dress and one on Saturdays and Sundays. Mum says Elaine, who has been her once-a-day carer for a while, has been bringing her a Sunday lunch when she's finished dishing out lunch for her own family. How kind of her. Why doesn't Robert do something like that to repay the ten years of her cooking meat and three veg and tart and custard every Sunday for him and his now absconded wife and children? He rarely goes near Mum, in case she needs something. If only she lived near me.

## SATURDAY MARCH 17 TH

Caught a train to visit Mum as a surprise. She was smartly and attractively dressed in her blue and white suit with its lightly padded shoulders and expensive buttons, the cut disguising her enormous bust though without a roll-on to squeeze unwanted flesh into sealed vacuum packed flatness. I don't think that she is able to get it on any longer. I remembered sneaking into Mum's bedroom as a child to stare with horror at this rubberised, elasticised foundation undergarment, the stiff carapace, which when not on her body, lay on her chair, its suspenders hanging down like cows' teats. These were to attach to that other repellent item of adult clothing, the nylons.

"Treat them as if they are gossamer," Aunt Gwen advised me.

"Always wear cotton gloves to put them on in case your nails should snag one. Roll them and put them over the toes, like so and then unroll them carefully up the leg."

Try as I might, my nylons sagged around my ankles, or after a few minutes I would feel a run, and have to apply soap or nail varnish, and go out with ladders turned to the inside of my leg and spots of pink every few inches to stop any further damage. No wonder I took to wearing trousers.

I dreaded growing up, as I thought that adulthood meant 'Ponds' cold cream, greasy looking 'Nivea', thick 'Panstick', red lipstick and having to make sure you applied even more powder if anyone other than the immediate family appeared, however briefly.

My mother and aunts' retiring conservatism, their belief that one was not dressed without hair dresser hair, a bra, roll-on, stockings and make-up made me feel like a misfit and an outsider. I always wanted to do something special, to wear something outrageous, to not conform.

My mother loves me, of course, but I've felt compelled to challenge everything, so we were destined to be different. She never managed to disguise the look of disappointment when we met at family functions:

"Haven't you got any makeup?"

"Haven't you got a dress or suit?"

"Yes," I would say, emboldened by independence. "But I made this ragged hemmed skirt and wanted to wear it."

We went for a walk down the country lanes near her home, and had a happy, chatty day together, just like old times. She seems to be managing now, which is a huge relief, though she invariably says, "Can't you stay the night this time? Aren't you on holiday yet?"

I admit that I have made up reasons not to stay ever since she moved here from our family home. There is a stiflingly yawning dullness about staying at Mum's. It's a modern maisonette with small patches of garden front and back and comfortable and warm, but it is not the house I was brought up in. It has no history for me, and I find just eating, sleeping and watching TV mind sapping.

Although I want to be helpful and loving, I don't want to give up my exciting, challenging job, my sport and social life or spend even less time with Mike and Cerys. That sounds so selfish, I want it all . . .

Mum saw her Consultant again last week and thinks that she achieved a high score in her MMSE (Mini-mental State Examination) test.

"Apple, ball, pencil," she said proudly. "I can *still* remember them!"

She has to have an MRI (Magnetic Resonance Imaging) scan next.

## THURSDAY MARCH 22ND

Mum fell in the kitchen this morning. She fractured a femur and was taken to hospital. Since the telephone call I've had to finish observing a class and writing a report. It's 10.30pm and I am off to see her tomorrow.

## WEDNESDAY MARCH 28TH

Came back again last night to see Mum. She was still waiting to have the very small fracture in her femur pinned. We chatted for an hour or so and she was thoughtful, calm, kind and interested in everything around her, as normal.

Saw her today after the operation. She was woozy, but otherwise fine. I'm on the train, on my way back to London.

## FRIDAY MARCH 30TH

Got back from work and the phone rang.

"Are you Ms A Williams, the daughter of Mrs Catrin Williams?"

"Yes." I said, fear gripping my heart. "What's wrong with her?"

"I'm afraid that your mother has had to be restrained. She is behaving violently and has threatened to take all her sleeping pills to kill herself."

"What? Mum hasn't got any sleeping pills. Where would she get those? She can't get out of bed. She's the most gentle, sweet woman and has never been violent in her life!" I was pacing up and down the kitchen, in shock.

"I am very sorry to cause you distress, but we have had to detain her for 28 days under Section 2 of the Mental Health Act 1983. We have written to you."

Not this doctor's fault, he tried to be kind. I'm in shock. How can she become like this after one small operation?

# SATURDAY MARCH 31ST

Came back to Wales this morning.

I was completely horrified and appalled, when I first saw her. My pale, wild haired, confused mother, tied to the bed with restraining straps, her baleful eyes darting around as if to find a soft target to attack. It was not the inhuman indignity, which upset me most, but the vacancy in her face. She did not seem to recognize me. "Where are they?" She slurred in a guttural, strange voice.

"What drugs have you given her?" I asked.

The staff on duty were pleasant, but had not been there the day before and were matter of fact as if this stranger was how she always was.

"Why would she have been raving and hallucinating? That would be postoperative confusion wouldn't it? Wasn't it the anaesthetic?"

They were guarded and defensive. I was almost crying with frustration at getting no answers. The doctor who had telephoned me was on leave; no one else seemed to know anything or could suggest what would help restore her to normality.

# MONDAY APRIL 16TH

"Why is she like this, a silent, floppy wreck, who can't hold her head up or feed herself? How can she lose all command of function and language after one small operation?"

"She has a severe urine infection."

"Should she have a catheter in her for over two weeks?"

"That is normal practice for someone who is bed bound."

"Is she going to die? What is the prognosis?"

I have spoken to everyone I can, but they are treating the urine infection with antibiotics and I cannot get any answers for what happens after that.

Mum seems to be struggling under a huge and heavy weight, she is so sedated and sleepy that she can do nothing for herself. I am despairing!

# SATURDAY MAY 20TH

"We all have our time," Mum said in a gratey gruff voice, as I sat crying by her bedside.

"Fight Mum, fight. Get yourself stronger so you can get out of hospital." I said.

Her body sagged even lower in the chair. Her head has hung down on her chest since the operation, too heavy for her to lift. I crouched down level with her eyes: "You are fighting aren't you Mum?"

She muttered something unintelligible. For much of the time she seems to be in a dream, not knowing where she is and thinking that she can come to Tenby or have a game of tennis with me. At other times her brain is razor sharp. She listened carefully when I read Michael Portillo's speech, putting himself forward to lead the Tory party, and made intelligent observations. Her hearing is perfect but her eyesight seems blurred, and she has little control of her hands and none now of her bladder and legs. She has been made immobile and incontinent.

Where is the humanity in her treatment? She has been drugged and imprisoned in the corner of a hospital room for thirteen weeks with a catheter. She has had a cycle of infections and has disintegrated into this pitiful sight. Her hair is filthy, her skin blotchy and unhealthy looking and she dribbles perpetually. She has no movement in her legs and can't lift her head up. Her teeth no longer fit. How have her gums shrunk so quickly?

She flushed as two male nurses came to wash her, a defeated look in her eyes. Her efforts to maintain her dignity exhausted. This hospital is uncaring, unkind, chaotic and dirty. It is understaffed, disorganized, and neglectful of the patients. I bit my lips and tried to smile at the men.

With no mental or physical stimulation, no reduction of drugs, how is she supposed to improve? I feel so helpless, she is dying from neglect.

# TUESDAY JUNE 19TH

No physiotherapy has been possible. She has been, and is too ill. Three months after entering this hospital she is an incontinent, inert wreck unable to stand or walk. Two other women, who were admitted at the same time with small fractures, have not been ill like Mum, but still cannot walk. Aren't hospitals supposed to make us better?

Robert does not understand how much she needs to feel that he is sewn to her, no matter how slack the stitches. He has become oppressed by his roles of breadwinner, father and son, and having lost Pam and his two sons, seems to also want to shed Mum. I think that he is suffering from depression. It is true that she has relied on him. When he changed a light bulb for her, she felt loved and supported, but he seemed to feel that she was being helpless just to bug him. This long illness in hospital is the final straw; he can barely suppress his anger.

I witnessed her having what looked like a slight stroke. Her teeth and hands clenched, her body went rigid and straightened as a wave of something passed through her. Suddenly she had the strength to hang onto the arms of the chair, as if she feared that she would fall, or be sucked downwards. A few moments before, she could not move those arms.

"I think that my Mum is having a stroke." I said to a passing nurse. She seemed unconcerned and when she eventually came, the effects had gone.

# Chapter 7—Catrin's Viewpoint

Who's that young man in his white coat standing over me? I'm jumbled, woozy.

"Are you feeling comfortable?"

What's happened to me? He's speaking to . . . Robert . . . Alys?

"The neurofibrillary tangles *hmm —hmm —hmm* . . . fracture was un-*hmm-hmm-hmm, buzz-buzz—buzz* . . . she should *buzz-buzz* recovery."

"There's nothing much wrong with our mothers brain!"

Alys gets so heated . . .

"We were doing crosswords and chatting about world affairs while she was waiting to go in for her operation. "She's only got mild Parkinson's or Lewy bodies and harmless hallucinations."

She shouldn't talk like that to a Doctor.

"It was only a very small fracture . . ."

Those large tinted glasses are dazzling like headlights; the blob of saliva bobs up and down on his bottom lip.

" . . . you should be up in a few days."

It's tossed into the air, up, up and down onto my blue blanket, but I'm no longer underneath, I'm on my way to the ceiling, squeezing through the air vent and over streams and squirrel woods to Tenby.

✳    ✳    ✳

It hurts, it hurts, don't force that tube into me.

"No, no, no!"

The strong, stocky is losing patience with me.

"Help, help." I'm too weak . . . a searing pain.

Events, people, scenes, past and present, swirling in and out. I don't know what day it is, what I'm supposed to do?

* * *

Why does Alys always look so serious?

"Mum, you've been committed for 28 days under Section 2 of the Mental *hum-hum*. Why did you say you were going to take sleeping pills to kill yourself?"

I haven't got sleeping pills. Why's she saying that?

"Mum, they're giving you more drugs to calm you down. I think the anaesthetic has reacted with your Parkinson's drugs, though I can't get them to admit it. Can't you talk to me?"

I want to speak, to move my lips, but a terrible weight's pressing down, my body, my dry, swollen lips won't move. Is that MY rasping breath?

* * *

"I'm taking you for an MRI scan Mrs Williams."

My bed's rolling . . . into the lift. How embarrassing . . . people are looking at me . . . where are we going?

"We're going to slide you into this tube. You mustn't move at all, Mrs Williams, not until we slide you back out again. Do you understand?"

"Not even the slightest movement. Relax please."

It's so small, I can't believe I'll get in there, is this my coffin? My breath's condensing on the roof. I want to scratch my head, everything's itching. It's so quiet, where did everyone go? Am I at my funeral?

It's dark.

I'm trapped.

I must scratch.

Move my arm.

I'm tense.

"Keep completely still, breathe normally and relax. Try not to move. It won't take long, keep breathing evenly."

Must lie still. Mustn't move a muscle. I'm made of unjointed wood . . .

45

*It's a perfect day, warm and sunny, the grass has been rolled and smells fresh and sweet. The lines are newly painted and the umpire is getting into her chair, all ready for my final. Big flowering rhododendron bushes echoing the colours of the boxes of begonias and busy lizzies. There's quite a crowd, they're calling my name encouragingly.*

*I'm moving well; I'm sharp and confident.*

*That was easy . . . five love. Only a few more hard drives to the corners and it'll be my set . . . ooh, I need to go to the toilet . . . I have to finish this game . . . pull up my pelvic floor . . . hold on . . . only one more point, I'll rush the net . . . ooh don't make me stretch . . . oh no, hot liquid soaking my legs . . . my feet. Did anyone see anything before I crouched down? Everyone's clapping, I've won the set. Rush to my chair; tie my cardigan's arms around my waist like young people do. I'll hold my holdall in front . . . go for a toilet break.*

*Oh no . . . I've forgotten to bring a change of clothes.*

*My skirt isn't too wet, but I'm going to have to play on with wet pants, socks and shoes. I'll douse myself with my Worth's 'Evening in Paris.'*

*She's giving me a filthy look for keeping her waiting.*

*"What's that terrible stink? Like cat's pee!"*

*Everyone's looking at me . . . Sniffing . . . Can they smell it?*

"Mum are you going to open your eyes?"

My opponent really is familiar,

"Can you see me Mum, who am I?"

I know I know her, "Gwen?"

"Muuum, it's ME, Alys, your daughter! I'm flattered though, she's so glamorous. She's been coming to see you every day, hasn't she? But this time it's me."

I haven't seen my sister for months; perhaps she's been visiting someone else.

Alys's talking to a nurse:

"My Mum is really ill, I want to see a Doctor. She must have another urine infection or the drugs you're giving her are much too strong. She's not used to taking any form of drugs, look, she can't keep her head up, she's like a rag doll and can't even speak to

46

me. Four weeks ago she was a healthy woman, with a sharp brain, looking after herself, cooking, using the phone, shopping, this just isn't right! I want to know why she's like this."

It's the stocky one, she sounds irritated and I sense her straightening herself up to her full height, Alys is very tall.

"Mrs?"

"Williams, it's Williams, the same as Mum, and it's Ms."

"*Miss* Williams, your mother is receiving appropriate treatment for her mental condition. She is behaving aggressively and rudely. She shouts and fights and scratches us when we go near her. She has had to have neuro *buzz-buzz*—anti—*buzz-buzz* drugs so that we can handle her. I'll tell Dr Martin you want to speak to him, but he has three other wards to visit before he comes here."

Her words drop like icicles. Alys sounds meeker. "Please tell him that I have to catch the 6 o'clock train back to London and I must see him before five. Mum has never, ever behaved like this before, she's a gentle caring person, there's something very wrong here!"

❋    ❋    ❋

Oh that's nice, Alys. My shoulders are so stiff . . . massage a bit there, yes, yes, mmm . . . No, my head won't lift, it's a dead weight . . . it won't lift off my chest. Can't speak . . . trying to answer you Alys . . . a gruff, slow sound is coming up from deep inside. "Errg . . ." *Is* that me? Thank you for bringing the flower . . . drawn, sucked towards the blurry yellow centre. Weightless, zooming towards the pincushion of creamy stamens . . . slipping inside their soft furriness . . . the heavy, musky perfume enters me, enfolds me. Mmmmmm.

# Chapter 8—After Hospital.
# June—July 2001

$\mathcal{J}$ had a phone call from Robert:
"The hospital want Mum out by the weekend, there's nothing else they can currently do for her and she's bed blocking."

"What? But she can't stand, can't feed herself and they've made her incontinent!"

"Well they say she's got to go."

"But she can't even hold her head up."

"She'll have to go into a Home. You ring Irene and arrange it."

"A Home?" My life seemed to be falling apart. I replayed the alternatives endlessly in my mind. Should I take early retirement to look after her? Could I devote my life to selfless physical caring? No, no, I can't! I thrashed about til dawn. Employing twenty-four hour nurses and carers, either at her house or in London, would cost more than my salary and we'd also need adaptations to whichever home she lived in. She would never agree to come to London, but going up and down to Wales was taking over my life. But a Home? "Don't ever put me in a home, kill me first," she has always said.

What would she want? To stay in her own home and be able to play tennis every day of course. She played until she was in her late seventies, and then watched all she could on the satellite channels, sitting all day long in her smart clothes, stiff hairdresser hair and full makeup.

I rang Irene. "It's just not possible for Catrin to go home," she declared. "There would have to be extensive building works to adapt her house and round the clock nursing care. No, impossible. There's a nice purpose built Nursing Home with a new Matron at Bryn Heulog, I'll see if I can get her in there."

I had no chance to vet Bryn Heulog, the Hospital would not discharge her unless she went directly to a Nursing Home, and they insisted that she leave quickly, to free her bed.

# FRIDAY 22ND JUNE

I took the train to Bridgend, packed two small suitcases of clothes from Mum's house and then walked the two miles to the hospital with them, so that I could travel with her in the ambulance. We drove down some country lanes and stopped at a low modern building, nestling in a copse of trees. The grass had been mown, the flowerbeds were full of summer colour and the staff greeted us effusively. The three lounges seemed quite pleasant and the only smell seemed to be of lunch. After the hospital ward, her bedroom seemed quite spacious and was ensuite.

"She'll soon settle in," said the Matron as I unpacked her things into the small wardrobe and chest of drawers.

"I don't want her to 'settle in,'" I thought, as we wheeled her into the lounge and she sat amongst a row of watery, vacant eyed, thin haired women in mismatched clothing. A line from Philip Larkin's 'The old Fools' (1973) came into my head:

*'Not knowing how, nor hearing who, the power of choosing gone.'*

I want her to get up and walk over to me and say, "Let's go home," and be back as I knew her before. Even though she is so quiet, confused and disorientated, amongst this company she looks refined and out of place. The more she 'settles in,' the more she will become another one of those ruined bodies and minds waiting here for death. She didn't reproach me for this terrible fate and stoically showed no emotion as she entered the faceless building and her gaolers came forward to receive her. Did she realise that this was a nursing home or was she in denial?

I walked back down the lanes, sobbing. How could I have allowed my private, reserved Mother, the person who brought me up and has been my friend and support for the last thirty years, to become Room number 61? To have to sit day after day in a row, decaying and inert, just another shapeless, slumped, dead eyed old person. She will be traumatised by communal living and without a role, her self esteem will sap away.

I have banished and abandoned her with all the baffled and fearful. She who has always worried about conforming and appearances. "What will, people, the family, think?" Has been a familiar cry. This guilt will never leave me, I sobbed for her pain and my impotence. "There was nothing else I could have done," I repeat to myself. "They all said, nothing else."

"I really do not feel that you could provide the standard of care your Mum requires and that you would have done a great dis-service to her, given her complex problems." Irene wrote to me in an e-mail.

Do I believe her, I want to. I try to believe it but the agonizing guilt is undiminished.

## SATURDAY JULY 14TH

I am sitting here in Tenby writing my diary and gazing out at Mum's favourite view, "I could spend hours painting this," she once said. I bought her pencils, a sketching pad, a watercolour palette, but she never did start. I teased her and encouraged her, but the whim was never more than that. The scene was already painted into her memory.

In front of me, this seemingly never changing view of blue to the horizon, the bobbing boats, the strangled cries of gulls and sounds of sea faring engines. A view, which she loves and has come back to for two weeks every summer since she was a little girl. Having grown up with it, I understand the infatuation, the timeless satisfaction of watching the light patterns on the sea, the soft waves lapping on the shore below, harbour life coming and going.

Ten years ago Mike and I bought this flat, looking out at that same view and every summer since, I have fetched her so that we can spend time in this place so dear to us both.

I need to stop writing and drive to Bridgend to see her. These notes seem to be turning into my catharsis, my occupational therapy. Haven't been able to write an entry for over three weeks, the college summer school took over my life.

Mum was watching TV, wearing an elegant, sleeveless navy and white straight dress; a light blue stole covered her shoulders.

"Hi Mum, what have you been doing?" I bent down to kiss her cheek. She has never been good at kissing and cuddling, but her face lit up and she angled it towards me with enthusiasm.

"It's lovely to see you at last! I've resigned from the tennis committee," she announced triumphantly. "They've been ganging up against me. I've been very busy, haven't had time to sit down".

"What did you think of the Wimbledon finals?"

She looked puzzled. "I think I missed them, I must have been doing something else."

"They weren't very interesting anyway and I don't think you like the players much, it was the Williams sisters and Hewitt and Nalbandian?" Her expression was hunted and vulnerable, I changed the subject.

"You were such a successful doubles player, but I don't remember you playing singles, Mum, did you enter singles tournaments?"

"Not many, no, even your father could beat me at singles!"

"I thought you let him win. You always told me that I mustn't beat men. And anyway, he didn't play."

"He did on holidays in Tenby. Don't you remember the court in that lovely garden? He'd do all these funny short shots and hit the ball up in the air; he always picked a windy day to play me. You and Robert amused yourselves in the summer house and picked apples."

Oh yeh, it's a car park and retirement flats now isn't it?"

We laughed together and I told her all my news.

"How's your back now Mum?"

"Oh fine."

She never complains. "It doesn't hurt when you go from lying to sitting?"

"Mmm, no."

"But I've seen you looking in agony for years."

"Yes well it can be a problem, but once I'm up."

Hum, I thought, 'mustn't grumble' Mum again.

She has had some huge setbacks, Dad and Tom, Milly, Lorna, David, John all dying, Roberts' vicious wife's' allegations against him, Parkinson's or Dementia with Lewy bodies, whichever it is . . . She has internalized all those blows and become quieter, sadder, and more watchful somehow, like a beaten animal waiting for the next kick.

We chatted for an hour or so, she is an attentive, encouraging listener and always so hospitable, "Can I get you a cup of tea?" she asked. "Or how about if I cook you a nice roast? I've got a piece of pork and fresh beans and peas. If you do the potatoes it won't take long." Her eyes glistened at the thought of pork and gravy.

"I'm sure I could find an apple to go with it," she beamed contentedly.

I got up to go. "No, I won't thanks, I want to get back to Tenby while it's light."

"Are you going on your own? Aren't I coming? Can't I come with you?"

I looked down at her blotchy face, hair in lank, grey strands, flat against her head, which seemed to be permanently drooping onto her chest, so her red-rimmed eyes focused on the ground. Her stiff useless feet, encased in their bandages protruded over the end of her footrest; a vague smell hung in the air of cheap over-cooked food, damp laundry and the unchanged nappies that she and so many other residents wear.

A badly cooked meal at midday and sandwiches for supper has been her daily fare since she fractured her femur. She no longer provides meals for those she loves. She has lost a skill that defined her. A skill, which gave her dignity and self worth

"Help, help," she said. "Help, help."

"I'm here Mum, why are you saying that?"

"I don't know, it just comes out. Do we have to eat all those carrots over there?" She gestured towards a spot beyond her feet. "There must be more than 20 lbs! Don't go yet, I'll get you a cup of tea."

Her weak, fluttery hands moved slowly, uncertainly, towards a cup, which had been by her side for some hours. I moved it nearer to help her and fumbling she lifted it shakily with both hands towards her face. Stopping inches away, she sucked, but the cup was not there. I lifted it with her, to her lips, but she was unable to tip it because she cannot lift her head off her chest. At last she said, "Can I have a straw?" Crying inside, I found one.

"I have to go now," I repeated.

"I'm sure I could come." she tailed off. "I'll just get up, if you could find my shoes?"

Tears filled my eyes and overflowed. I willed her not to look at me and moved behind her to massage her stiff, bony shoulders as I struggled for composure. She concentrated on her legs for a few minutes, but there was no movement, how could there be after three months of immobility?

She went back to restlessly, endlessly fiddling with the end of the rug covering her lap. Pulling, lifting, folding over. Offering me a corner she said,

"Take this, at least I can give you something to take with you."

Her eyes were two piercing searchlights of desperate pleading, cornering my guilty soul:

"You may need your rug, Mum," I said gently, not sure what she thought she was giving me and distressed at having to reject her gift.

"I'll come and see you on Wednesday. Keep practising your exercises, so you get stronger."

Walking away from her sitting helpless and alone with a brave smile but desperate eyes, is the hardest part. I institutionalized my mum, though at the time it did not feel like a moral issue. Social Services gave me no choice. I am carrying the burden of it and living with that reality ever since.

She has never asked me if there could have been an alternative, but has got on with this half life in the twilight zone, waiting to get better, waiting for visitors to help her forget where she is.

My (selfish) 'there is no other option' defence battles with my conscience, my instinct to protect her. So I have been coming from London to see her twice a week, thinking of things to tell her, to try and involve her in life outside the nursing home and pretend that she is still a part of it. When I say I am leaving, she becomes her most coherent and loving. She asks, even sometimes begs me to stay a little longer and forgets that she is not at home, that I cannot stay with her. I must, must, must get her off Olanzapine. I feel sure that this drug is killing her!

What sort of society do we live in? Certainly not caring. Old people are left lonely and nervous in their homes with pills and a personal alarm pendant to put around their neck to call for help. Then there is the dreaded Nursing Home. Thank-you Mum for never showing resentment at losing your home and independence. I know that your life was closing in, getting more and more difficult for you, but you could never have welcomed this. I think about her obsessively. Is illness the end?

No, I will think of it as the beginning of being open to whatever comes next.

On the way back to Tenby I tormented myself with how little I really knew of what she is thinking. How sad I feel that I could never be the sort of daughter she really wanted, who had won Wimbledon and then settled down near to her with a husband and a brood of children.

I desperately hope that being trapped in her little room with no control over her life, being fed poor quality food and having her nappy changed by people she doesn't know is not an unremitting nightmare for her. That what I am seeing is not what she is living. That she can live another reality in her head, of her youth, her happy times? Oh Mum!

Still thinking of her as I drove down the hill towards the little walled town and our flat overlooking the harbour, I felt that frisson of excitement that the sight of this dear place never fails to inspire. The sun was setting, but there were still people sitting on the beach and children running in and out of the almost motionless, blue water. The sky merged into the sea on the far horizon and I wound down the window to breathe in the tangy, salty air.

Was that us, that could be us, just there by Goscar Rock? Mum and Dad in coats with rugs and umbrellas (just in case), relaxing in their deckchairs, reading newspapers, my brother and I playing in rock pools. Mum, eating a steady stream of chocolates and ice creams, when she wasn't buttering rolls for us out of a Peek Freen biscuit tin, which held all the ingredients for our lunch and tea. Oh look, they are starting to play cricket. Dad doing his tricky googlies and Mum behind the wicket, leaving all the running to her long legged daughter. I could see her laughing, she had slipped off her coat and her arms were bare, smooth and tanned. I remembered asking:

"Is cricket your favourite game in the world, Mum?"

"I like it, but girls didn't play much in my day, or do athletics."

"Is that why you are always playing tennis?"

Her bare feet, tensed, then pushed off in the churned up sand as she leapt to take a catch from my brother's bat.

"Yes, I love tennis, I'd like to play all day every day, but *you're* the one who's going to win Wimbledon!" And she threw the ball high in the air between us. As we almost collided I caught a whiff of the perfume, which lived on her dressing table at home, before a little breeze whipped it away, across the sea back to our village in the valleys.

The sun slid beneath its orange blinds and the family finished their game and started packing up.

I drove on, watching the little boats returning as the shadows grew, and grieved for what was and what will never be again, finding no comfort, no solace, in this, her beautiful peaceful, timeless view.

# Chapter 9—'Bryn Heulog'

*J* can't go home yet.

"You haven't got your strength back Catrin. You won't be able to manage on your own. Until you get on your feet, I've got you a place at 'Bryn Heulog' in Pen-y-llwyd. You've got your own room and bathroom, a bit of privacy for you after ten weeks in 'ere."

Irene speaks so quickly in her soft Welshy voice that I can't take it all in, but I know I'm not going home.

"Annie is going there too, so you'll have some company." She's waving at a bed opposite.

Annie, who's Annie? My brain feels slow . . . blackness inside my heavy head. Can't concentrate; big breakers slosh around, washing my words away. People keep doing things to me, for me . . .

"Can't I go home Alys?'

Didn't she hear? Did I say it? I should get up.

"I've fetched some of your summer clothes Mum. The ambulance men should be here soon."

❊      ❊      ❊

Private, Irene said. Alys's left me with all these old people. This lounge isn't private!

"Hello love, just come have you, what's your name?"

"Catrin Williams."

"Here's a cup of tea, alright love?"

"Thank you, can I have a magazine from my room?"

"You'll have to wait, I'm doing the teas. Look here's a book from the book box, you can start on that."

'Best of Friends,' this might be my sort of book. I could just do with a cup of tea . . .

Can't drink this, it's nearly cold and much too sweet.

The words keep dancing away, blurring, the lines keep going on top of one another, I'll read them again. What happened at the beginning of the page? Why can't I sit in my room? Robert's brought my TV. I'm missing 'Neighbours', 'Home and Away' and all the tennis. There's the tea woman again.

"Can I visit the toilet please?"

"OK, coming."

I should have asked before, but its too embarrassing shouting out. Can't do that. Try and forget about it. Jesus lived for forty days and forty nights in the desert . . . this is a test, be calm, pleasant, relax . . . Oh, I'm getting quite desperate. "Excuse me, can I?"

"I said I'm *comin'* in a minute."

I shouldn't have drunk that tea, oh no, oh no, I can't stop it, I'm going! Can everyone smell it? I can smell it, so acrid. My Domani dress and the wheelchair . . . they're soaking. Is it dripping onto the floor? My face's burning. My chest, I can't breathe. What are they going to say? What will everyone *think*? My heart's going mad . . . My clothes are soaking, I'm so ashamed.

"Come on Catrin, time for the toilet."

"Can't a woman take me?" My voice sounds shaky, weak.

"Donna and Elaine are takin' someone else luv. You'll be all right. Won't take long, keep your feet up, in we go. Oh you've wet yourself have you? Your pad isn't on right. Sit on heya, I'll get you a change of clothes, 61 was it?"

I don't want to go any more. I'm sweating, it's so hot . . . . am I going to faint?

"Steady on, just sit tight on that toilet till Steve comes back, then we'll clean you up."

They're going to touch me, wash my bottom, I *must* smell. Going black . . . into a tunnel . . . rushing away. Can't I go out of this body? Leave it in a heap on the floor. *Please* inside me, come out. Why is this happening to me?

"Here's Steve now, are you sure you don't want to go again while you've got the chance?"

"My daughter asked if I could have women to help me, they wrote it down."

"We're a bit short staffed love, there's more women on the early shift. Open your legs, like this, come on now, gotta get you clean."

This doctor Alys's come with is very nice. He says I'm taking the wrong medicine.

Same old questions. My voice sounds gruff and growly . . . can't control the pen . . . The room's shrinking and shrinking, it's tiny and I'm looking down on it. Is my body here with me? No, there it is below with two of the staff, and Alys and the doctor are going out of the room.

I'm really floating now. There's Catrin being lifted and put on the commode. *I'm* not being demeaned, I'm floating warm and free and better than I almost ever feel down there. Expect Alys will get me on my feet soon and I'll have to go on long walks again, rain or shine. Where is she? Her car's gone. She's gone, gone without me again. Gone, just like that. I thought she was taking me with her this time. Aren't I going to Tenby this year?

"Time for bed, Catrin."

A flannel over my face and hands, this girl is so young. 'Have you just left school?"

"Ner, last year. Me Dad's a shit, had to get out of that house."

"Oh dear."

"Had to have a job . . . fucking fed up with me Dad."

I've no idea what to say.

"Have you brushed those bottom teeth? Open up, let's get yer top ones out."

"All right, all right."

"Are you going to sleep now?"

'I'll try."

"You do that. See you tomorrow."

I'm not tired, it's still light outside and I have to go to bed. It's just like being a child again. People say when you get old that you go through your second childhood. I want to cry like a child, shout, howl. I'm left behind, just like when I had measles that time . . . I was so looking forward to going. She should have waited for me. "Nurse, Nurse."

"Catrin, settle down, try and go to sleep, you can't have a sleeping pill every night."

Alys says I've been here for two months. I'm getting better. I can put my feet on the floor and push my wheelchair along. Not that they let you, they don't like you walking or moving your own chair. "You're too slow; you're blocking the corridor. Hop in Edith, save your legs Connie." They push those wheelchairs around, collecting people up, delivering us to the restaurant far too early. What's the time? Not even twelve? We shouldn't have to wait so long for the meal to be served.

The food's the best thing here. No one says much, except Mary, telling us over and over,

"My son's coming for me; he's taking me to live with him. I'm going to live in their bungalow; I'm only here because they've been on holiday. I won't be here much longer."

She's ninety-four; Connie says she's been here for years.

What's the time now? Twelve? Only five minutes gone. Time opens in front of me like the endless, bare desert . . . . no escape. No, I mustn't cry!

"Mornin' Catrin, alright are you?"

"Yes, I'm fine, thank you Charlie"

He's very kind giving me sweets and fruit all the time, but I wish he wouldn't keep saying to Alys: "I'm sweet on your Mum. Don't you worry about her, I'll look after her."

Or, "I go to the office every week and put her name down first for the hairdresser. Anything you want for her, just you tell me."

That was so embarrassing when Steve said:

"No, you can't sit on the women's table, leave the women alone."

He looks a bit like a wolf . . . long pointed ears and the bits of stubble. That first day I didn't know what to make of him, stooped over his stick, staring at me with those bright, hooded eyes.

Why do they put my wheelchair so I've got my back to him? It's awkward shouting answers over my shoulder, though we probably wouldn't have much to talk about. Not like with John, I didn't stop laughing when he was around. He said he'd never leave me, I felt so secure, so loved. Life's so fickle, so temporary . . . I don't know what women see in making love anyway, I don't miss it. Perhaps it was Gwen who put me off:

*"Boys have a sausage full of seeds between their legs. If you kiss them the seeds go into your tummy and grow into babies, so kissing is stupid." She tells me.*

*I've seen Tom's sausage, so I know it's true. It's disgusting, wee comes out of it as well.*

*I see Lizzie kissing spotty Wilf, "Are you having a baby," I ask her.*

*She's very cross with me: "Don't you ever mention that, ever again. If Mother finds out you'll be really sorry."*

*How is she going to have a baby without Mother noticing? I've been dreaming of having a boyfriend, but I don't want to kiss them.*

I suppose I'm standoffish.

Am I cold? Perhaps I could have been different with John. I wish I hadn't been so shy about him touching me.

After a good evening out I just wanted to go to bed, lazy really. I always thought that there was plenty of time for that, but there wasn't in the end. I didn't even get time to tell him how much I loved his company; how much I liked him.

That last day goes round and round in my head.

Lunch at The Ship.

Pork and apple sauce, peas and nice gravy.

"No tiramisu thank you, I don't like coffee."

"How about trifle?"

I love trifle.

Walking down the promenade, not too fast, so we'd get out of breath. I liked him holding my arm, warm, and the support. Though I was looking round in case anyone I knew could see us. He drove back and I unlocked the door, "Would you like a cup of tea?" I asked.

But he put his arms round me, kissed my neck, "Later," he said, leading me to my bedroom and closing my blue cotton curtains, "We don't need the light on, it's not dark." I wished I'd lined those curtains, I felt sick with apprehension.

He held my hand and traced small circles on my palm and the inside of my wrist. I shut my eyes as that unexpected tingling sensation shot through me.

Oh, stop now John, stop, but he was undressing me.

I was sweating, panicking, thinking about him seeing my wrinkled arms, my flabby legs and the folds of skin round my middle. I breathed in, sat up tall.

"I've waited a long time for this," he whispered.

The smell of coffee made me feel nauseous.

"You know how I feel about you," he said.

My breasts are so heavy; he was struggling to unclasp my bra. I didn't help him, I'm so weak now, I have to slide it round to the front to do it. He gave up and took off his shirt, grey hair and a beer belly, my eyes slid up to a fluttering pulse in his neck, then he gently pushed me down.

I did gradually relax and enjoyed cuddling and kissing . . . ooh, the memory is like a fingernail on my skin, I've got goosebumps . . . was it disloyal to Gareth? I thought I was past all that, but that once was all it was, three days later he was dead and I wish I'd not pushed him away all those years.

✳     ✳     ✳

I feel dirty, they don't wash you properly in the morning, they never have time. I used to shower every morning. That Matron is a really spiteful woman, she hates Alys. She's put me in this room for my meals with the people who can't feed themselves.

"Are you doing your best?" Daddy would ask us. I've always remembered those words; they help me cope with difficult times.

"Eat your food Catrin."

Not going to look up. I can replay my life on the dark screen of my eyelids . . . don't want to see that man with food all over his mouth and chin; it makes me feel sick.

Screw up my eyes . . . its like a snap from that Polaroid camera Alys gave me. He's blurred, then a young face, yes, the person he used to be. He's not bad looking . . .

"What's my Mum doing eating in here? Why isn't she with Mary, Annie and the others?"

Alys looks shocked.

"It's orders." They're looking sheepish though.

61

What's she whispering? "Mum, this room STINKS! And no one here can feed themselves. You look so dignified . . . out of place. Do you know why you've been put in here?"

"I asked for an extra bath. Don't make a fuss, please, please Alys."

✤    ✤    ✤

*Running down a wide street between large dark buildings, there's no traffic and my feet are flying towards a high red brick wall, two huge wrought iron gates. That's my tennis club; I'm late for a match. People everywhere, sounds of balls on rackets, people clapping, I can smell the newly mown grass. A gentle breeze caresses me lovingly, the sun is warm, I sing, "Skies are blue," There's Milly.*

*"Catrin, where have you been? We're supposed to be on the court now playing the final!"*

*I'm wearing my best tennis dress and my green flash are spotlessly white.*

*"Go and get your racket, I'll tell them we're just coming. There's such a big crowd, they won't want to scratch us. If we win you're bound to get picked for the County team, or even for Wales. Hurry up!"*

*There's the side door to the changing rooms . . . so many people I can't get through. "Excuse me, I have to play. Please let me through."*

*They're all looking me up and down with little spiteful eyes in their furry, pointed faces. I'll go round them . . . they're jostling me . . . swishing their tails . . . pushing me against the clubhouse.*

*"Hello Catrin,"*

*Frank, the steward holds the door open for me. "You look pretty today. Shouldn't you be on the court?"*

*Run down the corridor, down another corridor, and another and into room after room, but where's the changing room? Where is everyone? The tannoy booms "Catrin Williams, Catrin Williams, last call."*

*Running, running, where's the changing room? I'll be scratched, where is it?*

*All my partners, Audrey, Sonia and then Milly were picked for the county team, and they didn't win their matches on their own. So this time, this time . . .*

✳        ✳        ✳

When is Alys coming back from Tenby? Did she say? My memory plays tricks on me. It gets confused. At Alys's . . .

"Make yourself a toasted cheese and ham sandwich and warm up the soup for your lunch."

She'd say when she went off to the college. I didn't trust myself to remember what to do.

"What did you have for lunch?"

She'd ask later. "I had a few biscuits and an apple." I'd say. "I wasn't hungry."

"Mum!"

She'd say and be tightlipped and not want to talk.

What day is it? Wednesday, Thursday? I don't know the date. Where's my little pad? I asked her to write down when she was coming back. She asked:

"Are you OK Mum?"

No, get me out of here. Did I say that? Her face didn't change; the words must still have been trapped in my head. Can I beg her to get me out? I want my privacy, my own home, a phone, all my things around me . . . . everything I had before I fell and went in to hospital. Could I manage? Thinking about my home makes tears well under my eyelids. I'll close them tightly so nothing runs down my cheeks. I don't want anyone to see me crying. I'll smile as hard as I can and look down, I mustn't cry in public. Why did I get this Parkinson's, or Lewy something? It's not in the family. Mother and Daddy didn't have to come to places like this.

Why is this happening to me?

What did I do wrong?

Can't things be different?

Can I start again, and be fit

And everything will be fine.

When I'm better I hope I can keep myself going and never have to come here again. In my day we respected our elders and listened

63

to what they had to say. We were politer to one another. Some of the staff here are impatient, they haven't been brought up properly.

They get paid the minimum wage, Mum, that's peanuts for what they have to do, Alys says. They could still be polite though, couldn't they?

I'm resting quietly as much as I can to conserve my energy and then I'll get out of here and go home!

*'A cheerful heart is good medicine, but a crushed spirit dries up the bones.'*

*Proverbs 17:22*

# Chapter 10—Researching. The Home and Her Home. 2001-2

## SUNDAY JULY 15TH

This is the medical update, which I have been too busy to record until now.

In every spare moment I have been reading research articles from the Internet, the Alzheimer's Society library and the Lancet, particularly about Dementia with Lewy bodies (DLB), which initially has the symptoms of Parkinson's. Apparently, unlike Alzheimer's, DLB gives the sufferer *fluctuating* cognitive impairment as well as visuospatial problems and complex visual hallucinations. I made a major discovery, that anti-psychotic or neuroleptic tranquiliser drugs (that Mum had been prescribed in hospital) are extremely dangerous to those with Parkinson's or DLB as they induce rigidity, immobility, inability to communicate and even sudden death! A quarter of people taking them will die prematurely, often of a stroke. My goal is to get her off Olanzapine, which I believe has made her into a doubly incontinent zombie, and onto an acetylcholinesterase inhibitor such as Rivastigmine to reduce her symptoms and hallucinations, help her to concentrate and sleep better.

Unfortunately Consultant X who committed her under Section 2 of the Mental Health Act while she was in hospital and prescribed the inappropriate Olanzapine drug for her, has been off sick ever since. Trying to change his diagnosis and prescription feels like I am single handedly fighting the whole of the Dyfed Morgannwg Health Authority.

On Friday I complained by telephone and for the second time in writing to the Director of Mental Health Services.

## THURSDAY JULY 19TH

I have had a letter from X, saying that he has received my letters and faxes and telling me that Dr Shah was covering his workload during his absence.

The Director must have chased him up at home, but I have already been fobbed off by Dr Shah, who will not take the responsibility to rescind X's prescription for Mum. So back to the Director, I must keep pressurising!

Have been waking in the night, heart pumping and clammy. I'm not sure I'm coping with the demands of work and Mum's needs, though I can't try any harder.

## FRIDAY AUGUST 17TH

After more letters and phone calls, the Director has at last agreed that Mum could have a second opinion and that the consultant can come from a different Health Authority. So after this three-month battle, one came from the Cardiff Memory Clinic Health came to see Mum today. He was brilliant; he gave her the Mini Mental State Examination Neurological test (MMSE), talked to her and instantly recommended that she should not be taking an anti-psychotic drug. Hooray!

## TUESDAY AUGUST 29TH

As a result of cutting Olanzapine back and then cutting it out entirely Mum can now hold her head up, grip a cup, fork and pen, lift her legs a few inches, see the TV, stop dribbling, register what is around her and communicate normally. I am *so* thrilled. For the first time in over five months she has feeling and movement in her legs!

Now for the Rivastigmine.

Cerys says I've become obsessed. What else can I do? Leave Mum to rot in that horrible Home, that death row? I asked her if she would wash her hands of *me*, when I can't fight for myself. She said she wouldn't, but I am not so sure. I just hope I do not need her when she's bringing up the huge brood of children she wants to have. It seems to me that those growing out of life need as much attention as those growing into it. Glad I'm coming to the end of my career and have set up a strong system so that I can work flexibly. The image of Mum disintegrating in that institution is always in my head, I must not let the chance of helping her slip from my grasp.

## SATURDAY SEPTEMBER 8TH

Mum can write a sentence and guided me through Cardiff in the car today with clear and timely directions. My lovely Mum is coming back to life!

The main change is that although she can remember all the people she knew before breaking her leg, she is now even worse at learning new things, as she can't grasp any of the names of the staff in Bryn Heulog. She's also still having fantasies and at times seems unaware of where she is.

## WEDNESDAY SEPTEMBER 19TH

I read a poem on the train, and these lines summed up my feelings about Mum being in a Nursing Home:
*'There I sat*
*Imprisoned in my pity and my shame*
*That men and women having suffered time*
*Should sit in such a place, in such a state.'*
'Old Woman' by Iain Crichton Smith (1965)
There's rarely any conversation between the residents. Mum has tried, but seems to have lapsed into the same barely responsive passivity. She's in stasis, beaten down by boredom, and the sadism of the Matron, who has put her to eat with the severely demented. It's a foul smelling little room where 'they' are hidden away, out of sight of Matron and her favoured staff and where food is shovelled into 'them' as quickly as possible. I was absolutely horrified when I could not find her in the dining room today and was directed there. Mum had her head down, showing no emotion, saying nothing. My heart bled for her delicate sensibilities, her dignified carriage and table manners amidst those who no longer have any. How *can* she eat with the terrible

67

stench of urine from the poor hopeless human beings around her? The Matron told me that Mum had shouted so she was being punished. Mum told me that she had wanted a bath and hadn't had one for two weeks. I know that if I complain even more, Mum will be punished further. When a resident refuses to resign themselves to the fact that they have no rights and won't accept that they must drift quietly and politely towards the grave, they are made an example of. The Matron also knows I am one of many who have written to the Inspectorate about the lack of staff, lack of care, lack of activities for the residents and appalling management. Mum should be in the dining room with the people who can feed themselves and communicate. The carers agree, but cannot go over the Matron's head. What can I do? I want to scream with rage. I'll ring Irene, perhaps she can do something?

## MONDAY SEPTEMBER 24TH

Mum was still eating in that stinking room when I saw her yesterday, but Irene rang today to say that she had visited and commented on where Mum was eating and one of the carers took it upon himself to move her back to the main dining room. At last!

## WEDS OCTOBER 3RD

It was Steve who moved Mum, brave Steve. "Thank-you, thank-you Steve, "I said. He's not allowed to receive a tip or a present, so I'll give him Marks & Spencer's vouchers at Christmas.

During my train journey to Cardiff, I read Elsie Baileys' apt poem 'Visiting the Elderly,' and wondered if this is what Mum sees:

*'I open my eyes—and what do I see?*
*Several old Ladies just like me,*
*With sagging necks and wrinkled skin,*
*Red-rimmed eyes and unkempt hair,*
*Each frail body in a high-backed chair.'*

Does she?

Not many women in the home can manage to put on tights. Most sit with their scaly lifeless legs splayed open. They no longer bother with makeup and only a few have worked out the booking system for the Home hairdresser. 'Keeping up appearances,' is something they left behind when they entered these doors. It's no wonder that the handful of old men at Bryn Heulog find Mum attractive. As she recovers from the Olanzapine she's still determined, with help, to carry on the habit of a lifetime and put on her makeup and nice clothes every day.

She does seem to believe that she will get better and walk again. She still says when she wants to go to the toilet, though then has to give up and go in her nappy. A degrading experience for a woman so neurotically shy about her bodily functions. She has to endure the gross indignity of publicly sitting on a commode and a thrice-daily nappy change. Other people are invading the private places, which had previously only been known to her husband. She has withdrawn from the humiliation, blank-eyed as if she is somewhere else.

I still smart with indignation when one of the nurses tells a doctor within her hearing that she's incontinent. "Don't speak like that in front of Mum," I want to shout. What is she thinking, to be so described?

## WEDNESDAY OCTOBER 10TH

How many times has Mum been put through the MMSE neurological test? I have tried to go with her when she has an appointment with her Consultant, but the nurses at Bryn Heulog have not always told me when they are. Today I arrived to find Mum about to leave for hospital.

"Why do I have to answer these questions all the time, do they think I am stupid?" she asked me.

"No of course not," I muttered, remembering Lizzie's words: "She's the brightest of us all. She never failed an exam, in fact it was common for her to get 100%!"

"You're so lucky Mum, you've got such a good vocabulary and wish I had your photographic memory. You even remember the geography of places you went to fifty years ago. You're amazing."

For the first few times, before we went in to see the Consultant (always 'him,') Mum would make sure that she had rehearsed the answers. Although she no longer excels at maths and drawing shapes, she has unfailingly scored high because she has retained the facts that she needs and never forgets the three words she was told to remember at the beginning of the test. Then today, she forgot to ask me anything.

"What's the date? Where do you live, Mum? Who's the Prime Minister?" I tried to drum the answers into her while we queued in the waiting room.

The test is designed to identify people in the first stages of dementia, by examining their time and place orientation, recall, writing, and ability to copy a shape. Mum managed 20 out of 30 today. Not bad, but less than she has achieved before.

## MONDAY NOVEMBER 5TH

Consultant X came back to work a few weeks ago and agreed to see Mum to decide if she can be put on a course of Rivastigmine. It's not a cure, but there is evidence that it helps ameliorate some of the symptoms of DLB and does not aggravate the stiff joints of Parkinsonism.

I wheeled her in to see him this afternoon. He sat, his expressionless eyes and preening cat's face in place. There was another doctor with him, presumably to back up his diagnosis, because I had challenged his prescription of Olanzapine and had it overturned. I had been in such a state of nervous tension, worrying about this meeting but despite my sleepless night, my brain was buzzing and boiling, sharp and fresh.

"Where are you living?" he asked.

She managed to get this right.

"Where did I see you last?"

Mum was a rabbit in the headlights. He repeated his question.

"On a hill in Caerphilly," came out in a rush.

Where? She's hardly ever been to Caerphilly!

"You see!" he crowed to his colleague. "She doesn't know me."

"Yes I do,' Mum gabbled, desperate not to be wrong again. "You came to see me, you came in my room."

I backed her up. "Mum's already told me you went to Bryn Heulog to see her yesterday, why did you do that?"

Ignoring me, he continued with a superciliously sneering expression: "Take 7 from 100, then keep taking 7 from the figure you are left with."

"Ninety three," said Mum cautiously and stopped. He repeated the instruction and telepathically I sent her the answer, but there was no-one there to receive it.

"Eighty one?" she said eventually.

After this she was so flustered that I had to watch her score going down to something so low that X stopped his questioning. He looked triumphant as we exited.

## FRIDAY NOVEMBER 16TH

After the upsetting interview, he will not give me a full clinical assessment to substantiate his refusal to prescribe Rivastigmine for Mum. So I have been pursuing the matter through the complaints procedure and meetings with the Director of Mental Health Services, reinforced with copies of reports from the 'Lancet' and advice from cousin Alison (Lizzie's daughter who is a Consultant in Lancashire). After many communications and going over X's head, I have had a letter today from the Chief Medical Officer saying that the funding will be released for her to be prescribed an anticholinerase drug "if there is a clinical need."

One step nearer! Now I must get one of the other Consultant Psychiatrist's in the Health Authority to make this clinical decision. Obviously not X, his pride is more important than her welfare. I am devoting all my spare time to this crusade. Okay that sounds like I'm an unremittingly relentless person, but I am trying to additionally keep my life balance. I think Cerys could have a point though: I do get obsessed with my projects. It was feminism and now it is Mum and dementia. I know when I see my friends I bang on about it all the time. Am I boring and repelling them? To their credit they don't complain. Not to me anyway.

## TUESDAY NOVEMBER 20

I received a letter today from a Consultant Psychiatrist saying no.

"The Community Nurse says that her memory is not sufficiently impaired at this time."

I replied, "Mum is able to put on a good act for short periods. He has not met her before, so how can he judge her against how she was?"

## WEDNESDAY NOVEMBER 28TH

I have received another letter from the Consultant, not replying to my points, but with another excuse.

"Although 'the tablet' may relieve hallucinations and unusual ideas, the staff at the Home say that she has not had these type of symptoms for weeks."

I wrote by return. "Actually Mum does have increasing fluctuating cognition and hallucinations. I have no idea who has told you differently. Any of the nursing staff will tell you that sometimes she thinks she is playing tennis matches, or being attacked. When she returns from these fantasies she is thoughtful and intelligent and very worried about her worsening state. Perhaps you could let me know who has given you the wrong information?"

## MONDAY DECEMBER 3RD

Every time I feel that I am near to achieving the goal, another obstacle leaps into the path in our to and fro correspondence. The Consultant has now written:

"She cannot be prescribed an anti-dementia drug, because it must be closely monitored."

"Well that's okay then, there are nursing staff constantly on duty at her Home and regular visits from the local doctor and the Community Psychiatric nurse (CPN). Plenty of people who already monitor her!" I replied.

## FRIDAY DECEMBER 7TH

"Your mother says that she does not want to take antidementia drugs because of their possible side effects."

Oh dear, I know which Mum said that, the 'never admit you are ill' one. I wrote: "Someone must have frightened her by telling her that she might find no improvement and yet have deleterious side effects. Why don't we discuss this in her presence?"

I must speak to Mum and tell her she MUST accept offers of a drug, which can help her.

## WEDNESDAY DECEMBER 12TH

"Your Mother has reported to the CPN that she has changed her mind and does wish to take the tablet. Please telephone my secretary, so that we can arrange a meeting with the CPN and the Director of Mental Health Services also present."

## TUESDAY DECEMBER 18TH

Finally at this meeting a trump card was produced:
"There is a real danger that your mother will have a heart attack if we prescribe an anti dementia drug for her," said this Consultant Psychiatrist I hadn't met, but had been having the exchange of letters with.
WHAAAAT?

## FRIDAY DECEMBER 21ST

I have felt every shade of emotion these past months, from exultation to deep despair, and after that meeting on Friday it was a plunge down to the depths. But I am not giving up. Have read more and faxed again today. "This is a rare side effect and Mum has no history of heart problems, in fact she has a very strong heart, so this is very unlikely to happen. Have you evidence, or is your decision based on the fact that she is 82? Are you choosing who is to have a chance of a better quality of life based on age?"

Back came the answer:

"We consider that there is a real risk."

Is this defeat? How can I fight the entire Dyfed Morgannwg Mental Health Directorate?

So, do I think that Mum's so sudden chronic confusion after her operation was caused by neglect, incompetence, apathy or inefficiency? Well, yes I do, all of them, and malice too. Dr X prescribed an anti-psychotic or neuroleptic tranquiliser, which all the research shows should never be given to Parkinson's (or DLB) sufferers. He then refused to take her off it and to save face, tried to trick her into appearing more confused and demented in front of his colleagues. He put his pride above her welfare.

That strange Dr X may know from scans the molecular structure of the cell decay in her brain, but he has no idea of its effect on her, what it is like to be her or how much she understands. He has never attempted to find out but just tricked her into feeling a fool and to fail repeatedly. She is so frustrated when she is unable to communicate why has he been so unwilling to help her?

And through all these months of battling, why did no consultant or doctor bother to tell me what symptoms we should expect and what the long-term prognosis is? Why have I had to go away and read and research so that I am able to understand my mother's condition? I have understood too late to affect my sometime impatience with her or to successfully influence her treatment by the medical profession. Even a leaflet might have helped as we struggled to understand what was happening to Mum.

I have nagged her so often: "If you don't keep exercising every day, you will spend the rest of your life doing what you are doing now; sitting in your chair in front of your TV and you won't be able to move out of it."

Shouldn't someone have explained that the hardest lesson about a progressive disease is that it will inevitably get worse, no matter what one does and that neither Mum nor I could ever have done enough?

## TUESDAY DECEMBER 25TH

We wanted to give Mum a normal Christmas day with lunch and presents. Robert's house is nearby. He was not keen, but Mike, Cerys and I insisted. It was a miserable, fraught time. She hardly spoke and was blank faced, disorientated and unhappy. Has she become institutionalised?

We were unable to get the wheelchair into the kitchen/diner, so we ate on our laps in the lounge, taking it in turns to feed her. Robert will not help to lift her, saying he has a bad back. Mike, Cerys and I now all have them too, after a desperate struggle to get her into the tiny downstairs toilet, on and off the seat and hold her up for removing her nappy, bottom wiping and putting on a new nappy. I had to stand on the lavatory seat while the other two tried to lift, pull and push her into position from the front. Poor, poor Mum.

She didn't remember that she had been anywhere a few minutes after we returned her to Bryn Heulog. She remembered nothing of the day. Nothing at all.

## FRIDAY JANUARY 18TH

Did my usual walk to Bryn Heulog. It takes an hour from the station. The wind whistled through my jacket, the rain was driving down, soaking my jeans. Up through the empty back streets, onto the soulless freeway. No pavement and cars whizzing past. Why are there no buses? Everyone in Bridgend seems to have a car and no legs. I looked angrily at their expressionless faces as they sped past me, splashing me with surface water and making me wait for minute after minute to cross the endless roundabouts. It is a grey, depressing place, I hate it.

Gwen with Jake and Anna, who are visiting from America, came this afternoon. Mum had been dressed in her most expensive, lovely dress, which she has never worn before. She and I sat in her room waiting for them and I helped her put on her makeup. She looked beautiful. The anticipation was making her more and more nervous so she asked if she could go to the toilet. I found some of the staff, but instead of taking her to the bathroom opposite, they wheeled in a commode, just as the visitors arrived. We stood outside in the corridor, until the two male carers pushed out the uncovered receptacle.

Into her room we went, to be practically suffocated by a foul smell. I rushed to open the windows, and we bravely tried not to retch. Mum was heartbroken with embarrassment and so was I. What happened to her right to be treated with dignity?

75

## SATURDAY JANUARY 19TH

I slept at Robert's and when I went in to see Mum this morning she was still lying in bed, trying to attract someone's attention by banging on her metal bedpost with a cup she had managed to reach. No breakfast yet and it was 10.30! Her beautiful dress had disappeared. I was going to get it cleaned, but it was not in the laundry, or lost property. I started to look for a new Nursing Home; surely they are not all as bad as this one?

## MONDAY FEBRUARY 18TH

Lizzie and Rhodri came to stay with Gwen and visit Mum. The three sisters are very close, but Lizzie has had the easiest life, as Gwen never ceases to tell her:

"You haven't worked since you got married. I've worked all my life. I've had to."

Uncle Rhodri was a successful accountant, so they are comfortably off, though both have always done voluntary work at Abbeyfield and their local hospital. They play bridge, go to concerts and theatre, garden, have nice holidays, often with their two lovely daughters (Alison and Megan) and six grandchildren. Lizzie sings in two choirs and plays tennis and badminton. Whenever they come to Cardiff, Gwen takes Lizzie shopping:

"You've always been hopeless at choosing your clothes. With all your money you should look half decent!" She scolds.

Lizzie is a little overweight, despite her busy life. She has a sweet tooth, so there is usually a sponge cake in the tin and a Pavlova or trifle full of thick cream in the fridge for visitors.

"How lovely to see you." Lizzie greets everyone with a big hug and a beautiful, welcoming smile. Her astute, intelligent eyes shine bright with excitement and anticipation. She has more friends than anyone I know. I'm not surprised.

The three sisters have spent three afternoons chatting.

"She seems much better,' said Lizzie happily.

# SATURDAY MARCH 9TH

I'm trying to drive the one hundred and eighty miles every other week, rather than catching the easy, relaxing train, so that I can take Mum out in the car. Mostly I come on a weekday and then work evenings to catch up. Cerys has moved out to live with friends so Mum has become my new child. Taking her out is always stressful and painful for her, yet she keeps thinking that one day I am going to take her to Tenby, one hundred miles away. How could I get her out of the car? Into the narrow little flat in a wheelchair? Onto the toilet? I would need at least two burly nurses to lift her.

Every time we go out for a short drive she has first to be put on the commode, then a new nappy and out door clothes put on and back into the wheelchair, grizzling and grumping "Mind my feet, it's cold, they hurt." Then the huge performance of getting her into my little car, heaving and pulling and humping. It takes four of us. She is very heavy and can't help. Latterly she can't bend her legs at all and getting her long wingspan in, without banging her painful toes and heels, is becoming impossible. Carers are now supposed to use the hoist, but getting that outside would be an even bigger performance. Eventually, we manage to lift and drag her in, and off I drive. She always enjoys it, wherever we go, though there are so few places where a severely disabled person can sit in a car and see a view.

A few weeks ago I took her to her home, which she had left so abruptly. I cannot get her out of the car, so we sat chatting outside. She didn't want to look at it and showed no interest in her maisonette or the garden she had tended. Is it too painful to be reminded?

Today I took her to Ogmore and parked with a perfect view of the sea. Leaving her to listen to Classic FM and look at the beach and boats passing, I went off to find an ice-cream as she enjoys them, whatever the temperature. She loves Magnums and Feasts, but gets distressed at not being able to eat them quickly enough and I never seem to have enough cloths to protect her clothing and mop up the mess. I worry that her embarrassment at her inability to control an ice cream is taking away some of the pleasure of the outing, so we have moved onto Cornettos. She has never been very keen on them, but there is less ice-cream, and as it is contained in a cornet it can't melt all over her and fall off the stick. It feels like yet another example of the giving up, closing down, reducing nature of aging.

On returning, I was furious to find that an elderly couple had squeezed their car in next to us, only inches from the passenger door and had placed their deckchairs immediately in front of our car and Mum's view! They could at least have gone in front of their own car, but no, they were sitting there reading and eating with their radio on, apparently oblivious of the little figure behind them staring at the backs of their heads. Giving Mum her ice-cream I was just going to ask them to move to the space in front of their own car, when she begged me to say nothing.

"But they must have seen you there Mum, why should they sit right in front of you, it's so rude!"

"You will spoil my enjoyment of the day, if you say anything," she said doggedly. Forever the placater, the peacemaker. So we sat behind them, with me fuming and wishing them ill, the acres of chair-less, car-less grass to our right and left, which they could so easily have chosen.

Despite the pain to her bottom and feet of sitting in one place in the car for so long, Mum never wants her excursions to end. I saw her wincing in pain: "Shall we go back so you can lie down, Mum?"

"Oh, no, I'm not going to miss a minute of this," she pleaded.

So we went to Gwen's' and sat in the car park outside her flat. She brought out a tray of bone china cups and plates, serviettes, tea, sandwiches and cake. By then it had started to rain, so we huddled, cramped and uncomfortable in my little car. I felt helpless and ungenerous, that this was the best that I could do to give her an outing.

# FRIDAY MARCH 15TH

I bought a cushioned turntable to make the getting in and out of the car less traumatic and to save four of us doing the lifting. It is £30 wasted. We cannot get her on to it properly and of course, even with an extra cushion, it is too hard and uncomfortable to sit on. It doesn't work anyway on the soft sloping car seat.

When we go out we have normal conversations. Her personality reasserts itself, as if her different surroundings shock her into being her old self. Mum has always made people feel that their conversation is interesting and worth listening to. She is always on my side, my greatest ally, no matter how flimsy my position is.

Today, her expressionless face showed flickers of animation as we drove round the coast she knows so well. Glimmers of the person she used to be lit up her features and her eyes were open wide to absorb the passing world. By the time we returned, she had retreated back inside her blank face and immobile body.

## SUNDAY APRIL 7TH

Robert is going to move into Mum's house. He wants to sell his own as it has too many memories of Pam and his children. His idea of clearing her home is: "I'll get some mates and put everything on the tip."

I could not let him put her life into black bags as if she had never had one. Mike and I drove down this weekend and unlocked the door. The sun poured in through the big picture windows onto the scene she left thirteen months ago after she had fallen in the kitchen. It was neat, she had made her bed, the three clocks still ticked loudly on her bedside cabinet, she had never trusted just one.

Where to start? I opened a drawer, then another, all in the same disorder, old tights, packets of sanitary towels (she had worn in case she sneezed or laughed and wet herself), spent makeup containers, perfumes and hand creams, sachet of lavender unopened from Christmas's long past, thirty one sets of pearls, (only one intact) all jumbled together.

"Why did you keep over forty finished Max factor 'Crème Puff' compressed powder compacts?" I asked her later.

"I thought I might scrape them all out and make one,"

The wardrobe bulged with forests of clothes, many still with the shop labels and price tags attached. She had stockpiled outfits, bought at discount from Gwen's shop, ready for her retirement, sadly, less than two years ago.

Packing up her life was very unsettling. The guilt, sorrow and finality of moving on, mixed with the annoyance of sorting through clutter and summoning the courage to sweep away her belongings. I had to decide on the fate of personal possessions, many of which I remembered from my childhood. Keep? Car boot sale? Tip? It felt sacrilegious and brutal, but the things I thought that she would like to have, clothes, knick-knacks, furniture, jewellery, silver or china, were of no interest. The only thing she said, thoughtfully and with dignity, was: "I hope that some of them are worth something. Sell anything you can and get some money for yourself."

Unfortunately nothing is saleable, there are dozens of vases, elegant in their heyday, but out of place now. The silver is plated, the china cracked and she has ruined the tops of occasional tables with over watered plants. I want to give everything respect, but there is so much . . . I cannot take it all. My own possessions accumulated over my lifetime, have lately felt like encumbrances. I cannot have all of my mothers too, what would I do with them? How many vases, plates and teapots can one use?

The mantelpiece and almost all the surfaces in the lounge were covered with doubles tennis trophies, yet she barely glanced at the selection of them, or the tape and radio player, the jewellery, the vases and rosewood fruit bowl I took today for her room. Luckily, as it transpired, as all but the jewellery and trophies went missing while we were out in the car.

"Where are Mum's fruit wood bowl, vases and ghetto blaster Christine?" I asked her named carer.

"I think I've seen them in the staff room," she answered cautiously.

"Well can you go and find them please, they're for Mum to use."

She did not reappear and neither did her things. I knocked at the staffroom door, but no-one answered. I had had enough for one day and walked helplessly away.

Why does Mum show no interest in any of her possessions? Is it because if she allows herself to register the stripping of her house, she will not be able to cope with her reduced life? She has often blocked out events and memories, which did not fit into the way she wanted her life to be.

## SATURDAY APRIL 20TH

I found the ghetto blaster last time I came, but it has disappeared again. I have asked Steve to look out for Mum's things and have mentioned them to Deputy Matron. What else can I do?

I have been gently telling Mum that Robert is living in her house and when we take our excursions I offer to drive her past it, so she can see that he is extending it. But she still does not want to go there. She never mentions the absence of anything she owned, other than her bag.

## SATURDAY APRIL 27TH

Mum never fails to go on and on about her bag every time I visit. I do try to understand her anguish at not having it, though I am not similarly bag-addicted. She has carried one all her adult life, full of all sorts of things which she never looked at, but had been in there so long that they became part of the bag. When she developed the Parkinson's symptoms it became too heavy and she couldn't find what she wanted in it quickly enough so she had had to resort to a purse in her pocket and a light shopper. This didn't however wean her off the bag. It represents her life and her memories and she misses it terribly. I have not dared tell her that it disappeared in the first few hours after she had been taken to hospital nearly a year ago:

"You fell at home Mum, you were taken to hospital without your bag and you have never been home again. You haven't needed a bag, so I didn't bring it to you."

"I know I had my bag yesterday, I left it here and now it's gone."

"No, Mum, it has never been here."

"Are you telling me that I am making it up?"

"Yes," I said cruelly.

She subsided into slant eyed, tight-lipped muttering, frustrated and unbelieving. Robert, Aunt Gwen and I have had that same conversation with her, over and over and over. It never results in acceptance or even recognition of the repeated explanation. I have given her a small bag to put her makeup in and notebook and pencil, which she insists all visitors use, to remind her when they are coming again.

Her other fixation is with having some money to give the staff tips.

"Everyone else has money, why can't I have money?"

"No they don't Mum, no-one is allowed to have money here, you don't need it."

"Yes I do, I want to buy things, have my hair done and tip the staff."

"Everything you buy is recorded and I pay the bill at the end of the month."

"How can I tip the Hairdresser and the other staff?"

"I tip the Hairdresser for you sometimes Mum and I bought them all presents at Xmas."

"I see everyone else giving tips."

"You must have been mistaken. It says in all the literature we are given, 'no residents are allowed to have money. *No* staff are allowed to receive tips.'"

"Well they do, all the time, I see it," she is adamant. "Everyone else has money. *"*

Round and round, this same conversation repeated over and over again with all her family visitors. She will NOT accept that no money changes hands. Perhaps I am wrong, perhaps it does. Mum has attributed so much importance throughout her life, to having money to pay her way, why am I destroying her self-esteem? I did try to give a tip to a carer who has helped me hump Mum into the car innumerable times, it's an exhausting process. He refused it.

Absorbed in Mum's life, I read poetry, memoirs and novels about being old. Mum says she's lonely. I read a Dannie Abse poetry book on my journey here, and the lines of "Surprise, Surprise' (1970), seemed apt:

*'Talk not of loneliness, but aloneness.*
*Everything is alien, everyone strange.'*

"We're all alone Mum," I told her.

# Chapter 11—Trips out and time on my own.

"*J*'ve brought the car today Mum, so we can go out."

"Oh good."

"I'll get your coat and some of the staff to help get you in."

"Mind my feet, my legs, don't hurt my feet!" It's like a knife's going up my leg. "My foot, on the door!" I mustn't cry . . . I can't, I mustn't.

My bottom's hurting already, but I'm not going to say anything, I want to be out driving about.

This is the way to my house. So familiar, the Post Office, the Common . . . the grass has been cut. My street . . . ohhh . . . it's going through my eyes and inside me . . . my fence, my garden, the front door, the lounge curtains fluttering in my stomach . . . churning round and round, forcing their way down . . . jabbing, gurgling, rushing . . . I can't go to the toilet *now*!

Close my eyes, push them out, shut my mind down. Get out of me.

They're shouting, jostling to get in . . . I'm not going to look or listen.

"Robert has gravelled the beds, Mum. He hates gardening. Can you see?"

I'm not looking, I can't look. I can see the roses, the viburnum, and the holly in my mind. I don't want things to be different. I won't look!

What's Alys saying? I'm not going to look . . . She's driving on . . .

"This is perfect isn't it Mum, on the grassy bank, so you can see the sea? There's nowhere to buy an ice-cream around here though is there?"

I love having an ice cream, it brings back happy memories..."Why don't you go up to the village, you like to have a walk?" I can listen to the radio and imagine that I'm not looking at this tarnished pewter sea, this grey, cheerless emptiness of Ogmore, but beautiful sunny Tenby ...

After high tea we used to get dressed up and parade down the Tenby esplanade ... there were so many others, young and old. Tom often didn't wait for us, we'd take too long to get ready, he'd be off with boys he'd met on the beach. The best times were when Mother stayed in the lodging house and there were just us girls.

Then that last time the three of us were together when Father sent us to Tenby with our babies for the summer after the hospital was bombed ... Mmm what *were* the names of those officers we went round with? Lieutenant ... James was it? Yes, Bob James I saw a lot of him that time. Just as a friend of course. Just a friend. I don't remember any more names ... was there a Wilf and a ... Ted? That was a wonderful time ...

*"I'll give you my blue kid belt, if you swap with me tonight and let me go to the De Valence." Gwen's hazel eyes focused pleadingly on me.*

*"Oh, come on, fair play, just because I'm the youngest, I don't see why I should baby-sit two nights running."*

*"Pleeese," begged Gwen. One of her curls broke free and fell across her face. Her thick pale honey hair glistened where it caught the sun as she turned her head to considerately blow a mouthful of smoke through the open window. A large seagull shuffled further down the sill, casting suspicious looks into the flat.*

*"And Lizzie says you aren't to smoke indoors!"*

*"Only a few puffs, look I'll put it out," she grinned, grinding the butt on the windowsill next to the affronted seagull, who eyed it and flapped off in disgust.*

*The tide had deserted the golden beach for the evening. Two trapped fishing boats hovered on the horizon, waiting to return; a couple strolled arm in arm throwing sticks for their dog. How many days were there to Gareth's next leave? At least he wasn't fighting at the front like David and Rhodri. Poor Gwen and Lizzie.*

*"It's my last week. I'll be stuck back in Cardiff, sewing, modelling and trying to persuade ladies to use their clothing coupons to buy gowns, six days a week, ten hours a day with bombing every night!" Gwen's got quite heated. "And you and Lizzie don't even have to go back to the Bank."*

*I pictured that tiny, autocratic little Frenchwoman saying imperiously; "Catrin put your shoulders back, head high, you look like a sack of potatoes." I'd be frightened to death to have to work for Miss Antony and then not to see baby Jake all day as well. "Why do you want to go back and work for her anyway?"*

*Gwen tossed her hair. "Well, look what she's offered me. I'm not going to refuse being her top model. I've got to take my opportunities."*

*I shivered at the thought of all those pinning alterations and then sewing them in the workroom. "How come you two pretend you can't even thread a needle?" Gwen used to say to us in an annoyed tone when Mother gave us some sewing to do. "Oh, give it to me, you're both hopeless."*

*The late afternoon sun illuminated the scuffed, flower patterned wallpaper and the heavy brown furniture. I didn't want to stay in, but . . ."Okay, just this once, if you do my hair tomorrow night? I want your belt though . . ."*

*Lizzie came back from food shopping, and we sat down to eat bread and potted shrimp. For the next two hours they were getting ready for their evening out. I rag rolled Lizzie's thin straight hair and Gwen's unruly thick curls so they could fashion them into sleek pageboys held in place by carefully concealed hairgrips. Roll-ons, precious nylons and pinched in waists with tight wide belts. A layer of panstick, a touch of rouge, a dusting of powder, red lipstick and they pushed their feet into high-heeled, peep-toed slingbacks and tappy tapped off to waltz, foxtrot, tango and quickstep, to tunes played by old men aping Glen Miller, Duke Ellington and Victor Sylvester.*

*Out of the flat, along the front, past the stylish well proportioned houses built for wealthy Victorians, clip clopping down the cobble-stoned alley lined by houses once belonging to Tudor merchants and into Upper Frog street and the De Valence. Uniformed officers from the nearby army camp were waiting for them, pink shiny faces and hair slicked down with Brylcreem.*

*Alone, apart from the babies, I gazed out of the windows crossed with sticky tape and up at the cold, astringently clear sky and clusters of bright stars. No planes tonight. I pulled the thick black out curtains over the windows and went to check on the children.*

*Alys, stirred in her sleep and I longed to pick her up and cuddle her sleeping softness, breathe in her baby milkiness, but Father had said: "Discipline your children. Once they have gone to bed, never pick them up, no matter how hard they cry."*

*I looked anxiously at the three sleeping babies, how would I know if they were ill if they were never to be comforted? Then into the tiny, dark kitchen to make myself a cup of tea before settling down with my book.*

*"This isn't much of a substitute for dancing, perhaps I'll borrow Lizzie's radio for a while?"*

*Sneaking guiltily into her bedroom, I took her most cherished possession from her bedside table and carefully carried it into mine and Gwen's room and lay on the bed, still redolent of the sensuous perfume of Elizabeth Arden's 'Knowing,' which she liberally applied.*

*The news programme was followed by the daily round up 'Today at the Front.' Soon losing interest in the detail I carefully replaced the radio and curled into a comfortable embryo position to dream.*

*"Somewhere over the rainbow, Way up high."*

*I hadn't sung it since that last performance at the army camp outside Brussels, and it was on my mind all day: I missed singing, but not to people, not to soldiers. "There's a land that I dream of . . ."*

*I was so much more confident with Alys when I was with Lizzie and Gwen and their older babies and at my happiest in our family holiday town. The calm lapping blue sea, the wild flowers on the cliff tops, rock formations, rock pools, seaweeds, dressing up and promenading along the front, tennis at the little club, the shops, the walk-ways on Castle Hill and the De Valence . . . I loved every moment . . .* "Oh Alys, you made me jump!"

"Mum, what are those people doing sitting just in front of you? They must have seen you. There's acres of space for them to park and sit in. Why aren't they sitting in front of their own car? All you can see is the back of their heads. It's so rude! Hold your ice-cream, I'm going to tell them."

Her angry face is filling my head. Have the couple heard her shouting? I hate scenes. "Please, please Alys don't say anything. You'll spoil my enjoyment of the day if you tell them off. Please get back in the car."

"You're such a peacemaker, such a placater, you'd let anyone trample over you, why *should* we come to see the sea and then see nothing but heads!"

"Don't say nasty things about them so loudly, please Alys. I'll eat my ice-cream as quickly as I can and we can move on."

"Where do you want to go then Mum?"

"I don't mind, anywhere's a change for me. I don't want to miss a minute of this." Even though I'm in such agony with my raw bottom.

"We'll go to Sainsburys and get something for lunch, then you can direct me to Gwen's."

I haven't forgotten the roads around here.

✻     ✻     ✻

The nights are so long, restlessly waiting for the darkness to pull me under, watching the dust in the sunlight; slowly moving up the wall and away for the night, I never used to go to bed until 11.30, now sometimes I'll look at my watch and it's only 7 o'clock! The light through the open door makes dark shapes on the wall..

Is that moving?

Isn't it the chest of drawers?

Yes, yes, I know it is.

It is.

Definitely.

Such silence in this dead time. I'm sure I can hear wolves howling in the distance and squirrels jibber jabbering in their sleep . . . voices in bursts and snatches, like a radio being switched on and off, scraps of conversations as people walk past. I must have dropped off . . . what was that dream? It's unravelled . . . just vague recollections left, patches of fading colour, voices circling around as if they're trying to find their shadowy bodies. At least it wasn't one of my terrible dreams, making my heart race as if it'll jump straight out of my chest.

They're exhausting,

Draining.

Just thinking about them fragments flashing into my head makes me sick.

Did I doze again? Its cold. The light from the corridor's making a bright pathway to my bed. Who's there?

"Mother, is that you? Mother?"

*Her mid calf tennis dress is gleaming white against the light. "Are you going to play tennis?"*

*She's stretching a young, strong hand towards me and I'm floating up to meet it, slipping into my tennis clothes.*

*"It's time for your tennis lesson." The words ooze out of her red lipsticked mouth, sluggishly, like syrup, so each word sticks to the next. Mother's usually so brisk and quick, but she's taking long slow-motion strides along the lawn, past the geraniums and nasturtiums collapsed in golden heaps to the slatted wooden gate, pulling me behind her, my child's legs itching to go faster.*

*"Four of you and none of you played for Wales. It should have been you Catrin, you. Did I do enough? Children weren't so important then, 'seen and not heard' in my day. But I'm going to pass on my talent now. Come on Catrin, this time you'll be chosen!"*

*The blades of dewy grass glimmer in the sunlight like precious jewels, the leaves on the apple trees murmur in the friendly breeze. Mother hits the first ball and it's flying over the net, little wings appearing, a head, a beak . . . it's a baby dove . . . I can't hit that. I'll let it fly past.*

*"Catrin, watch the ball," she sounds irritated and impatient . . . hits another and another . . . they're flapping up high, singing beautiful songs. Shrink down very small . . . they swoop over and on.*

*The grass shimmers, the leaves fly off the trees and swirl down. They're grey with little red, evil eyes; their sharp teeth glint as they fall. My heart thumps so loud . . . cover my ears. The court is spinning round and away from me, mother's fainter and fainter and*

*I feel sick* . . . a creeping fear, a loneliness crawling all over me. Am I going to die? Won't resting, medicine, prayers, save me?

I've never slept in a single bed before. Always a double, with Gwen, then Gareth and on my own . . . spreading myself like a starfish . . . for the last . . . *twenty* years, is it?

Mustn't cry, mustn't feel sorry for myself, living with all these strangers . . . No one to touch, talk, laugh with, so many of my friends and family gone. I keep thinking, I need to tell John about that . . . the shock hits me afresh every time. He wasn't even ill! I'll curl my arms around my chest and close my eyes, so its like I'm being held. Gwen, Alys and Robert have their lives; I'm a burden to them.

Tears have come.

I know what I'm like.

I need to be secure.

Loved.

To have someone of my own.

A partner to love and look after me.

I know what I'm like.

I hate to be alone.

I know.

"We're all alone Mum," Alys says. "Dying or living, we're alone; no-one can live your life, or your death."

Why can't I get to sleep? Too many thoughts, whirling through my head . . . I'm losing track; my mind keeps going off somewhere else.

Is that what 'losing your mind' means?

How many times have I relived each moment of that day when I fell? Such precious moments, I breathe them, feel them, wishing and praying that I could change those few seconds, before, . . . . suddenly I was on the floor.

I should have walked more, tried to swim . . . I should stop my mind wandering about. What were the prices of tins from our shop? Middle shelf, fish: pilchard's small 26p, large, 48p, sardines 29p, pink salmon 99p, red salmon £1. 20 . . .

Did I drop off? My mouths like . . . eating ashes, this tongue isn't mine!

If I twist my shoulders and stretch my arms across, perhaps I can reach my drink . . . Oh, the duvet's slipped off . . . peer . . . strain to hear past the boundaries of my room and myself. Was that a nurse?

"Nurse, Nurse."

"Why don't you press your panic button Catrin?" I always forget.

"Why are you still awake? Are you OK love?"

The night nurse is always kind: 'Yes thank you. Can I have a drink please?"

"Up you come. Sip it. Ok? Try and go to sleep. Night, love."

My life's been quite ordinary I suppose. How much time have I got left? If I could just go back home, put on the kettle, answer the phone, choose what to eat, walk from room to warm cosy room. Though not John's bedroom. It was so quiet after he'd died. I didn't want to clean that room and suck up the last traces of him into the vacuum. I could go in there and breathe him in, that musky, spicy smell, Cougar was it?

Will I have any visitors today? I ask them to write down the days they're coming, but it's always a surprise when they walk through the door and I haven't had a chance to change or comb my hair.

"Would you like a cup of tea? A piece of cake?" I asked Winifred.

"Yes please, that would be nice." She smiled.

I called out for a nurse. But she said, "Wait for the trolley, you've only just had lunch."

It was really embarrassing

I'd love to see Lizzie and Gwen. I know it's a long way for Lizzie and she doesn't drive any more. It's not far for Gwen though, *she* could come. She doesn't like driving on motorways but she could get the bus or the train. If only she'd come.

Scenes rise in front of me like vapour, seeping into my every crevice, I'm a child . . .

*I clatter down the narrow stairs, jumping off the last but one, feet together to the brown linoleum of the hall and out through the door.*

*Mother is crouching in the shrubbery, filling a tin bucket with weeds. I know she's there because I can see the Golden Rod and the Hebe swaying as she moves and I can hear her busy trowel rattling against the small stones. Flowers are beautiful, but it's a lot of work making them grow. She's singing now: "Guide me oh my great Jehovah, pilgrims . . ."*

*"Mother. Mother."*

*I flip my hand as the drone of an insect stops and I feel the flutter of wings, the marching legs. I flip again and the cat starts and leaps, rush, rushing from the lawn to the gravel path and up into the laurel tree. It's Saturday morning and through the slatted gate the tennis net has been erected and tables and chairs are under the apple trees.*

*Her face appears above the dying hollyhock spires, its perfect heart shape framed by a headscarf.*

*"No, you are NOT going swimming with your sisters and the boys. You can't swim and you're too young."*

*"But I'll never learn if I don't go,"*

*"We'll teach you this summer," she says crisply, finally and her face disappears.*

*Don't suppose they would have taken me even if she'd said yes. I'm going to cry . . . run through the farmyard, across the field and into the copse at the far end. The path through the brambles goes to the little stream and the old wooden footbridge. I sit on the warm planks and weep. I hate being twelve and getting left out of everything. When I grow up I'll have the most handsome, clever, rich husband who buys me a beautiful house and we'll live happily ever after. I try to imagine him, but he's never more than a fuzzy blur.*

*The strong coconut smell of the nearby gorse wafts past me together with the damp, loaminess of the earth after last night's rain. The insects buzz and hum.*

*"I will have a handsome husband," I promise myself. "And make Lizzie and Gwen jealous."*

Well Gareth *was* handsome. I remember at Lorna's engagement party, talking to Uncle Percy, wearing Gwen's blue dress that Mother had altered, when he focussed on someone behind me.

"Let me introduce you to this fellow," he said. "Catrin, this is Mr Williams, Mr Gareth Williams."

My heart almost stopped and my brain went numb. He did the talking, well he was twenty-seven. How old was I? Twenty? I'd had both Alys and Robert before I was twenty-seven.

We danced. He wasn't Fred Astaire, but he held me firmly and I looked up into his open, clean-shaven face, at his grey amused eyes and thought how tall and good looking he was.

I could see my sisters and other girls looking at him. He said he played rugby and cricket for Newport, so of course he got on with Tom straight away. Uncle Percy took me aside and said, "Gareth comes from a well regarded and prosperous family, the 'Williams and Evans' of the fizzy drinks and the chain of grocers shops. He's sporty, he's done two degrees and now he's in management at Marks and Spencer's. He's a good match for you."

I *was* attracted to him. He was a refreshing change from my set. Time leapfrogged over itself after that first meeting, it was all so exciting. That period of my life, when I'd started working, it was all such fun, supper parties, beach parties, trips here and there, all too short and ended by the war. I can remember so little of it now, just snapshots and fragments.

It's funny, thinking back, how Gareth had a business degree, but he was no businessman. He was never interested in chitchat, which was hopeless if you're running a shop. When our customers gave us their weekly order, it was an outing, they wanted to sit down and gossip. I didn't like all that either, but at least I tried to listen. I think they thought we were a bit snobbish, well I suppose we were brought up differently . . . were more educated. Gareth didn't keep the accounts properly, or order the right things in. I was glad when he got the teaching job, so I was in charge of the shop.

I suppose our life revolved around sport, though he was keener on the socialising in the bar than I was. It's funny I got on so well with John, he was never sporty, but I was past playing when we got together. He made a lot more money with meat than we made with groceries.

It must be Christmas soon, I expect I'll be going to Alys's, or she can come to me. Perhaps I'll get a leg of pork for Boxing Day. I think I'll cook it myself, even if I'm at Alys's. It's quite nice the way she does it with the dried fruit; mushrooms, garlic and those herbs, but I do prefer the old plain ways of cooking. She'll make me do exercises every day, it'll be come on Mum, in and out and in and out and up and down and up and down, push those dumbbells harder!

How can I get presents if I haven't any money? "It's not allowed Mum, you're not allowed to have money here, they can't guarantee it won't get stolen." They say in irritated voices. I've seen other people giving tips, where do they get *their* money from then?

My shoulders are cold, it's light. I'll lie here a bit longer then I'll get up, have a shower and my breakfast and see if there's any tennis on the TV. What day is it? Hope it's not Monday, I'll have to rush to get dressed for the Day Centre bus. What's the time? Is that seven o'clock? Oh, this isn't *my* room, this is the HOSPITAL place. I have to wait to be dressed. My legs ache, I want to go to the toilet. I'm cold and I can't pull up the sheet. Someone's going past, "Nurse, Nurse!" Where's that alarm button, perhaps it's dropped on the floor?

* * *

Why is Alys showing me all these photographs? Who are they? I don't know these people. This is all too long ago. I don't want to think about them.

I'll make a joke. "My life's flashing before my eyes."

She doesn't understand and I can feel her hopefulness, her longing for me to enjoy them and tell her things about them.

I'm trying to be calm, but everything aches. Stabs of pain up through my body, heart flip-flopping, head swimming, her mouth moving. Whatever has happened to our closeness? I seem to be drifting away from her.

"You know I love you very much, don't you Mum?" She's crying. "Sorry Mum, but I get upset, thinking of you ill and alone."

It's so nice to be hugged. Her arms have left warm patches. "Yes, I know, but you must live your life, don't worry about me." I'm raging inside though and I know I'm going to cry when she goes, weep bitterly, with self-pity for what I had, what I've lost.

*That strange but familiar feeling of falling again. Falling up, not down. Up and up, skimming through the air, roaming the sky freely. The room, the building shrink to the size of a shoe box as I* pass chimney tops, skyscrapers, into damp, misty clouds, faster and faster. Can I stop? I don't think so; I'm not in control, maybe this time I've died. Is this what it feels like when you die and your soul goes back to soul heaven?

I'm out of the mist and there's blue sky all around. I'm calm, completely relaxed and comfortable as if everything is a big soft duvet and nothing will ever be painful again.

I'm so glad that there are these other possibilities, that I have two lives. What if I could choose where I am and create my own day? It's happening so often now, that I'm starting to believe that I could.

# Chapter 12—Reminiscing at Bryn Heulog. 2002

## WEDNESDAY MAY 8TH

*W*hen I cleared out Mum's home I gathered up her photographs, which had been scattered around loose in drawers or in corners in plastic bags. She had never seemed interested in sticking them into the albums I had bought her and I didn't know the where, when or even the who of some of them.

Attempts some years ago to get Mum to help me write the 20th century family history had always been met with resistance.

"But how many brothers and sisters *did* Grandpa have?"

"Well there was Auntie Elsie, Uncle Ted, Uncle William, Oh, I can't remember, don't ask *me*, ask Lizzie," she would say.

Begging and wheedling produced half stories, but she invariably became irritable and even cried if I persisted. However, having read how valuable 'Reminiscence Sessions' were thought to be for the elderly, I took along a selection of her photographs with me today. Would seeing them help her memory, would she be *more* interested now that she was losing it?

Mum was sitting with perhaps twenty-five others; all with their backs to the windows around the edges of the big lounge, rank with the smells of overcooked lunch, body odours and urine. Enid, Mary, Annie and John sat near her in identical red high-backed chairs with washable upholstery, staring into space, seeming to collectively breathe in time with the room.

She was wearing her royal blue Domani dress with the bands of green around the waist and hem. Another one of the lovely outfits she bought while she worked in Aunt Gwen's shop. It's infuriating how many have mysteriously disappeared from her wardrobe, despite the sewn in name tags. I understand why tights, stockings and socks rarely reappear after washing, they're difficult to mark. But where do they all go? Red, white and blue bare legs are the norm here.

Her face lit up when I appeared and we hugged.

"How are you Enid?" I asked the only other person who seemed to have noticed my arrival. We chatted about my journey, the weather and how they were both feeling and I got a carer to help me move Mum into a wheelchair so I could take her across the corridor, through the dining room and onto the small terrace for some sun and fresh air. The Mafia, as I call them, three of whom can walk and three with motorised wheelchairs were already occupying most of the small space. They have colonised their own lounge away from the others and seem to be almost part of the management. I manoeuvred Mum into a corner and tried to be chatty and charming to compensate the incumbents.

She was interested in all my news, knew the name of the flowers around us and seemed receptive to a photo session.

"Who are these, Mum?"

She stared hard at the curling, faded image of herself and her two sisters, marching down an esplanade accompanied by six smiling dashing young men. Mum was modestly dressed in an up to the neck jumper, a below the knee length skirt, and a toothy 'smile for the camera' fixed grimace. Tears pricked my eyes to see my young beautiful mother. Her two sisters were bare armed, firm legs below shorts, shaded gleaming flesh, looking as if it could burst like ripe fruit.

She smiled, as if remembering all the delights she has ever enjoyed: "Lizzie and Gwen," she started hesitantly.

I looked at the photograph, then at her, but somehow who she is escaped me and all I saw was a familiar blur. Has she always been like this, deliberately managing not to be known? Or is this my problem, loving her, but accepting the blur and not trying to know her? Come on Mum; give me some insight, I thought.

"Well yes I can see it's Lizzie and Gwen, but who are all these young men, where is it, how were you feeling?"

She looked perplexed. "I don't remember who they were. We were on a holiday in Jersey, staying in a hotel where there were mostly young people."

Lizzie and Gwen have their arms linked either side with the attractive men. Both smiling. Gwen with a sultry, elegant model-like confidence and Lizzie as always bubbling with happiness, as if life has been arranged for her pleasure. Mum although with the group, smiled shyly, reticently, holding herself guardedly apart.

"You look very young here, were you about seventeen?"

"Maybe, we went two or three times until the war broke out. Gwen only came that once, she was an apprentice at Antony's and couldn't get the time off."

"Yes, she was modelling and altering outfits wasn't she, learning the trade. What were you and Lizzie doing?"

"We must have been working in the Bank."

We looked at photos of Mum as a girl, and a lot of Dad in uniform with his regiment,

"Why aren't there any of you when you were in the concert party singing to the forces?" I asked.

I started to sing very softly, so as not to disturb the Mafia, a few lines of one of the songs I remember her singing around the house. Their words are still imprinted in my memory:

"Dear Mr Gable, I am writing this to you and I hope that you will read it so you know. Join in Mum."

"I can't sing now, my voice has worn out, it's gone."

"How about 'We will gather lilacs' or 'Somewhere Over the Rainbow?'"

She shook her head.

"My voice sounds, hoarse, tuneless, terrible now." She looked furtively at the Mafia, whose ears had pricked as if they sensed prey.

I tried to imagine this shy woman standing up there in the floodlights, alone in front of so many men. She said she didn't enjoy it, she found it too nerve wracking, and never mentions it. That whole part of her life has gone. Uncle Percy and Auntie Dolly, the real stars of those shows are long dead and will soon be beyond anyone's recall. I have two brass candleholders in the shape of cobras and an exotically carved mirror, which belonged to their eclectic collection of souvenirs from all over the world. Mum only went to Belgium and gladly gave up her concert party career as soon as she met Dad.

"How about a tennis photograph?" Mum stands, holding her racket, big bosom, solid legs, next to a skinny, pony tailed girl.

"You must be in your early thirties here Mum? How old was I when we started winning the club doubles together?"

In the bright afternoon light her eyes were cloudy, faded, so unlike this strong, clear, grey eyed, younger mother, smiling at the camera. She stared and stared as if she didn't recognise us. *My* head is so crowded with images I felt disorientated. *I* was sitting here remembering and wanting more, while she sat beside me forgetting and emptying. All those tennis games. She was very good, not flashy, fast or powerful, but steady, a good volleyer and so keen. Her tennis friends said that she was the best player never to represent her county.

When I was small, she would go off on the bus to play matches. Dad would be in the garden and I would sneak into their bedroom. It was one of the large bay windowed rooms on the front, my brother's little room sandwiched between it and the guest room, which my grandfather moved into when I was eleven. The door was always open, though I was not supposed to go in. It had a mysterious aura of secret grown up things, of a world I would inherit, roll-ons, nylons and huge bras, jewellery and makeup all mixed up together in the drawers. There was always a heavy smell of talcum powder and unopened windows. I remember the sun streaming in through the west facing dusty panes, a bedside clock ticking and the thrilling, daring feeling as I crept to the two most interesting places; the drawers of her kidney-shaped dressing-table with it's three-way mirror where I would be shocked at unaccustomed views of the sides of my face.

Or Mum's side of the bed on her bedside table were jars of Pond's cold cream, tins of Nivea and the nylon knickers, which held her hairdresser-set hair together in bed, between appointments. In the corner, a pile of handbags, not currently in use. A quick search would often unearth a Mars bar or similar, always battered, melted out of shape, bits of fluff and powder clinging to the chocolate protruding through the ripped wrapper. They tasted a bit odd, but I didn't care, I wolfed them down in the privacy of my own room, while lying on the bed reading. My favourite pastime.

"I taught you to play tennis," she replied. Her thin arm, with its sagging, blotchy skin trembled as she shakily put the photograph down on the table in front of her.

A blue overalled carer appeared behind us with the tea trolley. She offered me a cup, but I knew from experience than it would be too milky, too cool and the tannin would set my teeth on edge. I did not refuse the piece of sponge though, Pete, the nineteen-year-old cook, makes wonderful cake.

I brought out my favourite photograph, the one of the whole family at the farm for Christmas. We are posing in a corner of the lounge; the diamond shaped lead paned window behind on the right, the black metal fire-grate on the left, Christmas cards jostling for room on its mantelpiece. Two framed pictures hang either side of the corner on long cords. Whatever happened to that sinking ship scene, or the man on a horse? We are all in our Christmas best. My jumper and skirt knitted by my other granny, my pageboy the result of an uncomfortable nights sleep with my hair rolled up in strips of rag.

After the war, Tom, as the only son and the one to inherit the business, had carried on living here in the farm, with his wife Anne and two children, while the three daughters had had to live with their in laws. 'TE Williams and Son' the sign had said in black and gold above the grocery and butcher's shop.

I loved the farm. It had a staircase up from the front door and another spooky, narrow, dark one for the maids, from the little room off the stone flagged kitchen at the back. The stone walls were two feet thick and there were alcoves to sit in under each window. Nana kept the flagstones scrubbed, the iron grate gleaming with black lead polish and she would take only twenty minutes to cook an enormous rock cake for tea whenever we called. The rooms were small and the floorboards creaky, but the house had a happy family feeling as if it loved people and parties. Outside there was a beautiful flower garden, a large walled vegetable area, and an orchard, where my grandmother used to play tennis, but by then kept chickens instead. The farmyard had a granary, stables, barns and even a slaughterhouse. Fields spread beyond, with horses, cows and sheep. It was all pulled down before I was twenty and is now houses and flats.

Mum used to tell Cerys tales about her childhood, it sounded so idyllic. I'm sure it was. She found sport, singing and her schoolwork easy and her strict, sociable parents gave her a strong belief in family values.

"Who are these Mum?"

She glanced down at the large pasteboard rectangle and smiled almost that same sweet, self-conscious smile as her brown haired younger self, sitting in the middle row next to her handsome patriarchal father. Lizzie, the oldest child, photogenic, relaxed and sophisticated in the middle, their elegant mother with her wonderful poise and carriage next (grandmothers are so often described as beautiful—is it because of their proud poses, the steady look in their old fashioned eyes?) Then stunning Gwen in her stylish low, sweetheart neckline and earrings. The husbands and Tom all with ties and jackets stand straight backed behind, together with Anne, looking like the confident, capable, Chief Inspector of Schools that she was before marriage.

Mum smiled, was that wistfully? It is difficult to tell as DLB makes her face severe and expressionless. I was pricked by a wave of tenderness as she fastidiously tried to wipe the side of her mouth with a single curled over finger. I handed her a tissue and she concentrated hard to hold it in hands that are difficult to move and no longer grip. A huge effort just to check there are no fragments of her tea left behind.

"Only you three sisters and their children left now."

"They were all so tall and handsome,'

"Well you were, are," I corrected myself, "beautiful women. Do you think you would all have got married so young if there hadn't been a war?"

I had hoped that her memories of the past would be so powerful and vivid that I would have learnt more about my family this afternoon, but her secretive nature and the habits of her lifetime, of covering everything up, putting a brave face on, never telling anyone else your business was too ingrained. "Oh, I don't know," she said vaguely.

We both continued to gaze at the happy family scene of a Christmas over fifty years ago, unremarkable, yet remarkable in its contented conformity, each generation solid, dependable, churchgoing, passing on its Christian values of honesty, integrity and hard work. No one had ever really rebelled. Although most of us had lived with our partners outside marriage and some had taken time off to travel, we had all had professions and stuck at them, providing for the next generation. If anyone *did* have a deep dark secret, they had hidden it very well and I would never find it out from this mother of mine.

"Your Mother has jelly babies twice a week!" A tell tale voice was at my elbow. Lillian the Chief Mafiosi, who organises the tuck trolley, had sneaked up behind me.

"You like jelly babies do you Mum?"

She flushed, looked like a guilty little child. Come on, speak Mum, show some passion, show her how articulate you are! Why *are* you so passive, so accepting, uncomplaining, and always so equable? I thought, longing for her to fight back. Her submissiveness frustrates me. How I despise myself for the grudging way I have her to stay, or take her anywhere and then her gratitude, her not expecting anything from me, makes me feel doubly guilty. Not her fault, all mine. She is the one whose personality is nudging perfection. I'd hoped that she could join the Mafia because they're the only ones who go on outings in the minibus, but she was drugged and dopey when she arrived here and is still too quiet and subdued to be of interest to them.

"She has too many and she has chocolate as well, you must have a big bill," she purred, almost licking herself with pleasure at being able to snidely tell on Mum.

"It's fine Lillian, she can have whatever she likes." I said protectively, and to distract her: "How are the raffle tickets going?"

"Oh, Okay, how many will you have?"

I had arrived while they were in lunch, so had not been accosted in the entrance hall.

"None!" I said bravely. All the prizes were Mum's costume jewellery, which she had shown no interest in having: "I don't want to win all that stuff back again."

"She's *a Lesbian!*" said Mum loudly as Lillian rode away.

Horrors, I didn't know Mum even knew the word. "Yes, my friend in London *is,* isn't she?" I said quickly, not sure if Lillian had heard.

We were quiet for a while, it was slightly cooler and the Mafia had wheeled or shuffled themselves indoors. Mum turned her face to the sun and closed her eyes. I knew she wasn't sleeping as I could see her eyes flicking back and forth under her eyelids, as if she were reading her own thoughts. If only *I* could, would I *ever* know her?

The afternoon was nearly over; I picked up Mum's wedding portrait. We looked at one another for a long time, she looking shyly under her lashes, my eyes trying to bore into her soul. I will have to accept that to be personal has always been shameful, impossible for her. Irritated and disappointed at learning nothing from any of the photographs, I despondently packed them away.

When the cousins get together at funerals or weddings, we talk about who should update the family tree, old records of which go back to the late 14th century and Owain Glyndwr, the King of free Wales. We had our chance when we were young, but it wasn't interesting then, only the present and future had any importance. Our mothers must have a collective memory of so much that will be lost, but life rushes on and our chances are diminishing with Lizzie 87, Gwen 85 and Mum 83.

Why *do* we reach middle age and suddenly become more interested in our long forgotten relatives lives? Does knowing our ancestors feed us with a sense of perpetuity, help us to become everlasting? Why does the past matter, if Mum doesn't want to remember it and I never knew it, it's gone, without a trace, so what? But surely it's our memories that make us human, without a past, who are we?

Now that Mum can no longer read, and the TV is too far away, surely she entertains herself through the long days and nights by reliving her past? Hopefully it's a comforting refuge, even though I'm frustratingly excluded.

It's hard to tell how she feels about her incarceration, her shrunken life. The sight of her alien, institutionalised surroundings and her dignified, well dressed figure, sitting day after day amidst all those others in their twilight lives, all breathing, eating, existing and waiting for someone from the real world to visit and take them away is deeply upsetting.

"What are we going to do for Christmas?" Mum asked me.

"It's only May," I answered, but what can we ever do again after our failure at Robert's house. I pushed her wheelchair to her room to deposit the chocolates and magazines I had brought for her. She is number 61 on the ground floor. Everything she possesses must be marked with 61, no longer a name, but a number. All the rooms are painted in magnolia, with orange nylon bedspreads and melamine surfaces.

It was suppertime, so I wheeled her back to the next geriatric happening. A highlight in the monotony of the day for most of the residents. Parking her in her place between Enid and Annie, sitting meekly waiting, I prepared to flee.

"I'd better go now; it takes an hour to walk to the station. I'll see you again soon," I said.

"How am *I* going to get there? Will you wait for me, we may as well go together, have I got a ticket?" she asked anxiously. Every week, this heartbreak of explaining that she lives here, that she is not going anywhere, until, until . . . A nurse approached and distracted her with her pills in a small white plastic cup, "Shall I help you, Catrin?" Selecting one and holding it to Mum's mouth with the remnants of her very cold tea to wash it down, which I had left on the table earlier, for clearing away.

Is the pleasure she gets from seeing me for these few hours every week outweighed by the anguish we both feel when I leave?

"Bye Mum," I called, feeling upset and heartless as if this was a diversionary tactic, a trick to escape while she is trapped and helpless. I walked swiftly away to my life.

## THURSDAY JUNE 5TH

I am moving Mum to a new home next week. Bryn Heulog is appallingly run. Inmates are often left in bed for fifteen hours at a time, the smell of humiliation and need is unbearable and all her nice things have vanished. I feel that though some staff are excellent, they can't make up for the neglect and the grotesquely patronising way some of them talk down to residents. It's like a game; those who play along are rewarded.

It has taken me five months to find one that seems reasonable. Some were unaffordable, in others she would have had to share a bedroom, few had any organised activities. The majority of staff being foreign with poor spoken English seems to be standard. Riverside is near Mum's childhood home and Gwen's flat.

I feel guilty about taking her away from Charlie, but they have never exchanged more than a few platitudes a day. Charlie slips her sweets and fruit, brought in by his very glamorous sister and makes sure she is OK. They only meet in the dining room, and then all he can see is her back. The carers always place her with her back to the room and she can't turn her wheelchair round to see him.

"Are you OK Catrin?" he calls as he limps in, supported by his stick.

"Yes, I'm fine, and you?" The same platitudes are exchanged twice a day. The staff must know how he feels, because he is so often in the office putting her name down first to have her hair done and to see the dentist and optician, as he knows that my weekly visit would be too late for her to get places. Why have they never moved her position at the table, so that they can at least see one another?

Charlie never spends any time in the lounge. After lunch and dinner he goes off to his room to watch TV, so Mum has two other men friends to chat to, Ted and Jack. If she is placed next to women, she is quiet, but comes alive when near a man.

"Do you like Charlie, Mum?" I asked.

"He's very kind, but not particularly." Is her answer. I wondered if she was embarrassed because he had been a long distance lorry driver rather than a professional man. He is certainly the best catch in the Home. The only one who can walk, talk and doesn't have dementia!

Mum doesn't really want to move, "Whatever you think is best, I rely on your judgement," she said.

Charlie is heart broken, but understands: "I am very keen on your Mum," but he seems realistic enough to know that it can never be more than it is.

# Chapter 13—New Home and the beginning

*W*hat's this new place going to be like? "Right at the roundabout and left at the church."

"Thanks Mum, good job you know Cardiff."

"Yes, it'll be next left." I wonder if I could drive now? Have to get my heavy legs going first. I won't be wearing shorts and skimpy clothes like all *these* people though. My mind's hopping from here and now to there and then. "How was the party last night?"

"Uh, good, yeh, good. Though we ended up watching this weird DVD that someone brought, it was quite disturbing."

"Oh."

"Yeh, it was basically saying that there are loads of realities, but peoples brains are only conditioned to see the one they know."

"Oh."

"They said we are actually in more than one place at the same time . . . many places in fact . . . it's just we can't see what we have no experience of. I think that was it."

I'd like to tell her that I can be here and up there, but what would she think . . ."Sounds a bit far fetched to me."

"Yeh, I just can't get my head round it . . . me being in lots of places at once and not knowing."

Well I can be in two. "Oh, Alys, left and left again."

Must concentrate . . . nearly missed that turning. That pub wasn't there a few years ago, it was all fields. Is this it? Red brick, where's the garden?

"Here we are Mum,"

I know she feels guilty, well, when my legs are better, I'll go back to my own home.

"Let's have a big hug then Mum and I'll get out and ring the bell."

I can't say that it looks terrible or nice; it's just a building with no proper garden. I've never liked gardening, but I do like to look at pretty ones. Two nurses in blue coming out.

"Hello Catrin, I'm Joan and this is Marjorie. Welcome to Riverside, I'm sure you'll be very happy here."

"Hello." I won't tell her I'm not staying long. As soon as I can walk again I'll go home.

Joan has a kind, attractive face. She looks like May Edwards. I wonder where she is now? Perhaps Joan is her sister? "Do you know May Edwards?"

"No I don't think I do. Come and see your room, then I'll get you a nice cup of tea."

She's got a nice smile. Those coloured girls won't be able to get me out. "You're hurting me!" I'm getting cross.

"They're doing their best, Mum."

I've got heavy legs, I know, everyone tells me. Oh careful, don't pull so hard. Oh, no . . . no, wee . . . everywhere . . . it's on them. How has it come through the pad? I'm so ashamed.

"Don't worry," Joan says. "Lots of people do that. It's stress."

I'm mortified. They won't like me now. Two doors. "Watch my feet."

"Let me introduce you to Sheila and Mary."

Has Joan told them I've wet them all?

"Into the lift, you're on the first floor. This is your room Catrin; it's an inflating pressure mattress. Your son brought your TV and here's your bathroom."

It's quite pretty, but even smaller than the other place. My bedroom at home is four times this size, *and* I've got five cupboards, not just one little one.

"I'll unpack your clothes Mum, you need some dry trousers."

That was my case sighing as Alys opened it and my clothes sprung up.

"Here you are, you must be dying for a cup of tea and a biscuit."

Joan seems very nice.

✳     ✳     ✳

I'm lonely . . . feel strange. I wish Alys could have stayed longer. "No, I don't want to sit in the lounge, thank you, my sister might come to see me later."

I'm not interested in walking in Scotland but I can't seem to change the channel. I'd like to watch tennis or a soap. Is it always sandwiches for supper? They're a bit dry.

"You were being ill treated at Bryn Heulog, Mum and it was too far for Gwen to visit you," Alys said. But I had got to know it, and the food was quite good. I have to accept that I've no control over where I am; I have to rely on Alys's judgement. When I'm better, I *must* get better.

Gwen looks so stylish, so well groomed. I love those linen slacks and knitted silk top.

"Open your mouth, Catrin, you love green grapes."

She's taken the pips out; she's so kind and loving to me now. I must say she has changed, she was always telling me off when I worked in her shop. If I stayed with her on Saturday nights it was the same old script every time:

"How do we get through so much toilet paper when you come to stay?

I couldn't sleep a wink, you were shouting in your sleep again.

You eat me out of house and home!"

I'd smile and bite back my retorts; I knew she didn't mean it.

I'd wait all the week to see if she'd invite me and take my clothes to work just in case, and it was often late afternoon before she'd say "Are you coming to stay then?" I'd have to buy my share of the food in that expensive shop opposite, when I could have got it cheaper in Tescos if I'd known before.

"What did you buy that for?" She'd ask, and, "am I cooking again?"

I'd try not to annoy her; I always laid the table, did the vegetables and washed up. She's lived on her own for too long I suppose, David died . . . was it 25 years ago? She wasn't like that when we were young.

She used to say, "I always feel so inadequate, having two sisters who are brainy and good at sport. Why do I have to be so dull?"

It wasn't much fun for her staying at the convent when the rest of us went to High School. She didn't play in teams and do her school cert like we did. We didn't know about dyslexia then. She's bitter about having to work all her life and David dying young and never having much money.

Now she's so kind and loving to me, I'm grateful and I'm not going to think about the past.

✳        ✳        ✳

It must be dawn . . . the faint, watery light coming through the curtains making a path into my head. It's stopped raining.. I'll wait for half an hour, until the sun sucks up the mist . . . then I'll hit a few balls. Now I'm going to play for Wales . . .

The ceiling cracks are like paths . . . follow them, back and forth, back and forth, round and round. *Ooh, that breathless, constricted feeling, pulling me, lifting me up and up . . . faster and faster, stop, stop. Up, up and oooh, down. I'm in freefall, giddy, sick, plummeting, screaming down, corkscrewing, looping a wide endless loo-—op. Air currents lifting me . . . I'm a feather on the breeze . . . That noise in my ears . . . is it the blood in my head, my heart beats . . . the passing air as I fall?*

*Don't care?*

*I'm here, now.*

*Head full of . . .*

*What?*

*Shake my head to clear it, gulping in the breeze . . . There's twinkling lights, roofs, a huge still expanse of water, a road below, a coach, where am I?*

*Rushing towards the coach, help, heeelp . . .*

*"I feel so sick again!" Gwen's never been a good bus traveller; she's very pale, almost green really and her usually immaculate hair is quite dishevelled.*

*"We're nearly there, I've just seen a sign to Lake Muick, so it can't be far away. Keep taking deep breaths and looking forward."* *That's Lizzie's elder sister voice.*

*"We should have taken the train or I could have driven, I'm never sick when I drive. We've been on this coach, all day."*

*"Won't be long now Gwen. You'll be able to relax while we play."*

*"Catrin, you've woken up at last, you've got the programme, who are you playing?"*

*Was I snoring again? My throat's like sandpaper.* *"The over 55's and 65's are first at 11 o'clock. Then it's us at 1.30. Over 75's and over 85's Wales versus England, Scotland against Ireland. Then on this page all the names are listed, look, Over 85's, Catrin Williams and Lizzie Morgan."* *Lizzie Morgan? Lizzie? You're playing, I hope you've been practising.*

*No more towns and motorways just bowling along quiet country roads . . . a roofless, sightless skeleton of a croft and lakes and rivers sparkling in the soft evening light. Most people seem to be dozing.*

*"Look lights!" A cheer from the front. "It's the new Scottish tennis centre."*

*I couldn't be more excited and petrified . . . I'm going to play for Wales at last, even if it is with Lizzie; I'm going to have to carry her. I'll have to play well. I must, must, must.*

"Must what? Mum, are you going to wake up and talk to me?"

That's Robert's voice, I'm not asleep. What's *he* doing in Scotland?

"Open your eyes, Mum." He's looking at his watch again. "What were you muttering about?"

"Oh, nothing, can I have a phone at this place? I'm cut off from everyone."

"No, you can't have one here either, it's not allowed."

A chocolate into my mouth.

"It would have to be locked or everyone else would be using it, and who's going to unlock it for you?"

Such creamy sweetness, "Mmn ah."

"You can use my mobile when I'm here." He won't take his eyes off the annoying, beeping little thing.

"I don't *want* to use your mobile, I don't understand it and anyway they burn your brain cells. You shouldn't use it so much."

"What do you think's going to happen? Phones'll cause a geomagnetic storm so we go into meltdown? Don't be silly Mum, you've been reading science fiction."

"No I haven't."

"Oh, I know, you saw that item on the news about the sunspot. What could it do? Erupt solar flares to cripple satellites and radio communications, burn us all to death? Is that what you're on about?"

Am I?

"Well, you're being stupid, it's not going to happen. Who do you want to ring? Lizzie? I'll dial the number for you and all you have to do is hold the mobile."

"I'm NOT using one of those!"

Can't speak . . . mouth full of orange pieces . . . he calls so many people.

"I'm off now Mum, see you on Thursday."

He never stays long. I love my son, but he's so busy he's impatient with me. He takes too much on for that company, he shouldn't be on call day and night, but he won't listen to me . . .

✻       ✻       ✻

"Mum, mum, wake up, I've travelled for hours to see you."

I am awake, aren't I? I'm stiff and dry mouthed . . . where am I? What am I supposed to be doing?

"Mum, did you see the French Open final?"

I can see myself shaking my head.

"I told the girls at the desk to put it on for you, they wrote it down."

I wonder if she'll notice that she's talking to an empty person? But no, she hasn't paused for breath . . . something about a netball match. Floating on warm air currents, swooping and gliding. Am I on my way to Scotland or coming back? Shall I tell her I'm going to play for Wales? No, I'm too far away.

I used to feel so close to Alys, but now . . . she seems a stranger somehow, doing things I'm not that interested in . . . different lives,

110

and I always seem to say the wrong thing. I often go when she's here and by the time I get back, I don't know what she's talking about.

✳     ✳     ✳

*"This must be the court, our opponents are here already."*

*I'm so proud to be wearing my red jacket with the Welsh badge. "Our first match for Wales, Lizzie!"*

*Their supporters aren't putting me off with their chanting and clapping. In fact, they're firing me up for my serve. I'll jog on the spot and snarl in my head to get myself going. Grr, grr, here we go. We're only playing one set; this has to be a good serve, Whack. Poom. Puk, Whack!*

*"Well done Catrin, four aces. How did you make them skid like that?"*

*I'm playing the game of my life, this is so exciting . . .*

*"5 - 1 to Wales. Catrin Williams to serve."*

*I feel completely resolute, as if everything in my life has led to this moment. No amount of style or diversionary tactics are going to affect me. Up with the ball, a mighty swing, whack . . . an ace!*

*"15 love."*

*Only three more points for victory; I know I can do it. Toss the ball up high . . . the sky's gone blood red. Hurl my racket towards the ball . . . exploding. What's happening? Can't see . . . exploding ears . . . chest, has my heart stopped? The noise, the piercing noise . . .*

*Screams, terrible screams . . . fire . . . flames, it's the people, the people . . . burning like torches.*

*"Lizzie get back. The umpire and chair are burning."*

*That wind's fanning the flames from the English people onto the trees behind . . . All our Welsh supporters are inside that fireball, being burnt alive . . . "You can't help them Lizzie. Back away. Back away to the end of the court."*

*The plastic covering the fence is melting, the posts are glowing red and warping, we're trapped in this cage of terrible heat.*

*The pressure in my head is easing, it's not going to burst and I'm flying, floating on the wind. I've been looking down at the hideous*

111

*scene. Lizzie's cowering on the ground. Mouth's full of my dry, swollen tongue, drier than cream cracker biscuits, a desert, ashes. I want to cry, but there's no moisture left for tears, I'm dried into a shrivelled mummy. Force, pull my singed lids . . . my eyes pop open . . . I'm back.*

*"I can't believe it . . . our supporters . . . they're glowing charcoal, and we're still alive. And look at the English side . . . the trees, benches and people are still burning."*

*"How can you see? I can't open my eyes; they're so painful in this heat. I can't breathe, the smoke . . ." Lizzie can't stop coughing.*

*The flames are dying down. "Lizzie it's a normal beautiful day again, still and quiet!*

*"Can you see Gwen? Where's Gwen?"*

*"Don't know where she went. I don't think she wanted to see me have to serve for the match. Oh, your eyes are so bloodshot."*

*"Did she go down the slope to the lake?"*

*"Look, look, there she is."*

*"What's happened here? Those people are burnt." She's screaming and screaming . . .*

*Pulled backwards so fast . . . Breathless, dizzy. The screaming fades in the whoosh of my flight through the air . . . .*

Lifted, pulled roughly, needle stuck into me. Eyelids soldered down again with that heat. They're heavy trap doors.

※　　　　※　　　　※

Someone is boring a hole into my head. That's a blurry face I know . . . I want to soar up and away from this pain . . . I want to sleep again.

Can't speak, throats sore, tongue's like loft insulation . . . is that my heart thumping?

"How are you?" the hazy shape is asking.

Slowly, slowly, my tongue's softening. "Gwen? Where are we going to live now Gwen?"

"We both live here in Cardiff, dear."

"No, no, help." I want her to tell me where after the tennis match, but she doesn't understand . . . I'm sinking . . . sinking.

# Chapter 14—Settling in to Riverside. 2002

## THURSDAY JUNE 13TH

*I* arrived at twelve to pack up Mum's things and take her to Riverside. The secretary had gone to lunch, taking the keys for the safe with her, so I couldn't get Mum's valuables. She arrived back at two at the same time as Mum's replacement, who seemed to be fully occupying all the staff on duty. By two thirty I couldn't wait any longer, so they agreed to give them to Robert at the weekend and we drove off at last.

The new Home seems far better organised and is near to Gwen's flat. Gwen is now nervous of driving outside Cardiff so had rarely visited Bryn Heulog. I unpacked her twenty-nine nighties and negligees, her fifty-four pairs of pants and all her lovely clothes and crammed them into the five tiny drawers and half wardrobe. There is no room for her winter clothes; they've had to stay in the cases, which I piled on top of the flimsy cupboard. I hated leaving her there in this strange new place looking so scared, confused and vulnerable. Have I made the right decision?

## SUNDAY JUNE 16TH

Robert returned to Bryn Heulog to pick up Mum's jewellery from the safe, but they have lost their book in which all valuables were logged. Despite the descriptions I had left, of her rings, watch and bracelets they have been unable to find anything resembling them. I will write to the Matron and their Head office.

Mum looked up as I arrived, but didn't acknowledge me.

"What's the matter?" I said.

"I keep saying the wrong thing, so it's better to say nothing. Help, help, I mean hello."

"Why do you say 'help' Mum?"

"I don't know, I just say it, sometimes it's because I need help."

She fumbled with the little light blanket covering half of her lap. "Take this, it might be worth something."

"It's your blanket Mum, you'll need it."

"Oh I thought, I thought it was . . ."

She tailed off, conscious that she was always being made to look foolish and in the wrong.

We chatted for a while. I asked if she had been watching Wimbledon. She showed little interest and was confused about who had visited her and what they had said. Her memory has taken on the randomness of dreams, unconstrained by any noticeable order.

She started sentences with questions I was unable to follow. I know now that I must not correct her, it makes her feel frustrated, so I nod. Why do I insist that she recognises reality? Is it something to do with me being a bossy teacher? Eventually I said, "Not sure I understand Mum . . ." but then she agreed that she didn't either.

Being listened to and being understood would probably make her feel valued. I should just smile at her indulgently, agree with everything she says, and make our time together light-hearted fun, like Gwen and Lewis do. Why should she have to be rational and make sense? It isn't surprising that she is happier with them than me . . . I have tried, but we seem to slip back into our accustomed relationship, which is serious and discursive. We have rarely laughed together as she did so continuously with John. We settled down to watch the women's quarterfinals, where as usual she looked at a spot on the skirting board, insisting it was another TV. Can she see?

"What would you like to do with your time?" I asked after a while.

"Play and watch more tennis, win my matches!"

Had she felt trapped by the shop and her duties as wife and mother? I had thought that she liked her life to be secure, predictable and ordered. From one hundred and eighty miles away I thought I knew where she would be at any minute of the day. But was this not what she'd wanted at all? Had she been yearning for a different life of playing full time competitive tennis? When she was young, tennis was an amateur sport and the only professionals were coaches, very few of who were women.

She had been mumbling something for a few minutes. Should I be trying to decipher her ramblings? She sometimes seems to have a ravenous need to talk and to be listened to. If I talk her brain struggles to focus on my words. Where she is, seems to slide out of her mind. Do only old memories exist now in the tissues of her brain? Or is everything mixed up, circuits crossed and events spliced onto different scenarios? I am still convinced however, that her thoughts are clearer than the sentences she speaks. She becomes almost animated when she is telling me something I find incomprehensible. Confusingly, her speech patterns, the inflections and the tone of confiding secrets remain. If someone heard her talking without being able to hear the words, they would be convinced that she was communicating.

She seems to weave fantasies. There's the one where the Home is a tennis club and she is on the committee and the constant sound of buzzers seem to be reminding her of a college. She cannot, or will not remember that she is in a Home, but often talks about her class and how she will get back home when it finishes.

"Are you coming to the next lecture? I hope I don't have to sit near him!"

Yet, today when Gwen told her that three of her cousins were coming to Cardiff to see her she said: "I don't want to see them, it's embarrassing, three people trying to crowd into my little room, having to sit on the bed and I can't even get them a cup of tea or anything."

Ahaa Mum, so you do know where you are, I thought. Well you knew at that moment anyway.

# WEDNESDAY JULY 17TH

Mum was looking absolutely exhausted and upset as if she had played nine sets and lost them all.

"I just want a quiet life, with nothing to argue about," she said trembling.

"What's wrong?" I asked, feeling my pulse starting to race.

"The people were burnt to death." She shuddered.

What has she seen? Is she mixing up memories with TV programmes? Does it matter anyway? "Are you sure Mum? Was it on the news or another programme?"

"No, burnt bodies, like charcoal."

She was watching me now, waiting, I must not tell her she is talking rubbish. "Perhaps it was a nightmare, they often seem real."

She pressed her lips together into a bitter line, her eyes into slits.

"No." She said suddenly loudly. "And *you* don't seem to care."

I was lost. "Well, I didn't see it." I said weakly. She looked at me coldly, a long gaze.

"All. Those. Peo..ple. Dead!" She enunciated every syllable. "All burnt!"

"Yes, I said, terrible." There was a silence and I tried to change the subject, but she had switched off.

# FRIDAY SEPTEMBER 6TH

Bounding up the stairs after exchanging a few words with the nurses on their drug rounds, I rushed into her room, hot with the exertion from my brisk walk from the station. She was sitting in her chair with dead unfocussed eyes, her slumped position emphasizing her stomach, which pushed through the shirt, which had fitted her so well eighteen months ago. Her yellowish-grey skin was taut over her cheekbones and was so thin, it seemed as if you could poke your finger through it. Her stiff, twisted, useless feet protruded over the end of the footrest.

"Hello Mum, it's me, how are you?"

She turned her head towards me, staring vacantly with bleary, puffy eyes. There was no flicker of recognition. Is she ill? Is she cross with me for going abroad, because she never will again? I hate telling her when I am going anywhere, particularly Tenby, because she always looks crestfallen and upset.

"It's me, Mum, I'm here, say 'Hello.'"

"Hello." She said mechanically. She might say the same to a carer. Does she know who I am? She looked at me as if I reminded her of someone and then, more aggressively, "Where have you been?"

"You know I went on holiday, Mum, to Italy."

"Haven't seen you for years," she muttered.

"It's was only nine days and then we had enrolment week at College. I know that's the longest time we haven't seen one another since you fractured your leg, but I sent you a card."

I spotted it on her windowsill. "Look there it is, Florence. You saw it didn't you?"

She grudgingly admitted that she had.

"Ye..ess. I've been cooking for everyone."

"Oh, what sort of things?" I asked cautiously.

"Roast dinners, cakes," she giggled, "they love my cooking."

I kissed her and her old, stiff hands moved, slowly, flutteringly towards me. She so desperately wants to be hugged and touched. Mum is washed and her nappy changed regularly, so she gets physical contact, but not by hands that *want* to touch just her. She is starved of a loving caress, and I can feel her desperate need. No words, but a palpable longing and a look of gratitude as I responded. Standing behind her I massaged her shoulders, trying to pull the stiff coat hangers back to where they used to be. I rubbed her arms and hands, those claws, which can no longer grip.

"Will you unzip my boots?" she asked

"You haven't got any on."

A little later she asked again: "Can you take off my boots, I think I've unzipped them."

"You haven't got any on," I repeated. "Can't you move your legs?"

"Of course," she said huffily, "I do all the time! They're very heavy. It doesn't look as if Robert is going to get here."

"Why would he be coming?" I was puzzled. "He's in America for a month and isn't due back for a week. Gwen's away too, staying with Lizzie."

"He said he was coming on Wednesday."

"Well it's Friday Mum . . ."

## WEDNESDAY SEPTEMBER 18TH

Still no satisfaction from Bryn Heulog. Despite my letters and detailed descriptions to the new Matron and the Head Office, they are denying the existence of her jewellery. They had refused to give me a receipt the day Mum was admitted, saying everything was logged in the book. Very cunning, lose the book, then no receipt, no claim!

At Riverside the residents are not forced to sit in the lounge, so Mum has seized the opportunity of staying in her room, "in case I have visitors." I suppose I don't blame her, the few men also stay in their rooms and the eight or ten women sit silently in one row facing the row opposite, looking into space. They doze, (their thighs falling apart) or humour their contemporary, Peggy who comes in to play bingo or sing with them twice a week. Why do we think that this is the way to treat the elderly, containing them in their chairs with virtually no mental or physical stimulation?

On my train journeys I am deep into novels about older people, looking for hope, but finding none.

*'In the lounge—that hateful word—they sat about or slept with their mouths open. And if they had eaten too much, they made noises and sometimes smells.'*

Paul Bailey 'At the Jerusalem' (1987 p80)

Yes, yes, it is just like that . . . .

And though I had thought that her life was confined before she went into hospital at least she was able to move from room to room, watering her plants, making a cup of tea, looking at the TV Times to choose her programmes and plan her meals around them. Now her only options are 'the lounge' or being trapped in her room with the TV on too loud.

"Can you put the sound down?" She always says to me when I arrive. It was a programme about Glamis Castle, which I could hear from downstairs. She isn't the slightest bit deaf, but the carers put the volume up too high and she can't remember how to use the controls to adjust it.

The other residents seem to be so used to having everything done for them that they appear not even to be even thinking for themselves. For Mum, some memory remains: "Would you like a cup of tea?" she asked hospitably. "If you're going shopping, I'm a bit short of bread."

Then later, "what shall I get Gwen, Lizzie and the others for lunch today?"

All she wants is to be able to provide for us, to give her visitors tea or a meal, but she is stuck in that chair, hair a mess, stains on her front, her useless legs encased in their bandages sticking out stiffly, a huge, throbbing, unidentified hard lump on her left leg . . .

We ate a Marks and Spencer éclair each: "Lizzie doesn't make cake any more," I said, hoping that she would feel better about being unable to cook now.

"She doesn't need to, I'm always making them for her."

## THURSDAY OCTOBER 10TH

Mum had a urinary infection and was sent to hospital last Monday. Gwen said both times she had visited, Mum was asleep. When I arrived today she was being discharged, so I travelled back in the ambulance to Riverside with her.

I sat on her bed at the side of her chair and fed her strawberries and clotted cream. She wiped her lips carefully after each messy mouthful, still caring enough about her appearance, though of course she is not able to put makeup on, comb her hair or dress herself. Her nose looked hawk like and her cheeks sunk away towards her chin. She talked about friends who had died long ago, her voice barely audible.

Then, she had nothing else to say to me and I had exhausted all my news. We sat companionably and I knitted, popping chocolates into her mouth. Chocolates have featured quite importantly in our lives. Dad became an alcoholic, how could we blame him when we were so fixated on sugary self-indulgences? Mum's favourites were chocolate coated nuts and walnut whips. She could never have been thin with her sweet tooth; she always had bars stashed away out of sight, for secret eating. I studied her; she was somewhere else, so I scribbled the following in my notebook.

This notebook has become like a diary, an emotional crutch for me. It helps me make sense of the huge amount of time that managing Mum's life now takes up. My recent role of taking responsibility for and spending more time with a mother I had taken for granted, is making me look at her more closely, and do some character detective work. Oh, yes, her appearance is completely familiar, but even though I've spent my life in such close contact, I've always been looking outwards at the world rather than focusing on her. Now I'm looking *at* her and the words to describe her escape me. The closer I look the more the essence of her dissolves. Is she this, or that? Yet I know that when I leave, I won't hold onto, or even have grasped the essential her, she moves so lightly through her world, just the love I have for her. If only I *could* catch her, trap her, know her. Are mothers always hazy? Camouflaged by familiarity?

What *does* she think? Oh what does she *really* think underneath that layer of pretence and propriety? I've long suspected that she guards her thoughts and that they are more complex, imaginative and deep than her conversation. Sometimes I've caught an expression on her face, which looks as if she was translating something in her head, rehearsing what she says before she speaks. Unless she's joshing with someone, and then her repartee is lightening quick. But in normal conversation there's a pause, then out comes something perfectly ordinary. Was her original thought complex, poetic or contentious? What has she censored? Why did it have to be translated into this mild, simple sentence? I will never know now.

Mum seems to have lived in a serene, glossed over world of seeing what she'd like to see, always the best in every situation and telling people what she thinks they want to hear. She only presents an optimistic face to the world, so unlike me, I moan for Britain. Appearances and what the neighbours and family think count so much with Mum. When I decided to have a child, she told everyone that I was married. I have never known how she managed not to have been caught out, when the name of my 'husband' kept changing. Perhaps she was, perhaps everyone knew that I was actually a single mother.

To be fair, she has never made us feel that we were not the children she wanted, however much she longed for us to be different.

As a child I was ashamed of her posh voice, but proud of her manners. "Hello, how are you. How lovely to see you. Thank you for coming." She never swore or shouted, she was calm and unfailingly polite.

The last rays of the sinking sun suddenly beamed in like a strobe light, so her soft, white hair was a shining halo around her bony face. How to describe Mum? Well she had brown hair and a shy, but ready smile. She is tall and curvaceous, always hospitable, a wonderful listener and loves to laugh. She is so generous. How many times have I heard: "I'm paying for this." "Put your money away." What else? Reserved, circumspect, considerate and truly a Christian . . .

She never gossips or wanted to stand out, so thought that I should not either. This is probably why I remember best the statements she made which I rebelled against.

"You don't need to go to college, you'll get married and have children and it'll be a waste."

"Why don't you get a job in the Civil Service? That's a good job for a woman."

"Why did you win at tennis? Never beat a man at any game."

My parents were different from everyone else I knew in our village. They played or watched rugby, cricket and tennis and they had a shop. Customers came at the same time every week and perched on orange crates to gossip while they gave Mum their order. She listened, but has never repeated or exchanged gossip, not that they noticed, as they talked on and on, in thrall to everyone's ailments and misfortunes. Is this a Welsh thing? Were their lives dark and depressing, living nestled under the slag tipped mountains?

It has been hard to tell what her views are. Throughout her life she has managed to constrain them on almost all subjects, so that she never argues and is always a compliant companion.

"Always take the middle road," she has constantly advised Cerys. I suppose that is a view, as is the unsaid, but obvious belief that women should defer to men and make sure that they have the biggest helpings and the most meat.

My back is aching from sitting on this uncomfortable stool. I am going to stop and concentrate on Mum.

I am now on the train going home, writing again. I had stood up gingerly, my back climbing back into alignment and wandered out of the door, wondering why she was always in my head? However little I know her, she is there, pretending she hasn't heard a swear word, looking pained when I am abrupt or assertive with anyone.

Lewis, our favourite carer, had been coming up the stairs, thick, slicked down black hair stretched over his pink scalp.

"Just popping up to see your Mum," he breathed heavily." Shwmae Sweet pea."

Mum woke out of her torpor and giggled.

"How's my lovely girl then?"

Her face came alive, pretty, unlined and glowing, transcending her greasy lank hair, badly in need of a perm. "All the better for seeing you!" She answered cheekily.

"You're such a flirt Mum. Have I told you about the box of chocolates she sold three times in her shop, Lewis?"

"No, tell us, fach." Laughing in anticipation and mopping his brow. He was dressed in his cook's clothes, he must have been helping out in the kitchen again.

"Well, Mum was given this big box of Milk Tray chocolates for her birthday by one of her admirers and she was on a diet, so she put it in her shop to sell. Another admirer came in, bought the box and gave it to her, but she naughtily put it back on the sweet stand and would you believe, the same thing happened *again*! She gave up and ate them then, didn't you Mum?"

She smiled her shy Princess Di smile.

"Duw, duw. You're a one, aren't you!" He said admiringly and they giggled together.

"Yeh, Mum married my father when she was twenty one, and when he died she was only fifty eight? Fifty-eight weren't you Mum? Remember when we went to Tunisia when Cerys was two? The waiters were offering me dozens of camels for you and the fire-eater kept chasing you around the swimming pool. You're a magnet for men, it must be that big bust." I had looked ruefully down at my lack of one and we had all laughed.

# WEDNESDAY OCTOBER 23RD

I think that the sight of me makes her feel guilty, as she hastened to tell me how busy she has been.

"I'm always exercising. I've been for two walks today. I'm practising every day."

"Well let's do some more, I've just sat on a train for three hours."

The TV was blaring another programme about Glamis Castle, or was it a repeat? I switched it off and got out the dumbbells. We went through a routine of; "In and out and in and out and push those dumbbells harder." Her legs will lift a few inches with a great deal of concentration, but bending them is becoming impossible. She can't remember to exercise them every day, though she says, "I do this all the time. I've already done these exercises twice today."

If only she *could* remember to keep them moving, perhaps she could retain some mobility . . . We finished our routine and I gave her some cherries and grapes.

"I don't like getting up late, I feel lazy as if I should be up," she said. "I asked them to get me up last Saturday and they didn't do it. I feel as if I ought to be up. I shouldn't stay in bed for so long. I ought to be doing some cooking."

Sometimes when I leave her she cries, though protesting that she doesn't mean to.

"Oh, what time is it? Can't you stay a bit longer?"

"Mum I have to catch the 6.30, that won't get me home till after 9.30!"

"I know, I mustn't be selfish, I must be grateful you've come."

She says she's Ok and there's nothing else I could be doing for her, but the sadness in her face destroys my composure and I kiss her and walk away with tears welling up inside me, particularly when she says something selfless like, "Don't worry about me," as I leave her to wait for the next ritual.

How much can you do for someone you love? How much is enough? How do you measure something, which holds part of your heart? I cry almost every time I leave. Walking the two miles to the station along the empty pavements, tears stream down my face and I'm unashamedly uncaring of the anonymous cars. I am so upset that

I think and talk about her fate for the next few days, going over and over all the impossible options for her full time care at home with me, then absorb myself in my busy, wonderful life, until the next time.

## WEDNESDAY NOVEMBER 13TH

Mum is slowly disappearing, becoming progressively less capable. She goes from being lucid and sharp to incoherent and rambling or blank and unresponsive. Sometimes she interrupts loudly with an irrelevant story or comment. She cannot control a pen and struggles to feed herself. Her appearance remains the same, though DLB has clouded and emptied her eyes and rigidified her joints.

I feel embarrassed when she exhibits strange behaviour. The whole gamut of emotions surge within me. Love, sorrow, anger and impatience when I think she is not trying and terrible guilt ALL the time. Am I doing enough? What is going on in her head?

## WEDNESDAY DECEMBER 11TH

Mum slept through much of my visit. After an hour or so, having seen Lewis returning with Gladys in the minibus from the hospital, I wandered down to the kitchen to ask him for a cup of tea. He is one of those rare people who have perfected submerging his own desires and emotions in favour of effortless helpfulness to everyone. Generosity and gentleness swim freely in his bloodstream, they are part of him. He had his back to me, buttering bread.

"Duw, I've gotta get out of here. It don't pay enough to live and I'm workin' fourteen hour days!"

Rose gave him a hard grey stare as she wielded the chopping knife. "Ah, get away with you, yew daft bugger, you'll never leave this place."

Outside the pigeons cooed on the bins, and the traffic roared by. He finished buttering, and bounced his hands over his slicked back hair, joining up the escaping tendrils, which were curling in indiscriminate directions in the heat of the kitchen.

"Oh, shwmae Alys fach, didn't know you were here today."

He gladly made me some tea, then piled containers of the lunch onto the trolley and pushed it out past the nurse's station and into the lift. Margaret, who organises the training, was telling three new carers that they would need their NVQ's if they wanted to go on to work for the NHS or have a salary rise.

"It's a competence-based training. There are no entry requirements. You don't have to do exams. For Level 2 you're assessed here as you do your day to day care."

Ding! I could see a bell ringing in Lewis's head. Was this the answer, the way out?

He glanced out of the door, puffy little white clouds were scudding across the blue sky, and it was going to be a fine day. He smiled as the lift opened in front of him and humped the trolley forward.

## THURSDAY DECEMBER 26TH

I asked Matron, if I could borrow a commode and wheelchair to take with Mum to London for Christmas. She was very doubtful that we would be able to manage, but I was determined. I couldn't leave Mum in Riverside on her own, Christmas with her family is so important to her. We moved a bed downstairs and I fetched her on the morning of December 24th.

Mike and Cerys had taken the afternoon off work, but even with three of us, getting her out of the car was extremely difficult. We got her into the wheelchair and decided to keep her in it for the rest of the day rather than humping her in and out.

In the night I crept down to check on her every few hours. Though she was lying against the hot radiator and had a very warm duvet, she was always awake and cold. She never once complained. Her silence and loneliness pierced my heart. I rubbed her hands and feet trying to warm them up.

Christmas day was a disaster. She did not want to eat with our friends and us and sat grim faced like a spectre at the feast when we insisted. Did she feel demeaned because she had to be helped? Was she uncomfortable sitting in the wheelchair? She didn't cheer up in the present opening bonanza either. She loves giving and of course could not buy anything and all we could think of giving her were chocolate, nighties (she only has three left) and warm cardigans, reminding her of her incarceration.

I had intended to keep her for two more days, but drove the 180 miles back to Cardiff today. We were not coping, our efforts to change her nappy were difficult, degrading and panicky struggles and she seemed so lost and unhappy. She was quiet and uncommunicative throughout our three and a half hour journey. I felt deeply ashamed that I was not able to look after my mother and make her time in London enjoyable and comfortable. I had been so sure that if her little carers could deal with her then Mike, Cerys and I certainly could. How stupid I was!

When we arrived, she asked me what we were going to do for Christmas and could remember nothing of what was an absolute ordeal for us all.

# Chapter 15—The start of the journey

"<i>A</i>lys rung up to put the tennis on TV for you. She says you used to play really good." She looks sceptical, unbelieving. Oh good it's Tim Henman.

"Did you win cups?"

She's looking at my shields on the windowsill; don't pull the sheet so tightly.

"Is that what *them're* for?"

Her big clear eyes are trying to conjure up the sight of me on a court, running, hitting a ball. Obviously it's too difficult. Flawless skin, but she doesn't look like an athlete, too podgy.

"Well, enjoy."

She's turned the sound up too loud . . . Tim's so frustrating to watch, all that talent and effort, he needs a sports psychiatrist.

The sun's nuzzled its way through the curtains, its warm, just right for tennis. There's a light, bright foaminess jiggling and growing inside me. I'm going to burst if I don't have a game. I'll go and practice with my coach. Out of bed, on with my tracksuit, where's my racket? One two, one two, knees up, punch my arms.

"Your lunch, Catrin, you want? I put plastic."

Can't she see I'm busy? The bib thing's too tight. "Help, too tight."

"I been Manila, you been hospital, OK now?"

What hospital? I've been in Scotland cooking and training. "What?"

"Open mouth."

Can't eat all this shepherds' pie *and* a cake, I won't be able to play for two hours. Don't want that cold tea, I've got to go.

"I back, do change."

"I may not *be* here."

She looks puzzled, amused . . . such white teeth . . .

Oh no, here she is again. "Not that machine, I don't want that."

I hate being pulled and pushed, rolled and lifted, makes me feel like a baby.

"You heavy lady, hoist OK."

"Ow, ow, help, you're hurting me, help."

"Watch my legs, oh, my feet, my feet. Help, help, where am I going, where do I go now?"

I have to get back to the kitchen. They won't want to be without my roast dinner. I'll make a tart and a sponge for tomorrow. I'm putting on weight, I shouldn't have these meals here as well, they're not nice, not like my cooking.

✳   ✳   ✳

Living in this tennis camp has been everything I've always wanted. Though how can Lizzie and Gwen have two lives. Is that possible? Sometimes when it starts with wispy bits and ghostly shadows hanging in the air, it's like a dream. Then they come together, and they're people and places, and I'm training, playing and making all my favourite dishes, you're such a good cook Catrin, everyone says.

I haven't seen Alys and Robert for months, where's my notebook? Perhaps they wrote down when they're coming again? What day it is today? I'll play tennis. Who's that young man in the white flannels walking this way "Would you like to have a game?" *He's looking adoringly at me; I didn't know he played tennis. He must have learnt.*

*"I've been trying to find you. You weren't in your house."*

*He looks so handsome, black curly hair against his smooth tanned skin. He's rolled his sleeves up; his arms are so strong, so muscular. "How are you John?"*

*"I'm fine now that I've found you."*

*His hand is warm and smooth . . . he's real! "But you died."*

*"You think too much. Shall we go for a walk around the lake first?"*

*Weeping willows, carpets of bluebells, ransoms and wood anemones, a rushing brook to cross . . . so beautiful.*

*"Step here and here, I'll hold your arm."*

128

*I'm so happy to see him. "Life is such fun with you. Shall we play tennis now?"*

*His lively, dear face looks sad . . .*

✻    ✻    ✻

"No, we're not going to play tennis, Mother. You know I've never played and you're past your sporting days."

Robert's all in black, his shadow's a dark, lumpy shape on the wall behind him. He looks quite fat.

"Don't you want to know about my holiday in America?"

My mind's trying to go back to dashing John in his tennis whites.

"Are you listening Mother?"

Why can't I concentrate? I start thinking about something but my mind wanders off . . . It's hard to know where and who I am. There are so many words in my head, but they dance into a jumble before they reach my mouth. I can talk properly in my other life . . .

*Off for the south, leaving the tennis camp to look for our family, on this bright spring morning, with just changes of clothing, food, sheets of plastic and blankets. The trees are alive with birds courting and nesting, flashing back and forth carrying bits of their new homes. It's such a lovely day, so fresh and bright, but I've always hated walking, it takes too long. Never known Gwen do any either . . . she's always driven everywhere.*

*She's striding ahead on her long, slim legs, confidant and young looking in their shorts. I've lost a lot of weight and I'm faster and stronger on the court, but walking's different. This is exhausting, intense exercise.*

*"Gwen's too far in front, we mustn't lose one another."*

*Lizzie's voice is strained; it's too much for her.*

*After all this time I still haven't asked about their two lives, somehow we've always been so busy. "How do you get here each time Lizzie?"*

*She's looking confused. "What do you mean? I haven't come from anywhere. You know that. I've been with you."*

129

*"No, I'm not here all the time, and you live with Rhodri in Kent."*

*She's even more confused. "You are . . ."*

*Gwen's calling. "Come on you two."*

*"Don't you ever . . ." I was going to say . . . go back there? But she isn't listening; she's hurrying over the rough, uneven ground towards Gwen. I really don't understand. Are there two Gwens and Lizzies? I've seen them in both worlds, why don't they realise they have two lives? There must be two of each of them as well as two of me . . .*

*"Come on you two, down hill now."*

*"Can we have a rest Gwen?" Lizzie's little legs have had it.*

*"We've only walked a few miles!"*

*Since when did she get so fit? "Slow down Gwen, remember we have a long way to go." There's no break in her stride.*

*The end of the warm day is threaded with cold. I'm sore and shaky with fatigue. I want to stop. "Lets shelter here, in this tumble-down croft."*

*"We're going to be stiff tomorrow. I'll light the fire, if you two find the wood."*

*Lizzie's rubbing sticks together over some dry bracken, like the good Girl Guide and Brown Owl she used to be. "I'll have to have . . ." I was going to say a rest first, but I'm swooping away and she's no longer in sight. I'm weightless in black, airless space . . . It's hot, am I drifting too near the setting sun? I don't want to go yet . . . stretch my arms backwards . . . fingers straining, shoulders pulling at their sockets . . . I can't turn, I can't go backwards. I'm spinning and spinning into the blackness.*

Isn't that Gwen's Elizabeth Arden's 'Knowing?' I'd recognise her brisk swish as she moves and that perfume anywhere

"I love that cream suit."

When she smiles, her teeth are even, white. I'd forgotten they're false. "Tell them to take the lot out." Father said when she was fifteen and had a gum infection. She says it's never bothered her, she's used to the plate. Each to their own. Matching earrings, a loose knit cashmere jacket, her thick grey hair an elegant, shining cloud around her flawlessly made up face.

"I'd give it to you if you could get into it."

She's matching all my dresses with their belts and cardigans.

"Though you *have* lost a lot of weight."

She looks irritated.

"The green skirt with the blue and green jacket. I do this every week you know Catrin, but it's back in a shambles in no time. Look at all your nice clothes left crumpled at the bottom of the wardrobe. And whose is *this*? It's not yours. These girls really are the limit. They don't take any care of your clothes."

"I tidy that cupboard every day."

"Yes dear, I'm sure you do. How about a chocolate roll?"

I can feel my eyes glistening and the saliva gathering . . .

✲    ✲    ✲

Lizzie and Gwen are walking down an overgrown road leading south; it's strange that they don't know I've been away. This must have been a forest. Mile after mile of charred, black stumps, rising from heather and bracken a sad, desolate site. It's time to stop for the night.

*"We're not that far from Glamis Castle, remember how beautiful it was Catrin? It can only be a few more miles, can we stop there?"*

*Lizzie is a keen historian and royalist, as a matter of fact she looks very much like the Queen. "We didn't see any of them when we came before, they've got so many homes to choose from. How many years ago was it, anyway?"*

*"Our Scottish holiday? Mmm, fifteen? eighteen?"*

*"Do you think the Queen was killed, and all the royal family?"*

*"Hope not, Gwen. You've never been there have you? It was the Queen Mother's childhood home you know. Come on, it won't take long."*

*Lizzie's so excited; she seems to have forgotten her exhaustion . . .*

*"Look . . . there . . . the dark gothic turrets against the sky."*

*I'm shocked. "Those lovely gardens, all gone. Look . . . birds flying in and out of the windows."*

*Gwen is examining the moat: "Perhaps we can have a swim tomorrow."*

*"We'll watch you," Lizzie and I agree. We need a good wash, but we've never been keen swimmers and it looks freezing.*

✳    ✳    ✳

*Lizzie's sighing and rolling herself in her blanket. "Don't think I've ever been so tired, every muscle and joint is throbbing after two days of this walking. Night, night."*

*"Mmm," I can feel my eyes drooping shut.*

*I'm in a dream about a car journey and a wedding. All my relations are there. Alys is marrying Mike. I'm watching . . . no, I'm awake with prickles of alarm running up and down my body. I want to sleep, I want to go back to the wedding. What was that? A shadow passing in front of the fire. Is that whispering? Rub my eyes, breathe through my mouth to get rid of the stale taste. It's Gwen talking to someone in a long white dress with waist length hair . . . an embroidered hat. Who on earth is that?*

*Gwen's running her fingers through her curly, thick grey hair. The woman reaches an elegant hand up to touch it, she must be admiring it. Gwen always did have the best head of hair in the family. They seem to be getting on very well, Gwen's laughing self-consciously, she loves being flattered.*

*I'm really sleepy, my eyes are closing again. I want to snuggle back down . . . I'm probably dreaming . . . Gwen's moving after the stranger as she glides towards the stairs.*

*Shout Catrin, shout Gwen. Nothings coming out. "Gwen." A croak, but it's too late. They've gone. "Wake up Lizzie!"*

*"What, what's going on?"*

*"Come on, quickly, Gwen's gone off with someone!"*

*A rush of icy air meets us in the courtyard, swirling the white lady's gown as she and Gwen disappear in the distance. An enormous cold moon lights our path, but the tower staircase is dark and silent. Gwen has always moved quickly, this time, she must have flown.*

*"Gwen, Gwen, Gwen, where are you?"*

*"She's not answering and it's too dark to see anything."*

*Feeling our way, up and down steps in slow motion, like a horrible dream. My limbs, my body is starting to get weaker, weightless . . . submerged in calm, warm blue sea . . . floating up . . .*

Lying in cold wetness, "help, help."

The light through my open door dims as a figure stops in the corridor outside.

"Help, help, wet."

An irritated smile, glinting like steel.

"What have you been doing Catrin? Your covers are on the floor. Jyoti!"

No speaking, just washing me, rolling me one way and then the other, spreading the clean sheet under me, tucking in the corners, making it nice again for the disgusting person I must be.

"I'm sorry, I don't want to be a bother."

No one's moving or speaking. The cross one's flicked my duvet into place.

"Bother? It's our job. Your pad wasn't on properly. Go back to sleep Catrin."

I think there is a softer expression as the light falls onto her face. I'll close my eyes and hope . . . *there's a musty smell, we're holding smouldering pieces of wood . . . we must have been back to the remains of our fire in the kitchen.*

*"We've lost her . . ."*

*"Don't cry, she's got to be here somewhere, don't let's give up."*

*"Where are you Lizzie?"*

*Owls hoot and rats scuttle away. "Lizzie?"*

*"I've fallen into this room . . . it's so dark."*

*"Are you Ok?"*

*"Yes, can't see a thing though."*

*"Be careful. Feel with your hands around the floor and walls."*

*"Ooh, the walls opening, come and look . . ."*

*"What a beautiful room, like stepping back into time." Gwen and the white lady look up in surprise.*

*"Gwen!"*

*She's got on a beautiful Jacobean dress . . . a heavily brocaded deep blue and silver gown, fit for a coronation.*

*"Look at these exquisite clothes!"*

*In more than sixty years of modelling and fashion buying Gwen has probably never seen anything like this, she is completely entranced with this amazing wardrobe.*

*"Take that dress off and leave this room, now." Lizzie's really upset with her. "We've been searching for you all night, we were worried stiff."*

*Gwen looks surprised; she has a slightly dazed, vacant look. Is she stunned by the beauty of the clothes, or has the white lady put a spell on her?*

*"I am perfectly all right and old enough to do what I want. Lady Campbell's collection is magnificent, I am honoured that you want to show it to me." She's smiling at the elegant woman with the glittering eyes. "These gowns are worth a fortune, just look at the workmanship. Why don't you two go away, you've never been interested in clothes!"*

*Thank goodness, she's taking it off, but how do we make Gwen realise the possible danger without antagonising her new friend? My heart is thumping . . . I must be courteous . . .*

*"Lady Campbell, we are travelling to South Wales to look for our family. Please ask our sister to come with us."*

*The tiny, dignified lady has a sad, but soft look on her pale face. Lifting her gloved hand to her head with the gesture of a queen about to adjust her crown, she places it on her brow, shielding her lovely violet eyes, the same colour as her velvet gown. Seconds are passing, more . . . I'm sweating, what do I do next? She's straightening her shoulders, compressing her lips into thin lines, her voice is like a purr . . . ."Wars and disasters continue, the retribution that the sins of the world bring on itself. I will not add to them by taking Gwen, or harming you."*

*I'm light headed with relief. "Thank . . .*

*"For you who have only what you carry on your backs I may seem to have much."*

*She means the tapestries, the handsome furniture and marble fireplace.*

*"I have had such a lonely life and I wanted to keep Gwen with me as my friend. But you are three sisters and belong to one another, even though you now have more years than most humans are allotted.*

*Be always on your guard, your journey south will be fraught with dangers."*

*"Ooh! How do you know?" Lizzie nervously interrupts.*

*Lady Cambell looks piercing, suddenly angry.*

*"I do know." Her curt voice sent a shiver through me. "Be aware and strong hearted and if you solve this riddle you will find the sacred cauldron which can give you renewed youthfulness.*

*Where the fish flew from the otter, the hen pecks up a grain,*

*A ring now joins a cross, which you hold and hold again.*

*The highest one in Cymru guards a castle very fair,*

*Seek Cadw and Ceridwen, the world's spin changes there."*

*What's she talking about?*

*"Each of you must choose your final goal; youth or to join friends and family in the otherworld. Depart Gwen, I wish you every success for your journey, thank you for your visit. If you are ever in grave danger, wear this."*

*Is that a cloak she's given her? It looks as light as gossamer. She's gone . . . there's a strange stillness in her grand room.*

*"Why did you have to interfere, I was having such a good time."*

*Gwen's snappish, she seems to have recovered. "Your friend was accused of witchcraft and burnt at the stake, at least 400 years ago."*

*Gwen's gone pale. "I feel faint, let's get out of here."*

*Pushing the cloak into my pack, off we go into the grey, still dawn, the stars overhead and the moon hanging like a paper lantern, on our third day.*

# Chapter 16—Violent then cowed. 2003

## THURSDAY JANUARY 30TH

*J* organised a wonderful weekend (Jan 3/4th) in a hotel in Devon for ninety friends and relatives. To celebrate my sixtieth on the Friday, guests painted pots, played tennis, table tennis, snooker or squash, swum or walked. Then we had a champagne reception where everyone was given a card with three things that three people wanted to do, or be like when they retired. This got everyone talking, and then we had a meal, songs and speeches and square dancing. Mike and I got married the next day (after twenty years together) in a stately home with poetry, songs and more champagne. Friends have convinced us that we should marry for inheritance tax reasons. Mum came for the day with Lewis, (who disappointingly is talking about leaving to get a better job when he has finished his NVQ's). She managed to make a cross as a witness, we had tea and then she left before the dinner, cabaret, speeches and dancing. Her face was strained looking and she was quiet, as if in a dream. She can no longer cope with large groups of people, or a change in venue, she seems to go somewhere else in her head. However, my Mum came to the ceremony and has talked about it every time I have seen her since. She had waited so long for me to actually be a wife.

## WEDNESDAY MARCH 5TH

"I want you to find out what this means."

She looked harassed and preoccupied, the words seeming to sleepwalk out of her mouth, and barely noticed my kiss and hug.

"What Mum?"

"Cadw and Ceridwen."

"Where did you hear about them?" She didn't listen; her eyes were dazed and unfocussed. She has been watching TV again I thought.

"The highest cross in help Wales, a castle, help, help."

"Did you watch a programme about Celtic mythology?"

"I went to a party last night and when I went to get the taxi.."

Sometimes I feel very distant from her, sometimes even cross with her when she makes up stories and events, she seems unconscious that she's talking rubbish. Why am I writing that? It's not rubbish to her. I mean things I am unable to understand.

How many times has she told me, in an intimate, confidential whisper, "This place is closing you know."

"No this Home is not closing," Mum I say.

"Oh yes it is!" she replies sharply, looking at me coldly and critically.

Should I agree with her delusions? Her disordered brain puts things together that sound reasonable. Her dreams have become her reality. There's the one where she's in a camp with Lizzie and Gwen and lately she talks about walking every day. Those last months before her accident, when she was told by her consultant to walk daily, must have had a profound and lasting effect. Sometimes I change the subject, if I contradict her she is crushed and crestfallen and retreats back into her shell, then I feel guilty at my irritability. Am I punishing her for her inability to communicate? I'm glad that she is able to imagine something more interesting than this boring, miserable reality and I must treat her with more respect and dignity. Also remember that her impatience is probably due to frustration. Being institutionalised with nothing to do but stare at walls or a TV must be escalating the progression of her disease. She is changing, oh, she's changing. She's not fighting to stay in the life she has always know any more, and I cannot drag her back.

## WEDNESDAY MARCH 26TH

Cerys is pregnant, she and Andrew seem pleased, but they are not rushing to get married. Wonder if Mum's thinking, 'like mother, like daughter?'

Why *do* some older people develop paranoia? Mum has been going through a period of thinking people were stealing from her. She was right, but wrong too, the items she thought were being stolen were ones she had never had, like her bag. And where does the superhuman strength come from when she fights her carers? Is she raging 'against the dying of the light,' rather than going gently as Dylan Thomas wrote?

"Your mother did this," various slight Indian women have said, pointing at scratches on their arms and faces. *Her* legs are often covered with bruises and sometimes her face and neck, who does what?

Aunt Gwen popped in to the Home on Saturday, to find Mum surrounded by four carers. Her face contorted with rage, she was twisting and squeezing a black hand. He looked in pain and the others could not prise her hand off his. Seeing her sister she said spitefully: "And you can get out of here too," and continued to squeeze.

Speaking soothingly and persuasively, until she had penetrated the dark recesses of Mum's mind where the real Mum seemed to have taken refuge, Aunt Gwen managed to defuse the situation. I have witnessed these rages and though I too have managed to reassure her and calm her down, a separate self had felt a frisson of fear, fear of this sinister, possessed, unknown Mother. How is she suddenly so strong? She cannot hold a spoon a few minutes later. Sometimes, for a second I see fear and incomprehension in her eyes, occasionally a mutinous fury that chills me. Was I mistaken? It was only there for a second. Why this hatred and spite from a woman who has never in her life said or done anything unpleasant or hurtful? Why *does* she sometimes behave aggressively to Indian carers? She says they talk in their own language and do spiteful things to her.

Waking from naps, does she confuse them with the black, bat like squirrels with sharp teeth and scratchy claws she used to tell me she saw in her nightmares? Perhaps she is having fantasies of being attacked because she feels in constant pain? Or is it because it hurts when she is moved? The daily rituals are all too much trouble and she just wants to be left alone. She forgets that she is wearing a nappy and cannot move, she dreams of being as she was, looking after herself and they spoil the illusion.

138

What if the Matron refuses to have her any more? Sheila rang me a few weeks ago and said that she is biting and scratching the carers and shouting and swearing at them. I asked Mum why:

"Because they hurt me, look at all my bruises!" She showed me her currently bruise-free wrists.

"They won't like you if you are nasty."

"I don't care, they shouldn't hurt me."

I tried to explain that she is very heavy and cannot take her own weight, whereas the carers are slight and small, so might inadvertently hurt her when they move her.

"You never believe me, I'm always in the wrong!" She said bitterly. "Help, I mean hello . . . . ."

Another cruel manifestation of Mum's disease is the occasional loss of inhibition and use of an obscenity. She has never sworn before and I had never, ever, heard her say anything discourteous. In the first Home, she embarrassingly accused another inmate called Hilda of trying to kiss her all the time and was openly rude to her. I had been thrilled that Mum seemed to have found a friend and I was never sure what went on when I was not there, but I found Mum's total rejection of Hilda awkward and puzzling. Then there was last week when Lewis took us in the minibus to see the new Cardiff docks. We were pushing Mum along the quay, remarking on the cafes and new shops, when she suddenly said: "You're Homosexual, I know, I know," in a bitter, insulting tone,

I hoped he hadn't heard her rudeness and spite, when she should have been grateful. He obviously had because he went and sat in the minibus until it was time to go back.

It is difficult to convey how shocking these isolated incidents are. Her expression is so malevolent, so unlike the usual self contained, quiet and respectful demeanour of the person I have known and loved all my life. I wondered at first if this was a long suppressed facet of Mum's personality, which was emerging because of a loss of inhibition. But no, reading about aggression and rudeness in those with AD, it appears that it comes from an unused, primitive, survival part of the brain, which is kicking in as she struggles to emerge from the dark.

None of the staff understand that Mum has DLB and therefore fluctuating symptoms. Their treatment is always as a response to her worst periods. If she sometimes displays a vigour, lucidity and sharpness they are not expecting, their faces exhibit a faint disbelief, an amusement, as if her normalcy was an aberration, a freak moment.

In a nursing home everyone has power over the old. A 'care plan' is drawn up and shown to the nearest relative, this does not mean that anyone refers to it, but I am given the feeling that if I complain about anything and insist on things that they are not prepared to do, if Mum is not a 'good' patient they have the power to throw her out. After a few enquiries, which led nowhere, I find that I have to ignore her frequent actual bruises. She doesn't remember how they got there and do I want to invoke the complaints procedure? I can ask nicely about things I am not satisfied with, but not too forcefully and definitely not too often.

## WEDNESDAY MAY 21ST

"There's a good girl, you've eaten it all up."

Aunt Gwen was feeding Mum spoonfuls of Marks and Spencer luxury trifle; her tone was of a person being friendly to a small fluffy animal. I don't blame her. Mum can't move her legs, can't lift her head and can barely grip anything. She had sunk into her chair, eyes red and dull, and lips slack and shapeless. There is a smell of urine. I look at her and wonder hopelessly if the biomechanical processes taking her back into earth have begun.

The contrast between sisters couldn't be more marked. Aunt Gwen is two years older, but could have stepped off a page of Vogue. She is fit, has 20/20 vision, sharp hearing and is still an excellent driver. Poor drugged Mum. I constantly check her medication, and have found today that without my knowledge, she has been put on *two* different types of anti depressants, and *two* blood thinning agents. Why are drugs given so easily to pacify? I fought for months to get her taken off the anti-psychotic drugs, and I'm still fighting well meaning over prescribing doctors!

I rang Dr Crocker and asked him about his latest prescription for her.

"She was crying 'help, help' as she was wheeled into lunch. This isn't normal," he said. "She's a very intelligent, quiet, reserved person," I replied defensively.

"I can see that," said this man I've-never-met. "But no-one was hurting her, why was she shouting?"

I thought quickly, desperately, "Because she doesn't want to be where she is, she wants to be back at home, in her normal life. I don't want her to have to go to an EMI (elderly mentally infirm) Home.

"Well that *is* a possibility," he admitted.

"She was just having a bad day," I urged. "She thinks people are doing things *to* her, rather than for her. She has always had hopes that she will get better, but her ankles keep swelling up, she has sores on her heels and she can barely move her legs."

## TUESDAY AUGUST 5TH

Mum has yet another urine infection and was sent to Hospital yesterday. When I arrived she was asleep with her mouth open, her hair in greasy grey strands, stiff and flat to her head, skin taut and blotchy, as pale as if they had drained all her blood on admission. Her over night bag had disappeared before she got to the ward, so she has an ill-fitting paper nightdress carelessly revealing her left shoulder and breast.

I eventually woke her, but she struggled to speak to me. I talked, but my words were like the breeze passing through a colander. She was my closest friend and support and I bled inside for our lost rapport as the minutes dawdled by. An hour passed and we hadn't communicated. Her bed is near to the window; the sun shone through the slatted blinds, which moved gently in the breeze. A furious wasp stunned itself repeatedly against the glass, until it fell senseless onto the filing cabinet beneath. Tea arrived and I tried to get her to drink with a straw, but she had no strength to suck and when she did manage a little, started to choke. In the bed opposite is Rose, who cannot speak or move; she has been having strokes for twenty-six years. Her daughter sat wearily at her side, hoping for some kind of reaction, though experience has told her that there will be none.

Suddenly Mum did a huge intake of breath, a deep sigh, then slumped downwards and didn't breathe again. "Breathe Mum, please breathe," I said. Is this how a dead body looks? "Breathe!" Then she did, deep ragged breaths, which ceased completely every few minutes. The silence was unnerving. I didn't know whether to shake her or run for a nurse. And then she started again. Her body sagged with weariness, all energy dissipated as if her spirit was desperate to be released. My heart contracted, I am not ready to let her go. "Breathe Mum, breathe!"

I massaged the parts of her not connected to pipes drawing fluid out or dripping it in. Her skin was cold and clammy though it was another hot day and the other women in the ward were sitting in their chairs, dressed only in nighties. I pulled up the sheet and blanket to tuck them round her neck, which exposed her feet, jammed against the wooden bed head. They are now twisted and forever en pointe like a ballet dancer. How long have they been cold and crammed in like that? She cannot move them herself. I went to look for a nurse.

The staff do not like her. She is unresponsive and inert, cannot communicate and has to be fed, washed and changed. Being moved hurts her, so she screams, fights, swears and shouts.

"She called us every name under the sun," said two strong nurses who had forced the catheter into her. She has had things 'done' to her for two and a half years now. Some things are so deeply humiliating that she blocks them out. She doesn't show that she recognizes one nurse or carer from another, unless they are a man. She still flirts with male staff even now.

The women understand and are brisk and businesslike, but too busy to be bothered with talking to her. They said that yesterday they had to change her soiled nappy, which she resisted.

"She was so sure that it wasn't needed," one said.

I asked her about it. "I'm deeply ashamed. Mortified!" said my mother, who before 2001 was even reluctant to go into her toilet if there was someone else in the house.

Amongst the incoherent ramblings, the incomprehensible efforts she made to try to converse with me was a recurring theme. "What are we doing for Christmas?" Its only August, but Christmas has always been the highlight of her year.

What are we doing for Christmas? What can we do?

142

"I can come to London and stay for longer this time," she mumbled.

She cannot remember one thing about either of the last two Christmases, if only I could have made them enjoyable for her . . . .

# WEDNESDAY AUGUST 6TH

She lay, propped up on two pillows fiddling with bony, stiff, endlessly restless fingers at the hem of the yellow cotton hospital blanket, a blank, slightly cross look on her pallid, still blotchy face.

"Can I get in there, it's a bit narrow." She muttered incomprehensively, seeming to be plotting her escape and ensuring that all her possessions were safe first.

"Don't forget to take that piece of meat over there," she whispered.

"There isn't any meat Mum," I stupidly said. Her face took on that customary betrayed look. Why do I correct her? It doesn't matter.

"Do you mean to tell me that I don't know what I am doing? I only bought it on Monday." She said bitterly.

She is now past caring what she looks like, having had to give up her makeup routine some time ago. Her paper hospital nightie was off the shoulder again; her hair even greasier looking and she still had the appalling red rash all over her cheeks and forehead. Seeing her so reduced squeezed my heart. What were her desires, hopes and dreams for the rest of her life, which so abruptly ended?

I had brought with me a newly published book about the village where we had lived. She looked without interest at the four photographs of herself and Dad. Her eyes were dead and although she said she could see them, she had to have three guesses to identify herself in her WRVS costume and didn't recognise her husband and herself at a function at all. Neither did she know that the handsome young man, striding along with his father and brother, radiating sexual luminosity was Dad.

"Can't you see where you and Dad are standing? Whose shop is that behind?" I persisted with the last one. There they are, in front of their village grocery, looking drab and comfortably over weight.

Dads' smile revealing his lack of teeth; he refused to go to a modern dentist after his ancient chamber of horrors dentist died.

"Oh look Mum, here's our house."

We both stared at our big cream box on the hill, the village descending sharply from our garden wall. I used to run down the 1 in 4 gradient, past stepped terraces of colliers houses with their almost vertical gardens clinging to the mountain, pigeons sheds and vegetable plots fenced against the sheep. Round the hairpin bend I'd fly to the High Street of small shops, chapels, pubs and the cinema long since pulled down. The road falls again to the valley floor and the fast flowing inky black waters of the Ebbw, beside the dual-purpose rugby and cricket pitch and the monolithic Workman's Institute. The older villagers insisted that there was a swimming pool and skating rink underneath the floor of the theatre where we saw annual operettas, I can still sing most of the songs from The 'Pirates of Penzance' and 'Desert Song.'

"You were a much better singer and much more attractive than Miss Burge. Why wouldn't you be in the shows Mum? I'd have been so proud."

No answer and my eyes slid along the photograph to the steep bank of the hill opposite, where the dead lay, next to the allotments and the curve of the summit, changed forever by little buckets on high wires, tipping slag.

The wild, lovely hills and rivers of my childhood subjugated to nineteenth century coal owners desecration. All but three of the boys in my class at Junior School ended up working underground digging King Coal.

"I want to go to the toilet again. How do I get out of here?" Mum looked around purposefully as if to get out of bed.

I felt helpless and deeply sad so changed the subject. What could I say? "Do it in your nappy Mum, because it will take too long to get anyone to come and lift you onto a commode?"

She does seem to know when she wants to go, but has to resign herself to ignore those feelings. When the staff fitted a catheter to her, she told me every time she felt the urge, then I saw it sailing down the tube. How can it be made less undignifying for those who cannot walk?

I sat, heavy with quiet, consumed with anguished thoughts of how it could have come to this.

## SATURDAY AUGUST 9TH

The Hospital sent her back to the Home, minus her nighties, sponge bag and bed jacket, which were never recovered. She could remember nothing of her visit. "Everyone keeps telling me that I've been ill. I don't remember being ill."

Questions about the hospital, her visitors, and things we had discussed, the photographs I had shown her, nothing brought any spark of recognition. How depressing. But why should one want her to remember? To accumulate brownie points? Everything for Mum is now or long ago, she is frozen into the present tense. If she seems to be enjoying the visit at the time, that must be, that is enough.

## THURSDAY SEPTEMBER 18TH

Her skin is improving, Lewis, had painted her nails and put her makeup on. She was wearing an elegant green, blue and white straight dress, the effect spoilt only by her unkempt, unset hair. He popped in and out and they joked with one another. It is so good to see her smile; flashes of her mischievous, sexy little giggle reappear and then disappear as soon as he leaves. I rarely make her laugh. Does she only giggle with men? I'm too serious and loquacious. I have always used her as a sounding board, not expecting much response, other than encouragement.

She sat listening to my long-winded description of Cerys's baby shower, her mouth open, and jaw slack. She has never done that before, what was she taking in?

Gazing around her little room, I spotted the 'stress ball' which I gave her a few weeks ago, to strengthen her grip and to squeeze if she was angry. A piece had been bitten out of it.

"Mum this is for you to squeeze, why have you bitten it?"

"I wanted to see what was inside," she muttered guiltily.

Oh well, the two sets of dumbbells are still on her table gathering dust; I don't suppose that she would ever remember to have squeezed the ball anyway.

"Would you let me stand against that wardrobe to see if I can stand? You can't stand me up can you?"

I hesitated, not sure what to say,

"Can I try? I have to find some way of standing up."

If only she could!

## WEDNESDAY OCTOBER 22ND

In the last two years Mum has seen dozens of doctors and they all ask her questions which revolve around her IQ, not around her mobility and they offer no help. She has had an appointment this morning, which the nurses had forgotten to tell me about.

Poor Mum has had so many tests, how can they be made less demeaning and frightening? After lying or sitting in this little room for months, her bottom too raw for any position to be comfortable, she was suddenly told,

"We're going to the Hospital for tests today Catrin."

Whereupon, she would have been dressed and wheeled out, blinking into the daylight, into an ambulance to hang around for hours at a hospital. What if she wanted to go to the toilet? She would need three people to help her and only one carer goes to hospital appointments. What is the point of asking her wandering mind all those questions? The carer would not have thought to coach her beforehand.

"What date is it?"

How would she know, she cannot read papers any more, though she likes to try, she has no need to know the date. *I* rarely know the date, yet I work and read two papers a day.

"Where are you?"

Why would she want to know where she is? She usually seems to think that she is in college or in her own home.

"I want you to listen to these three words and then repeat them later when I ask you." the Doctor would have said.

She has always been good at this task before today. Did she remember them? Then she would have been given a pencil, which she can no longer hold.

When I arrived, she had returned and was confused, ashamed and upset. I assumed she had done badly. If only I'd been there.

146

We thought that all the scans, the tests; the visits to consultants had stopped. There was a flurry a few months ago after I had complained. A consultant came to see us both together and recommended her for a Memory Clinic. But she only went there twice.

Apparently no transport could be arranged for her. Riverside will not take her in their minibus; they cannot spare the staff to accompany her. I wanted to pay for a taxi but apparently there are none which can take a wheelchair with the person sitting in it. The NHS will not send an ambulance because she is in a private home, even though there is only one local authority home in Cardiff, which has a huge waiting list. It seems tragic because the clinic had seemed to like her:

"Catrin needn't wear a pad when she comes here, the Home is putting one on her because they don't take her to the toilet when she needs it." The friendly young nurse had said. "She will fit in well here."

"Is there nothing I can do to get her there?" I asked Matron.

"No, and in any case, her place has been withdrawn."

Did she wet herself last time? I cannot find anything out and Mum is not keen to go. It is all too little too late.

Everyone seems to have given up on her. Has she given up on herself?

## THURSDAY NOVEMBER 13TH

"I can be someone rushing around." She pronounced as I arrived. I have not written for a while, so am writing verbatim.

"What do you mean?"

"I don't know, where's the baby in the cot?"

"In London, Mum, remember, he's not mine, he's Cerys's."

"Help, help, help."

"Mum, if you can't stop saying that, don't say anything!" I say after an hour of this.

No response, I try to get her eyes ungummed with a tissue.

"I'll do it in a minute." She says testily. "Help, help, help. Do you think it's any good me trying again?"

"Trying what?"

"I'm trying to be helpful and make something, but . . . ." She says disconsolately, "I don't think I'm very clever at it. I'm trying to make a background. What are those two men standing there for? Can't you see my elbows are sticking out, my glass jug is surrounded? Would you like to have this one? Help, help."

I asked about her feelings, trying to make her focus on her past relationships. Dad was so suitable, sporty like her, parents in the grocery business like her, but what about John?

"Did you like John better than Daddy?"

"Yes. I don't know the pair. He helps, help help."

I ask the question again.

"It was a different kind of love. Well, shall I race or no? I'll break up a partnership. I'm afraid to go down there now. Help, help."

"What did you enjoy about marriage?"

"I enjoyed it all, help, help. There was a period when I didn't . . . I'm getting very irritable, help, help. I was going to walk around here . . ."

I gave up.

## FRIDAY DECEMBER 26

Lewis said that Mum spent Christmas day alone in her room, unwilling to join the others in the dining room. The first Christmas she has ever spent without her family. In London, we had fourteen for lunch and then Cerys, myself, her baby boy, Mike and Andrew, drove down on Boxing day, complete with a Christmas dinner. Turkey, sprouts, peas, beans, red cabbage, roasted root vegetables, bread sauce, roast and dauphin potatoes, and covered with lots of gravy, just how she likes it. Crackers, serviettes, a CD player to play carols and Xmas songs, quizzes and presents,

She was wide eyed and pale, "Oh hello, I thought you were never coming."

I kissed her. "We left at eight Mum, but, we needed to stop on the way, it was so cramped in the back seat and it's a long drive."

"Yes, sorry, I know it is."

Her face devoid of makeup was blotchy, the skin a lifeless grey between the patches of red, an undiagnosed allergy.

She greeted the rest of the party, coming in behind me, with recognition and pertinent comments and then when her audience had perched on her bed and the arms of the commode, she launched into. "Find out about Cadw and Ceridwen and where the ring and cross are."

"She's been watching TV again," I explained to the others.

"OK Mum, sorry, I've forgotten again. I'll look on the Internet when I get back."

# Chapter 17—Titan

*W*hy do they put me in this lounge with all these other women? Nothing to do but stare into silence with a dull, empty brain. I want to go back to my room. I'll say I'm having visitors tomorrow, so they leave me alone.

"Hello Mum, how are you? It's stuffy in here; shall we go out for some fresh air? You could do with some sun on your skin."

Suddenly, quite suddenly here she is. My daughter, blocking out everyone else. Are they looking? Wishing they had a visitor? She's saying something, I must focus. I want to say, no, I don't want to go outside. I want to go back to my room, but . . . I'm just watching her mouth talking.

The brightness hits me, I can't open my eyes, she's turning me around. I like to be warm, but my skin feels too thin, like paper, the sun's scorching it, burning it. This wheelchair's hard and uncomfortable. I hate this heat, it's dazzling. I can feel blisters of sweat, prickles of heat rash. I want to go back to my room. Why's she brought me out here? She always thinks she knows what's best for other people, rushing at things and battering them into submission.

I want to shout: "I don't have to be here you know. I've got a far better place to go to."

"Are you comfortable Mum?"

No of course not, but you don't want to hear all my problems and I'm not in the mood to listen to yours. "Mmm."

"Shall I tell you about my weekend Mum?"

I want to say no, but her eyes are too intense, her need to talk can't be repressed. "Tell me about the wedding dinner party again?" She looks disappointed, but I love to hear about her wedding day.

"Catch the bean bag Catrin!"

It's Lewis, over by the wall with the men in their wheelchairs. Where's the beanbag? It hit my arm, fell on the floor.

"Try again Mum. Get ready,"

She's dropped it onto my hands. How demeaning. I see myself as I was, running to catch high balls, taking them in the air with either hand. I'm trying to smile.

"Not much good today am I?" I'm embarrassed; better to hide myself in that room.

"Sweet pea, d'you want to do passing with Arthur and Bill?"

"No . . . thanks." Misery and loss are suffocating me. I've lost control of my body, my brain, my life and where I am. I want to be in Scotland, not here.

Myself and me, stuck here.

No time off so far today . . .

Stuck here . . .

I'm trying to stay serene, what was I thinking before that other thought? Lonely and frightened and tired of all this . . . my brain slowly clouding . . . stay serene, serene. Words, thoughts slithering away. I will get better won't I?

※　　　　※　　　　※

The tops of the trees sway, thin straight branches against the heavy, dark sky. It's going to rain. The roots will suck up the moisture and those bare sticks will sprout bright, fresh leaves. I want to walk on the springy turf, smell that age-old scent of humus, crunch my feet down on the crackling branches, the crisp brown leaves, feel the wind softly over my skin, while the day slowly unwraps itself. I'll do it, sneak downstairs and out, while it's quiet . . .

"Time for your wash, Catrin, then you can sit in your chair for lunch."

"No, no, it's cold. Don't pull off my blanket."

"Ooh your feet are *filthy*!" They can't have been washed for weeks. Look at these Titan."

Who's that huge man? What's wrong with his eyes? I don't want him touching me.

"Catrin, this Titan, he start today."

151

"No, NO No! Help, help. Give me my blanket." The giant's too strong. "Don't pull up my nightie, help." I can feel my nails digging into something soft, something warm.

"How did you get such dirty feet, Catrin?"

They're really hurting me. "Help, help, don't do that, you're too rough." I'm not going to tell them I'm trekking to Wales.

It's too bright, glarey, noisy. I'll close my eyes . . . I'm lifting up on a current of air. Relax . . . Away I go, far away from that room, that bed . . .

✻     ✻     ✻

*So weary. Through this endless forest, towards the setting sun and the grey-pink hill in the distance. The dying rays sneaking through the branches are casting a buttery light on the streaks of white in Gwen's grey hair, striding in front of us. A clearing . . . Lizzie is pulling her tracksuit collar closer to her neck against the cool breeze eddying around us. What an unusual stillness. No familiar chirping or flapping of busy birds and buzzing insects hunting for food.*

*"Why is it so deathly quiet?" Gwen sounds nervous. It's true, even the leaves seem to be refusing to rustle in the breeze.*

*"Shall we sing? Let's make up a tune for 'Where the fish flew from the otter, the hen . . .'"*

*"No, shush Lizzie, lets listen."*

*Nothings stirring in this dim, heavy quiet, everything seems to be holding its breath. I'm uneasy, sweating despite the chill.*

*On and on, through the silent forest, my every sense on edge. Ants have killed that beetle, they're breaking it into pieces to carry it away, death everywhere. Feeling shaky and light headed . . . must be brave and calm.*

*"At last, the hill." I've a strange sense of fore boding. The sun has gone down behind the wood and . . . "Wait a minute. Stay still under this rhododendron."*

*Why am I scared? There's nothing . . . what's happening? The last of the light is blotted out by a huge blackness gliding high in the sky towards us . . . nowhere to escape to . . . shrinking into one another, into the bush and the ground in dry mouthed terror. It's floating overhead . . . passing over the forest. Put my hand over Gwen's mouth . . . she's in spasms of shivering . . . she mustn't cry out . . . Circling slowly above us, its malign shadow darkening our path ahead. One more circle . . . it's disappeared over the forest behind us. All I can hear are our gasps for breath.*

*"How many of them are there?"*

*"Do you think it was looking for us?"*

*"What if it comes back?"*

*The forest is breathing and trembling with life again. "Listen."*

*All around us birds call, insects buzz and the undergrowths rustling as invisible small things scamper about.*

*"I'm sleeping here, here in this bush, I can't go on." Gwen's asleep already . . . The grass is so soft . . . I'm drifting into . . .*

✶    ✶    ✶

"I'm exhausted, Catrin, wake up now,"

"'I've only just gone to sleep. Why's Gwen awake already? She's looking so glamorous. Where did she get that beige suit, makeup and her *hair's* been set!

"I've had such a busy morning. I've been to town for Jake's birthday present, then back out to Sainsbury's and then the hairdressers. Edith and Ismerie are coming for drinks and snacks this evening."

What's she talking about? "Help, help." Where am I? I'm disorientated, confused. Listen to her news . . . smile and eat.

"I've stoned the cherries and I've got 'Battenberg' today for you."

My bottom's aching, can I lift my legs, turn a little, no, put up with it Catrin. Is that my voice? I want to ask about those flying squirrels but I'm saying jumbled, wrong things. Mustn't say help, it annoys people. "Hel . . . Lo, hello." She looks puzzled.

"Did you hear what I said? Margaret died on Wednesday, it was such a shock, she hadn't even been ill!"

"I had a long walk this morning. Shall we go on the train; we're not far from the airport? It's too early for me to have a bath. I'd like some sandals and some plain Irish whisky."

"Are you going to take up drinking?"

She's laughing . . . looking at her watch.

"I can't stay long today, I'd better go."

There's relief in her face. "When are you coming again, do you *have* to go yet?"

"I'll give you a kiss. See you on Tuesday, be a good girl."

She's rushing off to her busy life, her technicolour presence having made me feel like dull monochrome. A faint hint of her perfume hangs in the air.

✳      ✳      ✳

*The stars are fading . . . the blackness becoming cold, smokey grey patched with yellow. A lone bird soars and swoops as the grey lightens and lifts the dawn sun from its hiding place behind the trees. I'm stiff. It's so quiet I can hear the tiny insects, bustling through the damp ground beneath. Spiders wait hopefully, silver threads sparkling enticingly at prospective visitors. That powerful, unpredictable sky, changing colour and shape so high above me, makes me feel vulnerable and temporary, a speck in infinity. We've no food, inadequate clothing, we haven't hiked since we were girl guides.*

*The sun's breaking free of its pink cloud wrap, encouraging bigger insects to emerge to bask in its rays. Lizzie's finished her snoring symphony; she's wriggling under her blanket. "We should get to the coast today." She's speaking to that blackthorn bush above her.*

*"I wonder what fish we'll be able to catch?" Gwen is suddenly awake. She always lies still and unmoving, one minute asleep, the next awake. Like a light bulb, switched off, switched on.*

*"Shall we go?"*

*Up the rabbit cropped hillside and over, my nostrils full of the fresh, raw smell of aconites and celandines pushing through their green sheaths. The only sound the hoarse krekking of the ravens and the occasional wild, frantic wings of the disturbed game birds roosting in the heather. There's an icy stream rushing down to the sea. We can have a drink and I'll splash my sleepy eyes and puffy, creased just-woken face. Can't stop thinking about playing tennis . . . perhaps Gwen's thinking about clothes and Lizzies got a song in her head . . . but we must all be dreaming about food . . .*

*"I can see the seaaaa!" Gwen's chanting in a baby voice, and down the close-cropped hill she's hurrying, between wild sheep, charging away at the sight of us, bleating anxious calls to one another. It's like when we had our first glimpse of the sea from our Austin Princess, at the beginning of our holidays with Daddy and Mother. No buckets and spades, shrimp nets or cheese sandwiches wrapped in greaseproof paper secured with a rubber band, but in front the blue sea and on our backs the warm afternoon sun. Carefully down the rocky path onto the sandy beach, the imprints of our feet strung out behind us, the smell of salt and seaweed all around. Gwen's looking down into a rock pool, getting out her comb . . . I can see my face too, reflected in the cool, still water. She's touching those fronded anemones.*

*"Look they're closing like baby's lips over a nipple."*

*Lizzie's shouting. "Look there's shoals of little fish here. Give me a safety pin and the string Gwen, there might be bigger ones."*

*I don't like catching fish. I'll head back to those big smooth rocks . . . Here's one big enough to fit my body . . . Why aren't I thin after all this tennis and walking? The sea and sky are blurring together . . . I've never been keen on fish . . .*

*Mrs Harris is bringing in a big plate of fried fish and mashed potato. She plonks them on the table so that their gaping mouths and staring eyes are inches from me. 'I don't want any,' I say hurriedly, swinging my legs off the dining chair, turning my back, standing tall and looking hard at my flower puzzle on the little table in the window, so I don't feel sick.*

*"Don't be silly, Catrin, sit down at once."*

*Mother's voice has the no-nonsense tone, so I slide back onto the chair, but keep looking at my puzzle.*

*"You were starving a few minutes ago, what's happened to your appetite?"*

*But she knows. We've been in Tenby a week now, staying in Mrs Harris's house. She cooks the food Mother buys, but it's never right. Mother hates housework, she only likes gardening, music and playing tennis, oh and she and Gwen like making clothes. You'd think she'd be pleased not to cook, but she doesn't seem at all happy.*

*"Tom take this plate and cut the heads and tails off. Lizzie see if you can fillet the mackerel please."*

*This afternoon Tom and I were lying on our fronts on the edge of the dry dock, fishing for crabs with bits of fish the fishermen throw away. He doesn't mind breaking heads up and putting pieces on my line. Daddy said that when he was a baby he pulled all the legs off a crab and tried to eat it. Daddy was laughing, I think he was proud, because he wants Tom to be a farmer and butcher like him when he grows up.*

*The sun beat down on our backs as we peered down at the dark water. If we got a nibble, we lifted the line gently, up, up; hoping the greedy crab wouldn't notice it was flying. Sometimes they did and dropped off. Tom was silent and moved gently and smoothly, not like his rough rugby tackling, shouting, boisterous self. We got a whole bucket full, and then threw them back.*

*"Here you are Catrin, now eat this all up!"*

*I look down at my pieces of brown fillet and bits of scales on the mashed potato. I pick at it, avoiding the nasty bits and keep my eyes down so I don't see the big plate Tom and Lizzie have covered with the discarded remnants of the bodies . . .*

*My pleasant doze is interrupted by the disappearance of the sun. Must be a big cloud . . . No, it's an enormous man! My heart almost stopped, a tiny squeak comes out of my paralysed—with-fear vocal chords.*

*"Don't be afraid, I not hurt you!"*

*He must be 7 or 8ft tall. A sheep's face, big bony nose, and those eyes . . . the blue, kind one looking at me. Huge, uneven yellow teeth smiling.*

*"You old lady, what you here? No people come here. Titan no see people."*

*What a gentle voice for such a strange looking, massive man. He gave me such a shock.*

*"I, I," the words are catching in my throat like insects on flypaper. "I'm Catrin. Those are my sisters trying to catch some fish.*

156

*That red eye is on fire . . . he's snarling, roaring. "What's the matter?" He's got a rock . . . charging towards them, with huge, thumping giant's footsteps.*

*"Stop, stop! What are you doing? They're my sisters. Look out Lizzie. Gwen, Gwen!"*

*They've seen him. They seem to be frozen to the spot.*

*My legs won't move, they're heavy, unjointed wood. Move legs, move, move.*

*"Titan, Titan, please. They're my sisters, please don't hurt them!"*

*Legs in slow motion like in a dream, hurry, hurry. He's got Gwen . . . push myself between them. "Titan, please, what are you doing? You were so friendly, what's the matter?"*

*"I kill bad women!"*

*"Is it because they've caught a fish?"*

*Lizzie is hastily, carefully taking the thrashing mackerel off the safety pin, salty droplets flying everywhere. "Look we can put it back in the sea, it's still alive!"*

*"I give you fish, not sisters. I kill bad sisters."*

*He's got Lizzie's hair . . . knocked her head with the rock. She's deadly pale, tears sparkling in the bright sunlight. I'm getting hysterical, is he going to kill us? The sky's full of him. I'll hang onto his arm, look into his soft, gentle blue eye, "Titan, these are very good women."*

*He's gripping them tighter, he'll squash the life from them..*

*"Don't you believe in God Titan? He'll punish you if you hurt them."*

*"My Mother, she say God punish. Why God punish me this face?"*

*"When you smile, you've a nice face." I'm lying. "Leave them. Show me where you live and you can tell me about your mother." I know I'm gabbling desperately . . . .*

*"Go away quick, or I kill you. I friend with Catrin."*

*"Gwen help Lizzie . . . go away!" The flapping fish is still hanging from her shoulder.*

*Fear is creeping upwards from my soles, numbing my ankles, making my legs weak and wobbly. He's looking at me with happy anticipation. Am I going to my doom? Over the rocks and up the cliff, studded with sea lavender and sea pinks, to the mouth of this huge cave. He's disappeared into the gloom, could I run? I'm 87, he's perhaps 35, I won't get far.*

*"Come."*

*It's so warm and bright! Candles in what looks like pieces of sheep skull on ledges, a fire at the back, smoke meandering up into the darkness above. Sheepskins on wooden chairs, a fish hanging to dry at the side of the fire, with what looks like a leg of sheep. The mouth-watering smell from that pot is making my empty stomach churn.*

*"Sit. You drink tea. English people like tea, yes?"*

*Sip the warm, scented brew, mmm, sip again. I've never liked Alys's herb tea, it tastes like boiled sticks, but this is delicious. It's like peaches and strawberries . . . smells sweet and fruity . . . It's seeping into every one of my cells, warming and healing. Can't help the tears. Titan's seen them he looks upset.*

*Tears fill my eyes, colours and shapes whirling around and inside me . . . flowing down, making a bed of summer flowers: yellow petunias, red geraniums, and blue lobelia. The lush lawn spreads away to our wooden gate to the orchard. There's laughter, giggles . . . through the gate comes Gareth, his healthy skin glowing like phosphorus. His friend Winston and Lizzie and Gwen behind. I stop, but Gareth's eyes soften and he's smiling . . . I walk forwards, straining to see my sisters faces, but they're fuzzy, blurred and I'm covered with petals, soft and scented.*

*"Tell me why you're here." I'm so drowsy; I'll snuggle down into their velvety cosiness.*

*"My . . ." his halting words wash over and through me like sand through a sieve. I want to concentrate . . . my legs are numb, my head is full of the drone of his voice, I'm drifting away . . .*

"I feed you Catrin?"

What's Titan saying, am I not allowed to do anything for myself now? The blue plastic pinnie over my head. He frightens me. I won't open my mouth or speak . . .

Good he's giving up and going away. Here's Joan.

"What's this about refusing your breakfast? Aren't you feeling well?"

I'm saying nothing, I feel fine. I just want to be left alone.

"Well if you don't eat your lunch, we'll call in the doctor."

158

＊　　　＊　　　＊

*Have I been drugged, was it that tea? Heavy, dense, rooted, head full of sand. Titan must have been up for some time, that smells like fish stew . . .*

*How to escape goes round and round in my head . . . and crosses and cauldrons. How do I go from one place to another? It's strange, like living one life and watching myself in a film, in another one. It's not a dream is it? No, it's too vivid, detailed, coherent, too joined up. I don't understand it at all.*

# Chapter 18—Help! 2004

## WEDNESDAY JULY 28

*I*t's been months since I've written. I've been incredibly busy at College and also thinking about what I'd like to do when I retire. Researching has preoccupied me and there seemed to be nothing new to report. I haven't deserted my role as Mum's guardian, just the act of recording. I've also been wrestling with my new identity, as 'Nana,' and trying to find times to bring Cerys. Mum loves to see her grandson, but he's more interested in going up and down the stairs outside her room, (they live in a ground floor flat) returning only when she has food he can share.

Mum has been quietly deteriorating, but has good days.

## FRIDAY AUGUST 6TH

She's hiding behind a sagging, pallid, blotchy mask, a face no longer fitting on its underpinnings. Can it get any gaunter and skull like? Her voice any quieter? Her hair any stiffer? The Home hairdresser has been ill for weeks, so it never gets washed.

She is desperately keen to please, no longer shouts out and valiantly tries to feed herself and fastidiously tries to wipe her mouth after eating or drinking. Sadly she takes so long that her meals are cold and congealed before she's half way through.

She still sees things that aren't there: "I'll eat those two biscuits on my wrist."

"That's your watch and copper bangle Mum."

"Those ones there then."

Pointing to an empty area of the plastic table in front of her. As if to distract me from finding out how little she can see, she changed the subject.

"Went to church this morning. Grandpa was chatting to everyone, help. I don't think he and mother and I will be there much longer. Your writing's not right; it's a bit quiet. You want to take a few more lessons."

"Who from?" I asked.

"From the teacher. My toes tickle, I'm going to get chilblains. I wanted to say goodbye."

"Where are we going then?"

An intake of breath and a sarcastic tone, she enunciates slowly as if I am stupid,

"*Your* bed and *my* bed. Have alone the lights"

"What lights?"

More withering disgusted look and a long description of all the lights and the chicken one. This is really upsetting, I wanted to cry, but nodded understandingly and she seemed satisfied. She turned away from me and talked to the wall.

"I think Robert's come now." She pointed to her coat on the back of the door.

"Mum, I've come all this way to see you and you don't appear to know me?"

Back came, "'I know you, what made you think that?"

## THURSDAY SEPTEMBER 9TH

Mum had yet another urine infection and was very ill for three weeks. I couldn't seem to write then either. I just felt helpless and impotent because she couldn't communicate with me and looked so terrible.

Today she was sitting in her chair, her table spanning her lap is laden with drinks, fruit, chocolates, her glasses, magazine, notebook and tissues. I'm writing in between feeding her lunch, which is very poor quality fish and chips.

"I could do with another pair of tennis shoes," she says. "Help, I'll pay for ours if I can find my purse, it must be in the bedroom.

"What do you think about Mum?"

"I remember things that I used to do and what I have done and what I'd do if I didn't have a job. I think about people. I'd just

161

sat down for lunch when you arrived. I was surprised to see you. There's plenty to think about."

"Don't you get bored?"

"No, I don't get bored. Help. Help. Have you got a tissue?"

"They're in front of you Mum." She obviously can't see as her shaking hand goes towards a banana, and now she can't seem to coordinate the movements to let go of it. I say over and over, "further to the right Mum," but she holds the banana again. After five minutes I am losing patience, as her hand cannot get past the banana. Her mind is obviously playing spatial tricks, can't she see or feel anything any more?

"Can't you see, Mum?"

"I can see to a certain point."

I test her with big writing and she reads it slowly.

"Can you see your crisps?" I check her powers of observation.

She looks around: "There aren't any." Her bony claw reaches into the air, "Here they are."

There is no evidence that she can see anything on the table.

"Can you see your glass? If you wanted a drink, where is it?"

Both arms lift and fumble in the air, but neither goes in the direction of the drink in front of her. No wonder the fruit is always untouched and rotting.

"I'm trying to understand how you can read those headlines in the paper, yet you can't see anything on your table?"

She motions as if to stand, trying vainly to pull herself forwards.

"Are you happy, Mum?"

"Well I can't say I'm exactly happy, it could be worse. I sometimes wonder if it's alright for us to come here."

"Where?"

"Here, in this house."

"But this is a Nursing Home Mum, you need nursing care, because you can't walk."

"I walked a bit yesterday, in a wood, help, help, I know that I walked a lot."

If only. I feel so helpless, hopeless. "You haven't been able to walk for three years Mum." Why *do* I try to drag her back to reality?

"I know it's been a long time, but I'm fairly confident now."

"What can I do to help you?"

"You can't do anything. Help! If I was able to get around."

# FRIDAY OCTOBER 15TH

I walked the two miles briskly, arriving to see the Home's minibus slowly reversing down towards the entrance. The hall resembled a rookery; four black dressed carers and four inmates in their wheelchairs, poised for take off. I wondered who has died?

Mum lay in bed, bony, stiff and sobbing, no top denture and eyes sealed shut with pus. She looked gaunt and neglected. Apparently the Home dentist had come to her room and taken five teeth out four days before and I could see that she has contracted an appalling mouth infection, bits of dried blood and more pus kept appearing on her lips. Her voice was so deep it was unrecognisable, her breathing like a rasping, storm beaten seashore.

I was deeply shocked, her face was one of those dried up mummies in a museum, skin pulled taut over the cheek bones then sunken, her mouth a Munch scream. She didn't seem surprised to see me, as if I lived next door and was always popping in.

"Where's your son?" she demanded.

I explained yet again that Cerys has the son and I am his grandmother. It's a chilling shock when your mother no longer knows who you are. It changes your sense of self.

Time has gone on without her. I went to Italy, France, Scotland and Tenby this summer, while she has rarely been out of bed. We have had a General Election, two incidents of bombs in London, Wimbledon, and the US Open. "Did you hear that Henman might qualify for the Masters Cup?"

She looked blank, "Help." she said.

I stroked her hands trying to straighten her joints. After about fifteen minutes of stroking, massaging and gentle pulling, I managed to get her right hand looking almost normal. Her left is still a rigid claw. Neither can hold nor grasp anything now.

Eventually, she talked to me a little and seemed to understand the family news I was telling her, "Of course I do." is her usual retort when I say do you remember so and so?

I had at last remembered to look on the Internet.

"Mum do you remember you'd been watching a programme about Welsh fables and you asked me about Cadw, Ceridwen and a cross?"

No response, she seemed to have gone inside herself.

"Well some of the sources said that the tallest Celtic cross in Wales is at Carew and it's a memorial to the Welsh King Cadw, whoever he was. Do you remember it? In the car park, a high cross with a ring round it? You sat under it eating an ice cream when you didn't want to walk around the millpond and castle with Cerys and I?"

She suddenly looked as if she were following me.

"Not sure where the cauldron fits in though. You know the legend about that don't you? How Ceridwen left a young boy stirring it and he let a few drops fall on his fingers, so she chased him and they both kept changing their form until he became a grain in order to hide, but she ate him and the grain became a baby, so he was renewed. Perhaps *we* could get eternal youth if we knew where the cauldron was?"

No answer, so I peeled her a Satsuma. She loves fruit. She couldn't open her mouth enough for me to get a segment in. Then I managed to force it through her locked together teeth, and she chewed desultorily, mechanically, not seeming to savour it, thick spit foaming out and down her chin.

"It hurts," she said and pushed it out, so it hung on her lip. I wiped it away and sponged her eyes to help them stay open.

"It was all right; they had party night with female carrier bags. He's doing a lot of work on shoulders. Help, can I get in that side?"

"What have you been thinking about Mum?"

"Old school friends, finding family, things I did in the past. I made my mind up about. Help! Going to the parties and not, we had two parties and I wasn't invited. I can tell you I didn't make this up, help, the only person I rang and she asked me to hers, but otherwise I don't go."

I tried to change the subject, she's always saying there are parties happening and she doesn't get invited, but she kept returning to the same theme. We lapsed into silence. I ate my Marks and Spencer 'Three bean wrap' and feeling weary and stale, watched the dust motes dancing in the light and tried to remember a line from Michael Tournier's 'Friday' (1967). I looked it up when I got home:

*'Those fixed*
*points which thought uses for its progression, like*
*crossing a river on stepping-stones, are crumbling*
*and vanishing beneath the surface.'*

In came Joan the nurse and Mum pulled herself together to exchange a few sensible sentences, I asked for a Doctor to visit to prescribe antibiotics and then it was help, help, help again interspersed with incomprehensible stuff. When I questioned her about what she meant, she got irritated, a trickle of saliva coursed down onto her blue knitted Tricoville suit.

## THURSDAY NOVEMBER 11TH

Mum's Local Authority Community Care Worker came for her annual review. We had e-mailed one another and I'd told her about Mum's current state and my dissatisfaction with her confinement to bed for the last year.

"Hello Catrin, how are you?" The newly glamorous Irene asked.

Mum looked at her fashionable short blonde hair cut, her fitted jacket, long skirt and boots, "Hello," she said uncertainly, then muttered, "Help, help." Irene was visibly upset by this, but determinedly carried on asking her questions and Mum seemed to be following, but could not respond intelligibly. So we ended up talking around her, about her, as if she were in the audience. I hated this; Mum must have hated it more.

## SATURDAY DECEMBER 18TH

"Can the girls check Catrin?"

Joan was at the door. Did I sense reproach in her tone, that I was delaying their rounds, that they had to do what I should have been doing for my Mother? I waited outside in the ugly overgrown square of garden, with it's broken concrete fountain, no flowering shrubs and the stench of exhaust fumes from the busy road running past. Going back inside I felt an immediate assault on my senses. Firstly the smell, then the sounds of screeching, moaning and shouting. My mother's "helps" accompanying the hellish orchestra. Is her cry for proximal or existential pain?

Scottish Bill is in the room next door to Mum. As I reached the top of the stairs I could see into both their rooms. Both sitting in their chairs Bill keeping up a steady muttering, nodding his head from time to time as if carrying on a conversation with an invisible acquaintance, Mum mumbling, "help."

"OK Mum?"

"Help help. You've got TV?"

"Yes at home." While I was wondering what she was meaning, quick as a snake a retort came back.

"Well I wouldn't expect you to have it *here!*"

She then lapsed into continual helps punctuated only by answering the carer's comments to one another, which she can hear through the open door. She has excellent hearing and unfortunately as her bedroom opens onto the top of the stairs she hears everyone passing and whatever they are talking about. She has lost her spatial awareness, so thinks that they are talking to her.

"I think I can do it now, stand on my own, help, help, help."

"Mum you haven't stood for over three years!"

"Well, I'll show you. That was Charlie in Gwen and Bill's new car and most people are against it, help, help. Is that fly in here?"

"Mum, don't keep saying help please."

"Am I saying help? I am unaware that I am saying it. I'll try harder, help, help, help, help, mutter, mutter. Shall I get up? I'm sick of lying here."

"Do you want to sit in the chair?"

"They've got a lounge, help, help, help, help . . ."

"Mum, *please*, I'll have to go."

"Sorry, it's only words. Help, help, help, help, help."

"STOP it, say something else!"

"It's the only thing I can think about life in general"

"Do you mean you're saying it because your life is so awful?"

"No, I don't mean that at all. Help, help, help, help, help."

I flick through an old 'Daily Mail' my aunt has left for her, trying to breath deeply and *not* lose my temper. Seeing a coupon for 20p off 'I Can't believe its Not Butter.' I cut it out with my nail scissors. Why have I done that? I *like* butter! I ask if she wants a chocolate?

"Aren't I eating one? What's this in my hand?" She looks at her empty claw. "Help, help. Help, help."

"What do you want to do?"

"Well anything, not lying here, *you* choose something."

I have asked and she's not allowed to sit in her chair, her bottom is too sore. In any case, she hates being lifted out in the hoist and fights and shouts when it appears. No wonder the staff have given up getting her out of bed.

All she can say is 'help' and I become so tense that not even watering the half dead plants in her gift baskets can relax me. When she sees me ministering to them, she snaps, "I water them *every* day!" The filthy, stained carpet, the hideously stained pressure cushion on her chair that I had ordered from America for £200 and which I had never found her sitting on except when it was off, despite the huge notice: 'PLEASE TURN THE SWITCH FOR THE CUSHION OFF WHEN MUM IS <u>NOT</u> SITTING ON IT.'

All of it was getting to me. Poor Mum, she looks so neglected. I *have*, I *am* failing her!

"Can I pull the hairs out on your chin?" She is usually very keen.

"No. No, you'll hurt me!"

"I'll *cut* them off then shall I?"

"No, no, you might cut me."

"Don't be silly Mum, do you *want* hairs sprouting out? There's only three."

"No leave them."

"I'll cut your nails then."

"No, no," again.

I took her hand firmly to cut off the dead, yellowy-brown ends of her nails. She squealed and begun to cry, saying I was hurting her. She can't bear to be touched now; she'd apparently savagely fought off the carers who had tried to cut them a few days ago. Even more irritated I hung onto her hand and trimmed every nail. Big brown chunks flew up into the air accompanied by her wailing. "Ow, Ow!"

"I'm not cutting your finger off Mum; I'm *not* touching the skin!"

"It hurts, it hurts."

Do people who have no control over their limbs, become extra sensory in the dead bits?

Two sparrows ruffled themselves in the pools of rainwater on the cemetery path below her window. Luckily she has never looked out to see those gravestones and the scurrying, busy squirrels. She is petrified, paranoid at the thought of squirrels. I hope she didn't hear about that dog being ripped to pieces by squirrels in Russia! The worst thing was that when people tried to save it, the squirrels scampered off carrying bits of the dogs flesh. Yuck!

Her mouth won't close today so she is dribbling constantly. How many hours have I listened to help, help? Three and a half?

"I have to go now Mum."

"Where am *I* going, I have to go somewhere."

"Why can't you stay here?"

"Well you don't want me."

"But this is *your* home, not mine."

"Where would I go if I had to go, would they give me a partner?"

"Do you want to come and live with me in London then?" I asked yet again.

"No I don't want to live in London. I'm crazy, are you? Help, help, help, help. I'd better have your address on a bit of paper. I might be second hand, in which case. Can I go in there, down the bottom, by my feet? What am I leaning on?"

Lumps of brown stuff appeared every so often on her lips, caked blood, still coming out from her mouth and throat.

"Haven't you had enough of me now?" I asked.

"No, No. Help, help, help, help, help, help . . ."

"I love you, but I can't take you saying help any more Mum, I'm sorry, I'll have to go."

I don't need to go for another hour and a half, but checking that a doctor has been called, I prepared to slope off, deeply ashamed that I could bear my own mothers company no longer.

She pulled her dry lips into a gracious smile, as if automatically responding to some genetic memory. "Thank you so much for coming. Help!"

Then it was as if some chemicals, which her neural pathways had been holding back all afternoon, cascaded into her brain, she looked penetratingly at me, dissecting me, before allowing me to reassemble. I was disconcerted; she hadn't looked at me, not really *looked* for three years. Did she *know* that my train ticket was for 6.25, not 4.55?

I hugged her and hurried out into the cold, wet afternoon to walk the two miles to the station, letting the rain soak away the acrid stench of the Home and the terrible guilt in which I am steeped.

## TUESDAY DECEMBER 28TH

It takes a few seconds each time I see her to reconcile the skeleton in the bed with the image of Mum I've carried in my head for sixty years.

Her face was bleak, expressionless, rough patches scattered over papery, parchment skin. I didn't offer to make her up, as I so often do; I was scared the skin would tear.

"Help, help, help, help, help," she muttered incessantly.

She no longer seems to want me to touch her, stroke her hands or kiss her. She doesn't seem to care if I'm there or not. But, I thought, I'm going to stay, not because I have to, because I need to. I love her.

Visitors and staff go in and out of her room, she can have no influence on when, who or how long, what does that do to one? Impatient, hurried visits from people who can't wait to get away are the best she can hope for. And almost every time, she thinks she is leaving *with* us. It is so distressing to tell her that she isn't, that she can never escape her room. This is her fate."Help, help, help."

Dementia has often been compared to childhood—a sufferer seems to be experiencing things afresh each time. I have looked for that and though one certainly has to repeat oneself over and over. Are TV, flowers, food and so on delightful each time they are seen, smelt or tasted, just as if they were new? No, I don't think so, not to Mum anyway. Why couldn't her end have been more pleasant, not

169

lonely, demeaning, boring and as painful as it is. She no longer has anything to say to people visiting. How can she have? How can she be interested in anything outside this little room? After three years incarceration?

She always had hope, though I've realised recently that there never has been a way back. Everyone else knew that and now I think that Mum does too.

Cerys and I, our partners and her child had taken Christmas CD's, candles, crackers, presents and Christmas lunch to spend Boxing Day with her. All four generations together.

She didn't seem to particularly enjoy her food. The toddler looked longingly at his great grandmothers gravy dinner. I fetched another fork and fed them both from opposite ends of the plate. They stared solemnly at one another. Were they acknowledging their helplessness, or hoping that the other didn't eat too much? The clean sheet and the crammed page, complicit in clearing the plate. Mum was not interested in her presents.

# Chapter 19—The Old Men

*T*his hasn't happened for a while. There I am down there, the shrivelled shape in the bed by the window. My mouth saying 'help' but no one's coming. The breeze is lifting me gently . . . soaring over trees and fields in the hot, blue air. Wafts of freshly cut grass, coconut gorse and wild fennel instead of traffic fumes. I'll stretch my arms, paddle my legs and fly higher into cool vapour, out into sun, swooping, free and light . . .

"I don't know what happens to your blood vessels when I want to take your blood."

She's saying, faintly in the distance and suddenly I'm back, feeling her wrapping the rubber band tighter, watching her tapping, and digging the needle into my arm. She's looking at me strangely, as if she knows that I've just returned.

"Ah, here we go."

I should be used to this, but it hurts and I feel faint every time. Alys's said to her: "You don't need to take blood *every* week for Warfarin. Every third is plenty."

She carries on though, unless Alys is here.

"I've finished now Titan. Catrin can have her lunch."

Blue plastic bib, food pushed into my mouth. I'll close my eyes . . . it's delicious lobster and runner beans.

*In an underwater cave, weeds swaying and shaking amongst the pink coral and dark green water. A shoal of tiny, shining fish swims past. Titan fixes his unblinking eyes upon them and opens his mouth. They've swum inside. He's smiling a shark's smile . . . laughing . . . it's echoing, booming round and round. I'm sinking lower and lower, covering my ears. I want to cry, and I do, but it sounds strange sound like someone choking. I want to shout, but no shout comes, just a big air bubble . . . it's Gareth's face. I can't reach his hand. Fingers touching . . . floating up . . . this isn't Gareth, it's John. His strong, veined, mottled hand clasping mine . . . his face is gaunt, a scar running from under his eye to his chin . . . Charlie! Was that a stab of longing?*

*The rain beats down in determined, opaque sheets. How am I going to escape? Cloudy memories fill my brain. Scenes, words; all jumbled together; fishes, hens, rings and crosses spinning round with caves, shadowy people and Charlie.*

*'The highest one in Cymru guards a castle very fair.' How long have I been floating here? Titan must be drugging me. How can I escape?*

✻     ✻     ✻

A woman comes and speaks. I can't make sense of her words, I'll nod and, reassured she goes. My skin comes up in goosebumps, my teeth chatter, my body burns, buzzes, sweats, I'm ill, I want to cry . . .

"She should be over her urine infection by now. We'd better get the Doctor in again."

I don't care that they're speaking about me, not to me. I'm a baby balloon floating at the end of a long cord; I can't talk to you Alys . . .

✻     ✻     ✻

*I feel as if I've had a long sleep. I'll get up and have a wash . . . this is refreshing. It's a shock each time I see that this is my mottled skin, draping loosely away from my bones, these are my sagging breasts . . . is that Titan? Quick, cover myself. What's this? Oh, that cloak, wrap it around.*

*"Where you? Catrin?"*

*Why's he standing in front of me, looking at me and asking where I am? Pacing about looking everywhere? He's so agitated, has he lost his sight? Well he can see that sledge hammer, is he going to kill me?*

*"Catrin, Catrin, where you go, you not go outside!"*

172

*Why isn't he seeing me? I don't understand. Can't he hear my heart thumping? He was so close, why didn't he see me? Where's he going? Down to the beach, to look for me?*

*Shall I call him? No, I'll run away, escape. What if he's testing me, pretending not to see me? I'll go up the cliff. Shall I get dressed? No, just go, stuff things in pack, quickly, quickly. Scramble up, up the cliff path, faster, faster, oh, can't breathe . . . Along the cliff top, down and up and down and up, my breath rasping . . . gasping. Hurry, hurry, he's so big and fit, he'll easily catch me. I can hear myself repeating, "help" over and over in the rhythm of my footfalls, my pounding heart. "Help, help."*

*There he is, running along the beach, looking in the caves, behind the rocks. There's no trace of Lizzie and Gwen, the waves have sucked the beach clean.*

*Struggle up, up another rocky sheep track, here's a flat bit, go on, on. What's that ruined stone place? A hermit's or a shepherd's shelter. That's Gwen's' voice. Can't stop the tears.*

*"Gwen, Gwenllian, quick, we have to get away." She's looking around so wildly . . .*

*"Catrin? Where are you Catrin, where are you hiding?"*

*Has she gone blind, what's happening? I'll hug her. Why is she screaming? "Lizzie, I'm so happy to see you. Don't look like that. It's me Lizzie. Don't push me away Gwen, it's me!"*

*"Catrin, you're a ghost!"*

*"I'm here, this is me, why can't you see me?"*

*The cliff top, the sky and sea's spinning up and around and away. What's happening to me?*

*Going black, falling, my breakfast pouring out . . .*

"Hmm? Of course I can see you Catrin, open your eyes and you can see me too."

Gwen's wearing a turquoise jacket with matching earrings.

"How are you feeling today?"

Her face is immaculately made up . . . beautiful coiffed hair. Feeling? I feel outside this body, distant, sort of light headed, panicky, exhausted, I've run a long way.

"I've taken the stones out of these cherries, do you want one?"

It's plump, blood red and glossy. Sweetness fills my dry mouth, but its taste is less vivid than the taste of fear.

"Titan's after us with an axe, we should run, run now."

She's not listening.

"Cardiff should have won last night, they had two tries disallowed. Did you see the match?"

I open my mouth again and let my terror seep out as her words, her presence, soak up the room, so there's no escape.

✳     ✳     ✳

*"Can we sit down, just for ten minutes? I need to get something out of my shoe."*

*Lizzie's finding this pace hard. We can probably slow down now, we're miles away from Titan's cave. Lying here, the deep blue of the sky is a bright, warm blanket over me. The sun's rejuvenating my sluggish blood, melting my sagging fat, strengthening my crumbling bones, I feel eternal . . . and very lucky to have had the magic cloak to escape with.*

*"Come on you two, up you get, we'd better go on. Cover your head Catrin the sun brings you out in red blotches doesn't it?"*

*Gwen's enjoying this exercise, she's never been a walker before, but then, none of us have. Who's that? A shadowy apparition, grey and insubstantial in the sunlight. "Gwen, look out!"*

*"Have you come for us?"*

*Two small, meek, hollow eyes peer out from a bundle of dirty rags with a Rip Van Winkle beard. Terrified, she bats away his extended arm.*

*"There's another one!"*

*A tiny man with a wrinkled yellow head stops as a coughing fit shakes his body with wrenching violence.*

*"Are you taking us with you, are we rescued at last?"*

*The bearded one's crying, clutching Lizzie, well, she's the smallest and plumpest. "Don't let them get hold of you Lizzie." Gwen's muttering something.*

*"They look ripe for the scythe."*

*"Don't be so cruel. They're probably younger than us."*

*Lizzie's always kind and charitable; she's smiling warmly, kindly as if she were doing the book rounds at her local hospital, or helping at Abbeyfield.*

*"They're filthy, they've really let themselves . . ."*

*A taller, tougher old man . . . A strong body, but no top teeth, a scar, a face like a wolf, he looks like . . . Charlie, a fitter, more mobile Charlie. I'm shocked.*

*"Women! Where've you come from?"*

*He's looking at me and his face is freeze framed. "We're walking to South Wales to look for our family . . ." There's a smirk in his eyes.*

*"You're havin' a laugh ain't you? It's a thousand miles for Christ's sake."*

*Lizzie hates blasphemy. "Have you got any better ideas for getting there then?"*

*"You'll never make it."*

*"It's been nice meeting you, but we have to go to meet our friends."*

*Lizzies saying that, but she's the hostage of the two frailer men, old rheumy eyes glistening, almost salivating. Another one blocking our way . . . Short, swarthy, powerfully built, he's got no neck . . . ginger tufts sticking out from his sailor's cap.*

*"There is no fuckin' way, absolutely no fuckin' way that you three old crumblies can walk that far. On your own? Are you daft or somethin'?" Charlie's laughing at us.*

*"Why not?" Looking around at this peaceful copse, the sky blue above and birds singing in the trees, why not?*

*He's looking mocking, but somehow, appreciative, familiar. This sudden intimacy is confusing, wonder if he recognises me? That's an angry red scar on his face. "How did that happen?"*

*"Well it weren't fighting off a sexy grey 'aired ex blonde."*

*Yes, he remembers, I used to have my hair highlighted and he made my appointments for me. "If you wanna do the business, ladies, you need weapons and a bigger group. You have to keep watch at night. There's some bloody hungry creatures out there."*

*Lizzie always takes charge and looks after us, but she's gone very quiet. I think I'm realising that her 'big sister' persona is just an act, she's just as scared as Gwen and me. It's taken more than eighty years for me to understand that. It's going to have to be me who is strong and resourceful. "Sorry, but we must press on, thanks for your advice, we're off to meet our friends."*

*"Oh yeh!" I feel his eyes on me as I bend down for my pack. Pull my jumper down . . . feel self conscious . . . fat and frumpy, but somehow stirred up. His mouth and cheeks are twitching as if he's going to laugh . . . they're tensing in irritation:*

*"Well, we'd better escort you little ladies back to your friends. Perhaps we'll join up with 'em, safety in numbers."*

*Why do they want to come with us? Why did I tell that untruth? How embarrassing . . .*

✳     ✳     ✳

Robert always sits, paring his nails, not saying a lot, never telling me anything. If I ask him questions, his face hardens and the atmosphere goes rubbery, so that everything I say bounces back.

"Have you got a girlfriend now?"

"I may do."

"Are you dieting again?"

"Maybe."

Everything deflected. We sit stewing in our silence until he looks out of the window.

"Good job you don't go out Mum. There's so many squirrels down there. Look, they're jumping through the trees. I can see at least six, no eight, they're really big animals!"

That's not nice of him. Telling me. He knows I'm petrified of them. "That's not funny, you know I don't like squirrels." I'll tell him about the Home closing . . . he's not listening.

"Watch out for those squirrels."

He's gone. I used to be able to have proper conversations with people, make them laugh, they *liked* talking to me. Now no one wants to hear what I want to say, they don't try and understand me. Bored looks come onto their faces and they interrupt. I wanted to tell Alys that I was proud of what people said and did for her at her leaving party, but my thoughts were miles from my mouth . . . struggling through a swamp . . .

Robert won't talk about anything much, Alys wants to know everything. "Were you in love with John? With Daddy?" Personal questions.

Love? I'd feel guilty not being faithful to Gareth. He was as good as gold, even though he drank all our money away. Wonder what Lizzie and Gwen thought about John? He was such good company. He made me feel loved, protected . . . but, yes, guilty. The magazines say love means you don't notice what a person looks like or whether they're suitable. Could I be keen on a lorry driver? Mmm . . . Charlie's a bit rough and ready. I've got *two* real lives. What's real anyway? Can real be what you want it to be?

✲     ✲     ✲

*An unhealthy, cloying smell like old boiled socks is sucked into my gasping lungs as we cross the mountain crest. At last . . . a large group of stone farm buildings tucked into the heather and bracken below. But the unpleasant odour wafting in the cold breeze is growing stronger. "What's that terrible smell?"*

*I can see by the others uncomprehending, exhausted faces that they can smell nothing.*

*"Can't you keep up?"*

*Gwen's sick of waiting for the two, scraping and shuffling along with their sticks. I've no idea what to do. We're stuck with them and the light has been draining away . . . those scary shadows that hide under bushes in the day, have emerged for their twilight prowl . . .*

*Arthur's laborious breathing is now loud, rasping coughs, announcing our presence to anyone who might be in the farmhouse.*

*"It looks in good repair, perhaps there'll be water? Beds? People?"*

*Gwen's thick grey hair is matted with sweat; her once expensive, designer slacks hang shapelessly. After a lifetime of looking as if she had just stepped off a page of Vogue, this is so hard for her. "The door's wide open and look there's been a fire . . . doubt if we'll find people."*

*This must once have been a richly wood panelled hall, the marks where the wood was attached are still visible. A medieval stone fireplace with a carved mantelpiece and four arched openings, which once had doors. The ceiling mouldings are so thick with dirt that their subject is unrecognisable . . . a chill draught is swirling the piles of dust. A huge pile of charred wood . . . where a staircase once rose to the open floor above and what's this? It looks like a blackened thighbone; perhaps it's just a piece of wood?*

*"There's bones everywhere; it's like a graveyard. I don't like it here, let's go . . ." Ted looks petrified.*

*"Hang on, these bones ain't fresh, for chrissake, they're probably from fucking animals." Charlie's gone through another arch. My eyes are getting used to the dim light. "Look, you can see where pictures hung,"*

*"That room's full of shit, animal shit."*

*Charlie's gone into another.*

*"Get your butts in here. This kitchen's filthy, but there's runnin' water and wood to cook your porridge."*

*At the sound of 'water,' Gwen's rushed in.*

*The smell is not so strong here. Though the floor is covered with what looks like small droppings of animal faeces, leaves, dirt . . . Lizzie's found a broom.*

*"Lets clean the floor up a bit, I'm not lying down on that."*

*Gwen's cleaning the sink.*

*"Look, some soap. If I can cut off the filth, I'm going to wash my hair."*

*Even wet, it looks thick and glossy, it's a lovely silver colour and she's always managed to cut it into an elegant bob, so unlike mine and Lizzie's thin, flat, white straggles, deprived for so long of their twice yearly perm. The waters too cold for the rest of us.*

*The porridge tastes of nothing. I imagine winding a golden rope of syrup onto a spoon and circling it round and round on it, then eating from the edges to the middle. Delicious . . . .*

*Lizzie, always the perfect companion is* still *exuding her usual 'pleased to meet you' charm, smiling and chatting vivaciously despite her revulsion at the men's swearing. I must say she looks very pretty, with her rosy cheeks and bright eyes. Her skin is so unlined; this outdoor life seems to be suiting her. She's rubbing her cheek on her collar and closing her eyes, one of them must have said something crude . . . .*

*I never have much problem sleeping; I'm in a lovely dream about being in my home. I get up late, have a bath, open the fridge and there are all my favourite foods. I put the roast pork in the oven; quickly prepare the beans, potatoes, cauli and applesauce. There's blackcurrant tart and cream for sweet. I've a big bar of whole-nut chocolate to eat later when the tennis starts on TV. I'm feeling so happy at the prospect of my day ahead . . . but I'm awake?*

*I'm warm and sleepy, why did I wake up? Was there a scream? I want to go back into my dream, be sitting on the couch, waiting for lunch to cook. What's that thrashing noise? It's so dark, there's something moving, moving over Arthur. Can't Charlie and Bill hear it?*

*There are things on top of him, they're enormous! There's that smell again, and a choking sound. "Lizzie, Charlie, wake up!" I'll shake Gwen. "Wake up! There's big animals attacking Arthur." A wave of terror is rising, breaking and pouring down through me. My heart is drumming; I can hardly breathe for the squeezing in my chest.*

*That smell is suffocating. Why won't they all wake up?*

"Catrin, Catrin, wake up!" But I'm the one who *is* awake; my brain is sharp and clear, working out what to do.

"It's lunch time Catrin."

*Am I back in my nice dream at home, has someone come to visit? Gwen's stirring . . . she's shuddering. The others still haven't moved. A shape's rearing up . . . shining red eyes . . . baleful, evil. It's baring its sharp, pointed teeth . . . Is it going to attack me? It's gone back to its meal . . . huge bushy tail waving. They're as big as Alsatians!*

"Catrin, Catrin, do you want your lunch or what? Shall I get the Doctor? She's screaming and shouting, she won't wake up."

"No, don't worry, she's having a nightmare, Mum, it's Alys, open your eyes."

*What's she doing here? My eyes are open. Something is touching my hand.* "Get away from me."

"Please open your eyes Mum, I've come a long way to see you."

*That horrible smell is even stronger, open an eye, it's Alys, looking worried, holding a plate of grey coloured cauliflower cheese.*

"Don't you want your lunch?"

\* \* \*

It's dark, I'll try to get into one of my favourite dreams: the one where I'm a child at home in the farm, or I'm a pro on the vets tennis circuit, oh not again . . . *stiff and petrified with the sounds of chewing, champing, feeding and the acrid stench of blood. Oh not here, please I don't want to be back here.*

*Gwen is clutching my back, shivering violently, she's hurting me. My skin is cold, my blood moving more and more slowly, it's like a pool of stagnant water in my skull. I must think. We have to get out of here, breathe deeply . . . breathe . . . relax! The tightness in my chest won't go, my nerves and muscles bunched, paralysed . . . Think . . . I'll get the shovel and broom, they're just beyond my feet. The squirrels are so engrossed, they're ignoring me moving . . . all of us moving . . . Errr . . . that one fastened its jaws on a fold of skin and tore off a strip with a noise like ripping open a present . . . The others have all dived in . . . horrible sloshing, sucking, squelching noises as Arthur's organs and vessels release their blood supply. Tails high they are completely absorbed in the riches pouring forth.*

*"Quick, we've got to scare them off Arthur. Come on. Now!"*

*Ted's so slow getting up. "Don't back off Gwen, bang the broom and scream."*

*Bill and Charlie sound like ten men.*

*Five heads look up, insolently chewing, blood dripping from their squirrel jaws.*

*"Get away from him!"*

*I thought they weren't going to get off him . . . at last, slowly loping away into the shadows. I'm not going to look at the gory mess.*

*Lizzie is, she's crying. "I hope he died quickly."*

*"Let's grab our things and get out of here." My voice is cracking with relief and fear. The weak dawn light reveals another door in the far corner. Oh joy, it's not locked and we're outside in the farmyard with dead tractor tyres and rotting machinery.*

"Don't don't, let go!" Can't move . . . claws gripping me "Lizzie, Gwen? They've come back, they've got *me*!"

Trapped, crushed, aaaagh. "Help, help. Fight them, Charlie."

"Get off me, help, help."

"Too strong . . . can't move, help, help."

Try, keep trying. Terrors out of my throat like a roar . . .

"Stay nice and still."

A voice far away, cold, sharp pain . . . my arm.

"All . . . right love?"

My tongue's filling my mouth, huge and dry. A drink. "Tea, tea?" My voice a rough croak. "Tea?"

"Keep your hair on,"

A cup on my mouth, dripping down my chin, my neck. Can't move my arms.

"Catrin, we've had to put you in a strait jacket. I've given you a sedative injection. You'll feel calmer in a few minutes, try and relax, everything's OK, you've had a bit of a turn, relax, try and sleep."

A trolley going away, squeak, squeak.

My heart's thudding, pounding, I'm floating in weightless suspension in the thick black sky and the blackness in my head. What's happened to everyone? Voices . . . distant . . . sinking into nothing.


"What a night! Arthur having a heart attack and Catrin throwing a wobbly, I'm exhausted."

# Chapter 20—'It's no fun being like this you know.' 2005

*M*um was lying, frail and immobile, her faded blue grey eyes open and expressionless in the dark, oppressively hot and airless little room. Insulated from reality in the cocoon of routines: the pills, the tea, the meals, the nappy changes and ever-present TV. The antibiotics seemed to have cleared up her recurrent skin infection at last.

'Hello Mum.' I kissed her and dived to open the window to gulp in the cool, fresher air. Her lovely white, curly hair was greasy and squashed flat, so it stuck up at the back like a stiff fan. She shivered in an unfamiliar nightie, which hung open at the neck exposing too much sagging, worn skin. Where are the three I gave her for Xmas, the four last Xmas and the twenty-nine she came here with eighteen months ago?

I get blank, unbelieving looks when I enquire. I have a detailed inventory of her clothes, which I showed Sheila, the Matron a year ago when Mum lost three of her lovely winter suits.

"We'll keep looking around for them, I expect they've been mixed up with someone else's things."

"Everything's got her nametag sewn in."

"Yes, don't worry, they'll turn up," she said encouragingly, renewing her opaque smile. Indeed, when I complain, one item out of the many usually does come back, but never more than one.

Only one bed jacket left in her drawer, the distinctive pink, purple and orange one my friend Yvonne had knitted for her. I wrapped it around her bony shoulders and gave her a hug. I had been worried that she could have deteriorated in the last nine days while Robert, Gwen and I all had holidays. "How have you been, Mum? Has anyone else visited?" She said no, but then admitted that a few of her old friends had popped in.

"I've been given a job, I have to go to a meeting," she said importantly and chattered on in this vein for a while, interspersed with: "They asked me to make a speech."

"Who asked you?"

She looked perplexed, "The girl," she said eventually.

Go along with this, I thought. I'm lost; let her take this wherever she wants to. But she was looking at me as if I was slow on the uptake and was becoming frustrated at my lack of understanding. She gave up, and I stared over her head at a lone woman jogger, circuiting the cemetery below for the third time.

I asked if she'd had her lunch. She was quite definite that she hadn't. I persisted:

"I'm sure you must have had it by now Mum, what did you have?"

"Blue" she said, "It was blue." Then "mutter, world pin, mutter, mutter, blanket, I had his I think."

For the next half an hour she was completely absorbed in moving imaginary things from just in front of her to just at the side. Her lips trying to capture the thoughts speeding through her brain, as if they were ducks in a fairground that were flying past as she aimed her rifle.

I fed her with grapes and macadamia nuts. She stirred uncomfortably on her very raw bottom. The carers told me that she is not allowed out of bed to sit on her chair because sitting would be too painful. Her thin, bare, stiff legs and feet which she hasn't been able to move for at least a year must be hurting too, as she said:

"Take my shoes off, they wash them every so often, help, help, help."

We looked at a few old photographs of a holiday with her sisters, when she was about twenty. She remembered where four of them were taken and even identified two of the men looking admiringly at herself and Lizzie. She looked so vulnerable, so shyly pretty.

There was a noise like an outboard motor starting up, which made me jump and look around. Then I realised it was coming from her digestive system. It got louder and louder and I was starting to get worried, but she just went on with her usual 'helps' and it stopped after a while.

A little later, she told me gravely:

"One of them stood there and said Catrin Williams has won!"

"Won what?"

"Oh I don't know!" she said irritably. "We do this all the time, I say something, and then you say what do you mean? We just can't talk. I can't stand this. Help, help help."

Then she said with a flash of insight. "It's no fun being like this you know."

This self-knowledge really upset me and I was about to hug her, but two carers came in to change her nappy. The room is too small for all of us, so I sat downstairs and chatted to Joan the Nurse on duty.

"Don't worry about her," she said before she bustled away to answer a buzzer, "she doesn't know what's going on."

Oh yes she does Joan. Not all the time, but often enough and anyway how do we *know* what she's thinking? When she retreats into talking gibberish, she still conveys something of the subject of her thoughts.

I can still decipher fragments of what she is trying to say and then every so often she is back to her normal self. Why does everyone here forget that she has DLB, *not Alzheimer's*, so a bad few minutes can be followed immediately by good ones? Ideas obviously do come into her head, but as she starts to communicate them, they crumble and fall away, so that half way through the sentence a dazed look comes over her face as she realises that she has forgotten the idea with which she started out so bravely. All her memories and thoughts are trapped in her faulty circuits, so she can no longer hold meaningful conversations. But does she have meaningful thoughts? *Are her thoughts complete, unlike her sentences?*

Thoughts are so much quicker than the means of communicating them. Is this why she interrupts and tries to speak quickly? Is she trying to get the thought out before it disappears? I'm sure she still has conscious awareness, even if she's lost the means of expressing herself. She knows who she is and recognises and names everyone who visits. She still has personhood. And don't tell me that she doesn't know about her losses, she dreams of being able to walk about and of leading a normal life:

"Tell me when you're going, we can be company for each other, or are we going separate ways?" She said companionably, when I returned.

How could I tell her she wasn't going anywhere? "You live here Mum, in this bed," I said eventually.

"Oh," she laughed. "I keep forgetting that!"

She carried on, weirdly lifting nothing and putting it down near me, insisting that I take more. I've had enough, we're not communicating and feeling selfish and unloving, got up and packed my bag to go. "Bye Mum." She immediately snapped into completely normal mode, looked at me with intelligence, discernment and understanding and wished me a good journey. She still retains the cues, the openers and enders to conversations, which makes it very hard to leave each time.

On the train I read some Longfellow:

*'The leaves of memory seemed to make*
*A mournful rustling in the dark.'*

## WEDNESDAY FEBRUARY 9TH

Mum was pleased to see me; she lay in bed as ever in involuntary confinement. Blotchy face, blank, rheumy eyes, flattened, greasy hair sticking up at the back of her head like an ancient, straggly peacock. She coughed intermittently.

"Would you like to get out of bed to sit in the chair? I'll tell you my latest news about getting into universities to do research then?"

She pulled herself together and agreed, then listened intently to me. I knew that she was following as she gave me sensible advice and was proud and eager to know more about my wonderful retirement party from work.

Her lunch arrived and I fed her dry battered fish, cold chips and mushy peas. Her hands are always cold and rigid now. She can't grip her tea, but eventually managed to balance it between her stiff, unfeeling claws.

185

Robert won't feed her if he visits at mealtimes. He can't bring himself to cross into the uncharted territory of playing mother to his own mother. He talks to her brusquely, disguising any feeling he may have for her, telling her to "Try, you can feed yourself if you try. You're just being lazy!"

I thought back to a conversation we'd had last week. Mike and I had gone to visit him on the way back from a weekend in Tenby. He has lost his job and suddenly announced that he wasn't going to pay his share of the top up fees for Riverside.

"I never liked her anyway."

"Wha . . . a..t?"

Robert was sitting hunched over his coffee, in our Mother's chair, in our Mother's home, well, OK, she had paid the deposit, he *had* been paying the mortgage. "How *can* you say that?" I asked, in shock.

"I always liked Dad best and I can't afford to keep paying for her. I've got no income."

"Well that's not her fault! You're only in your fifties, you can get another job."

He gave me a filthy look. "I'm not going to work again."

"*How* can you keep going on holidays and driving a Porsche if you've got no money?"

"No *income* I said, I'll spend my savings how I want."

"It's only £90 a month each, and I pay the extras."

"She'll have to go into a local authority home."

"We can't move her again, and she'd have to leave Cardiff."

"She doesn't know *where* she is."

"She won't be near Aunt Gwen."

"Well that's tough. I'm not paying for her any longer."

"But she's your Mother, she's 87 and she'll die soon."

"She could go on another ten years, just lying there being waited on."

Like a blast from a fire-hose I switched into blind rage.

"You are the most fucking mean, selfish, cold person I have ever met. She's given you everything she has, you rarely visit her, you've spent all her savings and she *still* loves you! You'll rot in hell!" I screamed, grabbing my bag and storming to the back door. Mike picked up my coat and followed me to the car, where I was trembling with shock and frustration. Wrapping my coat around me and his arms around the coat, he said;

"Alys, let it go. It's not worth it. We'll pay it all, it's not much."

"It's not the amount. It's the fact that it's something we can both do for her."

I realised then that Robert was embarrassed by Mum's failing language skills, it made her less human to him, so it was easier to treat her with this cruel contempt. Easier to pretend she didn't exist. Life has dealt him cruel blows with his ex wife accusing him of abusing his eldest son after he had been awarded their custody. She lied, because she wanted the maintenance and settlement money, just as she had wrested from her first husband for her older children. He has been nasty to everyone since . . . .

"I could do with another pair of tennis shoes," Mum said ruminatively dragging me back to the present, as she finished the last morsel of her jelly and cream and only a stain of pink scum, the carcinogenic food colouring, was left on her plate.

"Did Cerys enjoy her couple of weeks?"

"Where did she go, Mum?" I asked puzzled.

She was flustered, "Oh she stayed with me," she muttered, "Help. I'll pay for my own if I can find my purse. It must be in the bedroom. Cerys came to me for about ten days, she had a lot of fun I think." The last sentence was so quiet; she had obviously lost confidence in its veracity. There was more muttering then, a bit louder, "It was quite a nice meal. Did you get that big parcel?"

Non-committal noises from me.

"It was well wrapped, you should have had it. Did you take two or three mushrooms? I saw that they had gone, they could have made a nice breakfast."

She was clawing at her table. What are you doing Mum?

"I'm helping you pick the blackberries."

## WEDNESDAY FEBRUARY 23RD

I talked to Sheila about why Mum was always in bed, rather than sitting out on her big comfy chair with the raising leg support. "I bought that inflating cushion for her. Different panels inflate every few minutes to keep her bottom moving. Yet I have never seen her sitting on it, or if she is, it's off."

"Don't worry, I'll speak to the girls again," she said comfortingly.

"I've put a notice explaining about it in big writing, above her chair, but even so, I invariably find it lying on the floor left on since the last time I visited."

"Yes, yes, we'll make sure it's used properly." Matron continued. "She hasn't been out of bed for a few weeks because her bottom is too sore. She finds it stressful to be moved out of bed."

"Mmm," what can I say? How can I insist on her sitting out, I'm not here to witness Mum's reluctance? I like Sheila, but feel she must have been on a Management Training course which has taught her to agree with customers to 'empower' them for that moment. But as for following through with action from the discussion, that is obviously not thought necessary.

"How has she been?"

"Oh not so bad, sometimes she understands and we can have a conversation, sometimes not. But she's rather restless at night. She must be having nightmares, if she hasn't had a sleeping pill she often wakes the other residents with her screaming."

Poor Mum, drugged up with sleeping pills to keep her quiet. I asked Matron again why staff can't stay on the same floor for more than a week so that they can establish a rapport with the residents and know their likes and dislikes and weren't always strangers to one another. She sidestepped my question and the phone rang, I trudged back to Mum's room, knowing that nothing will change.

I tried yet again to get her to talk about her relationship with my father.

"How did you know you wanted to marry Daddy, Mum?"

She half smiled, an 'I don't want to discuss this smile,' and carried on fiddling with her blanket. I tried to rephrase the question: "So why *did* you marry him?"

She sighed, and with a resigned, annoyed look said, "Because I was in love, I think."

She stopped and looked surprised as if she hadn't thought about love before.

"So,"

But she had looked away and switched off. I saw that she had gone somewhere else. Her eyes were open, but she wasn't there.

## MONDAY FEBRUARY 28TH

I entered Riverside today with the customary feeling of anguish, guilt and panic, and bounded up the stairs, what would I find?

She looked fogged and bleary; her pale eyes stared dully, blankly at me, with no recognition or welcome. "Hello Mum." I kissed her. "Can I turn off the TV, you're not interested in sea stories are you?" Her eyes swivelled back round towards the noise as if my appearance was just a fleeting distraction.

It was a programme about endangered species in our oceans. We gazed at the screen together, at the fin whale, which swims at 23mph and the leatherback turtle, which is threatened with extinction, because the beaches where it nested are now full of tourists. Apparently they are often found entangled in fishing lines, or they swallow plastic bags, mistaking them for jellyfish. The sea around the coast of north Wales has swarms of the harmless moon jellyfish in its warm waters, but these are normally accompanied by the much bigger species, Lions Mane, which has a powerful sting. The turtles come to these waters to feed and can grow up to nine feet long.

"Didn't you get stung by a jelly fish when you were swimming in Tenby?" She asked.

I was stunned. How did she remember this small incident? A downy feather of memory had floated back from over six years ago?

"Yes, you're right Mum, it was on my neck. I didn't see anything in the water. If it happened again I don't think I'd want to swim in Tenby any more. Can I turn off the TV now, the programme is finishing?"

It was quite a shock to find her speaking to me normally. I thought of the lines by Alexander Pope:

*'Lulled in the countless chambers of the brain*
*Our thoughts are linked by many a hidden chain . . .'*

Recently it's like making conversation with a stranger. Mum's lucidity is more shocking than her confusion, for it is not how I have become accustomed to find her, it is no longer normal. She seems surprised when I come and distracted and uninterested in anything I have to say.

## WEDNESDAY MARCH 2ND

A nurse rang last night to say they had had to restrain Mum with a strait jacket. A *strait jacket*! I was horrified. "But Mum can't move, how can she be a danger to herself or anyone else?"

"She was screaming and fighting the staff violently."

After a sleepless night I came today, but the jacket had gone and she could remember nothing about it.

## WEDNESDAY MARCH 9TH

Mum was quiet and unresponsive. It seemed from her eye movements and perpetual fiddling with the blanket, that she was thinking. Does she think in words or pictures?

The tea trolley had been outside her room for at least twenty minutes. At last it was her turn, and in came Pria with an ugly, heavy white cup of over-sweet tea and two fig biscuits.

"Remember, Mum doesn't eat dried fruit," I said smiling politely as I do *every* time. "She likes 'Rich Tea.' I'll come and change them. What's happened to the tall man with the strange eyes?"

"Gone." Mum said.

"He's gone." Pria agreed and pushed the trolley on down the corridor.

I held the cup to her mouth. The luke-warm grey liquid lay against her lips. I couldn't tell if she was drinking, then I saw it trickling down her neck, dripping onto her chest, onto the shabby, alien nightie.

She and I are so different. Mum has conservative tastes and takes pains with her appearance, I'm the opposite. It's a strange relationship, the one between mothers and daughters. I can't speak for her, but I alternately wanted to please her, annoy her, protect her or shock her. Contradictory emotions bound together by genes and limitless love.

Only Lewis lightens her face and makes her laugh. Now that he's cooking, he visits the residents when his duties in the kitchen are over. As usual, she was at her best for him.

"Shwmae, Sweet pea." He said with his eternal cheerful smile and caring, kind eyes. "Oh Shwmae, Alys fach, didn't see you."

I was sitting, leaning against the wall in the dark rind of the dim light.

Mum thought for a second, "Hello big heart." she replied.

How apt. How does she always manage to think of such appropriate responses?

"Let me have a look at those nails, biting them again have you?" He found her varnish in her messy top drawer and painted her nails.

"Remember when we were stuck in that Hospital last year, waiting for your appointment and I painted your hand and toe nails?" They giggled conspiratorially, like children. He spotted the hard sponge ball I gave her some weeks ago, which she had refused to squeeze for me.

"Ych a fi, I can see your teeth marks again! I'm wanting you *not* to eat the ball. Squeeze only."

She had come alive. Her eyes sparkled, her responses were quick, cheeky and jokey, as they chit chatted about places they would visit when the weather gets warmer. I don't make her laugh, I'm too serious, I try to force her back to how she was, which reminds her that she is getting worse and will never get better. We don't have fun together because I am not accepting her as she is. For these four years of her illness she has striven to retain her dignity, awareness of and participation in the life she knew. I think she has now realised that she will never recover and her old life is receding, becoming indistinct. She is giving up trying to keep track of my life, of anyone's lives, and seems to have faced the fact that it is gone and that she is becoming a different person and moving into a different world.

Lewis dashed off. I tried to tell her what I'd been doing and what was in the news, but she wasn't really listening, she wasn't interested any more. She composed the seam of her mouth into a grotesque fixed grin as if she was pretending to enjoy what I was saying for courtesy's sake. Then her eyes closed as if my news was not only boring, but soporific. I have to accept that she can no longer be the mother who listens to my endless moans and is always supportive and interested in me. The custodian of my family's history, betrayed by her brain, is preoccupied now in her own journey.

We sat, silent. I was full of anguished thoughts about being old and why it has to come to this.

"It's no fun being like this you know," she had said. The only complaint she had ever made about her illness.

# Chapter 21—Travelling by water

Gradually waking in the soft light of the frail winter sun peering meekly through the window. My other life's slowly fading and the terror gradually seeping out of me. Listening to the blood travelling through my head . . . eyes melting into the ceiling . . . circular patterns spinning in the dusty morning light. Spiralling out, swirling, sucking me into its dark vortex. Close my eyes . . . keep them closed . . . a tiny circle's wriggling under my lashes. Blink it away . . . no, shooting round and round . . . trapped in its eddies . . . imprisoned inside a whirlpool . . .

Now I can walk, I can go back home, take a taxi to town to do my Christmas shopping, be independent and private again. When I get up I'll tell them I'm better now. I'll ring Robert, ask him to warm the house and come and fetch me.

* * *

"Do you still have nightmares?" The woman's face is familiar. I know I should answer. Her mouth puckers, slackens and stretches into a smile. What's she telling me? I was going to leave, but I should answer first. Her face is familiar.

I know I should answer.

I'll push my thoughts from my brain to my mouth . . . go out . . . don't jostle in the front of my head. So frightening, this forgetting, things slipping away. It only happens when I'm here. If I let go of my other life, there'll be nothing of me left.

"Do you Mum? You must have been having a nightmare, you were very distressed and restless."

"No," I can't describe my life as a nightmare. I used to feel that heavy darkness around me closing in, when I closed my eyes at night. It was frightening, terrifying in fact, but now I'm not on my own . . . . Who's that beautiful girl?

"Would you like some of this chocolate cake Nana?"

Nice. Sweet, creamy, lightness melting slowly in my mouth. Close my eyes and drift away.

✳    ✳    ✳

*It's first light . . . the last pale stars are pricking the cold sky. I'm back, stumbling along the edge of a rushing river, ghostly boulders and shrubs looming at us out of the gloom. Blasts of fear running up through my body . . . Images of claws and teeth tearing at Arthur's body keep my legs going. What happens to people when they die? Does the soul go to the place it loved the most, like Lady Campbell? The person inside has to go somewhere. Mike says we're like computers and when we die, that's it. I don't believe that. Mother will still be dashing about somewhere, glamorous and vibrant, chatting non-stop while she throws together the unmeasured ingredients for a cake. Gareth will be playing some sort of sport and having a drink with his friends in the bar afterwards. John will be telling jokes and everyone will be laughing. All that energy and life force has to go somewhere . . .*

*Gwen's face is red and stained with tears. "Don't worry, they'll sleep off their big meal before they look for more. They won't catch us now." But a blast of fear is running up through my body . . . if only we could find somewhere safe to cross, somewhere safe to rest . . .*

*The river is wider and calmer here and . . . what have I found here? "Look three canoes, we can go down the river to the sea . . . ."*

*Gwen's paddling Ted. Bill's so powerfully built; his canoe is slicing through the water like a missile.*

*Charlie's shouting to them. "Come back, Bill and Lizzie. Let's stick together."*

*"Uh-huh." He's never much of a conversationalist.*

*This river seems so safe, so timeless, salmon struggling upstream past us . . . ducks, moorhen, swans. That's like Water Rats house in 'Wind in the Willows,' the river lapping on his windowsill. Charlie's smooth, even pull hardly disturbs the shallow, clear water. The sun's pouring down like hot glue, fixing me, warm, relaxed and peaceful, gliding along, with only the creak and drip of the oars to disturb my dreams.*

Everything is bright, close my eyes in the glare and I'm lifting on a current of air.

✳     ✳     ✳

*The night is cloudless and the full moon and thousands of stars light up the river and our camp in an eerie green brightness. The grass felt so soft when I first lay down, it's pressing itself into me. I can't get comfortable. Nothing's moving, just the shimmer of the moon on the calm black river. That's Charlie's voice "Don't you know how it is mate? You find the . . . and bingo!"*

*What did Bill say? Charlie's laughing;*

*"Are you two being disgusting?"*

*"Don't bleat on Catrin, this is men's talk, between buddies. We're feelin' chipper with all this exercise. You girls act like you're royalty."*

*His smile scatters his wrinkles, so his face is fleetingly young again.*

*Bill's sinking back, closing his eyes, his meaty face eloquent in its absolute expressionlessness.*

*Charlie's carrying on; "You're movin forward, then goin back. It's forward and back, forward and back. You're too old to play games."*

*His shining eyes like headlights have pierced straight into my heart. They're boring into me, as if my thoughts and feelings are displayed there in bright lights. Prickling sensations flash along my nerves. Despite my better judgement, I want to be closer to him. I'm astonished; I've never given way to sexual feelings . . . what would everyone else think? I can feel my face becoming pink, a dark shade of rose . . . it must be vivid scarlet by now . . . how embarrassing. I'll lie down again. I can't, I just can't tell him that I'm attracted to him. His strength and practical approach to life make his presence reassuring. Bill is too silent, irascible and if he speaks I have no idea what he's saying, Ted is doddery, but Charlie, I admit I get butterflies and feel quite sick when I think of touching him, being touched by him. I'll pretend to be asleep, I can't say anything, I just can't!*

*He looks so hurt, and what icicles for eyes. Bill's sitting up again . . . their voices are merging with the quiet sounds of the river. My heart's slowly stopping pounding and the strange feelings are receding. Is this lust? I'll never sleep now . . .*

*Waking to a watery grey light peering through the morning mist. Eyes and mouth gummed up; sweat's lying on my skin, cold and oily. I'll wash in the river . . .*

*There's my reflection. Tiny, shivery ripples break me up, stretch me out and sparkle all over me with the sun's rays. A shadow, Charlie? Two shadows.*

*"We haven't walked for days, we'll be stiff and unfit again, let's do some exercises?"*

*Gwen's bright this morning. Lizzie sounds half hearted.*

*"Up and down and side and side . . . Don't sit down yet, we've only just started. I'm surprised at you Lizzie. You've always been lazy Catrin. You wait you two, you'll be lagging behind and aching like mad!"*

*Tomorrow is another day.*

*I love this canoe. Gliding through the watery world. Through flat marshes where the only sounds are of the wind in the tussocks of grass, the clunk of the oars and the dripping as they rise out of the water . . .*

*"Let's dump the canoes and walk now," interrupts my dreams. "We'll cover them with branches in case we come back."*

Feel half asleep, but Charlie's off into a vista of green filled with a mass of silence.

✻     ✻     ✻

"We do your pad, Catrin," an Indian accent. I don't like this one, she's impatient. It's so demeaning, *why* can't they leave me alone . . . go away, so it's quiet and peaceful again.

196

✤    ✤    ✤

*Shooting up, up and down splitting the air apart like the slimmest of arrows, my vapour trail following behind. Their swirling bodies below. They're forming into clear shapes, moving slowly between the trees. That was a gentle landing onto the grass behind Charlie.*

*"You're looking fresh Catrin."*

*They haven't found anywhere to camp for the night, so they're still walking in the dusk. It's so eerily silent except for the muffled padding of feet on the long grass, wet from a sudden squall of icy rain. On and on, leafy branches slapping my face in stinging lashes. Into a pine forest, our feet scrunching and scuffing the needles, the moons rays illuminating the eyes of small animals and the frills of yellow fungi on the broken branches.*

*"What was that?"*

*Gwen's pointing through the shadowy branches. What is it? Oh no, a black winged creature flapping lazily above. It's a bat. One of those from my nightmares. My hearts starting to thump . . . can't control my trembling . . ." They're bats with dark, furry squirrel faces, sharp teeth and huge wings. They used to attack me in the night. I'm petrified of them!"*

*Everyone is looking at me in horror.*

*"Come on, let's move it, stick together and get out of here." Charlie's shepherding us all quickly on.*

*Up the hill, slipping and sliding on the wet grass, boulders and shrubs looming at us out of the gloom. On and on. The breeze tastes of salt, the sea can't be far away . . . we have to leave my nightmare far behind.*

*Plunging into this dense greenery waving and swirling in the wind, I caught a glimpse of three of them gliding above us again in the upward current.*

*A ten-foot high wall of old rhododendron bushes . . ."Shall we crawl under these? We all need sleep." Everyone's nodding . . . the humus carpet under us is so soft . . . .*

*What's woken me? I'm in one of those late dreams, the ones that make me feel exhausted all day. A biting, damp chill is cutting through my blanket. Lizzie is staring into the darkness. I remember this feeling, the still, expectant coldness, the air getting blacker, thicker and swirling menacingly. There's one, a dark shape the other side of the men, just outside our shelter. It's folding its wings and scurrying towards me . . . Help!*

*Bill and Charlie are too quick for it. They're smacking it as hard as they can.*

*Screams, spiteful eyes glowing red in the gloom, bushy tail flicking over its head for protection, it's attacking Bill. Charlie's swinging and stave and squirrel both in forward momentum . . . thud . . . They're finishing it off . . . I feel so sick; my heart has gone quite mad. I'm sweating and shivering. Ted, Lizzie and Gwen look as if they're in the same state.*

*"They're noc..turnal," I can barely speak. The sky is lightening; it's dawn, thank you God. I'm weak from shock and lack of sleep. Charlie's arm's around me, it's burning into me, my skin's sparking to his touch. Streaks of electricity are coursing through me, tingling and leaking down through my body. Glad he can't see my face smarting with confusion.*

*"Relax Catrin, it's over."*

*Wings of dark sweat have spread across his shirt, little rivulets still run down his forehead. He's cupping my elbow with one strong speckled hand, lifting my pack with his other. . His eyes are soft and shining. Be careful, Catrin, don't want to give him any ideas. On we go.*

✳    ✳    ✳

"I'm off on holidays tomorrow Sweet Pea. Can't wait!"

Lewis's face is flushed and sweating.

"Duw, haven't had a holiday for nearly a year. No cookin' for a week! Let me massage your hand. Your nails are too long Catrin, they're diggin in your palm."

"Where?"

"Look here, there's holes there. Have you been to Tenerife?"

"No," I say. But when he's gone I remember I went with Alys, Mike and Cerys. I didn't enjoy it much. It was too hot and Alys and Mike were always out on walks. I got Cerys to go on that boat trip with me, to see the whales. We were so sick and all we saw were waves, it was really frightening. I got a heat rash. No, I didn't like Tenerife much.

✳    ✳    ✳

*Up this last stretch to the coast, there's a tang of salt in the air. What a huge statue of Christ, one arm spread wide looking out at the grey-blue ruffled sea. There's the other in the grass, weathered brown by the rain and wind. A peaceful face, blank, disengaged eyes.*

*"Jesus bids us shine, with a pure, clear light. Like a little candle, burning in the night."*

*Lizzie thinks of a song for everything. All these years of trying to follow Jesus' teachings, ever since I learnt them from Morfydd Jenkins at Sunday school . . .*

*Gwen stares fixedly, checking out our new Sunday-school teachers dress. She sniffs, she can spot cheap material at twenty feet: "That's not silk," she hisses.*

*I haven't much interest in clothes, Miss Jenkins looks friendly and kind and I'm watching Uncle Percy's back, as his fingers press the keys, his shoulders sway and lift and fall. The sound flows out of the organ pipes high above us, pouring down on this big congregation in their Sunday best.*

*The hymn finishes and Lizzie pulls me up and pushes me quickly out of the chapel balcony, down the corridor to the Sunday school room. She goes to the far end to the 'Young Crusaders' group. Gwen will go up after Christmas, but now she's in Miss Jenkins' class with me. We give her our names, and she reads us a story about Jesus going into the desert and being tempted by the Devil. Then a modern story about not being envious or speaking badly about anyone. I dangle my legs on the wooden chair and shoot up my arm every time Miss Jenkins asks us a question. She smiles her special smile at me, where her eyes are soft and gleaming and right then, in that perfect moment, I feel a warm light suffusing me, as if Jesus were shining down, filling me with love and goodness. I remember that moment so clearly and it has stayed with me all my life. When we sang the candle song, I knew that I wanted to shine like a candle, to be clear*

199

*and pure, to love my neighbours and never say bad things about anyone ever again.*

*That was the only time I felt that Jesus was talking to me, nearly eighty years ago and I was such a little girl . . .*

*I've been going to chapel since I was small and have tried to live a Christian life. I've prayed so hard to get better and go home again, but I don't think God concerns himself with individuals. If he did, why are people killed indiscriminately, disinterestedly, even cruelly? I'm not sure now what I believe. Perhaps the Bible is just fiction? I do think that there's a God, but how could he listen to every persons' prayers? That sounds blasphemous . . . I don't know what to think.*

*Dumfries isn't beautiful like Tenby, but it seems familiar, I don't know why. Good, the clouds are clearing . . . the sun's pouring down like pale syrup. The palms are like ostrich feathers waving in the breeze. The tides going out, there are so many bits of boat lying around in the estuary, and bladder wrack like dead fish eggs idling in the rivulets. Is that why the seagulls are swooping about, looking for stranded prey? The men are miles away, following the retreating tide to fish.*

*"Come on Catrin, stop dreaming, we're supposed to be looking for wood and fresh water."*

*"Well have you found any yet Lizzie?"*

*Is that someone shouting? "It's Charlie, Ted and Bill from that boat on the sand flats, they're calling us."*

*"Leave your wood, come here . . . It's a quick way to get to Wales."*

*The stern is covered with barnacles but the masts and furled sails seem intact. Isn't it stuck in the sand? "How are we going to get it floating? And we don't know how to sail."*

*"Stop gasbagging, Bill were a merchant seaman."*

*Bill's rather blank, leathery face is looking towards the sea, up at the sky and out at the tide with an air of abstraction. He's rubbing his hands together with a dry rasp.*

*"Whit a weird bludy thing, the wee boat looks like it wirks. I rekin we've twenty minutes or so to push her off the sand bank, so she refloats onto the tide."*

200

*The tide's here now. Its fresh chill shocking my bare skin. I'm mesmerised by the bubbles breaking over my feet, by the sensuous drawing feeling beneath my soles as the water tugs sand out from beneath them. The seaweed and foam like rancid pea soup rushes away . . . I'm sinking slowly, and I'm disorientated, giddy with the tingling, drawing, sucking sensation.*

*"Move it girls, we've got to get this boat launched."*

*Charlie's broken my trance . . . pull my feet up and those almost orgasmic sensations are draining away.*

*Bill certainly knows what to do, it's like military operation.*

*"Ther ye go my gel."*

*Our boats floating free! The waters over my waist. "Pull me up please."*

*It's amazing, the sails billowing . . . we're skimming forwards against the tide, out to the end of the headland.*

*Now we're away from the protection of the cliffs, the sails are shaking and flapping like wild butterflies . . . the boats rocking, shuddering and swinging about to every shift in the gusty changing wind. I'm desperately sick . . . I hate the sea.*

*How much longer am I going to hang over the side, feeling or being sick. There must be nothing left inside me. Gwen's half waking with the dawn . . . a fountain of sick arching into the air . . . she's always thought she was a good sailor. It's making me feel worse, sliding about with the rocking of the ship. She's shivering, encrusted sick on her cheek and foot. I'm longing for a few seconds of sleep. I'll try to get into my favourite tennis dream . . ."whack, poom, pac, game to me, whack, poom, pac, game to me," in time with the rush of sea under the boat . . .*

"Good morning Mrs Williams. How are you feeling today?"

Who's this? I must be staring blankly.

"It's Doctor Pietrowska, Mrs Williams, I understand you've been unable to keep your food down. Can I see your tongue?"

That stethoscope thing's cold.

"There could be quite a few reasons for your sickness. I won't prescribe anything just yet, let's see how you get on with plenty of fluids and plain food for another 24 hours."

I say nothing though my senses are still sharp. I can hear what he's saying to Matron, she's adamant it's not food poisoning. Have I been ill? The food is flavourless slop anyway, it all tastes the same. Alys keeps asking why I can't go back to proper food, but I never do. I've lost interest in food.

Sleepy heart rate
No feelings.
No body.
I'm unclear about my edges.
Don't know where I stop.
Am I seeping into this bed?
Dissolving away?

✳      ✳      ✳

*Nothing inside me to sick up. I must have lost weight, I feel so weak.*

*Charlie and Bill are trying to get into the lockers.*

*"Gotta smash this padlock, gimme that."*

*They're banging and crashing. "It's off!"*

*"It's like all our birthdays. Biscuits, chocolate, tins and dried food."*

*"Blankets, waterproofs, water, ropes, fishing gear, a hatchet, first aid kit . . . what a haul."*

*Charlie and Bill are very quiet . . . they're downing a bottle of whisky for breakfast.*

✳      ✳      ✳

"Breakfast Catrin."

I'll open my eyes a crack. The light's glinting on the girls' gleaming dentistry . . . she's la la'ing a strange tune.

"Shush now Priti." This one has lovely hair, I must say, thick, black, a tapering rope down her back. Surely that diamond stud in her nose is painful?

"We are eating the breakfast now?" What a calm, melodious voice.

"Tea?"

Its cool, thick and too sweet, so's the porridge. I'll open and close my mouth . . . . must focus on this noisy world.

That was a lick and promise with a flannel . . . Now I'm ready, for what? I can feel her scanning my brain to see if I'm here. "Thank-you." Satisfied, she's picking up the bowl, leaving me to my thoughts.

※　　　※　　　※

*"We've hit a shoal, we've hit a shoal!" I was beginning to think that there weren't any fish in this sea. With the breeze licking the surface . . . it seems alive*

*"Careful."*

*The lines and net are full . . . the deck's a frenzied floating slaughterhouse. Gulls in ravening circles . . . Slithering fish everywhere, flapping and jerking, eyes staring in terror, gulping the air they can't breathe, twisting and writhing. I feel nauseous.*

*Everyone seems to be looking greedily, rapaciously at the haul. Why do I feel so squeamish about them dying? I never used to worry about things like that . . .*

※　　　※　　　※

*Tom's helping Fred, to bring in the calves and hold them still, while Daddy shoots the bolt into their brains. Their little legs buckle and they crumple down and twitch on the bloody floor.*

*Lizzie looks up from her book and I shoot Teddy with the piece of wood that looks like a gun. Bang, teddy falls into the straw. I shoot Gwen. 'Bang.' She looks at me witheringly.*

*"Why can't I help Daddy?" She says again.*

*"You're dead." I say.*

*"No, I'm not."*

*"Yes you are, I shot you. Lie down."*

*She grabs my gun and shoots me in the head, like the calf.*

*"Well you missed me and now I've shot you!"*

203

*There's no point arguing, she always gets her own way, and I want to play with her more than she wants to play with me: so I fall back into the straw and we look down from the hayloft to see the next calf being led in.*

*Life and then death were part of our lives. The farm animals being taken into the slaughterhouse in the centre of the farmyard was a spectator sport. Sometimes I loved a calf, piglet or chicken, gave them names and petted them as if they were my babies. It was a shock that time I realised that I wasn't eating pork, but Winnie. But it didn't make me a vegetarian like Cerys, I just didn't ask whom I was eating. When I got older, watching animals die didn't seem fun at all.*

*Fish dying is a different matter; they're not supposed to feel. I think those did. I'm glad Cerys isn't here; she would have been throwing them all back.*

*The time on this ship passes so slowly. The weather is unpredictable, the cold penetrates our bones and my hands are so raw, the wet ropes have levered off chunks of skin. They feel too sore to use.*

"Come on Catrin, hold your cup, like this, you're not trying."

My hands won't grip; they're stiff and hurt, my bottom's on fire from all this sitting.

"Open your mouth."

Open obediently, open, close, chew and swallow. What am I eating? My senses have silted up; nothing has smell or taste . . . everything grey. I don't want this tea. "Enough, go away!"

"What you say Catrin? Come; open your mouth for tea. You don't want? I take."

"What is she writing on that piece of paper? Where's Gwen, or Alys or Robert? I haven't seen them for weeks. No visitors, no fruit and chocolates.

My mind's drifting out of control. Thoughts flap in my mind like chaotic butterflies, words flit past like birds . . . try to capture them before they disappear . . . speak them, before they evaporate like snowflakes on warm ground.

In a harness.

"You don't want to stay there."

The fat, grinning white-overalled woman swings me round.

"I'm very well trained, don't you worry."

"Help help," that rubber band going round my arm again and a needle jabbing underneath.

"Stop, stop, that's enough . . . You took blood yesterday."

"And the day before."

The sweating, flabby face is laughing.

"No shouting if you please. I'm very well trained for this."

I'm trying to be serene and patient, but I want to get to Tenby. It's not a dream; they're fragmentary and fuzzy and fade away when I wake up. My journey is real, vividly, palpably real. It must be . . . Sometimes, when I'm basking in the breeze above, I want to shout, "I'm not there you know, I'm here." And see them look upwards, startled. But perhaps they'd be able to stop me going and I can't have that.

*'Beareth all things, believeth all things, hopeth all things, endureth all things.'*

St Paul 1 Corinthians 13.7

# Chapter 22—'I can't do it all!' 2005

## WEDNESDAY MARCH 16TH

*A*fter my brisk walk from the station, I arrive hot and breathing deeply. Today, on pressing the buzzer and opening the released door, the stink of failing bodies hit me. Of full nappies, damp laundry, sour flesh and cheap, over-cooked food, swirled into a heavy, cloying mixture, which filled my head, stuck to my hair and clung to my clothes. Riverside is usually relatively stink free, but not today. It was so immediately the last home for desperately frightened, anaesthetised dependents.

I ran upstairs, calling a greeting to the nurses at their station as I passed. Into Mum's room at the top of the first flight. A shrivelled, gaunt, skinny shape, closed eyes sunk into their sockets, mouth hanging open in sleep or vacancy, barely dented the bed she rarely escapes from. She seemed to have diminished, collapsed, gone to dust from within. A desiccated figure, mimicking life.

"Mum, Mum," I called, "Hello, it's me."

Her eyes flickered open, blank and expressionless, but she said triumphantly, "I won, I won!"

On closer questioning she said she had been:

"Praying for the family in chapel, we can be taken, help help, I don't want to throw my life away, do I? Help! I go to Chapel all the time and when I get home and change, I'm tired out. Help, help."

At some angles her face is smooth and beautiful. Mum's appearance used to be so important to her. I put on her makeup and told her she looked pretty. It's hard to put it on for others, especially when they can't purse their lips.

Peggy the powdered, red-lipsticked, plumped up cushion-on-legs pensioner, who comes in every week to organise activities for the resident's, popped in. "Hello Catrin." She shouted at the skeleton in the bed, then looking at me: "Poor old thing, shame isn't it?"

Mum grimaced graciously, ignoring the aside which she must have heard, and said, "I haven't seen you for a while."

Peggy smiled pityingly at me, "I always come in to see her, *every time!*"

Then her face crumpled and a tear trickled from her pouched eyes and over the lapped folds of the pendulous mauve sacs, accentuated by an erratic black line, and congregated in a small black pool on her powdered chin.

"My husband died suddenly, five weeks ago and I've been so busy sorting out our affairs. A terrible shock," she said. "But I'm back to help the ladies again now."

So Mum was right, I thought as Peggy exited, heading for the lounge.

Ten minutes later and there was some hoarse cawing, just recognisable as the resident's unaccompanied hymn singing.

We were talking, or rather, Mum was and I was filling in the dips and hollows of her monologue with platitudes or grunts of agreement, when her eyes slid around me.

"Help, help, hello."

A male voice said; "Shwmae, Sweetpea. Hi Alys," and Lewis bustled in, his cooks apron over his baggy black and white squared trousers and white polo shirt.

"Hi," I said back, smiling happily. Mum beamed with excitement. We cheerfully discussed taking her out when the weather was better, but as she has rarely been out of bed for the last year, how could she sit in a wheel chair with those legs like two broom handles refusing to bend and her bottom an open wound? She was disorientated and embarrassed at what she had become when we pushed her around the Cardiff docks last summer, how could she cope nearly a year later, having not left her bedroom and bed for so long.

"Duw, we have a lot of fun when we go out in the minibus don't we?" He giggled.

Mum nodded and laughed and gave him one of her looks, but he'd already disappeared to respond to an insistent buzzer.

I told her about meeting an old school friend, whose mother is in a Home in the Gwent valleys, where we used to live. "She is lucky, she can still walk about," I said.

"I can walk about; I hope you've noticed," is the immediate response.

"Where?"

"I've been walking a lot, to Wales. I had two or three goes at having kisses from sponge people. She had a big scotch on her."

She dribbled. I'd been feeding her grapes and she tried to spit a skin out into the air. It got as far as hanging on her bottom lip. I removed it.

"You're not easy to talk to," she said suddenly indignant.

"Me?" I asked in surprise. It was true, she hadn't stopped talking since I arrived. She hadn't been interested to hear anything I had to say, so I'd encouraged her chattering, as the alternative of 'Help' was so irritating.

"Well don't expect me to do any more, I've done my bit!"

Is she alluding to the fact that she had been conversing with me on a range of different subjects for the whole of my visit and she had now had enough? She continued her endless wrecked monologue, her mind scuttling around like a crab from corner to corner:

"I'm looking forward to my Xmas dinner. Who's coming for Xmas this year?"

It's March, so I changed the subject. "Wales are playing Scotland at the weekend."

Quick as a flash she showed that she knew about the match.

"Yes away, on Saturday. I've got my head down on my feet, help, help. Have you got any knitting needles suitable for me?"

She looked at her hands as if it were she who was knitting, not me.

Her tepid afternoon tea arrived. I found a straw and pushed it into her mouth, "Come on Mum, suck."

"I can't do it all," she complained. Nothing was going up the straw.

"Suck Mum, suck. Do you want me to tell you about anything?"

"No, I don't think so."

She stared ahead like an unblinking owl. I tried to get her to sip her tea, as the straw was a failure. Why do I feel so helpless? I have watched her gradually deteriorating, gradually slipping away from me.

"Her bottom is too sore for her to sit out of bed."

"She didn't want any lunch."

"She made a fuss about getting in the wheelchair."

"She didn't want her hair washed this week."

"Your mother shouts, fights and scratches."

"Look what your Mother do!"

A brown arm with a deep scratch. How do I know what goes on when I'm not there? I can't accuse the nice, cheerful carers and nurses of neglect or malice, but I see Mum's horribly bruised legs and the nasty bruises she often has on her neck and face. Are they hitting her, or is it because her skin's so thin?

Mum lives in a world of shifting shapes where the real and the imaginary seem to blur into one another. Why don't Nursing Homes try to keep their clients mentally and physically active? Stimulating them in any way is not what homes do. Well not any I've been able to find anyway. And of course so many have closed, why should they offer more than they have to, there are certainly plenty of customers. And there is always the threat:

"We haven't put your fees up much this time. We're having to ask families who can't afford our fees to take their relatives away."

The home is a place where people go to die, and speeding up the process makes economic sense as they can charge more for the next round of inmates, I thought cynically.

Robert, despite his complaints has continued to pay a share of the fees.

## THURSDAY APRIL 14TH

Mum was lying quietly when I arrived. How much more gaunt and skeletal can she get? Her skin is waxy and blotchy, her lips thinner and nose sharper. She seems to have retreated even further below her surface. When I ask if she is in pain, she always says "No," and never complains, never says anything self pitying. She seems to have gone to another place, from which she feels nothing and our voices and concerns are faint and insignificant.

"Hello Mum, how are you?" No answer, she looked at me blankly, then at last,

"Help, help!"

The noise in the corridor behind me increased as two carers shouted at a deaf resident going into the toilet opposite and a nurse with a drugs trolley shouted at the handy man just passing. Mum looked confused, all these noises so close must be scrambling her brain. She has lost her judgement of distances and spatial awareness and cannot filter out the hubbub to concentrate on me. She resembled a disorientated animal caught in the headlights, the sounds must have been reverberating around, bruising and blanking out her thoughts, so she didn't know what to respond to. It must be so tiring living in this noisy room.

Her nightdress was gaping open at the neck, she felt cold. I found a bed jacket and managed to get it on her, but she is so thin, bony, stiff and difficult to move. She started crying. "Isn't that warmer Mum?"

"No! Help, help, help."

I rubbed her arms and shoulders, her face was set in agony, she cried help repeatedly. I tried to give her a drink, but she wouldn't open her mouth, it was clamped tightly shut. In came Jean the nurse with a plastic syringe,

"I got her to drink some of her apple juice with this earlier."

She filled it and shouting; "You won't be able to gossip with your daughter if your mouth is dry," managed to squirt in three mouthfuls of the drink.

When she had gone, I offered her some of the scone that I had brought, but she wouldn't try it, wouldn't or couldn't unclamp her teeth.

"Do you feel ill Mum?"

"No, why should I?"

How do you feel then? But she didn't answer, just repeated and repeated, "help." She wouldn't open her eyes and had clenched her cold, stiff hands in front of her face. Her hair can't get much worse; it's dry, straight, stiff and filthy. She is so frail and still has an open wound on her bottom, so that presumably she can't have a bath or sit in a chair for her hair to be set or permed.

"Are you talking to me?" I asked desperately.

"Yes of course I am, help help. Sea sick, help, help."

"What are you thinking?"

'I don't know, I'm going down hill, I can't do it all. I firm bits of fur. The help, help incident belongs to the green hair."

A carer came in and said that she wouldn't eat any lunch or supper, so I nagged her into eating some mashed banana, though having agreed, her mouth was clamped shut when I tried to force it in. Then she launched into an incomprehensible jumble of words and helps during which I managed to squeeze in a few spoonfuls of banana and even a grape.

She managed to take in a few sips of tea, though most trickled down her chin onto the waiting saucer. I gazed out of the window at the bleak scene of untended graves below.

## WEDNESDAY MAY 4TH

Mum endlessly lifted and weakly pulled at either her sheet or blanket, with her deformed, blue veined claws. Pull, lift, lift, pull, with all the concentration of a craftsman, marking out the proportions to create a masterpiece, the whole four hours of my visit.

Two of her distant cousins arrived with chocolates and a yellow begonia. She seemed to recognize them, but was unable to utter any sensible sentences, so I chatted to them for a while. Mum sat quietly, a strained grimace representing a smile, her tongue moving inside her mouth. Winifred, conscious that she was being excluded, asked, "How is Gwen, Catrin, we haven't seen her for a while?"

The reason for the tongue action became obvious as her top plate fell as she opened her mouth. I hunted in vain in the bathroom and through all her drawers for her denture adhesive, and then went downstairs to ask the duty nurse where it was and why the dentist *still* hadn't been in to see her. Gum shrinkage and disease have loosened her bottom teeth and made her top plate far too big.

Mum was unable to communicate other than tell me my name. After three weeks, her dentures are still not back from being relined. Her thin, greasy hair was stuck to her scalp and her face drained of expression. She was placid and faraway.

Our conversations are going in smaller and smaller wheels. What can I say to her? She has been institutionalised for so long, she has little to say to me and only shows interest in talk about her grandson. I told her everything I could think of relating to him. She concentrated on my face, her eyes shining, but then dulling as I moved onto other topics.

Has she exhausted herself trying to keep up the appearance of leading a normal life? There were none of the "I went to Church yesterday," or "I've just been out for a walk," type remarks today. Perhaps the dull life she leads is redemptive. Perhaps reducing life to a few simple choices enables one to think more deeply, go onto a higher plane, so that day-to-day life becomes trivial. What *is* she thinking?

It was a sweltering day, the room was hot and airless, I stripped to my tee shirt and rolled up my trousers yet her skin was cold and clammy. Her bottom is apparently too sore for me to take her outside to the cheerless 'garden'.

"You used to make me wear a liberty bodice on hot days like this, and say: 'Cast not a clout til May is out.' Do you remember Mum?"

Cheered by her slight nod I reminisced.

"On sunny Sundays like today, you'd get out your Peak Freen biscuit tin, fill it full of sandwiches and Dad would drive us off to Southerndown. Do you remember Mum? We always managed to get into the long, narrow grassy car park. It's tiny when you see it now, people park on the slopes of the Dunraven Estate, where the sheep used to graze behind signs saying: 'Private, Keep Out,' and 'Danger.'"

No response, but I plunged on:

"We'd pick our way over those huge pebbles, onto the sandy beach, carrying your deckchair, our buckets and spades, the cricket bat and of course the food. If the tide was in, we'd sit on the rocks, people watching and listening to the sea slapping the rocks and sucking back the sand, until the waves receded. Sometimes a steamer would pass and we'd collect glistening shells and have winkle races until there was enough sand to play on."

Her eyes were closed, have I bored her to sleep? I sat regretting things unsaid and my inability to prevent her increasing helplessness, for the rest of my visit. Both she and I have always thought that there was a way back. Which one of us realised first that there wasn't? We've kept up the cheerful pretence for so long that she could get better; that her legs, which have no movement, could one day be normal.

"You should clear out her wardrobe. I tidy it every week, but everything's jammed in. She's never going to wear some of those clothes again." Gwen has nagged me repeatedly, pulling her mouth into a jag of disapproval. But I couldn't and can't. She might improve. Do I believe in miracles?

"Throw money at it, there must be a way to keep her mobile," Mike had said.

But by the time she had recovered from the Olanzapine I should have known really that it was too late and the frantic bursts of activity to get her a particular drug, an appointment with a consultant or physiotherapist, a link with a day centre or better place to live, were all hopeless and ended in tears and frustration.

## WEDNESDAY JUNE 15TH

Aunt Gwen, Robert and I all turned up together. It was too much for Mum, who was actually sitting out. She smiled at me and said "Hello. Do you . . ." Then her mouth stopped moving as if it were frozen solid, beached on a multiple memory track, on something she couldn't express. Her top plate still wasn't back. I asked yet again for the dentist to be telephoned.

The thin sheet slipped away from her legs, they are two twisted blue broom handles, her toes curled under, forever on points as if she had been a ballet dancer. How can blood circulate around these muscle-less, immovable, hard sticks?

I felt uncomfortable with all of us there, everyone trying to include Mum in the conversation, but rarely waiting for her to finish her contributions. She, alive to the dangers of social exclusion, piped up with helps and other incomprehensible phrases, but we were too impatient. We wanted to exchange news and she was fit only to receive our gracious bounty, as we shoved grapes, chocolates and drinks into her. She can't really suck any more, her top lip recedes back from the bottom, with no teeth to hold it out, her tea and orange juice run down her chin, she struggled for a few sips then gave up.

Her concentration came and went. "Who's that you're with, I don't know him," she indicated Robert, who was rather affronted; he doesn't need much excuse not to visit. "You don't look like my son. Would you like to take my skirt off? Help, help. Well. I'll have to go to the toilet."

Did she want us to leave while she filled her nappy, did she want the carers? The moment passed.

I tried to cut her nails, but she cried out that I was hurting her again. Big, brown chunks of nail flew into the air, "Ow, Ow!" she said. I had uncurl her fingers to get at each nail, perhaps that's the thing that hurts?

"If the ham's no good, what are we going to do?" she asked Robert. Then plunged into a long monologue ending; "I never did like the sea, help, help."

## WEDNESDAY JULY 20TH

All the excess flesh of Mum's face has wasted away to leave grey lunar hollows like the dead landscape of the moon. What is going on behind this mask? I smile, there is no reaction from her. We sat, still and silent, absorbed in our own thoughts. Mine, that I am made of this same decaying matter and am moving towards this same end.

Lewis came up the stairs, back from fetching people from hospital. Both Mum and I brightened at the sight of his rubbery face with its usual mist of sweat, topped by slicked back black hair sticking closely to its owner.

"Can I get you a cup of tea, Alys fach?"

I felt a surge of warmth, after my three and a half hour drive; there was nothing I wanted more. I turned from the window, which

I was struggling to open wide enough for a draft to flow into the stuffy room.

"Oh, yes please Lewis, but aren't you too busy?"

"Ner, and I'll do that Alys. How are you cariad?"

Mum glowed.

We tried to change places in the foot of space at the bottom of the bed, his tubby tummy jammed me against the wall.

"Duw, duw, you're awful tall aren't you Alys. You're a tall girl too aren't you Catrin?"

Mum giggled and almost preened, then with a heave we got past one another and he wrenched at the window.

"How's Mark?" I asked

"OK, we're off to Blackpool in three weeks, Mark's ever so fond of Blackpool. Can't wait. Four days holiday."

Brute strength tamed the window and he bustled off to do more good works after a few more jokey comments to Mum. I love that man.

## FRIDAY SEPTEMBER 23RD

Still no top denture of course and the bottom ones are exposed to the bottom of their roots, like rotting mushrooms on long brown stalks. As she deteriorates and becomes a travesty of what she once was, her appearance is upsetting, even for me, who loves her so much. Her occasional desperate attempts to appear and behave as she used to, even more poignant.

Always in bed, though I ask every time if she can get up. The pressure cushion was on and lying twisted under a leg of the chair.

"Hello Mum."

"You haven't got a mother," she said. "I haven't seen you for three months."

"Two weeks," I corrected her. I asked her about a friend of mine who said he had called to see her when he came to Cardiff for a rugby match.

"That's right, he did come and see me, I think it was after the match."

I was shocked by this memory, she doesn't remember any of her family visiting ten minutes after we have left.

"Hello!" she bellowed in the direction of the door.

"There's no-one there Mum." Unfazed, she carried on.

"Have you had any news from this place? I think we're going to lose our jobs, that's going to come soon."

We lapsed into silence. I felt as cold and empty as her vacant, faded eyes. I thought about the school reunion I went to last week, the first one since the people in my year had left at either 16 or 18.

"How's your beautiful, clever, sophisticated mother? She was the most stylish, poised, cosmopolitan woman I knew." Gwyneth had said.

Clever? Stylish? My brain had reeled.

"Yes, remember those wonderful parties she organized for your birthdays?" Carol asked. "All those delicious cakes and games I'd never played before. She was so creative, a brilliant party giver." Helen nodded in agreement.

What? I was pole-axed. These women I had not seen since we were girls had seen my mother entirely differently from me. Had she really been like that and the later mother replaced my earlier memories? I looked at my watch:

"I've gotta go and catch my train now Mum."

"Wait for me then, have you got me a ticket? Don't go without me, take my hand and pull me up. I don't want to go alone, we can go together."

"But Mum, you live here," I said gently.

She looked searchingly at me, the terrible shock of self awareness and despair in her eyes, as yet again she realised that her visitors can come and go, see friends and family, go to restaurants and shops, while she has to lie here trapped in her stiff immobile body.

"Shall I put the TV on for you Mum?" She nodded, her face a bitter, sunken, disappointed mask. I hugged and kissed her. "I love you, can't you smile for me?" I begged as I moved towards the door. Her eyes were cold and defeated; her down turned mouth was set and reproachful.

What can I DO Mum, I thought for the thousandth time. If I visit and talk about things she can't do I feel guilty, if I don't tell her I am conscience stricken. Whatever I do I feel that I am at fault, that I could have, should have, should look after her? Should? CAN'T!

I half ran the 2 miles to the station, because I CAN!

# Chapter 23—Still Sailing

*T*he gulls shrieking travesty of a morning chorus woke me. Landing on the mast, malevolent yellow eyes and cruel beaks full of squirming life, or rotting dead. I'm wet. That thick lid of sullen grey cloud keeps discharging stinging showers . . . fat, heavy drops making bullet holes in the sea and battering our skulls.

"It'll brighten up soon," Lizzies trying to be comforting.

I must have dropped off again . . . the winds stronger . . . surrounded by tossing waves . . . foam and cold droplets of sparkling flying spray.

Charlie's shouting above the wind. Can hardly see him through the curtains of drizzle.

"Bill says to lash ourselves to the boat."

The wind's worse, it's a gale, whipping the waves into foamy peaks . . . higher and higher. Help, the swell's rolling the boat . . . pitching everywhere. Where's the rope? Help, are we going over? That was Lizzie's scream. She's gone . . .

"Lizzie, Lizzie!" She's not a good swimmer. She'll drown. Deep breath Catrin . . . into the icy darkness. Kick, kick. Ten-foot high waves . . . Dive through them like Gwen taught me. Sucked into the trough . . . lifting . . . battering me back. Can't stop swallowing and coughing . . . salty, freezing . . . being swept further and further away from our boat, where is she?

Mustn't panic; keep kicking, kick, kick, kick. Keep floating. Into the wave . . . there she is, under the water, hair fanning out, limbs moving feebly. She's going into the under-tow . . . I've got her hair. "It's Catrin, float, Lizzie, relax and float." Hand under her chin; I've got her, kick, kick . . . numb . . . where's the boat?

Gasping huge breaths . . . bitterly cold water seeping like death into my eyes, nose, mouth . . . Heart's bursting . . . Choking . . . Lungs *full of water. Kick legs kick, don't seize up . . . starting to black out, is this the end? There's the boat, oh thank you God.*

*"Hold on Catrin, hold on."*

*I must open my eyes . . . Bill is pressing the water out of Lizzie. Chattering teeth, can't speak, I saved Lizzie, I saved Lizzie! We're safe. Freezing cold, exhausted, but safe. A blanket round me, Charlie gently drying my face and hair.*

*"You daft girl, you could have drowned!"*

*"I didn't think." Eyes meet and everything around us retreats.*

*"You know," he sighs, as if whatever he was going to say, he'd prefer not to . . .*

*"That was incredibly brave, Catrin, I didn't know you could swim so well." Gwen looks really shocked.*

*Can't feel my lower half or my arms, but the intense cold seems to have cleared my brain.*

*"You know the line; 'A ring now joins a cross' . . . what if the ring was the rim of the cauldron, you know, like the circle around the cross? Then if a person held the ring and cross, 'holds and holds again,' would this be the same as immersing in the cauldron? Would it give them eternal youth?"*

*"Mm, that's possible, that's clever Catrin. Eternal youth?" Her eyes gleam for a second. "If we ever get to Wales."*

*I'm so stiff and freezing, but proud. There's gratitude and love in Lizzie's eyes . . . the winds dying down at last . . . clouds joining up into one long crease as the hazy sun fills the horizon.*

✳     ✳     ✳

"I saved you," I say happily.

She looks at me uncomprehendingly, looks at Gwen, to see if she understands.

"You were drowning." I try to tell her, but some other words come out . . . She's not wet, her hair has been set and she's wearing a turquoise jacket with matching earrings. Her manicured hands stroking my arm. Drag yourself back from the boat . . . try and smile . . . concentrate on what they are saying.

"You did remember I was coming down to stay, didn't you?"

218

"Of course."

"I've brought you these."

That's a big expensive looking flower arrangement. It's very kind of her, and chocolates too.

"Are you still on your mushy food diet?" Gwen looks anxious. "Because we've brought you grapes and cakes. I'll go and speak to the nurse."

Better than raw fish and dry biscuits, I'm trying to say.

"Why are you shouting help?"

✲      ✲      ✲

"How's my girl today?"

I feel as if I'm hundreds of miles away . . . well I am . . . I was.

"You been watching yor telly?"

His fat, splayed fingers expertly smoothing my bed covers. His smile cheers me up. "Busy are you?"

He's not answering, but his eyes are spyholes. He wants to complain about something, perhaps being put upon, but he's checking himself, his eyes are clouding and he's organising his features into a less vulnerable expression.

"Always busy, you know me Catrin fach, always runnin'."

There's that insistent scream of a bleeper: "Just comin', I'll see you later, when I get off. Hwyl, Sweet pea."

"Bye." I used to talk to him a lot. He'd tell me about his job 'in the print.'

"Wasn't my sorta job, a friend got it for me, good money though."

I've told him about my life in the past . . . never talked so much . . . he asked so many questions: "Tell me again about your big house on the hill and your shop down the bottom?"

I described the two acres of ground, the vegetable garden, the soft fruit, orchard, the chicken and geese paddocks, taking the bus down the valley to play tennis, and him gently asking questions all the time.

"Am I talking rubbish?" I'd ask.

"He'd giggle, so I was never sure how much he'd understood.

It's quiet; I'll close my eyes and hope to go back to the boat . . .
A squirrel as tall as the door walks in, with a shiny smiley face. I'll
try not to be frightened, "Can you sit over there?" Her full, red lips
are parting . . . out comes a squishsome, sucky tongue.
"I'll just give your table a wipe."
Slurp, slurp, my chocolates and biscuits disappear.
"Just a lick and a promise today."
With a swish of her tail she's off.

✳       ✳       ✳

I've no idea of the date, it doesn't seem to matter. I'm not tested
any more: 'What's the date today? Who's the Prime Minister? Where
do you live?' Doctors have given up on me, I'm like the old rotting
things the tide leaves on Tenby beaches. Memories swirl through
me like a blizzard. Events, colours, scents, voices, warm summers,
evenings by the fire. I can see my family and friends; Fathers calm
face and tender eyes. He lifts me up onto his shoulders and we go to
the farmyard to feed the pigs and chickens.

Those voices, that's not Father, no it's outside my room. They've
pushed themselves into my head, driving away my thoughts, I can't
block them out. Why don't I get better, so I can leave this place and
go back to my warm, comfortable home? How long I've been here?
I must ask Alys, time goes so quickly. I seem to have lost interest
in Alys and Robert's lives, though they *were* more important to me
than anything. They're not as real as my other life. I never thought I
wouldn't be interested in my children. That somewhere where they
don't exist, would be more pleasing. Well, that's the way it is, the
world without them is more satisfying, more meaningful to me.

The need to leave this place is growing and growing, so it fills
my entire mind and there's no room for anything else. Visitors used
to be remissions from the tedium of the day. Now they distract me
and keep me where I don't want to be. They want me to listen, and
respond. I've always tried to be a good listener and not talk about
myself, but listening can be quite boring sometimes and I find them
irritating now. I try and tell the staff things and make jokes but
they either don't speak good English, or shout platitudes and rush
off. We've no common interests and they don't have time for me.

My mind melts into the room and I can sense people's thoughts, their feelings become mine, swimming around me like schools of colourful fish. But I can't tell them what I know, words which don't belong to me come out when I speak. "Am I talking rubbish again?" I ask and I can see by their faces that I am. They come from their busy lives with their gifts, but can't cope with being here. I can't entertain them, so I can see that after a very short time they want to go. There is nothing left to tell me and I have nothing to say. They make me feel like a leper, an untouchable, with no life outside this room. Boredom sets in and they want to flee from their guilt and what I am now, here. Does anyone stay special when they're old?

✻    ✻    ✻

Alys keeps talking, she's so serious. What's Crones? She's disturbing me. I don't want to listen. We must be nearly at the Welsh coast.

"Cerys has been told it's inherited, but no-ones had it in our family in the past, have they Mum?"

The past, why's she worrying about the past? She's said to *me* so often: "Nothing stays the same Mum."

The past. So many people and places, all gone. Our farm . . . the lead-paned windows, the flag stoned floor in the dark kitchen, the farmyard and paddocks. The autumn days in the orchard with the rich, sweet smell of apples. Mother cooking an apple tart in her ancient electric cooker, or a cake for tea, just the same as Alys makes now. Father's gentle smile and kind, bright eyes, everything's still in my head. Those memories I've carried inside me all through my life.

"Cerys is taking massive doses of steroids, they supposed to make you fat, but as she's like a walking skeleton."

"Mmm." Must keep moving my lips, perhaps the words will come? Alys loses patience when I don't talk. Shall I tell her about my busy life? Can I put thoughts into her mind, by thinking them hard? Alys, I'm on a boat with your aunts and three men . . . can you see the sea all around? She's staring at me, as if she's mesmerised . . . Alys, I saved Lizzie from drowning . . . no, she's not understanding.

I'm tired of trying to communicate, words coming out jumbled and twisted and the blank looks, uncertain expressions.

I'll close my eyes; leave Alys's forlorn face. Why doesn't she wear makeup? She'd look so much better if she did. Close my eyes tightly . . . bury myself deeper and deeper into my mind, until I hear nothing. When they go away, I do too . . .

*"Are you free tomorrow? Could you possibly spare the time to play in a county match? A player has gone down with food poisoning."* The South Wales tennis captain, sounds stressed, begging . . .

*"Well, what time is it? I may be able to fit it in . . ."*

✳     ✳     ✳

*"A brilliant performance Catrin, you inspired the whole team! We've never beaten Kent before. You certainly made Virginia Wade look ordinary."*

*"Thank-you, you're very kind, but I must rush. I could do with a cup of tea before I go?"*

Someone's laughing?

"Right on cue, Mum. I had to wait ages, and then Lewis came along and made it for us. We can eat the éclairs I brought, with a nice hot cup."

What's Alys doing here? She wasn't playing. I can't get her out of my head; she's there, cramming the room with her words. Talking, always talking, words stream everywhere.

"Half a sugar, or have you got used to two?"

My stiff arms won't move. Can't hold my cup. They're stuck in space, my hands clenched so my nails hurt my palms.

✳     ✳     ✳

*"Would you want me to look after you in Wales?" His voice is so gentle. "Like live together?"*

*I'm shocked, can't read the expression on his calm face. He's so close, I can see the patterns of tiny capillaries in his eyes. So close, breathe out and our molecules of air dance together. My heart's hammering, the wind's lightly stroking my hair. Breathe deeply, slowly, breathe in the cool clear air, be calm. Why am I feeling like this? Is it*

222

*constantly being together on this boat? Embarrassed . . . can't look at him, look at the heavy, slug coloured sky.*

*He's touching my hand, so gently. Lizzie's pulling her blanket over her head, like Gwen's done, and leaning back against the side of the boat. I can't hold his hand, I'll give it back, like something I've briefly borrowed. I want to say, "Yes," but out comes, "Of course you never knew Gareth." As if it were a misjudgement on Gareth's part to have died before he met Charlie. As if I'd need his posthumous opinion on whether living with a man not interested in sport could ever work.*

*"I dodon't know," Trail my hand in the sighing, shushing sea below.*

*"OK," His voice is casual, but I know he's hurt or angry, he exhaled a sigh and his eyes darkened. "Well no worries, you're loss. Don't want to follow your heart eh?"*

*He's going to the other end of the boat, beads of water shining on his head like diamonds, as the sun briefly appears.*

*Did Lizzie or Gwen hear any of this? They haven't moved, they must be dozing. I'm being a fool to myself.*

*The afternoon is merging into night and we're sailing into a rolling mist, the only sounds, the creaking of the boat and the occasional voice, reverberating back at us from the curdled air.*

*The fog's starting to clear and it's raining, the whistling wind blasting sheets of rain across the inky sea. Pull my waterproof closer, cold droplets down my neck.*

*Why do I care so much about what my sisters think of me? Are they thinking anything? The raindrops prick my skin, puncture my eyes, I weep with the sky for the thoughts I've never named, but which lurk in the recesses of my brain. What did they think when Gareth started drinking, when we had no money . . . when I had to take over the shop?*

*Dredge up those unwanted thoughts that cripple me, torture me, imprison me. Dig them out of my head. The icy water's scouring and wiping the corners of my mind, gone. Gone. No more. No more memories, only now . . . Clouds hide the moon and stars, everything has disappeared from sight . . . only the pattering of the invisible rain and the hissing, tossing sea.*

The night is melting away taking the rain. I can feel the light on my eyelids . . . pull and pull but they're glued down. Flicker my lids, like blinking . . . panicky . . . they're firmly stuck. There's a numbness inside me, wrapping round my words, smudging their meaning, muffling their sounds, like this heavy sheet over me, pressing me down into the bed. I want to call, but all the thousands of words that make up a thought stay inside my head, they're floating together . . . silently suffocating me. I want them to burst out of my head . . . oh, they are, "he . . . elp!' Spurting to the circley ceiling, unravelling down the faded flowered walls, looking for the meaning of my thought. Slipping and slithering. No words left. No meanings.

My hands won't reach my eyes, be calm, but tears are coming, self-pitying tears and my lids are working loose . . . Keep them open, wide open, don't fall into a fog, don't . . .

"Catrin is *still* on a soft foods and thickened drinks diet."

How can I hear this? I'm not there; I'm looking down on my body, on the women standing by my bed, with a pail and towel. There's no flicker of life on my face.

"Oh sweet Jesus, she looks like she's going very soon. Not much hope for her."

"Get out, she just sleeping."

She pulls off my sheet with strong brown hands. I shut my mind as well as my eyes.

✳    ✳    ✳

*Terrifyingly immense sea and sky stretching endlessly to the horizon. The sun fading like a dissolving pill in the sky. Most people are dozing. Sleep is sucking me down its slippery slope . . .*

*I'm cold and stiff, sore necked, my back hurts, my bottom's sore from sitting, I can't get comfortable. Eyelids stuck down again. Rub them . . . the edge of the sky's changing colour as the air slowly fills with light. The sun's splashing through the little clouds, making sparkling patterns on the water. What was that bump? A brownish shell covered with algae . . . the green head of a large sea turtle poking out of the sea, an ugly old man's face, two holes for a nose and black eyes looking straight into mine. It nodded to me . . . it's flipping lazily away . . .*

*An electric shock, a cold and liquid tingle shooting through me . . . a triangular fin slicing through the water. Help! On the other side of the hatch Gwen's head has slumped onto the side of the boat; her arm is trailing in the water. The fin is changing tack, scything towards us . . . the speed . . . I can't get to her, I can't . . . Quick, the oar, smack the water with all my strength. Splat! Freezing water all over Gwen.*

*"Wha, what's happening?" She's screaming, outraged . . . the fin veers away. Glaring at me, she's furious.*

*"What are you doing? I'm soaking. That's not funny Catrin!"*

*"Look" . . . the fin is heading off into the distance. Her angry face is melting; she's going so pale, trembling.*

*"I'm going to faint! Oh my god, it nearly had my arm? Oh, oh my arm. You saved me."*

*Lizzie's seen it too. "You've saved us both now, Catrin, you're a heroine. Gwenny, let me rub you dry."*

*"My arm! Thank you, thank you Catrin. Come and have a hug."*

*She's crying in relief, what a soft, loving look . . .*


*Land ahoy! Bill's gruff voice.*

*At last, land in the distance. Is it a mirage? No, everyone can see it . . . at last. Sailing gently closer and closer . . . the welcome sound of vigorous waves crashing down . . . like applause . . . sucking up the shingle as it pulls back, then spitting it out, drowning our words.*

*"Come on."*

*"I'm so stiff."*

*"Ouch, it's freezing, takes your breath away."*

*"Come on Catrin, put your feet in."*

*Down, into the icy surf, sinking to solid land, ouch, shingle . . . at last. Shaky weak legs . . . buffeted by little foam capped waves "Ow." Bare feet connecting with tiny sharp pebbles and broken seashells, seaweed wrapping and unwrapping itself around my legs, so stiff from lack of use.*

*"Ouch. Ooh"*

*Sunlight glittering on the sea, the welcome shingle and sand beach ahead. Lizzie and Gwen are there first, looking so happy to feel it unmoving beneath them.*

*"That was a complete nightmare, I never want to sail again."* *Gwen runs her comb through her hair, sapphires for eyes. "And you're a star Catrin, saving me from that shark."*

*Fresh, sharp vegetation smells, my pulse is speeding, muscles twitching to be on the move. I'm so excited to be here. "Come on, let's go." Oh, my legs, my head, I can't faint, no.*

*"Sit down Catrin," Charlie sounds cross. "You're not used to being on land."*

*"But I want to shout and sing. Wales at last!"*

*"Don't we pass near to Carew on our way to Tenby?"*

*"No, Gwen, it's further west. I thought we'd decided not to go there?"*

*"Well I was thinking that having a younger body would be very nice."*

*'Unable to love the old, we approach them via sentiment, duty and an eye to our own eventual decline. We make sure that they are housed, fed, medicated, and seated facing their favourite channel. We see ourselves in them and they see—what is it that the aged see?'*
Ronald Blythe, "The View in Winter' (1979 p13)

# Chapter 24—Waiting and Leaving. 2005

## MONDAY OCTOBER 3ᴿᴰ

Recently it's like making conversation with a stranger. Mum's lucidity is more shocking than her confusion, for it is not how I have become accustomed to find her, it is no longer normal. She seems surprised when I come and distracted and uninterested in anything I have to say.

I couldn't understand what she was trying to tell me so I fetched her top teeth from the bathroom and with a thick layer of the fixative I had brought, managed to get them to stay up. She was rambling incoherently, so I smoothed Nivea onto her red, inflamed skin pulled tight like thin paper over the bones of her face. I was shocked by the prominent hard ridges her eyebrows rested upon. The flesh is sunken away behind, leaving two rocky ledges overhanging the deep hollows which hold her eyes. Her face is becoming like the bare skull it will soon be. I gently stroked on compressed powder, applied lipstick and combed her dry hair. She even let me pull out a few hairs on her chin.

"Lunch Catrin."

The new Indian carer put down a tray of tepid food; mince and mushy grey vegetables, red jelly and already scummy tea. I have complained so often, what was the point in fighting again today, when they can give her what they like when I'm not there.

I went to the upstairs dining room to get her a spoon and fork. Past the patient, passive rows of slumped figures, delivered early to the tables, heads bowed in sleep or stupor. All waiting; for the next meal, for their visitors, for the Doctor, their next pill or a miracle? How must it feel to be in a place where everyone breathes, eats, exists, but look backwards and can never be useful again?

Why can't the residents be given little tasks, so they feel useful? Why can't carers sit with the residents and eat with them? That would ensure that the staff had a meal in their long day and ensure a more social, normal atmosphere.

Mum ate uncomplainingly but without enthusiasm. As I spooned in the mush, I let my gaze go past her towards the usual scene below her window, but my eyes focused on something much nearer. A huge spider has built a palace of gossamer thread, colonising the top panes. It too sits waiting for its next meal. I idly wondered if flies have different flavours.

I told her all the family news. Her face was a blank, she didn't seem to be taking anything in, not Lizzie's husband, Rhodri dying, the funeral, Cerys's serious illness, nothing. She was lying there patiently, as if waiting.

I talked to her about her career in the Bank and singing in the concert party; "You gave over a hundred concerts to the troops didn't you Mum?" She tried to answer and a few words came out, then it was "help, help, help," lots more helps and more unintelligible words and something sounding like "washday."

A vast, almost tangible silence settled around us and scenes from the women's world of my childhood flooded into my head. All those routine domestic chores, crowned by the worst time of the week, Sunday morning washday. Up came all the mats from the quarry tiled kitchen floor and I filled our 'modern' washing machine with a jug, while Mum sorted the washing into six piles by colour. All six were washed in the same water where the central paddle moved a few inches clockwise and back, thump thump, thump thump. The progressively greyer, soupier water pushed the clothes a little one way, a little the other and then out they came, one by one and through the mangle. "Watch those buttons, Alys," Mum would cry, and I was rinsing each item in the sink, mangling again and then humping them up the sloping garden to the washing line. It always seemed to be freezing and windy, so the wet sheets flapped all over me, the shirts flew off onto the bare soil and I prayed to change into a boy so that I could disappear with Robert and Dad.

The only pleasure from this wet misery was in singing, with Mum harmonising. This was the only time I ever heard her sing, apart from in Chapel. I was allowed to choose the songs, which she had often not heard before, but could immediately harmonise with, in her lovely contralto voice. 'Catch a Falling Star,' 'Magic Moments,' or the ones she had sung on stage, 'Dear Mr Gable,' 'Somewhere Over the Rainbow,' or 'We'll Meet Again.' We sang song after song for the first few hours, until we got to the pants and socks and by then we were both in bad moods.

Is Mum in pain? I sat watching as she endlessly fiddled in slow motion with the cellular blanket, her curved claws with their translucent sheathes too weak now to lift it. Poking and prodding throughout the tediously long afternoon. She winced sometimes: she cannot move her body or legs to change her position.

"Are you in pain Mum?"

"No," though her face was a sour grimace.

"Is your bottom painful?"

"No, it's much better today."

Her memory is so patchy, so unreliable; does she remember the pain from a few seconds ago? If one has sporadic memory, can one feel continuous pain?

The Home had settled into its afternoon torpor. I slumped on a stool wondering where she was, behind her dull eyes, which seem to be looking inwards. Mostly now, it's as if Mum has gone and someone else is inhabiting her body. A stranger, who doesn't know our past life or me. If what we are is the sum total of our experiences, an unique store which we dip into to pull out a memory and make new connections, Mum must feel as if she is going into someone else's dark and unrecognisable store. If memories are not being revisited and no new connections are being made, do they fade away? How much can you lose of yourself and still be you?

Is there a level below which she will no longer be a person? What does constitute a self? Obviously Mum is not anyone else, but disease has changed her because her brain has been damaged. Most philosophers agree that without the characteristics of self awareness, linguistic capacity and rationality and the ability to reason and respond, there is no personhood. So how could she be

229

defined? Is there something, someone inside a body that is more than biochemistry? Are our thoughts and feelings really just produced by neurons, so when they die the self dies with them? I prefer to believe that her identity is intact under her clogged, tangled and misfiring brain cells and it will soar free at death.

If she has given up the struggle to communicate, hopefully it is to escape her miserable reality and she is living a more comfortable fantasy. By letting go of all her attachments perhaps she is achieving a state of happiness. In her dreams she can be as she was.

Jung said that we probably dream all the time but that our consciousness is so noisy that we don't realise it. Perhaps she has switched off the noise, in which case her visitors are dragging her back. This could be why she is sometimes irritated by our questions.

I thought of that poem 'Look Closer Nurse,' reputed to have been written by Phyllis McCormack:

*'But inside this old carcass*
*a young girl still dwells,*
*And now and again*
*my battered heart swells,*
*I remember the joys,*
*I remember the pain,*
*And I'm loving and living*
*life over again.'*

## THURSDAY OCTOBER 20TH

Mum was in bed, hair and face drained of colour, her nightie stained, her hands and arms blue with cold. I stood for a moment feeling unbearably sad at how hard she has striven to maintain her dignity despite being unable to move; having that deep and painful wound on her bottom and having to be lifted with a hoist to have her nappy changed. Dignity, what is it like to have none?

"Hello Mum, how are you?"

She looked up and a glutinous softening touched the edges of her mouth as the shadow of a smile flickered across, like that described in a Thomas Hardy poem.

*'The smile on your mouth was the deadest thing*
*Alive enough to have the strength to die;'*
('Neutral Tones.' 1867)

230

She tried hard to talk, struggling to get her sentences out, losing the sense half way through, but I felt exhilarated and happy that she was trying, until the 'helps' started again. However, buoyed by her improvement, I asked the nurse on duty if there was any way that her filthy hair could be washed. A few minutes later Sian and Priti appeared with a blow up bowl and jug to wash it in bed. I worried that Mum would make a fuss, but Sian seemed confident and they asked me to sit downstairs as the room is too small for all four of us.

I waited, gazing idly around before opening my novel. The matron's whyteboard had a list of all the inmates, I read the first column: Phyllis Price, Dilys Phillips, Winnie Evans, Gwen Thomas, Margaret Evans, welsh *women's* names all the way to the bottom where there was Bill McShane and Ken Parry . . .

At last, Sian called me upstairs and there was a glamorous Mum. Clean, blow-dried hair, face made up, a pink stole disguising her bony shoulders and a pleased expression.

"Thank you," she said to Sian and Priti.

"I'm much better now, I might, help, help, help, I want to help, open the car door. One two, three, four, five six, please will you take one? Help, help, help."

"Do you know you're saying help?"

"No, I don't think I do, help, help, help, help. I've got to eat fish, what are you selling? A juicy steak I think, help, help, help, help..

I looked over her bed at the grey sky through her dusty window. Would I be any more coherent if I were trapped in this hot little room for so long? She closed her eyes and fell asleep, that Munch scream again. Is she almost at the end of her journey? Is this shell of my Mum, waiting to die? She snorted and opened an eye: "Bye love, thanks for coming," she said, and my fourteen hour day had been worth it, every bit.

# FRIDAY 11TH NOVEMBER

Mum looked pretty, her face smooth and unlined and a good colour. She appeared to be with me and was talking about her sisters, so I asked how she would describe them.

"Lizzie is a good doer, she enjoys doing things for people. We have never, ever argued, mumble, mumble."

I asked about Gwen.

"She was very quiet and had things I wanted, which I normally managed to get. Lizzie was much cleverer than Gwen and she always worked hard, which I never did. When I get to Tenby I'll find someone is . . . . I found out how much Gareth had spent. I thought I could persuade him to give it up, but it doesn't work that way."

"Who's Gareth, your husband?"

"Yes of course it is, I'm not in your fantasy world!" she said sarcastically. "I know he's going to be there in Tenby itself, I can't seem to get him to realise, he shouldn't use the money."

I am mystified. Is she talking about the money he spent on alcohol? I thought that she had successfully brushed Dad's drinking under the carpet; did the cost of it still rankle? I wish so much that I knew what their relationship was like. It is all a blur to me now. I don't remember much physical contact, though I'm sure that he was faithful. Her shy smile entered his heart on their first meeting and stayed there the rest of his life. She continued:

"I must try and go to the hairdressers tomorrow."

Then lapsed into incomprehensible muttering and helps until her lunch appeared, a mountain of cold mashed potato with a tiny spoonful of baked beans on top. What disgusting cheap ingredients. Where are the meat, fish, green vegetables?

"I know that you have nothing to do with preparing the food, but why would she want to eat this?" I asked the gentle, beautiful carer who brought in the tray. Her English was not up to a discussion, so she directed me to Amanda, the crewcutted, arms-like-anvils cook.

"Well I dowanna give her thar rubbish either. I wudn't eat it. I gave her sandwiches for tea one day and gor told off. I have to stick to the sheet see."

So I approached the nursing station for my fourth discussion on Mum's diet. They have been unable to find the written diagnosis, which put Mum on mush and thickened drinks three months ago and are starting to think that it might have been one nurse's decision.

"Well if you made the decision in the first place, you can decide to give her proper food now, as there is plenty of evidence that Mum has never had difficulties swallowing. She has never choked and eats grapes, cherries, apples, nuts and drinks as if she is desperately thirsty when I give her juice. Why does she have to have that horrible thickener stirred in to her drinks?"

Their compunctionless faces stared unblinkingly at my anguish. Setting their lips in thin lines, their eyes, like those hard, bright stones washed up on the beach, narrowed.

"Alys," they said, as if they were about to explain to a child that she should not play with matches: "You can give her what you like, that is not our responsibility. We're not prepared to take her off her diet until the speech therapist comes to see her. She's the only person who's qualified to say what she can swallow."

Their polite smiles snapped back like rubber bands. I kept trying:

"That's what you said two months ago, well this is getting ridiculous. What pleasures other than eating has Mum got in her life? There is obviously a huge waiting list; it might be another six months. I want you to give Mum proper food now. You can change a directive that no-one knows who made or why."

They brought along a Doctor who had popped in to see another patient, so that she could remonstrate with me before I left. She understood my point of view, but the only lifeline she handed me is that she will write to the speech therapist encouraging her to make Mum a priority. We stood over Mum discussing her as if she was not there. I was shocked by their inability to give me even one reason why she cannot have proper food, The Doctor and chief nurse exited and I said to Mum, "Do you understand what we were discussing?" But she looked past me blankly. Had she tuned off, or did she not understand? I explained the situation to her, but she was not taking it in, she was looking around. She hates rows. If she does not care if she eats and drinks mush, why am I so upset and upsetting the Nursing Home staff?

I rung the hospital speech therapy dept and spoke to a very sympathetic and helpful speech therapist, who confirmed that they are not the ones who prescribed her diet and that Mum was sixth on the list to be seen. She would try and get the department to class Mum as an emergency.

# WEDNESDAY NOVEMBER 16TH

Into her room I went and smiled as our eyes met. What I saw was her, but also not her, as her dead eyes with their papery lids, seemed like a mirror reflecting back my gaze. I felt so alone. She is leaving me, not all at once, one moment she is here and the next she's gone again and I'm left wondering if she will return and where she goes when she leaves.

Witnessing Mum's demise by slow degrees is agonising. It is protracted, on going grief. Who called dementia 'the long goodbye?'

After four hours we still had not communicated. It is as if her words are the branches of a tree in the wind, sometimes the branches touch and connections are made and a whole sentence might emerge, but mostly her thoughts are scrambled. She used to search assiduously for the word she wanted; now she seems too tired, it's all become too hard. Why do I come so often? I make no difference, my presence doesn't matter. She knows that I cannot change her situation. No matter how many people tell me that the disease is going to progress, no matter what and that I could never do enough, I'll always blame myself that I didn't do more. All I remember now is what Robert and I did not do and what we should have done while she was well. This disease is so cruel it sets family members against one another, makes them want to blame someone, mostly themselves.

It was a dark day. A moth slammed itself against the overhead light bulb, and then fluttered fruitlessly around inside the glass shade, trailing dust from its damaged wings.

"Mum," I said. "I've come all this way and I've waited for hours, but you're responding to me as if I were a stranger, I'm not even sure you know who I am. Who am I Mum?"

Her pale eyes focussed on me, steadily, meaningfully, she looked as if she was trying to say something comforting, something which would make up for the last four hours of non-communication. Seconds passed, a long minute, then lifting her left claw to her chest, she said blankly,

"I think I'd like to have something up to the neck!"

On every visit, leaving is the hardest, as then she comes closest to being the woman she once was. Why, I asked myself for the hundredth time does this person I visit every week, who often does not seem to recognise me, suddenly metamorphose into my mother when I am leaving? Having not said a sensible, communicating word she will say: "Are you going? Do you have to go? Can't you stay the night? Don't you have any holidays? Don't go yet, can't you stay? What am I going to do? Who'll be with me?"

And on my last visit: "Can't you even wait for ten seconds?" A betrayed look on her gaunt but still pretty face. I had to walk out of the door with her resentful expression as my last memory.

"Where do I go now?" she asked me as I stood up to go.

"This is your home, mum," I reassured her.

"No it isn't, I don't know it."

"Mum this is the nursing home you have been in for nearly three years." I said under this suddenly keenly intelligent gaze. "I'll be back next week."

"I may not be here," she said. "It's too early for me to have a bath. I want to go home."

If only you could Mum, if only you could.

I walked to her door feeling as if I was abandoning her yet again. I was going away AGAIN, I cannot do enough, be here enough, but I *can't* give up my life to look after her. "I'll be gone soon," she had said. I PUT YOU HERE MUM, to be controlled and contained, that is my agony, which never goes away.

She stopped pleading, but looked at me with big, soulful, puppy eyes staring into my soul, and as I wrenched myself away, the guilt followed me padding insistently behind. Down the stairs, out of the door and on the two-mile walk to the station, my heart felt heavy, haunted by the memory of my mother and the sight of her now. I found myself weeping bitter tears at leaving her behind yet again, to her shrunken life in the hot, tiny room, which she has never recognised as home.

# Chapter 25—Travelling by land

*I* ought to go and visit Maisie and Winston. I could give Winston some of Gareth's cricket trophies . . . he'd love that. Wonder if they're still going to the opera? Perhaps they'll take me. I haven't been for such a long time. I'll get dressed and go and see them now.

"Mum, what are you doing?'

Alys looks perplexed. "See Maisie, help."

"Mum, she died four years ago and Winston died two years after, remember?"

I'm shocked; my eyes swim with blots and tadpoles of summer light. Winston thumps a six. Maisie and I cheer as the ball lands behind us on the clubhouse. "Let's go and get the tea made, he's only got to make another five and they'll all be clamouring for it." We get up, only she disappears and hot tears are running down my cheeks. "Why didn't you tell me?"

"Try this drink Mum, it's raspberries and mango juice."

Sliding down my throat, mmm, saliva oozing into my dry mouth, that's nice, that's delicious.

That was such a nice dream. There he was in tennis whites, shining eyes, beckoning, bouncing a ball. We played a few points, I was moving well, then my love turned away as if to go.

Plastic bib around my neck . . . mush into my mouth, no taste. Swallow cold glue, don't bother to chew, just lie here and swallow it.

*"Wait for me, wait for me." He's moving so quickly down the long, dark corridor. Run after him. Which door did he go through?*

*This one with the rim of light around it? There he is, winding tape onto a racket handle. "Here you are!"*

*A bell. Who wants to come in? The bell again and I'm here, not there . . . jerked out of the thin, dreaming sleep of just before waking . . ." come back my love" . . . I want to be with you . . .*

Why is Alys arguing with those women? She shouldn't get so angry. Be calm Alys, anger won't do you or anyone else any good. Don't wave your arms, don't shout like that.

"Your mother's condition fluctuates daily . . ."

"I know, of course I know that, and not just daily, hourly, and even by the minute."

Alys shouldn't interrupt.

"It just isn't possible to make a care plan to suit her range of conditions."

"Yes, yes." Alys really should calm down." I *know* there's no doctor here to make diagnostic decisions *every* mealtime. But, she *never* has a problem swallowing!"

"We're not convinced of that." She's looking at her watch and the door.

Alys sounds as if she's begging. "How many pleasures in life do you think Mum has? Everyone else has had fish and chips for lunch; Mum has had potato mush and thickened tea. Would *you* want that?"

"I'm sorry, I'll write to the hospital to ask them to see her urgently, that's *all* I can do.

Don't get so upset Alys. I eat roast pork, that soft, salty sweetness, the crispy, crunchy burnt edges. I suck the crackling, hold it in greasy fingers, lick the salty fat off afterwards. And steak and kidney pie, duck and orange sauce mm, the smell of the duck, with peas, gravy and runner beans, mmm.

* * *

*"This wind's vicious! It's knocking my breath out of me, cutting through to my bones." Lizzie's words come racing towards me.*

*"My eyes, my eyes!" Gwen's covering them with a hand, fruitlessly trying to hold her hair with the other, as the wind's fiendish fingers*

*whips it into tangles. Scrubby pieces of bush hurtle at us, ripped from the sparse soil by this savage gale. No sun, just thick grey cloud. Surely nothing can live in this bleak landscape.*

*It's ominously silent except for our gasps . . . the wind snatching our breath away. No bird calls or insects vibrating hum . . . The sky is a slash overhead in this narrow ravine . . . A huge black shadow from this column of rocks. I'm sensing something evil. Tell them Catrin, shout.*

*Don't go any further, stop, stop . . .* Stop! . . . The words are still in my head . . . I'm floating . . . who's that dressed in white?

"I think you should wake up now Catrin, it's eleven, you've slept right through breakfast."

"Can I have some tea?"

"I'll get you some then the girls can give you a wash and get you up."

I'll have a shower, wrap myself in my two big, fluffy towels, 'Nivea' my face, make it up, comb out my hair, what shall I wear? Mmm, am I playing tennis today?

"What . . . ? A damp flannel . . . scraping my face, my neck, my hands. "Don't pull me up.."

"Drink this Catrin, open your mouth. You said you wanted tea."

"I'm going to put my makeup on now."

"What? Drink this tea. And here's a piece of toast. You're lucky I'm so good to you. Open your mouth."

Suck the dry piece . . . the morsels hiding in the back of my mouth.

"Open your mouth Catrin, drink your tea."

"Where's my makeup? I hate to be seen without my makeup."

"Hello Mum."

Alys?

"You don't have to use that stuff, it clogs your pores and you're pretty without it. How are you Mum? Let me give you a kiss and hug."

She looks so pale, so old sometimes. Makeup cheers up the face.

Sleeping pills make me feel woozy half the day. My eyelids are drooping . . . my breathing getting heavier . . . sinking down, down into slushing, watery sounds.

✻     ✻     ✻

*What's happened here? Blood on Bill and Charlie, on the ground. Where's Ted? Everyone looks in shock. What's happened? I can't ask, they'll think I've gone mad . . . why couldn't I have stopped this happening?*

*"Let's get out of here before they come back for another of us."*

*No one's talking. Walking, just walking. All I can hear is our crashing progress and the blood pounding in my ears.*

*"Listen . . . They're coming again."*

*Who are they? Is my heart going to burst out of my chest?*

*"I can hear them, can't you hear them?" Gwen's gone white. "Listen, they're getting nearer and nearer."*

*Crashing sounds . . . coming towards us . . .*

*"What're we going to do?"*

*Roll my shoulders back, stick out my chest and let out all my fear . . . a primaeval howl . . . vibrating down the barren valley. Was that me?*

*It's curling back seeping over the rocks as a soft echo. I feel so brave . . . breathe in again and out of the bottom of my abdomen bellow a fierce conquering call. Everyone is staring at me in horror. "What?" Starts Lizzie.*

*That was a quieter, frightened response . . . Another one further away, like scaredy yelps . . . our pursuers have met their match. Horror's turning into admiration. "You've frightened them off!"*

*"That was unbelievable!"*

*"Just being positive . . ." but I'm amazed at myself, was that really me?*

*Trudge on, muscles stiff and tight. The air is still, melancholy, chilled, my breath flares in the sunlight. I'm moving awkwardly, picking my way through this rocky terrain. Up, up and we're looking down into a verdant valley . . .*

*Down, down and these lush woods are dense, green and secret.
Birds flock together and drop down into the trees in front of us,
twittering like a group of children. Willows trail in a river.*

*"It looks clear, lets have a drink and a wash."*

*"You're not going in there are you Gwen?"*

*"Yes. It's freezing, but come on, have a quick paddle."*

*The shock of it is clearing my brain . . . the sun's warmth's
lightening my blood, it's frisking around my body.*

*I'm feeling so much better . . . light and bouncy with
absolutely no stiffness. Jump up this hill, leap from boulder to
tussock . . . confidently landing with a twitch of excitement. I'm not
afraid of this sheer descent . . . plunge off, somersault . . . float like
thistledown, land so lightly . . . I barely disturb the springy turf. The
others look jealous, plodding down as I soar and sail above them.*

# Chapter 26—'Neither sense of life, nor joys.' 2005-2006

## MONDAY DECEMBER 5TH

$\mathcal{M}$um has retreated so profoundly inside herself, that she has shorter and fewer periods of lucidity. The link between thinking and speaking has been faulty for some time, but now it rarely makes a connection. On the train I was reading Oliver Sacks 'The Man Who Mistook His Wife for a Hat (1985).' He cited various examples of people who continued to think and feel long after they have lost their language skills. But it is so difficult to have a satisfying relationship with someone who is only talking rationally sometimes. It's as if a switch is turned off and then mysteriously turned back on again. She begins a thought with the cues, the openers and enders to conversations but by the time she's got through a few words she has forgotten where she is heading:

"I really think . . ."

"This place is . . ."

"I don't think he should be allowed to . . ."

"I think you should know."

"Did you hear?"

"Thank you for coming."

"Tell me, what do I do about your 'furl'?"

"What's a furl, Mum?"

A wave of irritation at my stupidity passed across her face. She looked frustrated as though she was trying to tell me something, but her ideas were flying about in threads and fragments. There was a desperate longing to be understood in her eyes. It's probably the reason that she has given up responding to questions or news.

Has Mum still got a sense of self? If not, how can she know me as her daughter. She often gazes at me blankly and then turns back to the TV. She is simultaneously aware that she should recognise me, yet struggles to do so. Although she gets a feeling of familiarity when she sees me, my appearance and our past are all mixed up with everything she has ever known in the jumble of her mind. Her eyes see, but do they know? There is no feeling of warmth from her, no emotions, I feel abandoned, does she too? Do I believe Luis Bunuel who wrote in his memoirs?

*'Life without memory is no life at all . . . . . Our memory*
*is our coherence, our reason, our feeling, even our action.*
*Without it, we are nothing.' (1982)*

No, I don't want to believe that, it is a different life, but surely not 'no life at all?'

Later she started to make sense and talked inevitably about Christmas. I explained about having to go to Cerys's partners' family this year as they had come to us for two years. I was thrilled by her response:

"Don't worry about me and bringing a dinner for me,' she said, her face full of concern. "I don't want anything, you've spent enough on me."

As supportive as ever.

"What would you actually like for Christmas, Mum?"

"I'll have some kidney beans. I've done my exercises for my elbows, hands and back, so you can't say I haven't done them, because I have."

She knows what I *want* to hear. Perhaps she had done them, what seems like half a lifetime ago, when she was first diagnosed with Parkinson's.

"Is your bottom painful?" I asked as a fleeting twinge like a veil passing briefly across the moon, briefly creased her face.

"At times, very much so. My bottom gives me the worst pain."

I get up to go, "I'll see you downstairs in a bit," she says.

On the train back to London I read Oliver Sacks book again. He interestingly suggests that people with neurological problems are heroes, victims, martyrs and warriors and more. *'We must say they are travellers to unimaginable lands—lands of which otherwise we should have no idea or conception.'* (pxi) He goes on to write *'that a disease is*

242

*never a mere loss or excess,'* but that the individual compensated *'however strange the means may be.'* (p4)

Certainly Mum struggles to see what is there and sees something completely different to me. Perhaps in the same way, she is thinking and experiencing unimaginable events? He continues by saying that it is too difficult for even the most sensitive person to understand *'the inner state, the 'situation', of such patients, for this is unimaginably remote from anything he himself has ever known.'* (p8).

If only, if only I could . . .

# MONDAY DECEMBER 26TH—CHRISTMAS

Mike and I drove to Cardiff on Boxing Day with Mum's Christmas lunch. She was sitting in her chair, makeup on and hair done. She had her top teeth in at last and looked attractive, but her mind was somewhere else. I think she knew me, but we had no sensible exchanges. Then at two o clock, in bustled Lewis, the little fat man with the huge personality. They beamed at one another.

"We had a nice day yesterday, didn't we Catrin fach. You enjoyed your lunch didn't you?" He wiped his wet brow as she smiled in agreement.

"What are you doing now, Lewis? Going to a party I hope." I asked.

He let his breath out, shaking an exhausted head: "I'm going home to sleep, I've been up at 5.30 and here over twelve hours a day, all this week." He turned, "Hwylfawr sex bomb," he called to Mum and blowing kisses to us, hurried off.

Mum's elation gradually receded; her eyes grew duller as I desperately searched for interesting things to tell her which might bring her back. I tried a story about her grandson, this always seems to strike a chord of interest and I was immediately rewarded by the alertness and joy in her gaunt face. I continued with a less interesting anecdote, and the light faded, leaving her eyes as empty as before.

I have learnt too late that Mum often reflects the mood of her visitor. If I had been told just that one simple fact it would have lightened my visits. If only I hadn't been so serious. Lewis is much more fun than me.

We were both filled with guilt at our inadequacy to communicate with one another. Mum did not seem to be understanding the meaning of the words I was speaking, but she seemed to be able to feel my torment and irritability at her distance from me.

## FRIDAY DECEMBER 30TH

Mum's eyes were dead and unseeing and she looked dishevelled with filthy hair and food around her mouth and down her front. I pointed this out to Joan, the nurse on duty, and asked why her teeth were not in. When I got home, I sent more pocket money and asked if they could ensure that Mum was out of bed for a few hours every day, sitting on her inflating pressure cushion.

## SUNDAY JANUARY 15TH

Today and last visit, Mum looked lovely. She was sitting in her chair dressed nicely, with clean hair, makeup, jewellery, the lot. She even held her own drink; her right hand seemed a lot stronger and more flexible. "I'm improving," she said. "Can I have another chocolate?"

## WEDNESDAY FEBRUARY 22ND

Visiting for the last five weeks has been stunningly boring, as Mum cannot communicate at all. Sometimes she was asleep, her eyelids fluttering over her dreams. What are they? Where is she? Her breaths are little shallow girlie puffs. There are no intelligible sentences, apart from the polite conventions, which she still retains to offer to the carers and nurses. "Thank-you so much, how are you today."

Her blank eyes were on me, her lips moved continuously in 'help, help.' A desperate, helpless, begging mother behind those dead eyes, focussed on me, but what does she see?

I crammed delicacies into her willing mouth and wondered how she could have borne lying here for four years, unable to move. I have found it very hard to cope with this place for four hours a week.

Whatever I did for her, such as get the sleep out of her eyes, she said immediately: "I did this just before you came."

When I tried to put her makeup on,

"I was just going to do that."

She looked towards me with that empty, spatial stare, as if I were part of the wall, then broke her gaze, and slowly, thoughtfully began the usual picking and pulling at her blanket.

## TUESDAY MARCH 15TH

I have made visit after visit to this stranger, who just looks like my mum, and then today, she had partially returned. I told her some grandson adventures and she smiled.

"Oh, he's a lovely little boy. No. I'll be honest and say, help, parsley rooms and he's walking now whatever he's got. Hello, Bill. What we didn't have any fireworks today. Are they all coming tomorrow? Help, help."

So that is it for the perception and making sense, I thought.

"Where's your wedding ring?" She suddenly asked. She can see then.

## TUESDAY MARCH 22ND

"I feel I ought to go to the funeral."

"But you can't bend your legs Mum, how are you going to get in a car?"

She thought for a moment.

"I think you'll find I can now," she said aloofly.

"Don't worry Mum, I'll represent you." She looked completely blank. I repeated this three times, then eventually she said: "Which horse, where?"

Ethel, one of mum's greatest friends who was very active and fit and had been awarded an MBE for her work with disabled swimming competitions, elderly exercise and her church, had suddenly, so surprisingly died.

I tried to make Mum face reality. "You can't really go can you Mum?"

"Well I can walk now."

245

"Hmm." I held a glass of fresh orange juice to her mouth, which she drunk thirstily, then she consumed a bunch of grapes. No problem with her swallowing mechanism then. Matron was passing. "Look Sheila, Mum can eat and drink normally."

She stood at the door looking unconvinced.

"The speech therapist is coming in two weeks, you'll have to wait for her to decide."

I boiled inwardly.

"I don't remember having lunch." Mum said hopefully, as I bit into my usual three-bean wrap.

"Well you won't like this (she's a true butcher's daughter and loves meat), how about a chocolate éclair?"

In between bites of squidgy cream and chocolate, Mum reflected.

"I had two jars of Bovril at five past. I don't know who sent it; it was one of those they put on peoples."

She then carried on talking incomprehensively for half an hour. I felt suffocated by the heat and smell. "You must be so sick of this little room. Aren't you?"

She looked shocked, puzzled, "N—O!" she exclaimed emphatically, enunciating each letter.

"Why?"

"I certainly wouldn't want to move onto the street!"

She shivered, her arms were really cold. I had opened the window a crack because it was so stuffy. I looked in her wardrobe; four of her knitted bed jackets were missing. I wrapped her in a pashima, wondering if I should make a fuss or ignore this constant theft. I chose the latter. "When you were a little girl, what did you want to be when you grew up, Mum?"

"What I am now."

"Well if you'd had to work rather than marrying Dad and then having to run the shop, what would you like to have done?"

She shrugged. "Something to do with animals."

"But you don't like animals."

"He didn't know that."

We lapsed into silence and I thought about her lack of interest in animals. She had ignored all the pets Dad bought for us children and I never saw her feed, or pat any of our succession of bulldogs. It's true

246

they weren't that appealing. They had squat powerful bodies, foul breath and huge, black lipped mouths, from which a pointed canine and a lolling tongue dripping saliva protruded. No, not appealing, everyone in our village was petrified of them.

A vicar and vicaress walked past and into the lounge, just past Mum's room.

"We're going to have a service." He announced loudly. "You enjoy that, don't you?"

"No we don't," said a loud voice. There was complete silence from everyone else.

"We'll turn you all around so we can have a singsong."

We heard, "No, no!" and "All right, all right, I'm going."

I couldn't understand what Mum was telling me.

"Help, help and he promised me he wouldn't."

"Number thirteen, number thirteen we're starting with today," the Vicaress suddenly shouted.

"What did Dad promise, Mum?"

"He kept drinking, help, help, help, he got salvation, they came from and it frightened me."

"Ready to sing?" A scream from across the corridor. The response was silence again.

" . . . kept thinking, what will happen if . . ." Mum continued.

Then suddenly beautiful, tuneful singing filled our ears. I was gobsmacked! I went out and peeped in. Only Dorothy and Kitty's mouths were moving, nine other ladies stared into space. Then I realised that the Vicaress was singing along with a recorded choir.

"We blossom and flourish, like leaves on a tree. And wither and perish . . ."

Music memory is stored in a different area of the brain from language and lines of the song came back to Mum so we sang too, with gusto.

"tis only the splendour of light hideth thee."

The Vicar prowled up and down the corridor outside, like a black bat searching for prey. We heard him swooping on a reluctant lamb next door and exhorting his captive audience. Then it was the prayer. The lady with a voice like a rook cawed loudly. The Vicaress went up an octave and bellowed deafeningly to drown out her competition.

We sung number fourteen and then I slipped downstairs to get a cup of tea from Lewis in the kitchen.

"Singin's thirsty work," he giggled.

I told him about not being sure if Mum had at last admitted that Dad had drunk too much. "Oh bless." he said. "There is a woman in number 31, who shouts 'Jack, Jack' all day. I go in and say Duw, he'll be comin' along now in a minute.' Or 'He's missed the bus, he'll be here soon,' even though he's been dead for years. Then one day she looked at me and said, 'No he wun't, he's carrying on, en he?' I'll never know if *that* was true or not." He laughed.

## TUESDAY APRIL 11TH—THE SPEECH THERAPISTS LONG AWAITED VISIT:

My train was late, so I ran the two miles to find Tracey the hospital speech therapist sitting in the entrance hall, waiting with her forms. We went up to Mum's room, to find a statue sitting in Mum's chair.

"Hello, Mum, here I am, you look pretty today, are you going to open your eyes for me?" I gave her a kiss, she was immobile, her eyes and mouth tightly shut. Her breathing was so faint, that she might have been an angel occupying this rigid, skeletal body.

"Hello Mrs Williams, I've come to see you, I'm Tracey, I need to see you eating and drinking so that I can tell if you can go back to a normal diet."

I massaged her arms, her shoulders, her face, talked over and over to her, but there was no sign of her having heard. Tracey had gone to get the nurses on duty, so left alone with Mum I frustratedly shook her, pulled her face into a smile and begged her to wake up. No response.

In came the combined might of the Home, the matron and chief nurse. The powerful Sheila and Joan shouted questions at her, Lewis popped in and tried, but she was as stone. My thoughts were swirling, whirling. "Has she had a stroke? Was she given sleeping pills last night? This morning?"

The nurses had no answers and didn't seem concerned. Half an hour passed and conscious that Tracey had to go, I managed to get the sleeping form to sip some orange juice, "Look you can see she's swallowing OK, even though she's asleep!"

Tracey filled in her form, noting the food Mum's relatives give her and pronounced that based on the information from me, "I can see no reason why Catrin cannot drink normal fluids and eat normally as long as the food is not tough, for example, beef, pork, skins of some fruits and possibly white bread."

I almost kissed her. She went off to inform the nurses.

Ten minutes later in came Joan, "Not much change then is there? She can have normal drinks, but the food is much as she is having already."

"What do you mean? Tracey said she could eat normally as long as the food isn't too dry and tough."

Joan looked doubtful, and then she looked down, not meeting my eyes.

"That means she can have fish and chips rather than that mushed up potato stuff?"

"Not chips, no, she won't be able to chew them." Her polite smile snapped back like a rubber band.

I ground my teeth in anguish behind my smile. "But she's eating grapes with tough skins, apples, ham sandwiches, anything I bring for her, what's the difference?"

She looked immovable. I resolved to ring Tracey, how could we have such different interpretations of her recommendations?

An unworthy thought went through my head; did the nurses drug her, because they had to prove me wrong?

Half an hour later Lewis popped in. "D'you wan yor lunch Sweet pea?"

Her eyes fluttered open, she smiled sweetly at him, "Yes please."

"How come she's speaking to you," I shouted. "That's not fair."

"Why didn't you open your eyes for me?" I asked when he'd gone.

"I didn't think it was important. Will I be able to have bacon now?"

Is she serious? Was she acting, was she exerting the only power she has, to not respond? Aunt Gwen laughed when she dropped in on her sick visiting round.

"You ought to have been on the stage, dear."

Her lunch arrived and Mum ate every morsel of it with sudden greed. The pureed meat and potato and all the jelly and melted cheap tasting ice cream. She even drank some of the cold, milky tea. It took ages, she had to be persuaded to open her mouth each time. "Have you finished Mum?"

"No," she'd say testily.

"Well open your mouth then. Open your mouth."

"What?"

I repeated this request over and over, and each time she reluctantly parted her lips a crack.

A new carer came in to collect the empty plates.

"Who is this, Catrin?" pointing at me.

"I don't know," said my Mother.

"It's your daughter," she shouted. "What's her name?"

Mum concentrated on my face. "I can't think at the moment."

"Try," came back.

"I'll think later."

I pushed another grape into her mouth, which she sucked with a self-satisfied, owly expression.

Then she gave me a disdainful look. "How many of you are here?'"

"Only me Mum."

"What time are we meeting those two girls you said?"

After four hours, I had to go. "Thank-you for coming," Mum said. The first sensible thing today.

"Thank-you for not speaking to me for the first two hours and making my journey almost a waste of time," I grumbled.

She looked surprised. "I've only just come," she said. "And wait, I'll come with you."

250

A skeletal smile, skin gleaming like alabaster. She was in her chair, legs like ramrods, the sheet supposedly covering their bony, thin skinned, bruised rigidity had slipped off.

"It's nice to see," she said and smiled again.

My heart soared, she's recognised me, and she's pleased to see me! When she smiles, a blurred version of her beauty and charm survive, which together with her sense of humour, make even strangers warm to her. I sat down happily.

She leant towards me as if to confide a secret, her eyes dancing, girlish giggles emitting from wide lips.

"I think I should tell you," her voice dropped to an unintelligible whisper. "I put a small acorn, help, help . . . long, mutter mutter, mutter." She laughed loudly and looked at me waiting for me to join in. I smiled weakly, having no idea what she had told me.

Mike had arrived from a walk around the nearby park and was sitting on her bed, unable to hear her secret. "Tell *me* now," he encouraged. She repeated the story, her face aglow, almost as lively as it used to be. She looked flushed, pretty and naughty, her voice went down to a whisper. I still had no idea what she was saying, but he nodded sagely. "When did you do that?"

"Not so long ago, help, help," said she coyly.

"Why?"

"I was fed up with, I thought they'd probably get over it, help, help, and it worked." She laughed. "Help. Help. Mutter. Wonder if I've got a funny sense of humour?"

"You didn't get found out then?"

What *are* she and Mike talking about?

She shook her head. "I was very relieved I took that risk," she giggled and looked at me proudly. I tried to smile.

"We're off to Tenby now Mum, we're off then." I hate telling her we're going there, it's reminding her of her inability to come with us.

Her animated expression faded. "I've got some clothes I bought thinking I was going. I can lend you jumpers, blouses, a skirt," she tailed off. "Help, help."

Is it a good thing that she knows what she has been and what she used to do? Possibly, but certainly good that she seems not to know what she has become.

In the car Mike enlightened me.

"She said she slipped something in two people's cups of tea. I'm sure she said: "They didn't pick me for the match and I wanted to play.""

Oh, so *that's* what she was talking about. Nobbling some of the team so she got picked. Well she never did get to play, so it was wishful thinking. Has she really been so keen to play a county match that she considered poisoning the women selected? Wow!

I sat dozing as Mike drove the hundred miles on to Tenby, dreaming about tennis and Mum. So ambitious for me, that is of course as long as I didn't beat the opposite sex. How could she have lived her life so retiringly, so shyly, yet have been so confident when it came to tennis? I've always been so nervous in matches, but for some reason, she never was. If I asked her why she wasn't nervous, she'd say:

"I love playing. I love matches. Competing makes me play better."

What a pity she never played for South Wales, she would have been a natural.


Copying up these notes, I re-read what I wrote in March. Should I have written so irreverently about the Vicar's visit and the resident's responses? Perhaps not, people with dementia are easy targets for humour. They can't defend themselves, so any treatment can be meted out to them: minimum care standards, cheap, badly cooked food and love and respect withdrawn.

Is this why there is no political will to improve elderly care? There is no legal requirement to do so, many are too ill to vote or complain, so any attitude is excusable. We lock them away out of sight. They're deteriorating so why bother to do more than leave then in front of a TV, until they give up living?

Or am I beating myself up too much? Perhaps humour gets carers through the long days. Though it seems exploitative, perhaps its just one of the range of emotions a carer goes through?

On the way back from Tenby, we called again at the Home. It was a beautiful hot June day and the nicest, most helpful nurses were on duty. "Mum hasn't been out of her room for nearly a year," I ventured. "She's in bed. I know her bottom is sore again, but do you think I could take her outside in a wheelchair for half an hour?"

"'Why not," they said smiling cheerfully and Jyoti dashed upstairs to get some helpers to dress Mum and get her downstairs for me. Peeping through the door I saw her sitting in a sling being hoisted out of bed, stiff sticks for legs.

"Help, help," she was shouting. "I don't know what to do." She never gets used to the hoist.

Ten minutes later a grumpy looking mother emerged, dressed with care in her expensive Jaeger black and white two piece. I wheeled her complaining into the small lawned area outside. Her skin seemed to crumble as it met the sun. "I want to go back," she said.

"But look Mum, I've got raspberries and cream for you, just eat a few first. Look I'll turn your chair round so the sun's behind you. You're warm aren't you?"

I felt her hands, which are usually cold. She felt warm. I chatted to her cheerfully and encouragingly. Eventually she ate a few raspberries, but no chocolate, she seemed to be sulking, diminished by bewilderment, dazed by her helplessness and reliance on others. Embarrassed by what she has become, humiliated and humbled by her reduced life. I tried to get her to register her surroundings, by pointing out visitors coming and going, or cars going into the recycling centre next door. She wouldn't eat or talk, but gradually relaxed and accepted being outside.

What has happened to our love for one another? I never feel warmth any more. She seems switched off, uninterested in me and in anything I have to tell her. Is she blaming me for her being here? Can she feel my impatience when she can't communicate? I have read that the people with dementia are no longer moved by things, they feel detached and the emotions are lost. We sat in silence and I opened the poetry book I brought to read on the train. I found John Clare's (1793-1864) poem, 'I am,' written during the twenty-two years that he was in a mental asylum. I didn't read it to her, but the middle verse wrenched my heart:

'Into the nothingness of scorn and noise,
Into the living sea of waking dreams,
Where there is neither sense of life nor joys,
But the vast shipwreck of my life's esteems;
And e'en the dearest . . . that I loved the best.
Are strange . . . nay, rather stranger than the rest.'

She was looking miserable again and had found no pleasure in sitting in the sun. I pushed her back to her oppressive little room. It seems the older one gets, the narrower and more confined life becomes, till it ends, in a box.

Before I left, Mum smiled, or was it a grimace of pain? Was she remembering all the delights that she had ever enjoyed? All those blissful moments which unlike the ordinary ones were exciting? Was she longing for everyone she loved to be living and to have her life all over again?

# Chapter 27—Owain

"$\mathcal{H}$ ello Mum, do the staff think you're deaf? I can hear the sounds of battle from the entrance hall downstairs."

Alys? I didn't know she was coming. It's nice to be hugged.

"Are you watching this Mum, it's not your sort of programme is it? Can I switch it off?"

"Yes." Though it was quite interesting. In fact I enjoyed the parts set in Wales except for King Arthur fighting dragons and wolves. "Owain Glyndwr is our relative."

"Yes? I think you've told me that before. Can you *see* the TV?"

I can hear it. "Of course." Alys looks doubtful.

How are you Mum? I went to see Lizzie and she gave me some money to buy something for you. Is there anything you want?"

"Some sandals and some plain Irish whiskey." Why am I saying that again? I don't want those. Why won't the words come out right? I start and then it comes out wrong, but I blunder on and . . . it's . . . . I don't want to try and talk to anyone any more.

✯      ✯      ✯

*Down this deeply rutted, ancient lane, its time to stop for the night. Round the bend, and . . . that's our old farmhouse and our granary! It's been neglected. The walls weren't covered in that tangle of honeysuckle and dog rose, or the roof with moss and stonecrop. The lovely old lead paned windows are filthy . . . Is it our farm? Ours wasn't called 'Ty Sycharth.'*

*The grass on the lawn is so high, there's no trace of Mother's neat flower beds . . . or Daddy's vegetables and soft fruit . . .*

*They've opened the door . . . It's so dark and dirty but it is our hall. I can smell black-lead from the grate and carbolic from the flag-stoned kitchen, mingling with the soapy smell of Daddy's shaving cream and the rose petals from the bowl in the hall. I don't understand, this isn't Cardiff and our home was pulled down years ago . . .*

*Lizzie's in the lounge, playing the piano . . . The same maroon velveteen couch and all the so familiar objects from our childhood. There's the sinking ship painting and the watercolour of a man on a horse. I feel like a child, so safe and secure here. We're home, our home, a proper home at last.*

*"Fuck! Running water, tins of food and candles." Charlie's in the larder. "No power, but a wood burner range."*

✵    ✵    ✵

Light shining in my eyes. Don't care, go away, this is *my* home . . . too many people. I'm quite tired, a thump hiding in the back of my head. All that talking . . . Don't feel like answering.

That scolding, impatient voice again. "Mum, will you wake up PLEASE!"

I'm yelling, "Go away," but my voice has no sound. I'm soaring with exhilarating speed up into blueness and lying on the wind. I can see them down there . . . perhaps I'll never go back. That's Lewis; he's come to visit.

"Why didn't you open your eyes for me?" Alys looks annoyed.

"I didn't think it was important. Will I be able to have bacon now?" The thought of a crusty white bread bacon sandwich.

Mmm.. hot and salty, soft and crunchy warm fat oozing out into my mouth . . .

✵    ✵    ✵

*"Didn't think I liked corned beef. It's delicious mixed with tinned tomatoes." Lizzie's licking her spoon . . . scraping it again round her dish.*

*"Are you coming up?" Gwen's upstairs. "Our bedroom and Daddy and Mother's looks just the same. Tom's and the back bedroom are so tiny. Come on up, what are you doing?"*

*She never eats much. Shall I open another tin?*

*"Come on, you two."*

*"Alright, OK, coming."*

*Drawing the shutters back, years of darkness evaporate as the dying light reclaims the room and there, through the stale air are our beds, seemingly untouched since our childhood. Lizzie shakes the rugs out of the window, dust flying back in the breeze.*

*"I've washed my hair and these clothes, but don't know if they'll dry, it smells damp."*

*"Come to bed Gwen." The persistent rain sounds like a lullaby . . .*

✻      ✻      ✻

*What woke me up? Where am I? The journeys back and forth are often when I'm sleeping . . . I'm not conscious of travelling, but when I get here life continues as normal. It's warm and comfortable, so why am I so tense and alert in our moonlit bedroom? There's only the wind and Gwen's even breathing next to me. What was that? Sounded like a window downstairs banging shut. I'm really awake now and so uneasy. It's just the sounds of the house . . . the cracks and creaks of an old building. Nothing frightening. I'll sit on the window seat and look through the lead panes, like I used to do. The rain has stopped, a few last spectral wisps of vapour floating across the chill, bright stars. I'm still scared . . .*

*What's that? Shadowy shapes moving through the orchard towards the house? I want to go back to a safer world, now, please . . . They're huge! Can they get in? Are they wolves or horses? They're underneath the window . . . what shining, evil eyes . . . Oh! What touched me?*

*"What are you doing up in the middle of the night?"*

*"Shhh Gwen, you scared me to death . . . look down there!"*

*Fear and horror in her face . . . she's seen them.*

*"How many are there?" She's in shock, can't speak. I'll crouch down and peep over the sill . . . can they see me? Five looking up at me, white fangs bared and gleaming in the moonlight.*

*Gwen's like a statue, hardly breathing . . . shivering uncontrollably in the shadows.*

*"Are we going to die?"*

257

*I must be calm. Breathe deeply, breathe. Why can't I get out of this world into my other one?* "Lets wait, perhaps they'll go away . . ."

*Frozen right through, its dawn . . . So stiff . . . seem to have been praying for hours . . ."*There's nothing there now, they've gone."

"D'you think they've got inside?"

"Don't think so, but I'm not going down to look. Let's wait til we hear the men going downstairs."

*At last, voices, footsteps and sounds from the kitchen. The sun is shining, a thrush sings in the overgrown fruit trees, pigeons scuttling and a dove cooing on the roof above.*

"Let's go down . . . ooh..I can barely stand my body's frozen stiff."

"Lizzie's still asleep. Ok, Gwen wait for me."

"Wolves as big as horses? Cut the crap girls. You been dreamin',"

*Charlie's doesn't believe us.* "What both of us? If squirrels get bigger, why not wolves?"

"What are we going to do? They're enormous, they'll tear us all to pieces." *Gwen's getting hysterical.*

"Get out and find their footprints then. That ground is damp and soft, right? Show us their fuckin' prints."

"I'm not going out there." *Gwen is adamant.*

"Well, we didn't hear them." *He looks so sceptical.* "Come on, lets look."

"How can that happen . . . that there's none under the window, on the lawn, or in the orchard? How is that possible Gwen?" *I don't understand it.*

"I don't know. We were so happy to be here, why is everywhere we go so dangerous and terrifying?"

"Try and forget last night, it was probably a dream."

"Its OK for you Lizzie, you slept through it all. We definitely couldn't both have been dreaming the same dream." *Tears are shining in her eyes. "Can we move on now it's light, I don't want to spend another night here."*

*"Come on Gwen, this is a good spot to get our strength up for the last lap. Stay calm. Here, drink this." Charlie has made herb drinks.*

*I'll sit outside the kitchen door in the sun with my strange tasting brew. Mother's blue hydrangeas stroke me in the little breeze. Rub my hand across them . . . it smells of their breath, that fresh, sharp mixture of dew, air and sap.*

✻ ✻ ✻

"Time for a wash, Catrin."

Two girls with a plastic bowl and flannel. I don't want them doing it, it hurts. I'm not in the mood for this. "I'm washing myself."

"What? You want to get washed and dressed for when your daughter comes don't you?"

"No, no, help help, help."

"Just a quick wash."

I'll wash myself. "Don't pull me." . . . a wet flannel . . . rub . . . chocolate coloured woman, gentle. "Thank you Mother." The little hollow in her neck is deep and dark. "Where are we going Mother?"

✻ ✻ ✻

Haul myself out of my tennis dream . . . where am I?

"Open your mouth," Alys says.

I thought I'd just eaten. "Shall I tell you what I did?"

Alys moves towards me.

"I wanted to play for South Wales, so I gave my partners some poison in their tea." I lower my voice. "I *poisoned* them, but not with too much."

"Oh?"

Alys isn't shocked. Doesn't she understand? "They weren't ill long and then I played. *I* played a county match!" I can't help laughing. Why doesn't *she* laugh? Why's she so agitated, running

259

her hands through her hair and looking at Mike. What's the point of me talking to you Alys, if you're not going to listen?

I wonder if I can put thoughts into her mind, by thinking them hard and staring at her? She stares back as if mesmerised, then looks at Mike again.

"What did you say Catrin?"

He understands. I want them to go away now, I feel sleepy. They're going to Tenby; well I should get there soon.

✳     ✳     ✳

*"Move over you two. I hope you were imagining those wolves."*

*"Can't you sleep in your own bed Lizzie? We're much too squashed." Though I'll never sleep, I'm too tense. It's like waiting for your execution. It's like daylight with the full moon.*

*"We probably were dreaming." I'm trying to be comforting, but I don't believe we were . . .*

*I must have been dozing, is that tapping? Tapping on the window? "Ohhh!" A huge wolf face, saliva dripping from its fangs. "Scream." A squeak came out. Lizzie and Gwen scream and scream . . . The gleaming red eyes turn to Charlie and Bill at the door.*

*"What the fuck?"*

*"Shite!"*

*"It's enormous, Charlie, is it standing on something?" Lizzie cries.*

*"I ain't going to get close enough to look. Lets close these shutters before it smashes the glass. Jesus that's a big animal."*

*The shutters bang shut blocking out the dreadful face. "Don't go . . ." They're swearing in Daddy and Mother's room, there must be more . . .*

*Help! Our window and shutters are smashing as if they were matchwood and paper. "Come on, let's get downstairs." Wolves pressed against the lounge window . . . run, run out of the back door . . . Across a field towards that mound, covered with trees and bushes. Why can't I switch this world off, go back to my safe one? Concentrate, visualise my room but I'm just getting slower and slower. I'm moving in slow motion, straggling behind the others.*

*"Come on, Catrin," Lizzie pants.*

*Charlie's looking back, "Move, woman!"*

*Gwen has been deathly quiet; she's suddenly sprinting towards the hillock, singing hysterically in her tuneless voice:*

*"Birds fly over the rainbow, why oh why can't I?"*

*Her body's jerking; her arms flapping wildly as if she's taxiing for take off. The moon makes her seem unearthly, translucent.*

*"Gwen wait, let's be together." But she's going faster and shouting louder:*

*"That's where you'll find me."*

*She's crumpled into a heap under the tree, shaking and shuddering, seeming to fold into herself, smaller and smaller.*

*"Everything dies Gwen, everyone dies in the end . . . shall we pray?"*

*The grass is lush and sprinkled with sleeping daisies and clover, imminent death makes everything more beautiful, more precious.*

*They're here. Snarling and salivating, as if they're exacting the last minutes of pleasure from our agony. I'm instantly calm, floating upwards . . . at last . . . leaving my body and the others paralysed with fear below. Is this what happens to people at death?*

*Who's that? Strong figure in chain mail leaping in front of the wolves . . . holding that enormous axe aloft? That biggest wolf isn't scared . . . snapping ferociously at the air between them white fangs bared and gleaming. It's snarling crouching, ready to spring. The honed metal of the axe glints in the moonlight. I can see their eyes, one pair red, evil, the other fearless and shining.*

*"Why are you desecrating my home, evil spirits?"*

*The powerful beast is so much bigger than the man . . . it's tensing to take off! Look! Row after row of men appearing behind our saviour. Some are wearing helmets and carrying wooden shields and swords, some with staves or big, long-tined forks.*

*The wolves are hesitating, but it's too late, the horde of men are chopping them into pieces. Blood everywhere . . . their massive bodies thrashing in agony. A writhing mass of fur and blood. I can't look at the gory slaughter.*

*Relief and joy! I can see myself sinking onto the dew damp grass, weak from shock, light-headed, shivery. Who are these medieval dressed men? Shards of memories of a bloody, romantic past are flitting in and out of my brain . . .*

*There's our saviour . . . blood-spattered and breathing deeply, a look of triumph on his face.*

*"I am Owain Glyndwr. I would not let harm befall you, Catrin, or your two sisters. My descendants, you have the hearts of true Cymro."*

*I'm back in to myself. "You saved our lives!"*

*"Croeso!"*

*Suddenly, this mound we're standing on has a fine manorial hall surrounded by a high fence of wooden palisades and a moat.*

*"This is like a dream."*

*His eyes smile at us and his strong face, so like Daddy and Tom's, softens.*

*"You are where you want to be. It is only with the heart that you can see what is invisible to the eyes. You have come almost to the end of your quest. These men from Pembroke and Kidwelly who want to return to their homes will escort you. Enter for some rest and refreshments."*

*Through the massive wooden door, we're in a large, long, beamed room lit by tallow candles, minstrels playing in a gallery above. A stout table extending the length of the room, with a cloth of crimson and gold, is covered with food and drink. Owain apologises in his powerful baritone to the guests for the delay to the banquet. His grey-blue eyes, so like mine, smile at me and his face is lit by a magic radiance that I have never seen before.*

*"My wife, Margaret, children Meredudd, Dafydd, and Catrin, of the burnished brown tresses and moonlight eyes. This is her wedding feast."*

*They smile, we smile, we understand, but don't speak the Welsh very well.*

*"I've never seen so much meat." Lizzie's eyes are shining." Goose, boar, hams and what are those little birds? Try a sip of this mead Catrin."*

*"No, I just don't like alcohol. Might be partridge, pheasant or quail?"*

"Or wood pigeon. This is a very jolly evening, I'm going to sleep like a log tonight."

Waking, it's light and the rain is falling in a monotonous drizzle, spattering against the window in the wind. Spiders are creeping around in my skin.

"You must drink, Catrin. Try and drink won't you," call Lizzie and Gwen well groomed in cream and green suits with matching earrings, as they walk away.

Why? I've never drunk alcohol, they know that; it's got such a nasty taste. People rush past my door, no peace. This world is an uncomfortable place where the simplest things are a nuisance and nothing has a name. I'm not opening my mouth. I feasted too much last night, I need nothing now.

"Come on Catrin, just a sip of tea?"

I want to escape into the silence behind my eyes, but someone comes and talks on and on, looking at me hopefully for a response. My heart's thumping . . . . my brain skittering about from her words to mine, to my other life, here, there and where I want to be. This chocolate's nice. That's nice, nice. Saliva running down my chin . . . my arms won't lift to my mouth; they're lost in space. She's wiping it away, I'm ashamed. "It's OK Mum, it's Alys, I love you."

The Indian women wait at the door, their eyes masked, indifferent, what are they seeing? "Catrin need change," they say.

I feel free, beyond attachment, beyond this stiff, painful, emaciated body, this room I never leave. There is no reality except what I hold inside me. My eyes are wide open to my other world . . .

"'This is your energy drink Catrin, try and take a little. You'll be ill if you don't eat and drink."

I *am* ill, I've been ill for too long, why don't they go away and let me sleep. I smile, but keep my mouth closed.

"Alys asked us to wash your hair Catrin."

No, leave me alone. Don't lift my head. Everything silent apart from the sloshing water on my head.

"Does your neck hurt Catrin?"

Grit my teeth, everything hurts, leave me alone. Rubbing my head . . . that's nice, nice.

"The hairdryer's not too hot is it Catrin?"

Smile, that's nice, warm, nice. Combing my hair. They go away and it's all silent, just throbbing in my head. Shake it to clear it. 'Birds fly over the rainbow,' throbbing and humming, thudding, heavy waves thud down and stream away.

"How do you feel now Mum? That's better isn't it?"

A question, must move my lips, grab the thuds, wait and I'll answer, red, red lips.

"Good." Did I say it? Yes . . . red lips smile . . . use the right words for a smile.

Lips coming towards me, pursing, turn my head, but they touch my cheek, smile. The doorbell, who's coming? Is it time for my lesson? Am I in the right classroom?

# Chapter 28—Mum Switches Off. 2006

*I* looked into her blank, pallid face for some sign of recognition or enjoyment as her mouth opened and closed for the spoonfuls of raspberries and cream.

"Who is your mountain?" she asked in a gratey, gruff voice.

"Who makes your cake?" Then without stopping for answers. "I can see you're going to have a highly entertaining help, standing in the clock. Is that Owen behind the door?"

"It's your coat, Mum, it's just your coat."

She swallowed the last spoonful of fruit as two carers came to the door and I was asked to wait outside while they changed her. I hung around outside the door, nowhere to sit, so I leant against the corridor wall and tried to concentrate on my book. One carer came out and I saw before the door closed, a stick being held up to be flannelled.

"I've always had big, heavy legs," she used to say. Well not now Mum, not now.

"Your mother might have scabies, we're treating it with sulphur ointment," Joan said coming up the stairs with a container of something.

"How would she develop that?" I asked.

"A few other women have it and she has a rash, so it might be scabies." Joan passed on down the corridor.

"I thought everyone had their own personal flannels and towels?" I muttered to her disappearing back.

Going back into the room I wondered how many more trials Mum would have to put up with? I stroked her shoulder; her skin on her arms and chest had a red, raw rash.

"Does this rash itch Mum, is it sore?"

She ignored the question. "I'm not going to see you again."

"Yes Mum, I told you, I will be back next week. Gwen will be here after lunch, and when I'm not here I think about you."

"Help, You can do very well without me. Help."

"No, I can't Mum, I don't want to. Stay strong, give me a smile."

Her gaunt features and down turned mouth didn't relax, but her washed out, pale blue eyes focused on me. "Come on Mum." I smiled encouragingly, but there was no smile, no expression as I waved and blew her a kiss.

## SATURDAY JULY 22ND

"She was so spoilt, got away with everything," Aunt Gwen said with feeling. "Just acted helpless so we did things for her."

We paced around outside Mum's door while the carers changed her 'pad', and we were talking about Mum as we usually did.

"But I'd spoil her for ever if she could just recover a bit, so we could have sensible conversations."

"Was she spoilt because she was the youngest? Did you all spoil her?" I asked, though we have discussed this so many times before. Then Gwen delivered a bombshell, why have I never known this?

"It was always Mother and Catrin, giggling together in Mother's bedroom with the door closed. Lizzie and I were never invited in."

I was shocked. I had thought it was her siblings who spoilt Mum.

"But I thought it was you who were the favourite?"

Gwen shook her head. "Perhaps Daddy had a soft spot for me, but she always got what she wanted."

I looked at her and suddenly I knew. Underneath the love and support the sisters show for one another there has always been a frisson of jealousy. The spoilt younger sister, who was the cleverest, best at sport, best singer . . .

Aunt Gwen was deep in thought:

"His parents owned shops, he was sporty, had degrees, handsome . . ."

I felt faint, as if all the air had been sucked out of the corridor. My head was pounding with my discovery. "But you loved *David*," I said faintly.

"He'd been my boyfriend years." She straightened and looked at me, her social face back in place.

"Of course. I'd always loved him. He was a good husband and would do anything for me, but he should have stayed in the army. I had to work until I was eighty!"

'Did you fancy Dad then?" I gasped.

But she had regained her composure and was giving nothing away.

"He was attractive," she said cautiously, "but David was my childhood sweetheart. Everyone rushed into marriage because of the war."

The door opened and out came Swamini and Pria: "You come in now."

## SUNDAY AUGUST 13TH

Mum was asleep. Mouth agape, minus her top teeth. Eyes deeply sunken, her hair in stiff, uncombed strands. I wondered how long she can last, so pale, shrunken and helpless, her breath so shallow and slight, coming in small unsteady sucks.

She seems to be desiccating, from within, dust mimicking life. A James Blunt song came into my head:'
*I'm watching you breathing for the last time.'*
Am I?

"Mum, Mum, I've come to see you."

She opened her eyes slowly, showing no surprise or pleasure. I told her with a pang of guilt about our weekend in Tenby, assuaging it by cramming soft fruit and chocolates into her mouth. She ate with no apparent enjoyment and was far away, as she often was, a long, long way away, in that unseeable space that I cannot imagine or follow her to. Her eyes were empty wells. She is lying there but she may as well have gone to the moon.

Lewis had seen me arriving and brought in a pot of tea and biscuits.

"Bore da. How are you Alys? He asked brightly.

267

"Fine, fine. But Mum's so switched off, she doesn't really want to see me."

"Don't worry fach, it's just one of her bad days. There now, she'll be alright."

The encompassing kindness in his voice made me aware that there were tears running down my cheeks.

He went and I sat wondering how long she will hold on for, it's been five years already, but her organs and heart are strong and her health has always been good. Presumably she'll go on until the DLB makes her forget how to swallow, then breathe. How naive I was, not realising what a disease like this can do, that Mum would be so diminished that I'd lose her long before I actually have . . .

I held her hand and stroked her stiff, curled fingers. Her eyes were closed and she breathed those quick, light breaths, as fragile as a glass thread. What if she went into a vegetative state, clinging to life with her brain seeming not to function and they ask me if they should resuscitate her, as they have done already, 'for their records.' Would I allow them to let her slide away as tranquilly and unremarked as she has preferred for her life? No, of course I would not. How can I make the decision when it is time for her to go? I told them then, "Yes, resuscitate her," and it would always be "Yes, yes, yes!"

Why was I thinking like this? Because she is going further and further away from me? She opened her eyes and started to talk. I strained to understand her jumbled words, but had no idea what she was saying. If only I knew if she is locked in that crumbling body and tangled sieve of her mind, or if she sometimes escapes to a better place? How many times have I sat by her bed wondering if there was more to her life than lying there? I want her to be having wonderful dreams in which she can make herself understood, where there's meaning, enjoyment, where her soul soars? I believe that the value of her life, the essential her will not die, just this worn out body, but where will she go? One minute here, the next, where?

I took out my tweezers to distract her from her unintelligible stream of words.

"Can I pull one hair out on your chin?"

"No, no," she said. "No, no."

"Why not, Mum, you're usually keen."

"It's keeping me *warm.*"

Still got her sense of humour, her repartee then.

She lapsed into complete silence and I could think of nothing else to tell her. We sat for half an hour, a poem 'Going to Heaven,' going round and round in my head:

*Going to Heaven! —*
*How dim it sounds!*
*And yet it will be done*
*As sure as flocks go home at night*
*Unto the shepherds arm!'*

Emily Dickinson (1830-1886)

Then I made my excuses: "It's a long drive, Mum. I want to get back before it gets dark."

She said nothing, no reproach, she didn't ask me to stay longer as she usually does. Does she think I have given up on her and can only bear to flit in and out, push a few things into her mouth and rush off? Instead of travelling by train and spending the day with her, my visits this summer have all been in passing. On the way to, or back from Tenby, with Cerys, Mike and various friends. We rarely stay long, wanting to get to the coast for a swim or to London before the evening rush. My heart was gripped with guilt as I said, "Yes, I've gotta go now Mum." She looked at me, no expression, not anything. Was that a pleading behind her eyes? It seems such a long time since we really communicated. What was the point in sitting not talking? Are my visits a pleasure for either of us? Or have we both adjusted to how it is and stepped away from one another? If only I knew.

"She doesn't know how long you've been there, don't worry, she has no sense of time," Mike said as we drove away.

Mmm doesn't she? I'm not so sure.

What a terrible way to die, you certainly do not 'earn' the sort of death you get. Mum didn't deserve this lingering end. I knew a horrible human being who died hitting the most perfect volley to win a tennis final. Though perhaps that was worse for those who loved him, one minute being full of vivid life and then the next dead. Would one be able to accept that he was gone for ever as I am having time to do with this person I have loved all my life, as she so slowly disappears, leaving a shell which looks like Mum and needs care?

# Chapter 29—August

$\mathcal{B}$right morning sun on my eyes. Have I slept for a long time? Open eyes. Glistening raindrops on the window, sparkling in the spider's web. Open eyes. Want to sleep. Mustn't sleep. Open eyes, open wi..de.

Strong brown arms.

"Up Catrin."

Float up, up. "Shall I creep into your tent with lobster and lamb? Pork and gravy?"

"Come on Catrin, open your mouth."

Choking, choke, can't breathe. "Don't squirt that into my mouth, help, help, help."

"You *have* to drink Catrin."

"I'm still full, help, help" Her brown gentle face, white teeth, so close, too near.

There's Owain. "Thank you for saving our lives, are you coming to South Wales with us?"

"I am full of hiraeth for my green and pleasant land, which is no more; I will go back to rest cariad. You will be safe with these men."

That squirrel is making a jibber jabber clackety sort of sound.

"Are your teeth falling out?"

It's opening its mouth to speak and out drops every tooth, cling, bing, clitter, clatter. Stooping, its sucking them up, one by one and smiling its animal smile as it lopes away.

"This not eating and drinking must stop Catrin. Do you want to be ill? Drink some of this now." I know that voice.

Coolness seeps into my mouth, trickles in my throat, swallow, no swallowing, why don't I swallow? I do and suck the liquid greedily.

"Yes, Mother." Her black satin high-necked dress has a little white frill under her chin, she sits proud and erect. She looks beautiful.

"You have been very brave Catrin, keeping your sisters safe from every danger. You're nearly home, we'll play tennis again, you'll still be the best. Now eat this banana, eat up, you must be strong to finish your journey. Yes, good girl."

And Gwen smiles.

"Where's Mother, Gwen?"

"Shh, just eat up dear."

"Where's Mother?"

Gwen has had her hair done; it's thick, grey and glossy. "Is that a new coat? *I'd* like a new coat, does grey suit me?"

Voices. "Well done Gwen. How about your lunch Sweet Pea?"

He smiles, I smile. "Or some ice-cream?"

I nod; he's squeezing my hand . . .


"It's a chest infection, let her daughter know."

Taken my eyes . . . can't see . . . see through my nose, sing through my nose, don't whisper, speak up.

"Do you feel Ok? Are you in pain?"

Gwen's voice is echoey, far away; the words land noiselessly before they reach me . . . she's blurry at the edges. I'm light, transparent, the air's thin. My heart pulses, thump, thump, there's a humming in my brain.

Rising upwards, flying higher and higher, circling in a warm air current, plunging through a cloud of wetness . . . higher and higher. Looking down at twinkly lights in the inky blackness. Will I float so high that I'll see the earth spinning below? And be sucked towards the sun and explode into a million fragments?

Do I want to return? Well, just for a while . . . air rushing past . . . falling to nowhere . . . try to catch the air . . . too fast . . . breathless, dry mouthed, dizzy . . . climb into bed for a sleep.

❈　　　❈　　　❈


*I feel refreshed for the journey. Can I ride on that sledge through the glistening snow? Sit; warm in my sheepskin boots and woolly slacks while dry flakes hurry downwards and the moon hides veiled and sinister behind the scurrying clouds. Charlie stands in the snow, his breath like smoke.*

*"Well girls, you don't need us no more, you've got these guys."*

*"Where are you going?" I feel a sharp pang of loss. "Why aren't we all going together?"*

*"You'll have your family. We've no reason to go to South Wales. Might stay around here. I've looked after you for long enough now."*

*Rush of warmth flowing through me, heart quickening . . . reach out my arms to hug. Don't want him to go. Snow in my face, blinding me . . . fighting back tears of loss. Sinking into a hole, so cold, jump up, watch those icicles inside me . . . Charlie waves in stripy pyjamas. Squirrels and wolves pull us along, whoosh, across the snow, get out, dance, twirl, leap in the sun, in the snow. Quick, close the curtains.*

*Thump, thump, thump. Why's Alys holding that photo so close? "Yes, I can see, I know that's a baby, honey or jam? Hold the photograph . . . is this Mother? Or Daddy?*

*"Am I going to Tenby now Owain?"*

*"Seek Cadw and Ceridwen, the world's spin changes there."*

*No, I'm impatient to see Tenby, my family. Travelling on and on and on, the sleigh crunching and creaking on the snow.*

*Thump, thump. The sun slides across the grass, gleaming in the puddles and sparkling on the spider's webs, birds flash past, beaks snapping for insects. Snap, snap.*

*There's a woman sitting, stirring a cauldron? Is she Ceridwen? Head bowed, her long brown, velvet cloak pulled close around her.*

*She turns and she is me. That was my cloak, those were my pearls. My hair is pretty; I like my face, it's open, clear, soft lips, big grey eyes.*

*"Where have you been?" She's smiling, "I have been waiting." We laugh together. I wonder what she is thinking of my thin, grey hair, my sagging skin, myself now.*

*"At Caereu you can drink this broth and be me again," she says slyly. Her voice echoes round the snowy valley and the wolves and squirrels in their harnesses shrink away, burrowing deep into the snow.*

*"No, No. I want to get to Tenby, now."*

*A warm wind is blowing, melting the snow and whirling away the cauldron and myself. The squirrels and wolves are bursting apart into millions of tiny round pieces and disappearing into the earth. Lush leaves and flowers spring out of the bare trees. I smell the mild, sweet air.*

# Chapter 30—Tuesday August 22nd 2006

$S$aw Mum last Sunday and then two days later, developed lower back pain. Was it that long car journey? It got worse playing tennis and became so painful I could barely sit or stand. By Saturday, any movement, even lying down was agony and then the Home rang to say she had 'bubbling' in her chest and wouldn't swallow anything.

"I called the Doctor and he's put her back on antibiotics."

How many dozen times has she been on them in the last five years I wondered?

At 7am on Sunday morning. I tried to get up to go to the toilet and the pain was so horrific that I was losing sensation in my right foot. I couldn't stand, it felt as if my back would snap in half . . . the pain . . . the pain! But I can't wet the floor! I was determined to get to the bathroom, falling awkwardly onto the toilet seat, in horrendous agony.

Mike was asleep; somehow, I *had* to get up off the toilet seat. I breathed out and pulled myself up by clinging onto the basin, crooked, bent, sweating and blacked out.

Some time later I found myself lying on the floor in the narrow gap between the toilet and bath, shivering and shaking and with a sore head.

The next few hours were a blur. I couldn't move. Mike covered me and gave me the phone and I rung up NHS Direct and within 20 minutes paramedics were giving me gas. This immediately relaxed all my muscles and I was able to get up, be dressed and walk to the ambulance.

Later, back in bed, stuffed up with painkillers, anti-inflammatories and muscle relaxants Riverside rung.

"We've called the Doctor in again. What do you want him to do?"

They're asking me if I want them to let her die I thought.

*'She may be fading away: fading out into nothing and nothing at all, as we do, as we all do, as it happens,'* as Ken Smith wrote in 'Here (Shed Poems 1980-2001, Bloodaxe),' but:

"I love her, I want her to live," I said. "I can't make the decision for her to die, only she can make that."

"We'll send her to hospital for assessment," they said.

Why is this happening to me now? I should be with her but I can only get out of bed with a great deal of pain and assistance.

'Assessment' continued through Monday and she was 'comfortable.' Robert had visited both days.

This morning 8am; I telephoned and she was more alert and looking around.

"The speech therapist is coming to do an assessment later. She refused to open her mouth yesterday," said the Sister.

"Tell her I love her and no matter what, I'm coming to see her tomorrow," I said.

I bought my rail ticket and planned to take as many painkillers as I had to, to get myself there. At 4pm I rang again and asked the nurses to tell her I was looking forward to seeing her in the morning.

# Chapter 31—Somewhere Over the Rainbow

"*I*'m quite tired." They're pulling up my nightie and lifting me. They're strong; they turn me over and strip it off. Turn me back again. A man with very short-trimmed hair . . . a syringe in his hand. "What's that for?"

I want to get up, but the needle is spearing my arm. Why is he doing this? Robert's holding my hand. Is he crying?

"Are you ill Robert?"

"Hang on Mum, Alys's coming soon, she'll get you eating. And Cerys is bringing her new baby, your great grandchild, at the weekend. Try and drink something, open your mouth, drink. Please try and drink."

I'm awake, or perhaps I've dozed. Eyes stuck, mouth gummy, what a horrible taste. Throbbing head. A watery grey light peering around the curtains. I'm sweaty and my whole body aches, especially my bottom, always my bottom.

I'm watching a very old woman lying still, in a bed, tubes and pipes from her nose and mouth. Her face is hawk like, eyes so deeply sunken, they can surely never open again. Is she breathing? She must be alive, there's a heavy looking man sitting at her side. He's holding a hand, stuck stiffly at an angle, another tube attached to the wrist . . . Her hair is greasy, stiff, her skin transparent, she looks at deaths door. Poor woman, not much life left there.

A nurse, with a syringe on a metal tray, swabs the scrawny arm not attached to a drip and injects her. I shiver, it's so cold.

Two more nurses . . . rolling her onto her side. I hear myself groan, the pains all over my body subside.

The fields are covered with frost, sparkling as the sun climbs over the trees and the grey dawn changes to blue. Brown and gold leaves drift down.

What's buzzing at the back of my head? Move my lips, open my mouth, where have my words gone? Help. What's that dog doing? Is it Holly, Gareth's dog?

"Go and look for your master, go and look, dog."

The TV thumps in my head, flashing on and off, so loud, always so loud.

Another dog, floating, baring its teeth, "Can you catch squirrels?" It's tail's cut short, like a screw. Screw screwing into my eyes. "Put the TV off please."

Women in blue, don't take my knitting away from me; push a spoon at my mouth. My lips won't open . . . can't speak. Don't turn me over again . . . cold . . . can't breathe . . . head throbbing.

Am I here? Or there? Is this me? It's so quiet, just throbs in my head. Move my head, shake the throbs out. "Dog, did you find Gareth? Help."

I'm looking for him too, and Alys and Robert. No, not Alys and Robert. Mother, Daddy, my grandchildren and nieces and nephews. "Alys, where is your father?"

She's singing a song. I know that melody, 'Somewhere over the rainbow.' Shall I try it? I'm floating up, opening out; I've become so light.

Thoughts running through my head like sand, running away. I'm asleep, awake, light shining in my eyes . . . What's left in my eyes? Will I be home before dark?

"Up we go, come on, up."

Hoisted up, pillows behind me. I'm cold, cold; I go and hide in the top of my head. Help.

There's a humming in my brain, shadows, faint, blurring at the edges:

"She's on her way out I'm afraid, her organs are failing, she can't swallow,"

Who?

No food in my mouth. Open? No food. What's biting? Bite what? Bite voices, dogs, eyes closed, no squirrels, men, hundreds of men, walking, I'm walking, not far, no snow, cold.

I flight, float, hollow, lightning. Marching, marching, arms swing. Lizzie and Gwen hold my arms." Thank-you for looking after us, for saving our lives." They're looking at me with love, with gratitude. Where the fish flew from the otter . . .

I float, fly, gravity not working. No faces, men, faceless marching to Tenby.

Down the hill, marching. I know this hill, these gardens, a bend, this slope down. Gwen strokes my hand, she has cake, I don't need to eat. Marching. Sweet, soft, melting chocolate. We're singing hymns, singing together, the men sing, I harmonise. My Sunday school teacher with smiley eyes says, "Well done Catrin you're a heroine. Let's sing, Jesus bids us shine."

Gwen goes across to the other class, out of the door to Lizzie's class. Out of the door. Out to the car park. Up to the cross. Carew cross. Youthful cross.

March on with all the men and Miss Jenkins, marching, marching: "Jesus bids us shine like a . . ."

Down to the last bend, breathing in the salty air, seagulls above. I can see the sea. I can see the blue lapping sea, the sky and the sea reflecting one another. People on the hard, golden sand below. Down, down I stretch out my arms, to Charlie; no he's not here . . .

There he is in army uniform, strong body, sleeked down hair, it's John waiting for me. "Here I am," he turns, he smiles, it's Gareth. "My love." Arms out-stretched, rough khaki cloth against my cheek. I breathe him in. We run. Arm in arm, down the beach, down a bright white corridor to a tennis court, apple trees all around. We play, not speaking, slowly, dreamily, he serves, I hit, the wind blows, he laughs, he always wins in the wind. We swing and sing, the wind blows, I'm home.

# Chapter 32—The Day After she Died. Wednesday August 23rd

*A*t 6pm yesterday our phone rang. In trying to reach it from bed, I dropped it and lost the connection. It was Riverside and I couldn't get them back, my calls kept going on to their answer phone. Because I had spoken to the Sister of Mum's ward less than two hours before, I didn't realise that the nurse on duty in the Home was ringing to say that Mum had suddenly deteriorated. Eventually they got hold of Robert and she died that evening (Tuesday) with him there. The first but final time that I wasn't there for her, to hold her hand and tell her how much I loved her.

Robert was there and I wasn't. Robert held her hand and I didn't. I let her down, and I'm in agony. But then I also feel that perhaps she didn't want me there, that she somehow had the power to make my back go into spasm on the day that she became ill, she had *never* wanted to cause trouble to anyone. How could it have happened that neither of us knew about the other's problems and that we each became worse and worse together. How *could* we have ended up in hospitals, me in London and she in Cardiff, on the same day? More than coincidence, surely?

I came, painfully, stuffed up with drugs, on the train this morning. Robert picked me up and took me to the Hospital:

"What happened Robert, describe it, please?"

"Oh . . ."

"Was it as if the air was slowly leaking out of her? She was like a punctured ball, flat beneath the blankets? Was it, was it?"

"We..ell . . . ."

"Was her skin like parchment, stretched tight over those prominent bones which are so sharp that they could almost cut the blanket covering them? Greasy hair stuck to her head in tufts, her nose a pointed beak?"

"Y..e..s, I *suppose* so."

"How did you *feel*?"

"I was frightened, lonely, it was raining quite hard."

Robert's face had melted into a puddle of loose, pouched, moist, grey skin.

"Was the wind lashing the rain against the windows, the drops running silently down?"

He sighed. "She said, something like: 'Where shall I go?' You don't have to go anywhere, I kept telling her not to go anywhere, you were coming and Cerys. 'Hang on Mum, Alys and Cerys are coming, Cerys is bringing her baby girl, she's only four weeks old, you want to see her don't you?' But she might have been beyond hearing. A nurse came and pulled the curtains around us, and I was scared, alone with my dying mother."

"What did you see? Come on Robert remember. Please."

"A pulse was jumping in her neck, she was swallowing with difficulty. Oh, I, I don't know, she was quiet, then her mouth gaped, she whispered 'help, help.' Then she did a sort of deep wheezing as if her tubes were blocked, with the odd gasp, or snort and then huge terrible breaths that went on and on, then a big violent one and no more."

"What did you do?"

"I made myself put my hand out to touch her hand on the sheet. Though with her fingers all curled in, it was more like a claw. There was a sigh and I felt something like . . . the life force, a little gust, flow out."

He looked as if he was going to cry and I remembered that Christmas when he was a little boy, opening his stocking while it was still dark and taking out a joke present wrapped by Dad, a chicken claw. His screams shook the house. He never ate poultry again. I imagined him staggering out into the quiet wet, night, dazed and bewildered that everything out here was the same, though his life had changed. I imagined a gust of wind lifting his hair, like a caress from his mother and him calling out, "Mum, I'm sorry I didn't do more." Then walking on, tears coursing down his cheeks.

I went down to the bowels of the hospital, having asked to have her brought from the fridge so that I could see her. She lay in a pink bed, covered with a pink, flowery duvet. I wondered if men were taken to a blue room? I held her rigid shoulders, hugged her with all the love I have for her that now has nowhere to go. Then I leant over to kiss her cold, damp, waxy brow, her tightly sealed eyes. As I did, I felt a transmission of energy and I was inside a scene.

Mum was dressed in her tennis whites against a background of apple trees and summer flowers. She was laughing, concentrating on the ball as she hit it low over the net to the far corner of Dad's side. He laughed too and hit it up into the wind. The ball circled around, almost landed, and then flew off and over Mum's head as she ran forward, to bounce behind her. Robert and I bit our apples and giggled, Dad's won again.

They embraced at the net, eyes shining with love for one another. Then they faded away and away and Mum was stiff and cold under my lips.

I straightened up and stroked her icy, stiff hair. "Bye Mum, I love you, I'm so very sorry I haven't been with you. I love you, and I'll keep on loving you, even though everything that you've thought and are, has gone somewhere else."

Then I realised that my back had no pain, no stiffness, it was completely normal. The drugs would have worn off by now, how could this have happened, how?

Eyes smarting and wet, but feeling calm and peaceful, I turned and walked away from her, singing 'Somewhere Over the Rainbow,' at full volume in my head.

I'm back on the train going home, drained by grief, writing and thinking of how she accepted her lot without self pity or anger, and of the journey we took through her memory loss, incapacity and the erosion of her identity. Of the world we entered, of hospitals, homes, drugs, catheters, nappies, cheap badly cooked food and the terrible boredom of her long incarceration. I am numb, exhausted and so tired of all the train journeys and the mental efforts of trying to get the best for her, but more than *anything* I wish that she were still alive and we could go back to the beginning of her illness and I had another chance to make it better for her.

# Addendum

 here are between 7 and 8,000 people in the Uk who have been diagnosed with dementia. It is characterised by a loss of nerve cells, but there is no definitive diagnostic test until after death. There is no cure.

The most common form of dementia is Alzheimer's or AD (62%), which could be caused by a build up of amyloid plaques and tau tangles.

Vascular Dementia (27%)is the second most common. This is characterised by problems with the blood supply to the brain, it is often accompanied by AD and also strokes. Remembering, solving problems and concentrating are affected.

Dementia with Lewy bodies (10%.) is related to AD and to Parkinson's. We do not know why the tiny spherical deposits of protein disrupt the chemical messages, but there are attention, hallucination and movement problems and the symptoms fluctuate.

Posterior Cortical Atrophy (1-2%), is often misdiagnosed because at first it affects only literacy, skilled movements and vision, eg, recognising colours, shapes, faces and words.

Fronto Temporal dementia (2%) affects language, behaviour and emotional responses and can return sufferers to childlikeness and childishness. It is a rare form and often affects younger people. The best known of a range of conditions is Pick's Disease, which causes massive personality changes. There are genetic links.

Until very recently, the National Institute for Health and Clinical Excellence (NICE) would not recommend the NHS to prescribe drugs to help sufferers in the early stages of dementia. Those people who were able to afford, or whose doctors did prescribe, Aricept, Exelon and Reminyl have often reported amazing gains. It can be as if a fog is lifted, their memories have improved, they become less depressed and agitated, can drive and remain independent for longer, and start enjoying life again. These drugs can ameliorate the problems for some people and are now only available because of the relentless campaigning by the Alzheimer's Society and so many individuals who have fought to get NICE to reconsider. I am conscious that I have made a judgement in the last paragraph, that people whose lives have suddenly been reduced by extreme neurological disfunction are not able to enjoy their lives. When my Mum said that she was happy rarely moving from her bed, I was shocked and disbelieving. However the French Association for Locked-In Syndrome have recently completed a survey with 91 patients with chronic LIS, like Jean Dominique Bauby (whose royalties from the book he wrote by moving one eyelid—'The Diving Bell and the Butterfly,' has established and funded the Association), and surprisingly found that 72% were happy and 68% said that suicide never crossed their minds. I am glad that I never made the decision not to resuscitate Mum. I can now accept that she was able to be happy in circumstances that seemed unbearable to me.

Out of £833 million of research funds made available by charities and governmental organisations in 2007/8, 71% was devoted to cancer research, 20% to Coronary Heart Disease and only 6% to Dementia. Yet the social care costs are huge, easily equal to the total cost of care for cancer, CHC and stroke. Although dementia means brain failure, patients in homes have to pay the full costs of their care, unlike patients with heart failure in hospitals. Dementia is not seen as a priority, perhaps because of stigma and ageism.

Anyone who has had experience of care homes, or saw Sir Gerry Robinson's TV programmes (2009), will understand how woefully inadequate the majority are. In too many there is a failure to recognise the person with dementia as worthy of respect or physical and mental stimulation. Resident's clothes and possessions are 'lost', they wear other peoples ill fitting clothes, have 'prison' hair cuts, pressure sores and no teeth, are over sedated, bruised, dehydrated, fed bad food, dehumanised and even hit. They may be our relatives or friends and unless there are radical changes, may also be us, frightened and crying for help.

For six and a half years I was traumatised and angry with myself at being unable to make the last years of my mother's life better for her. I was angry at the NHS for poor and uncaring treatment. Angry at the government for callous and inadequate funding and the lack of an integrated policy for health and social care. Angry at local authorities for their constant cutbacks and with social services for not providing clear information about entitlements.

And I am conscious that being angry and frustrated when one is old is too late, as age and illness bring fear, lack of confidence and resignation. We know that providing a life that every old person deserves would need a massive increase in funding and which other budget should be cut? Education? NHS? No politician would agree to the sort of increase necessary, as people with dementia rarely vote. So what could change our current system? It will have to be the selfishness of the baby boomer generation who will want something better for themselves.

To donate to the Alzheimer's society, call 0845 306 0898, or download a website donation form from alzheimers.org.uk.

# Some Memoirs, Novels, Short Stories and Ethnography in which dementia sufferers or the elderly feature:

Akin Charlotte A. (2000) *The Long Road Called Goodbye—tracing the Course of Alzheimer's.* Creighton University Press. Omaha, Nebraska.

Appignanesi Lisa (1999) *Losing the Dead—a Family Memoir.* Chatto and Windus, UK.

Bailey Paul (1967) *At the Jerusalem.* Bloomsbury Classic, London.

Barnes Julian (2004) *The Lemon Table.* (Short Story—Appetite 159-173) Jonathan Cape, Picador, London.

Bayley John (1998 ) *Iris.* Gerald Duckworth & Co. Ltd, Great Britain.

Bawden Nina (1991*) Family Money.* Virago, London.

Bennett Alan (2005) *The Candlewick Way of Death.* In *Untold Stories.* Faber/Profile.

Bernlef J (1988) *Out of Mind.* Faber & Faber, London.

Blank Louis (1995) *Alzheimer's Challenged and Conquered?* Foulsham, London.

Boden Christine (1998) *Who Will I be When I Die?* Harper Collins Religious, Australia.

Blythe Ronald (1979) *The View In Winter—Reflections on Old Age.* Harcourt Brace and Jovanovich, New York & London.

Bronte Charlotte (1897 ) *Jane Eyre.* Oxford World's Classics, Oxford University Press.

Brown Audrey (1998) *A Matter of Timing.* The Book Guild Ltd, England.

Bryden Christine (2005*) Dancing with Dementia.* Jessica Kingsley Publishers, London.

Bunuel Luis (2003) *My Last Sigh.* Translated by Abigail Israel, published by University of Minnesota Press, Paris.

Byatt A.S. (2003) *Little Black Book of Stories* (The Pink Ribbon 233-276). Chatto & Windus, London.

Chabon Michael (2005) *The Final Solution.* Harper Perennial, London.

Chia Josephine (2002) *Frog Under a Coconut Shell.* Time Books International, Singapore.

Cobbold Marika (1993) *Guppies for Tea.* Black Swan, London.

Davies Stevie (2007) *The Eyrie.* Phoenix, Orion Books, London.

Dean Debra (2006) *The Madonnas of Leningrad.* Fourth Estate, Harper.

DeBaggio Thomas (2002) *Losing My Mind.* The Free Press, New York.

Dibdin Michael (1993) *The Dying of the Light.* Faber & Faber, London.

Erdrich Louise (1994) *The Bingo Palace.* Flamingo, Harper Collins London.

Faulks Sebastian (2006) *Human Traces.* Vintage, Random House, London.

Forster Margaret (1979) *Mother Can You Hear Me?* Penguin Group, London

Forster Margaret (1990) *Have The Men Had Enough?* Penguin, Harmondsworth

Fine Anne. (2001) *All Bones and Lies.* Bantam Press, Transworld, London.

Franzen Jonathan ( 2001) *The Corrections.* Fourth Estate, London

Fredriksson Marianne. (1998) *Hanna's Daughters.* Orion, London.

Friel McGowin Diana (1993) *Living in the Labyrinth.* Elder Books, New York.

Gale Patrick (2000) *Rough Music.* Flamingo (HarperCollins), London.

Genova Lisa (2009) *Still Alice.* Simon and Schuster, UK.

Gillies Andrea (2009) *Keeper.* Short Books, London.

Grant Linda (1998) *Remind Me Who I Am, Again.* Granta, London.

Grant Linda (2002) *Still Here.* Little Brown, London.

Hadley Tessa (2007) *The Master Bedroom.* Vintage, Random House Group.

Harvey Samantha (2009) *The Wilderness.* Jonathan Cape, London.

Hegarty F (1996*) Let's Dance*. Harmondsworth, Penguin.
Hill Reginald (1987*) Exit Lines*. Grafton Books, London.
Hope Chrisopher (1992) *Serenity House*. Macmillan, London.
Ignatieff Michael (1993) *Scar Tissue*. Chatto and Windus, London.
James Ken (2000) *Strew on her Roses, Roses—a Memoir*. Fourth Estate. London.
Jennings Kate (2002) *Moral Hazard*. Fourth Estate, London and New York.
Lee Janine (1991) *13 at the Table*. Mark & Moody Publishers, Stourbridge.
Lessing Doris (1984) *The Diaries of Jane Somers*. Michael Joseph, London.
Levine Judith (2004) *Do You Remember Me*. Free Press, New York.
Long Kate (2004) *The Bad Mother's Handbook*. Picador, Macmillan Ltd, London.
Lively Penelope (1998) *Spiderweb*. Viking, Penguin Group, England.
Lurie Alison (1998) *The Last Resort*. Vintage, London.
Kingsolver Barbara (1992) *Animal Dreams*. Abacus, Great Britain.
McDermid Val (2004) *The Distant Echo.* Harper and Collins, London.
Mck. Stewart Linda (2004) *25 Months*: *A Memoir*. Other Press, New York.
Millen Julia (1984) *Dilemma of Dementia*. Lansdowne Press, London.
Miller Sue (2003) *The Story Of My Father*. Bloomsbury, London.
Mistry Rohinton (2002*) Family Matters*. Faber and Faber Ltd, London.
Moggach Deborah (2004)*These Foolish Things.* Vintage, London
Moore Jeffrey (2004) *The Memory Artists*. Weidenfeld and Nicolson, Orion Publishing Group, London.
Moskowitz Bette Ann (1998)*Do I know you? A Family's Journey Through Aging and Alzheimer's*. Taylor Trade Publishing, Maryland USA.
O'Farrell Maggie (2006) *The Vanishing Act of Esme Lennox*. Headline Review, London.
Roach Marion (1985) *Another Name for Madness*. Houghton Mifflin, Boston.
Slack Patricia & Mulville Frank (1988) *Sweet Adeline*. Macmillan Education Ltd, London.

Smith Ray (2004) *Amazing Grace: Enjoying Alzheimer's.* Metro Publishing Ltd, London.

Rose Larry (1996) *Show Me the Way to Go Home.* Elder Books, California.

Roth Philip (2006) *Everyman.* Jonathan Cape, London.

Rowntree Kathleen (1997) *Mr Brightly's Evening Off.* Doubleday, London

Rowntree Kathleen (1994) *Outside, Looking In.* Black Swan, London.

Rubens Berenice (1998) *The Waiting Game.* Abacus, London.

Russo R (1994) *Nobody's Fool.* Vintage, London.

Sackville-West Vita (1931—reprint 1983) *All Passion Spent.* Hogarth Press, London.

Sarton May (1983) *As We Are Now.* The Women's Press, London.

Snyder Lisa (1999) *Speaking Our Minds.* WH Freeman and Co, New York.

Staincliffe Cath (1997) *Go Not Gently.* Headline, London

Stevens Ann (1996) *November Tree.* HarperCollins, London.

Tan A (2001) *The Bonesetter's Daughter.* HarperCollins, London.

Tan A (2003 ) *The Opposite of Fate.* Flamingo, HarperCollins, London.

Unsworth Emma (2006) *Care.* In *'You Are Here.'* Edited by Bill Broady and Jane Metcalfe. Redbeck Press, Bradford.

Vine Barbara (1996) *The Brimstone Wedding.* Harmondsworth, Penguin.

Walker-Blondell Becky (1995) *In My Mother's Arms.* Scythe Publications Inc, Nashville, Tennessee.

Walpole Hugh (1924) *The Old Ladies.* Hogarth Press, London.

Wearing Deborah (2005) *Forever Today.* Corgi, London.

Weldon Fay (2000) *Rhode Island Blues.* Flamingo, London.

Whitman Lucy—ed (2010) *Telling Tales About Dementia.* Jessica Kingsley, London.

Wilkins Christopher (1999) *The Horizontal Instrument.* Anchor, Doubleday, London.

Woodhouse Sarah (1994) *Meeting Lily.* Michael Joseph. London.

Woodward Gerard (2007) *A Curious Earth.* Chatto & Windus, London.

Lightning Source UK Ltd.
Milton Keynes UK
UKOW02f0720120716

278170UK00001B/87/P